DIVISIBLE MAN™
THIRTEEN MOONS

by

Howard Seaborne

ALSO BY HOWARD SEABORNE

DIVISIBLE MAN
A Novel
DIVISIBLE MAN - THE SECOND GHOST
with ANGEL FLIGHT
A Novel & Story
DIVISIBLE MAN - THE THIRD STAR
A Novel
DIVISIBLE MAN - THE FOURTH SEASON
with ENGINE OUT AND OTHER SHORT FLIGHTS
A Story Collection
DIVISIBLE MAN - FIVE MAN CREW
A Novel
DIVISIBLE MAN - SIX HARD RULES
A Novel
DIVISIBLE MAN - SEVEN BLACK ROBES
A Novel
DIVISIBLE MAN - EIGHT BALL
A Novel
DIVISIBLE MAN - NINE LIVES LOST
A Novel
DIVISIBLE MAN - TEN KEYS WEST
A Novel
DIVISIBLE MAN - THE ELEVENTH HOURGLASS
A Novel
DIVISIBLE MAN - TWELFTH KNIGHT
A Novel
DIVISIBLE MAN - THIRTEEN MOONS
A Novel
DIVISIBLE MAN - FORT NIGHT
A Novel - 2026

REVIEWS

DIVISIBLE MAN – THIRTEEN MOONS [DM13]
"*FIVE STARS!* Seaborne delivers another unforgettable entry in the
Divisible Man series…this novel doesn't just continue the series, but
elevates it, proving once again that Seaborne knows how to mix genre thrills
with heart and humor in a way few authors can." — *BookLife*
"A smart, fearless thriller with a shocking twist!"
— *BestThrillers.com*

DIVISIBLE MAN – TWELFTH KNIGHT [DM12]
A *BookLife from Publishers Weekly* Editor's Pick:
"A book of outstanding quality."
"A swift vigorous action thriller in a series that continues to soar." —
BookLife

DIVISIBLE MAN - THE ELEVENTH HOURGLASS [DM11]
A *BookLife from Publishers Weekly* Editor's Pick:
"A book of outstanding quality."
"*FIVE STARS!* A brilliant, action-packed thriller..." — *Readers' Favorite*
"Seaborne's text is thrilling and full of fun."
— *BookLife from Publishers Weekly*
"Lean, fast-paced, and unpredictable…An accomplished supernatural thriller
from a series that keeps on delivering…**Will Stewart is one of the most
believable unbelievable characters currently running in fiction**."
— *Kirkus Reviews*
"…thrilling…an effervescent pace…littered with slabs of wicket humor…
relentless action…full of fun…truly compelling."
— *The BookLife Prize from Publishers Weekly*

DIVISIBLE MAN - TEN KEYS WEST [DM10]
**"The best possible combination of the Odd Thomas novels of Dean
Koontz and the Jack Reacher novels of Lee Child."**
— *Kirkus Reviews*
"*FIVE STARS!* A gripping read...the outstanding writing had me hooked…"
— *Readers' Favorite*
"Seaborne keeps the chatter fun, the pacing fleet, and the tension urgent. His

secret weapon is a tight focus on Will and Andy, a married couple whose love—and bantering dialogue—proves as buoyant as ever." — *BookLife*
"The author's skill at pacing is razor-sharp—the book is a compulsive page-turner…" — *Kirkus Reviews*

DIVISIBLE MAN - NINE LIVES LOST [DM9]
"*FIVE STARS!* A blend of action, mystery, and love of flying and airplanes...this is a highly recommended read." — *Readers' Favorite*
"Seaborne's latest series entry packs a good deal of mystery…A smart, diverting tale of an audacious aviator with an extraordinary ability."
— *Kirkus Reviews*

DIVISIBLE MAN - EIGHT BALL [DM8]
"*FIVE STARS!* An exhilarating thriller filled with suspense and unexpected twists…another captivating and memorable read highlighting the series' consistent ability to deliver engaging and through-provoking thrillers." — *Readers' Favorite*
"Any reader of this series knows that they're in good hands with Seaborne, who's a natural storyteller…Another riveting, taut, and timely adventure with engaging characters and a great premise."
— *Kirkus Reviews*

DIVISIBLE MAN - SEVEN BLACK ROBES [DM7]
"*FIVE STARS!* Seaborne has got his series down to a fine art at this point, masterfully weaving a complex narrative filled with suspense and high stakes that challenges the heroes we know and love more than ever." —
Readers' Favorite
"Seaborne is never less than a spellbinding storyteller. Will himself is an endearing narrator. He's lovestruck by his gorgeous, intelligent, and strong-willed wife… A solid series entry that is, as usual, exciting, intricately plotted, and thoroughly entertaining."
—*Kirkus Reviews*

DIVISIBLE MAN - SIX HARD RULES [DM6]
A Kirkus Starred Review – "A book of exceptional merit."
"Seaborne shows himself to be a reliably splendid storyteller in this latest outing. The plot is intricate and could have been confusing in lesser hands, but the author manages it well, keeping readers oriented amid unexpected developments…His crisp writing about complex scenes and concepts is another strong suit…The fantasy of self-powered flight remains absolutely

compelling…Will is heroic and daring, as one would expect, but he's also
funny, compassionate, and affectionate…
A gripping, timely, and twisty thriller." —*Kirkus Reviews*

DIVISIBLE MAN - FIVE MAN CREW [DM5]
"*FIVE STARS!* Seaborne never ceases to amaze with the smoothness of his
narrative, and his natural ability to blend high-octane action with intricate
plot twists to keep the reader hooked from the first page."
— *Readers' Favorite*
**"Seaborne continues his winning streak in this series, offering another
page-turner**." —*Kirkus Reviews*

DIVISIBLE MAN - THE FOURTH SEASON
With ENGINE OUT & OTHER SHORT FLIGHTS
"This engaging compendium will surely pique new readers' interest in
earlier series installments. A captivating, altruistic hero and appealing cast
propel this enjoyable collection…" — *Kirkus Reviews*

DIVISIBLE MAN - THE THIRD STAR [DM3]
"*FIVE STARS!* A gripping, suspenseful read that was difficult to put
down." — *Readers' Favorite*
"Seaborne…proves he's a natural born storyteller, serving up an exciting,
well-written thriller. He makes even minor moments in the story memorable
with his sharp, evocative prose…Will's smart, humane and humorous
narrative voice is appealing, as is his sincere appreciation for Andy—not just
for her considerable beauty, but also for her dedication and intelligence. **An
intensely satisfying thriller—another winner from Seaborne**."
—*Kirkus Reviews*

DIVISIBLE MAN - THE SECOND GHOST [DM2]
"*FIVE STARS!* A suspenseful ride...difficult to put down...I was captivated
by the plot's thrilling twists and turns from beginning to end…**This story
was masterfully crafted and will stay with me for a while**."
— *Readers' Favorite*
"Seaborne…delivers a solid, well-written tale that taps into the near-
universal dream of personal flight. Will's narrative voice is engaging and
crisp, clearly explaining technical matters while never losing sight of
humane, emotional concerns. Another intelligent and exciting
superpowered thriller." —*Kirkus Reviews*

DIVISIBLE MAN [DM1]

"*FIVE STARS!* Fast paced and action-packed...This page-turner had me on the edge of my seat...a nail-biting book...difficult to put down." — *Readers' Favorite*

A *BookLife from Publishers Weekly* Editor's Pick:

"A book of outstanding quality."

"A crisply written thriller. Will's narrative voice is amusing, intelligent and humane; he draws readers in with his wit, appreciation for his wife, and his flight-drunk joy—**a great read**." —*Kirkus Reviews*

"Seaborne has knack for tension in crafting this thrilling journey...a must-read for fans of suspenseful thrillers..."

— *Readers' Favorite*

"Seaborne's crisp prose, playful dialogue, and mastery of technical details of flight distinguish the story...this is a striking and original start to a series, buoyed by fresh and vivid depictions of extra-human powers and a clutch of memorably drawn characters..."

—*BookLife*

THE SERIES

While each DIVISIBLE MAN [TM] novel tells its own tale and can be read on its own, many elements carry forward. The novels are best enjoyed in sequence. The pivotal short story "Angel Flight" bridges the second and third novels and is included with the second novel, DIVISIBLE MAN - THE SECOND GHOST. "Angel Flight" is also published in THE FOURTH SEASON short story collection along with other stories offering additional insights into the cadre of characters residing in Essex County.

SUPPORT YOUR LOCAL BOOKSELLER

The entire DIVISIBLE MAN [TM] series is available from many local independent booksellers who offer online ordering for in-store pickup or home delivery. Visit your favorite bookseller's website and look for online ordering.

Search: "DIVISIBLE MAN Howard Seaborne"

For advance notice of new releases and exclusive material available only to Email Members, join the DIVISIBLE MAN [TM] Email List at **HowardSeaborne.com**.

Sign up today and get a FREE DOWNLOAD.

If you enjoyed DIVISIBLE MAN, please share your feelings by posting a review. Reader reviews give an author's work greater visibility and help propel the book to a wider audience. Reviews are deeply appreciated.

Post your review with your book's retailer or at www.GoodReads.com.

Blue skies!

HS

ACKNOWLEDGMENTS

This thirteenth Divisible Man novel follows in close formation with its sisters. The flight crew varies little, but it is no less important to acknowledge their roles. I've said so a dozen different ways: nothing leaves the ground without a host of good people contributing to the effort.

I'd like to thank my editor, Stephen Parolini, for expertise that constantly teaches me to be a better writer. Thanks to my first writing mentor, the late Victor Zilbert, for his ruthless blue pencil marks. Thanks to Arnie Freeman for a lifetime of ego refueling and friendship. Thanks to Denise Kohnke for pointing me in the right direction at the beginning. Thanks to Stacey Brandt for medical expertise that keeps the story real.

Those brave souls, my beloved beta readers and lifelong coconspirators, Rich Sorensen and Robin Schlei, deserve special thanks for their seemingly endless willingness to read one more novel.

Much gratitude goes to the crew at Trans World Data—to David, Carol, Claire, April, and Rebecca for keeping the machine running—and to Kristie and Steve for taking over what I used to do so I can do what I do.

I can't say enough about my sharp-eyed copy editor and eternal partner in every aspect of this adventure. Thank you, Robin, for always knowing I need to fly.

H

AUTHOR'S NOTE

Dedicated readers of the DIVISIBLE MAN series will recognize the prologue of this novel, a short story called "A Way In A Manger" that appeared in the *ENGINE OUT & OTHER SHORT FLIGHTS* collection. You are forgiven if you remember the story and skip over it in this iteration. On the other hand, a refresher never hurts and you never know what may have bearing down the road…

For 50.47 percent of you.

PREFACE

THE OTHER THING

It's like this: I wake up nearly every morning in the bed I share with my wife. After devoting a religious moment to appreciating the stunning, loving woman beside me, I ease off the mattress and pick my way across the minefield of creaks and groans in the old farmhouse's wooden floor. I slip into the hall and head for the guest bathroom two doors down—the one with the quietest toilet flush. I take care of essential business, then pull up to the mirror. The face offers no surprises. I give it a moment, then picture a set of levers in my head—part of the throttle-prop-mixture quadrant on a twin-engine Piper Navajo. The levers I imagine are to the right of the standard controls, a fourth set not found on any airplane, topped with classic round balls. I see them fully retracted, pulled toward me, the pilot. My eyes are open—it makes no difference—I can see the levers either way. I close my hand over them. I push. They move smoothly and swiftly to the forward stops. Balls to the wall.

For a split second I wonder, as I did the day before, and the day before that, if this trick will work again. Then—

Fwooomp!

—I hear it. A deep and breathy sound—like the air being sucked out of a room. I've learned that the sound is audible only in my head.

A cool sensation flashes over my skin. The first dip in a farm pond after a hot, dusty day. The shift of an evening breeze after sunset.

I vanish.

Bleary eyes and tossed hair wink out of the mirror and the shower curtain behind me—the one with the frogs on it—fills in where my head had been. The instant I see those frogs, my feet leave the cold tile floor. My body remains solid, but gravity and I are no longer on speaking terms. A stiff breeze will send me on my way if I don't hang on to something.

The routine never varies. I've tested it nearly every morning since I piloted an air charter flight down the RNAV 31 Approach to Essex County Airport—but the flight never made the field. The airplane wound up in pieces and I wound up sitting on the pilot's seat in a marsh. I have no memory of the crash. The running theory is that I collided with something—something I recently found under a crush of broken trees in a winter forest. I believe that object—whatever it was—saved me and left me this way. I may never know how or why. The object is long gone. As time passes, the memory of its discovery plays like a dream.

Since the night of the crash, whenever I picture that set of levers in my mind and I push them fully forward, I vanish. Pull them back, and I reappear. It applies to things I wear, things I hold, and even other people in my grasp.

A gimmick? A party trick? A useful tool for espionage—assuming I knew anything about espionage? I don't know.

There's one aspect of this *thing* that I may never understand. On a fogbound Christmas Eve I held a dying child in my arms and made us both vanish. I found out later that the child stopped dying. That when this *thing* envelops a child fighting cancer sometimes—often—it leaves the child whole and healthy.

This *thing*—what I call *the other thing*—allows me to disappear. It defies gravity. It cures where there is no cure. It saved me.

It may kill me.

That doesn't scare me.

Losing someone I love scares me.

PROLOGUE

Last Christmas

"Don't forget to stop at the hardware store and pick up an outdoor timer," Andy reminded me.

"Digital or mechanical?"

"What's the difference?"

"Never mind. I'll take care of it. What time does the service start?"

"Six. And please don't be late."

"I won't. Love you," I said.

"You, too."

I ended the call and pocketed my phone.

"What service?" Arun asked. I had stopped in his office to tell him that I closed and locked the main hangar and to hint that he should go home. The desktop pile of grant applications to the Christine and Paulette Paulesky Education Foundation seemed to grow at his touch, rather than diminish.

"Christmas Eve Eve."

He cocked a skeptical eye in my direction. "Is that a thing?"

"Andy's church likes to put on a Christmas Eve service and potluck dinner, but attendance has been dropping off. Too much competition with family travel plans. This year they bumped it up one day. 'Tis the night before the night before Christmas."

"I did not take you for a religious man, Will."

"Church is Andy's thing. But nobody flies for a living without getting a little religion." I zipped my jacket and waved to him. "Thus, I bid you a Merry Christmas Eve Eve! I'm off to purchase a replacement timer for the Nativity scene. Baby Jesus needs a nightlight."

Outside, light snow quilted the silent airport. The green and white rotating beacon swung around and around. Falling flakes solidified the beams of light against the night sky.

I brushed fresh snow from my car and made the run to Ace Hardware where I confronted a dizzying array of indoor and outdoor timers. I settled on a mechanical type that used green and red plastic pins to map the hours of darkness and light.

A line formed at the single open register. I checked my watch and calculated the time needed to reach the church, install the timer, and seat myself with Andy for the service. The line moved slowly. I might have to slip into the pew during the first hymn.

A young woman ahead of me laid a coil of garden hose on the counter, then added a candy cane from a countertop jar. She dug into her pockets, pulling out crushed bills and a fistful of change. I caught a whiff of body odor and noticed greasy hair tucked into her stocking hat. She wore an old letter jacket over sagging workout pants and blown-out sandals over wet socks. Her attire contrasted sharply with that of the church full of worshipers I would soon be joining—good Christians decked out in their holiday best.

"Seventy-five, eighty, eighty-one-two-three." The teenaged clerk counted out the last pennies from the spill of pocket change. "Uh…looks like you're twenty cents short."

The woman stared at the coins, willing them to reproduce.

I laid the timer on the counter.

"Put the candy cane on mine," I said.

The kid looked at the woman for confirmation. She did not raise her head but instead lifted the hose off the counter and scooped up the candy cane. She turned abruptly and hurried out the double doors.

"Merry Christmas to you, too," I muttered, instantly wishing I hadn't.

"Yeah, really," the kid at the register agreed, doubling my regret. "Who needs a garden hose at Christmas?"

He waved his scanner over the bar code on the timer box.

I fished my rewards card from my wallet. The unpleasant scent lingered.

. . .

I CAUGHT up to the woman in the parking lot. She crouched beside a rusted Dodge minivan, struggling with a clutter of clothing, toys and unidentified objects that had spilled into the new snow from the van's open side door.

"What were you doing, Casey?" she demanded, kneeling to gather up the debris.

A small girl leaned out. "I was building a fort! Please don't be mad, Mommy!"

"Shush! You'll wake the baby!"

I tossed the timer in my car and turned to lend her a hand, but she was too fast. She scooped up the laundry and shoved the pile behind the front passenger seat. She picked up bits of plastic, a flat cereal box and a few other items, shook the snow off, and tossed them in. Her mountain of possessions threatened a fresh avalanche. She avoided disaster by yanking the sliding door forward. It groaned on its rusted track. She put her shoulder into it and forced the door to latch, then hurried around the van. The Dodge cranked reluctantly to life, and she wheeled out of the lot. Watching her go, I thought her night stood a good chance of getting worse. She drove with one taillight out.

THE ESSEX UNITED Presbyterian Church is a country church, founded by the farmers who settled Essex County when President Tyler doled out land grants. The church dominates the northwest corner of the intersection of a county road and a narrow town road. The pastor's manse faces the church from the opposite corner. The congregational cemetery takes up the northeast corner. Cornfields and hayfields abut the borders of the church property, isolating it. The white steeple, when lighted, is visible for miles in each direction, especially in winter.

Tonight, Christmas lights in the windows and the spotlighted Nativity scene on the front lawn supplemented the holy spirit with holiday spirit. At a distance, the white wooden church looked like a decorative miniature in a snow globe.

I pushed the speed limit on the empty county road. My watch said that the organist was warming up and Andy was taking her seat with the rest of the congregation. If installing the timer gave me any trouble, my arrival might not be covered by the first hymn.

Two miles from the church, a single brake light flashed on the road ahead. A right turn signal flickered. The lights disappeared quickly. Between the snow charging into my headlights and my preoccupation with the looming task of finding the extension cord running from the church to the Nativity scene, I hardly took note.

Except to wonder.

Who needs a garden hose at Christmas?

When I reached the intersection where the vehicle turned, I glanced east, down the side road. A puff of exhaust bloomed red around a solo taillight.

A small park sits between two cornfields, donated to the county by the farmer who owns the land around it and billed as a meditation spot in memory of his mother. It's not much more than a three-car gravel lot, a picnic table and a half acre of mowed grass that ends where a stream passes at the back of the property.

The red light glowed briefly before turning into the tiny park.

I lifted my foot off the gas and pumped the brake. My car slid to a stop. The engine and I sat idling.

Wondering.

My built-in time sense warned that Andy's beautiful eyes would judge me harshly for showing up late, but my hand closed on the shifter and threw it in reverse. I retraced my path through the intersection. I stopped, shoved the car in gear, spun the tires and turned east.

Approaching the park entrance, I slowed to a crawl. I squinted through my wet side window. The dark boxy shape of the minivan crouched on the snowy lot. The park entrance sloped and had not been plowed. Deep tracks suggested that turning around and driving back out again might be challenging, especially in an old front-wheel drive minivan.

I eased my car to the side of the road.

I killed the engine and climbed out for a better look.

Winter landscapes, especially under falling snow, bear a signature silence. Or should. This silent night was broken by the steady hum and occasional wheezing of the old Dodge's engine. A cloud of exhaust billowed from the rear of the van.

I walked back to where her wheel tracks left the road.

You're going to scare the poor girl, I warned myself. She probably had a perfectly good reason for stopping.

I wasn't crazy about hiking down the snow-covered slope in my freshly polished and buffed boots. The footing on leather soles can be slick. I considered vanishing and floating across the snow. A BLASTER power unit and propeller nestled at the ready in the pocket of my leather jacket. Yet disappearing carried with it the complication of reappearing beside her vehicle—or creating cause to question why I left no tracks.

I trotted down the slope and trudged up behind the one-eyed rear of the minivan. Snow and moisture glossed the dark fogged windows. Dashboard lights lent an interior glitter to wet drops accumulating and freezing on the glass.

I stopped.

A curved line in the snow began just below the tailpipe. The indentation snaked past the left rear of the van and then forward, parallel to recent tracks. I followed the line to the driver's door. There, the newly purchased garden hose rose out of the snow. It hung from the driver's window, which had been nudged up to secure the hose end. Clothing had been stuffed in the gaps on either side of the hose.

I retraced my steps to the rear of the vehicle, to the exhaust pipe. The garden hose had been inserted in the pipe, but it must have been a poor fit. The hose end lay in the snow.

Shit.

I thought of the little voice that begged, *"Please don't be mad, Mommy!"* Mommy wasn't mad. Mommy was *Done.*

Mommy found the end of a road I could hardly imagine. I thought about the mountain of possessions, the odor, the scramble for change and surrender of what must have been her last dollar for a last resort.

I thought about the candy cane she couldn't afford but couldn't do without.

The snow falling on my shoulders suddenly acquired weight.

I walked back to the driver's door and closed my left hand on the handle.

Fwooomp!

Vanished, I put my right hand on the minivan for leverage and pulled open the driver's door. It creaked angrily. I let it swing to the stops and held on.

She startled.

She lay across the front seats with her back to the passenger-side door. A golden-haired bundle of mismatched snow pants and oversized winter jacket curled up against her shoulder. She clutched a smaller bundle in a blue blanket against her chest. The van smelled sour and dank, but with a hint of peppermint. I've smelled better barns.

Red-rimmed eyes flared on the woman's elfish face. She had been pretty before the road leading her to this final parking spot drained her face of softness and light. Glaring into the darkness, a mix of fear and guilt embossed her expression.

"Who's there?!" she cried, tightening her grip on the children. "Who are you?"

"The name's Gabriel," I replied.

She jerked the children closer and sat up. Her head shot from side to side, searching the windows.

"Where are you? What do you want?"

"I'm right here." I reached for her feet and tapped her ankle. She jolted and pulled her foot back. "Hey, relax. You're the one who called me."

"I didn't call anyone!"

I reached up and wiggled the hose end dangling through the cracked-open window. "Uh, you kinda did. This is what you wanted, right? To end it all?"

She blinked.

"Fast acting. Painless. I'm here to take you the rest of the way."

She swallowed.

"Mommy, who's there?"

"The name's…uh…Gabriel, Casey. Sorry you can't see me. I'm an angel."

"How do you know my name?"

"Come," I said. "Come outside."

The little girl obediently shifted to crawl out, but her mother pulled her tighter. "No! Go away! We're not—done yet!"

"If you weren't done, would you be talking to me?"

She said nothing.

"Okay look, I may have intervened here. The truth is, if you finish *this*— you're technically committing a couple of crimes I'd rather not name in front of Casey. And that might send you off in…let's just say another direction."

She stared at the empty open doorway.

"It's okay. You're going to be okay. Trust me. Come."

Trust came slowly. She let the little girl go first, then slid across the front seats and eased out of the van. Sinking her sandaled feet into the snow, she pulled the small girl close and frantically scanned the empty lot.

"I'm right here," I said. I gripped the steering wheel and leaned in to turn the key in the ignition and kill the engine. "No point in wasting gas."

She whirled around and stood wide-eyed. "Are we…?"

"Going someplace warm? Where there's food? Yup."

"I'm hungry, Mommy. Are you really an angel? Why can't I see you?"

"You can't see me because—well, because it doesn't work that way— because if I appear, I'll get my wings all full of snow. And then I can't fly. Here. Do you feel that?" I reached out and touched the little girl's cheek. She broke into a bright smile.

"It's magic! Mommy feel it!"

The mother blinked at her daughter. I didn't want to touch the mother's cheek, so I squeezed her shoulder instead. She shivered and jerked away.

"Okay, here's the deal," I said. "We need to travel. And what's one thing angels love to do?" I directed the question at the little girl.

"Angels can fly!"

"And you can, too," I said. "I'm going to give you all a hug. Ready?" I pulled the BLASTER power unit from my coat pocket and snapped the prop in place.

The young woman's lips quivered. Wet drops ran down her cheeks. She scooped the little girl off her feet. The move split between defensive and compliant.

"Are you ready?" I asked again.

She dipped her chin twice.

I closed my left arm around them. The woman stiffened, but I pulled the collective bundle into a hug. I gripped the levers in my head and pushed.

FWOOOMP!

They vanished in my arms.

The woman shrieked. She tightened her grip on the small girl and baby. *The other thing's* cool sensation replaced the biting cold that seeped under my coat and through my clothes. Gravity let go. The woman sucked in a harsh breath.

"It's okay," I said softly. "You're gonna love this."

I flexed my ankles and pushed gently. We broke contact with the ground and rose, which ignited a gasp.

"Mommy, look!"

I held the three of them against me with my left arm. I rotated us and extended my right hand and aimed the BLASTER unit.

"Get ready! Here we go!" I pushed the power unit slide control. The prop hummed. We eased forward across the fresh snow, rising slowly.

"MOMMY! MOMMY! Look! We're flying! We're angels, Mommy!"

The woman whispered, "We are, honey! We are!" A choked sob shook her against my grip.

"Do you know Santa?" Casey asked.

"We're best friends," I replied. I aimed higher. The snowscape fell away. The minivan, a dark blot on virginal white, receded. My own car sat by the road in puddles of parking light illumination. I hoped the young mother wouldn't notice; if she did, she might question Gabriel's arrival via worn-out Toyota Corolla.

"You know Santa? Really?"

"Angels can't lie," I lied.

"Mommy! He knows Santa!" The young woman squeezed her daughter in reply.

We glided across the small park, over a fence and across corn stubble smothered in fresh snow. I navigated beneath a set of power lines and veered right to follow the road, skimming six feet above the pavement. I set a course for the beacon at the next intersection, the white steeple towering over fields of snow. The illumination broadcast to the four corners of the compass gave the winter scene a ghostly serenity.

"Mommy, the angel knows Santa!"

"That's right, I do," I said when the woman didn't answer. "If you tell me what you want for Christmas, I can tell him myself."

"Mommy!"

I steered to the front of the church and eased to a landing on the concrete stoop beneath big double doors that wore twin evergreen wreaths. On the lawn, the Nativity diorama glowed, turning the falling snow into a cascade of sparkles. Spotlights aimed at the steeple filled the sky with glitter.

"Easy now," I said, ensuring that the woman had her feet firmly under her. "Get ready."

Fwooomp! I let her go. She snapped into view and wobbled on the salted concrete. I held my hands close, ready to catch her, but she found her footing. For the first time, the baby cooed and squeaked. She quickly adjusted the blanket over the infant's face.

"Go inside," I said. "They're waiting for you." She didn't move. She looked for my voice in the air. "Go on."

I fixed a grip on both handles of the big doors. Using one for leverage, I opened the other.

No question. I missed the first hymn. The pastor's voice carried, amplified by speakers in the small church lobby.

"…so Joseph went up from the town of Nazareth in Galilee to Judea, to Bethlehem, the town of David…"

"*Go ahead,*" I whispered. "*It's okay.*"

Bewildered, she stepped into the candle-lit church. I pushed her gently.

"Wait! Wait!" the little girl cried out. In the church congregation, heads turned. "Where are you? You have to tell Santa!"

I pulsed the power unit to lower myself. I bent my knees, dropping to face her. I reached out and put a hand behind the child's head, then kissed her cheek and whispered in her ear, "You can tell me."

She lifted a hand and found my chest, then traced my neck and cheek. She leaned closer, cupped my ear, and whispered loudly, "*Tell Santa I want a house for Mommy.*"

"*I will,*" I whispered back.

The woman fought off a sob and gently tugged her daughter forward. I let the door close behind them. Alone outside—

Fwooomp!

—I reappeared. Silent snow fell, dusting my shoulders and hair. A trio of wise men, a camel and a cow loitered on the lawn, ignoring me, enchanted by an infant under a rundown shelter.

At least they had a barn.

I'm not sure why, but it kinda pissed me off.

I gave it a long minute, then opened the door and hurried into the church. The scent of fresh-cut pine boughs and green bean casserole warming in the basement kitchen greeted me. The pastor continued his Christmas story.

"…but the angel said to them, 'Do not be afraid, for I bring you good news that will cause great joy for all the people…'"

She hadn't moved. If anything, the young mother stood more frozen with fear than when I'd found her. I stomped the snow off my boots, which caught her attention.

"*Hi!*" I whispered loudly. "*Merry Christmas!*"

She didn't answer. She dropped her eyes and pulled her daughter out of the path of the stranger, making way for me to pass her by. It occurred to me that I wasn't the only one able to exist unseen.

Andy, seated on the aisle four rows from the front, leaned out and turned her head. She fixed a questioning look on me, then shifted it to the woman with the small children.

"Why don't you come and sit with me and my wife? And then we'll eat."

She examined her shabby clothes and shook her head vigorously.

"No way!"

I smiled. I held out my hand for Casey, who took it without hesitation.

"Way," I said.

PART I

1

Monday Night

The hotel room door slammed open the instant the hot shower stream hit my head. The bathroom door, locked out of habit, resisted entry then took a hard blow and banged open against the stop.

Blurred movement filled the frosted glass—a figure grabbed the shower door handle. I had no time.

Fwooomp!

I vanished under the steaming stream. The figure jerked the door open.

I gripped the shower head and pulled myself backward. Hard tile impacted my back. The move cleared me from the stream. Water fell in an orderly rain to the floor drain.

Behind the muzzle of a heavy handgun, the intruder leaned in. A man. Military haircut. Beard stubble. No glasses. He wore a sports jersey over dark sweatpants. He glanced at the water falling to the floor and into the drain, then conducted a careful scan of all corners of the tiled cubicle. He leaned back.

"Clear!"

In the hotel suite, male voices repeated the word.

"What do you mean *Clear*? Where is he?" A second man entered the bathroom. An angry bald orb of a head rode an expensive-looking gray suit and black shirt. His lime green tie screamed under his clean-shaved chin.

Sports Jersey man reached in and rotated the control knob. The stream stopped. Both men examined the shower where I pressed my body against the wall. My arms strained. I held my breath. They looked straight at me.

"Where the hell is he?" the second man asked the first.

No answer. The men turned and left the bathroom.

"He's not in here," another voice reported from deeper in the suite.

"What the fuck!" Angry Bald Man again. "Find him!"

I gripped the shower head.

Thinking.

At check-in, the hotel clerk produced a broad smile and told me I had been upgraded at no charge to a three-room luxury suite. Something about construction on the floor I had originally been assigned. Like I'd won the lottery. I didn't complain. Now I linked this intrusion to the fortuitous upgrade. They knew exactly where to find me and how to get in.

Noises from the two bedrooms told of every door and drawer in the suite being opened and closed. Zipper sounds signaled a search of my overnight bag and my flight bag.

"How is he not in here?" Angry Bald Man demanded. No one answered.

I calculated the risk of poking my head out for a look. Andy's inevitable questions rang in my head.

How many?

What did they look like?

Were they armed?

Did you get a license plate?

Despite its extravagance, the suite had limited spaces. It would be easy to run into someone. Plus, I had no means of propulsion. My BLASTERs nestled in my flight bag. At best, I could kick myself to the ceiling, but from what I could see and recall, nothing on the ceiling offered a grip. I might easily bounce off the plaster and drift down into one of these guys. On top of everything, I was naked. Colliding with a hostile intruder while wet and in the buff held no appeal.

I stayed put.

A man I had not yet seen entered the bathroom and checked the shower again. He cultivated the same tough guy look and attitude as the first intruder, but this one wore business casual under a nylon windbreaker displaying a logo for McGinty Heating and Air Conditioning.

I pondered the eclectic apparel. Black tactical gear might have suited their behavior, but a cliché like that would be difficult to explain in an upscale business hotel. Except for oozing attitude and the weapon that I'd seen, these guys could have been ordinary guests.

HVAC Guy studied the ceiling, probably calling up movies he'd seen in which people pop open lightweight tiles and climb into two or three feet of empty space to hide. No one seems to consider the fact that the person hiding above a drop-ceiling is kneeling on the same lightweight piece of acoustic foam they just shoved aside. In any case, there would be no hiding in the ceiling of this hotel room. Ten feet high and made of plaster, it offered no tiles to shove aside. The single heat vent in the bathroom looked like it might accommodate a baby raccoon and nothing larger.

Dissuaded that I had escaped into the building infrastructure, HVAC Guy pulled open the bathroom cabinet doors. I lifted myself for a look over the top of the glass shower door. He crouched and searched under the sink.

Seriously? Even if I squeezed in there, I'd never get out without the fire department taking an ax to the woodwork.

He closed the doors and checked the drawers. Satisfied that I wasn't hiding behind the handheld hair dryer, he gave up his search and left.

Someone in the suite asked, "Now what?"

"His clothes are still here. This is what he was wearing when he checked in."

This referred to the clutter of jeans, t-shirt, socks and underwear that I left on the desk chair when I stripped down to take a shower.

How do they know what I was wear—?

Of course. I'd been watched.

"Maybe he changed."

"Whatever he did, he ain't here."

"*Bullshit,*" Angry Bald Man cursed. "We had eyes on the whole time."

No one spoke. Sounds that I interpreted as a search ceased. Nothing moved in the short hallway outside the open bathroom door.

A moment passed.

Angry Bald Man spoke. His tone changed. A phone call.

"It's me. He's not here."

"I don't know. He's not in the suite."

"No. One door. Nothing adjoining."

"Of course we did."

A long pause.

"What do you want us to do?"

Another long pause.

"Okay. Got it."

The conversation ended. The man who made the call barked orders.

"Keep the eyes up in case he comes back. Take everything. Find this guy and finish him."

HVAC Guy said, "What about the team in Essex?"

"Green light. Finish her, too."

HVAC Guy trotted back into the bathroom and scooped up the Ziploc bags I use for travel toiletries. He gathered my toothbrush, deodorant, and razor and carried the works away.

THE HEAVY HOTEL door snapped shut. I waited.

I ventured into the empty suite. Floating naked above the carpet, I assessed the damage. No clothes. No overnight bag. No flight bag. No phone. No room keys. No wallet.

No airplane keys.

And only one screaming thought in my head.

"Green light. Finish her, too."

Andy!

2

Sunday, Eight Long Days Ago

"She's missing."

Andy's sister Lydia spared none of her flair for the dramatic. The expectation embossing her face cried out for Andy to leap to her feet, pull out her phone, and issue an all-points bulletin. I pictured hand-cranked sirens and cops in blue wool tunics clutching Tommy guns and riding the running boards of Capone-era sedans.

Andy tipped her head back to let the early October sun warm her cheeks and neck. Shortened days snip sunlight from both ends of the clock as Halloween approaches. Diminishing bursts of bright blue sky and tantalizing final breaths of September's summer-like air separate chilly mornings and cool nights.

We lazed on Lydia's deck overlooking Leander Lake, a tabletop of blue jewels sparking under the afternoon sky. An artist's palette of gold, red, and green foliage lined the western shore. On Lydia's property, majestic maples silently dropped crisp colored leaves. A few of the errant paratroopers landed on the wooden deck, then skidded under the patio furniture at the behest of a light breeze.

"Your friend?" Andy asked Lydia without opening her eyes.

"No. Her daughter. I'm talking about her daughter."

Lydia lured us to her deck with the promise of leisure, cold Corona, and a brisket she had lovingly smoked herself, an act so incongruous to what I know of Andy's sister that I came prepared to order pizza. No one was more surprised than me to see Lydia's gas grill wheeze tendrils of smoke laden with stomach-stirring scent. Assured of a good meal, I spent over an hour chasing my deadly nemeses in and out of the brushy woods on either side of Lydia's property in a life and death game of Ditch It in which I seemed to always be It. Lydia's daughters—Harriet, who would turn 7 in a week and two days, and Elise, who insists she is "almost five" even though her birthday lay months in the future —gave no quarter and showed no mercy. When I collapsed on the grass utterly spent, I found myself under a pile of squirming, tickling girls.

"No! No, do not eat me," I cried. "I taste like boogers!"

My pleas ignited giggles and renewed attacks. Even after fighting them off, I had to drag one of my tormentors, still attached to my leg, all the way back up the hill to Lydia's deck. A cookie bribe finally freed me from the vicious duo.

Andy smiles when I'm in my glory with my nieces. Plowing into the third trimester of her pregnancy, my relationship with Harriet and Elise says something to her about me as the father of her child.

At least, I hope it does.

I remember paralysis each time Lydia tried to play life instructor by handing me her newborn third child, the Infant Princess Grace. The first time she thrust the wrapped bundle into my hands, I froze, terrified that I would drop her. Or that I would dent her soft skull or not hold the baby's head properly and cause—I can't even say it.

My shameful performance eroded any confidence I had for when Andy's and my own newborn crashes the party.

On Lydia's deck on a glorious Sunday afternoon, said inscrutable Princess Grace stared at me from her collapsible playpen. Now eighteen months old she is less terrifying but no less a mystery. She looked at me as if she knew a secret and intended to engage in blackmail.

I tipped my Corona in her honor. Without taking her oversized dark eyes from me, she lifted her formula bottle to her lips in a return gesture.

Drinking buddies. That's progress.

"Her daughter," Lydia emphasized, growing perturbed. "I'm talking about her daughter."

"And who is this again?" Andy asked.

Lydia, who could pass as Andy's twin sister despite a three-year difference, scooted her chair closer to where Andy stretched out on an expensive leather lounge chair. My wife rested her hands on what she had just this morning referred to as her beached whale.

"Caroline Gaffney. We were friends in college. She married a guy I dated before I met and married the son of Satan."

Andy lifted her hands and formed the sign of the cross with her index fingers. Her eyes remained closed.

Lydia nodded her appreciation of the gesture.

"We stayed in touch after she moved to New York. I invited her to join an online survivor group that I belong to. God knows she needed help. Her husband left her and three kids for a paralegal in his office."

"Disgusting," Andy opined.

"They're both lawyers. You can imagine how that divorce went."

This felt like a good time to slip away. My beer neared the empty end of the bottle. I had recovered most of my wind. The girls had long since demolished their plate of cookies. I calculated that the burden of full bellies improved my odds against them. I was about to tap Harriet on the shoulder, call her It, and make a run for the woods when I heard my name.

"Will, you should take Katie up to see Caroline." Use of the childhood name Andy once adopted for herself occurs with suspicious frequency when Lydia wants something.

"Wait, what?" Andy opened her eyes and shaded them with one hand. "See her?"

"I told Caroline that my sister is a police detective, and that you could help."

"A police detective on maternity leave, Liddy. And…help with what?"

"Find her daughter."

"Where?" I asked.

"Well, if I knew where, she wouldn't be missing," Lydia replied.

"No. Take Andy where?"

"Oh. Up north. Three Lakes. Caroline followed my lead and bought a lake house after the divorce. I believe her settlement left the ex-husband a cardboard box under a freeway off-ramp." Lydia clasped Andy's hands. "Fly up and have a chat with her. That's all. Just talk to her."

"How old is the girl?" Andy asked.

"She just turned eighteen."

"Liddy," Andy said, mustering patience, "the list of reasons why I would be of no help starts with this." Andy pointed at the beached whale. "But okay, not to play the pregnancy card, let me point out that I'm not on the job, that I would be out of my jurisdiction if I were on the job, that I'm not licensed as a private investigator, that a non-critical missing person's case is the least likely of any to garner law enforcement resources, and—"

Lydia interrupted. "How do you know it's non-critical?"

"Because the girl is eighteen. That means it's not critical if the girl is merely missing from home without credible risk of harm. And even if this situation warranted the attention of law enforcement, under no circumstances would I step on the toes of an agency engaged in an official investigation. Liddy, I don't know the woman. Or her daughter. Or the circumstances."

"Details, details."

"Yes," Andy said. "Details. Has your friend reported the girl missing? What are the circumstances of her last known whereabouts? Is there reason to believe she is in danger of harm? There won't be an Amber alert because of her age. Is the ex- involved? Is the ex- in the picture? What about shady friends? Has the girl emancipated herself? I have a thousand questions."

Lydia smiled pointedly at her baby sister.

Well played, Lydia.

3

"This is going to bug you," I said when Andy and I entered our rented farmhouse. It's been nearly a year since the building was repaired after being shot full of holes, yet the scent of new woodwork and fresh paint still contrasted with the fresh outside air. I dropped my keys in the bowl in the mudroom and followed Andy into the kitchen.

"No," she lied. "And yes," she confessed. "There are a few things about what Liddy said that might not add up—not that I think for a moment that my sister has the facts right, or in anything resembling the proper order."

I locked a steady gaze upon Andy without saying a word.

"What?" she protested. "I'm just saying…I mean…even at eighteen the girl is still someone's child. Look at you. Thirty-something and you're my first child."

"And how is that going?"

Andy touched my cheek. "Darling, it's because of how it's going that I thought I better try again."

She peeled off for one of her frequent bathroom visits. I considered topping off a superb afternoon and pleasant evening with one more Corona but opted for ice water instead. The temperature sank with the sunset. Hints of Indian Summer lingered. I made for the front porch and settled into my cheap version of the expensive Italian leather lounge chair that Andy had occupied on Lydia's deck. (Mine featured duct tape.) In the front yard, dry maple leaves blazed against the twilight and whispered to the dying breeze. Few had fallen. At peak color, the trees held their breath.

Andy slipped onto the cushion beside me.

"I'm not getting sucked into this," she announced.

"Are you saying that for my benefit? Seriously, Dee, don't hold back on my account. If this sparks your interest, go for it. Might do you good to occupy your time with something—" I stopped speaking, what with my foot firmly lodged in my mouth.

"Really? You think I need something to occupy my time?"

"No, love, I just meant, well, you know, maybe something more akin to police work instead of, I don't know, picking out—oh, shit, I'm going to shut up now."

"The first smart thing I've heard in this conversation. For the record, we have a child arriving in this household in a little under fifteen weeks, give or take. Do you understand what still needs to be done?"

I feared that the full list danced on the tip of her tongue.

Think fast.

"You know…I was running around in the woods with the girls when Lydia explained her friend's situation. I missed most of it. Tell me…what's the deal? Is her daughter really missing? Or did she run off with a boyfriend? Or is this a parental kidnapping by the ex-husband?"

"Nice try, ace. We shall continue our discussion about the many unfinished tasks in this household. Capisce?" Her hand slipped up the side of my rib cage toward my insanely ticklish armpit—Andy's intimate equivalent of sliding back the missile silo covers in North Dakota.

"Capisce."

She retracted her hand and settled in against me. Our unborn child lounged against both of our kidneys.

"Liddy's friend is from New York. Lydia used to commute from D.C. to shop and dine with her back in the bad old days—mainly to get away from The Worthless Bastard." Andy nurtured nothing kind in her soul for Lydia's dead ex-husband. "The friend has three kids, a girl and two boys. The girl is the oldest. She turned eighteen a few months ago."

"Ah. So, you did discuss the details with Lydia."

"Yes. The daughter is your classic teenaged girl story. The New York rich kid version. Private school. Entitled. Looking for attention and limits. She has everything so nothing means anything. Top of her class. Tremendous potential. A model child devoted to pleasing her parents until they betray her with a bad divorce, at which point she acts out the feelings she cannot share with her mother and father. She abandons all the right kids to take up with the wrong crowd. She gets in trouble. The parents try counseling. A top therapist. Real love. Tough love. They get compliant apologies one day. Violent revolution the next. In other words, the behavior you'd expect of a teenaged girl in a disintegrating family."

"She sounds like a mess."

"Five alarm. The busted marriage lit the match. A protracted divorce battle threw gasoline on the fire. The girl ran away numerous times. Hitch-hiked as far as New Orleans once."

"Sounds like a genuine head case."

"Not necessarily. Before everything went haywire, she scored good grades against a respectable academic load. She got accepted to top schools. But after the shit hit the fan, she failed half of her classes, and her college prospects fell apart. Alumni donations only carry so much weight. I'm not sure she graduated from her expensive private high school, but if she did, the rails were greased by mommy and daddy."

"Drugs?"

"Dabbling, mom says, but not the root cause."

"Mom is probably deluding herself."

"Maybe…"

"Dee, this doesn't sound like she's 'missing.' This sounds like she split. Homelife isn't peachy. Dollars to doughnuts, if you met the mom, you'd probably give the girl bus fare."

"Maybe," Andy said, probably recalling battles with her own mother.

"I take it back. What I said about this giving you a…distraction. I'm not sure you should get involved."

Andy didn't reply for a beat. I waited.

She said, "On the parenting, I fully agree. When Lydia spelled all this out for me, I figured at most I would try and get the mother to understand that law enforcement involvement is limited. For someone of age, unless there is evidence of imminent harm, there's not much we can do."

"But?"

Andy drummed her fingers on my diaphragm.

"Lydia said the girl took off from a camp."

"A camp? What kind of camp?"

"The expensive kind for girls with issues. Some exclusive rich kid resort-camp in Upper Michigan. Apparently, the girl's high-priced New York therapist recommended it. Probably accounts for mom's move to Three Lakes."

"Michigan? Really?"

"What?"

"I don't know. Sounds a little weird to me. New Yorkers sending their troubled kid to a camp in the Midwest? Why not the Catskills? Or upstate New York? Doesn't that seem weird to you?"

Andy shrugged. "Liddy said the camp is the kind of place you only get into because you know somebody who knows somebody. Liddy said the mother called in favors from friends and begged with her checkbook until the therapist pulled strings to get the girl enrolled. They shipped the girl off the day after her senior year ended. The girl went missing a few weeks ago."

"Went missing or took off?"

"Not sure. Either way, she's been gone a couple weeks."

I whistled. "That sounds like a lawsuit looking for a lawyer. Didn't Lydia say the mom was a lawyer?"

"Yes, but one of the covenants of this camp is that the girls of age may come and go as they wish. The camp makes no promises to the parents to either hold the kids there, or to notify the family if they leave. I know—it sounds irresponsible, but they play it as being essential to building trust."

"What's the track record? How many girls take off?"

"How would I know? I'm not the investigating officer."

Yet.

I stroked the smooth skin on the back of her shoulders. Andy read my mind.

"I'm not going," she protested. "I know Lydia wanted you to take me up to talk to the mother in Three Lakes, but I'm not going."

She snuggled in.

"Nope," she added. "Not going."

I waited. The silence between us begged the question I eventually asked.

"But?"

Andy sighed.

"But?" I repeated.

"A phone call. I promised Lydia I'd make a phone call to the mother."

4

Monday

"Who put a nickel in him?" Rosemary II asked from behind the Essex County Air Service front counter. She watched Arun Dewar hurry down the hall from the flight instructor offices and out the front door without so much as a wave. He wore a silly grin and stepped lightly across the ramp toward the Christine and Paulette Paulesky Education Foundation hangar on the other side of the tarmac. Arun walked like someone pumping upbeat music directly into his brain through earbuds. The rhythm to which he marked time wasn't coming from any device.

I said, "A—I think you know the answer to that. And B—is that something your grandfather used to say?"

Rosemary II produced an exaggerated frown. "He's been like that since summer. He waltzes in here first thing in the morning. Brings her coffee and pastries. Hangs around and gets underfoot."

"That's terrible." I leaned on the office counter and stirred coffee I had stolen from a batch she made for the FBO office. "Nobody waltzes anymore."

"Pidge had a 4 a.m. departure last week and he came in to see her off. I know he was here. I smelled that cologne he smears on."

"Tell me about it." I sipped my coffee. "It's not as bad as it was. It used to be eye-watering. Pidge finally said something to him. I swear he was bathing in the stuff."

"That ain't all that girl is teaching him. You can tell by the way he walks. That boy is growing up."

Rosemary II let her gaze linger another moment, then reeled her attention back to the intriguing invoices or bank statements or work orders cluttering her desktop. I loitered and watched the ramp where one of the Essex County Air Service instructors guided a new student through preflight procedures for one of Earl Jackson's Cessna 172s.

"He is indeed," I agreed.

Arun Dewar had been a timid young man with wet ink on his business administration degree when Sandy Stone hired him to attack the mountain of grant applications facing the recently formed Education Foundation—my current employer.

Indian by birth and British by upbringing, Arun proved to be a human supercomputer. His debut act was to lift the stack of paperwork off Sandy's desk. After a few months, he took over administration and investment of the one hundred million dollar fund. After just under a year, Sandy made it official and named him Director. Technically, that makes him my boss, a dynamic I neither admit to nor encourage.

I joined the Foundation as chief (and only) pilot because I persuaded Sandy that a private aircraft offered the most efficient way to visit remote, small-town schools applying for Foundation grants. As much as I loved flight instructing and flying air charter for Essex County Air Service, the Foundation job seemed like a better fit following my accident and the near miss I had with the FAA over my license and medical certificate.

A lame half-truth.

The Foundation job fits better with *the other thing* in my life.

The other thing.

Andy insists that my ability to vanish needs a better name. I humor her. I'm way better at naming things than my wife. She also insists that too many people know that I can wink out of sight in a split second.

Pidge, my former student who stepped into my shoes as chief pilot for Essex County Air Service, knows I can vanish. Earl Jackson, the owner of Essex County Air Service and my former boss, knows. Rosemary II's teenaged daughter Lane knows, but her mother does not. Special Agent Leslie Carson-Pelham of the Federal Bureau of Investigation knows. So does Andy's boss, Tom Ceeves, the chief of the Essex Police Department.

Arun Dewar does not know.

"I'm thinking about telling him," I recently and very casually mentioned to Andy. Letting Arun into the circle of trust offered conveniences, if not outright benefits.

On overnight Foundation trips with Arun, I slip away to visit hospitals with cancer wards specializing in the treatment of children. Arun has come close to catching me. I've had to explain myself a few times. In other words, lie. Arun is honest to a fault. He has a good and open heart, which only frosts my lies with shame.

Bringing Arun in on the joke would make things easier.

"Absolutely not," Andy responded without hesitation. "For countless reasons, Will. But let me boil it down to a single, selfish reason. Do you really want to lose him? Arun has impeccable logistical skills and he's a whiz with the Foundation's investments. He's the glue that holds the Foundation together."

I hate arguing with my wife when she's irrefutably right.

Arun is a buttoned-down linear thinker, a left brain acolyte of black and white organizational charts who doesn't just look for order in the universe, he attempts to impose it. Explaining to him that I can vanish and escape the grip of gravity…? I think his head would explode. For Heaven's sake, the guy skirted a nervous breakdown when the Silver Spoon Diner changed their menu.

Andy nailed the coffin shut on the idea.

"You're already tangled up with the FBI and with Spiro Lewko. What happens when they find out Arun is involved?"

"Are you going to hang around here all morning woolgathering?" Rosemary II interrupted the debate replaying in my head.

"Woolgathering? Did you wake up in the wrong century this morning?"

"Language is the apparel of thought. I choose not to go out in public naked."

"Wow." I downed the last gulp of coffee. "You are your daughter's mother. I see where she gets it."

"Her brains *and* her great beauty. Now scram. And rinse that coffee mug before you go."

No one defies Rosemary II, Goddess of the Schedule. I did as I was told.

Before leaving the FBO office, I jogged down the hall and found Pidge at her desk in the cramped chief pilot's office.

Pidge creeps into her mid-twenties looking like a teen who should be helping with chores on the family farm. Some of her too-young appearance can be attributed to her petite size. In high heels she barely tops five feet tall.

Some of it comes from her pretty pixie looks and short blonde hair. First impressions of Pidge belie her most significant attribute.

Cassidy Evelyn Page is the best pilot I ever taught. I'd like to have met the greats like Doolittle and Yeager because I would have introduced them to Pidge. She can aviate circles around pilots twice her age and experience level. She also curses like a sailor with chicken pox. Pidge earned the nickname Pigeon as a student pilot because she flew like a bird and talked dirty.

"Heads up." I leaned into her office and tugged her attention from the copy of *Sport Aviation* spread across her desk.

She tapped the magazine spread. "Did you see the P-47 this guy restored? Do you see how big this thing is?"

"When fighter pilots transitioned from cramped Spitfires to P-47s they said if a German ever got on their tail, they would avoid enemy fire by running around in the cockpit."

She looked up at me. "Did you decide?"

"Decide what?"

"Don't fucking mess with me."

I leaned on the door frame and examined my fingernails. "Andy says no."

I expected an argument. Pidge had recently favored telling Arun. She surprised me.

"Probably for the best. It would scare him."

"What are you tal—?"

"Hell, you scared the crap out of me when you showed me."

"Exigent circumstances." I wasn't sure that my hearing ever fully recovered from Pidge screaming in my ear when we leaped out a broken window on the thirty-eighth floor of a Chicago high-rise office building.

"I'm serious, Stewart. Arun is a delicate flower. You start popping in and out of sight or heaving him off tall buildings and it might leave him in a catatonic state."

"Wow. You hopped on Andy's bandwagon right quick."

"Because your wife is always right. The only reason I sided with you telling him is because I don't want to say something I shouldn't when we're making the beast with two backs."

"Jesus, Pidge. Do I come to mind when—?"

"Fuck you. Where are you taking my boy toy today?" she asked.

I shrugged. "Best thing I ever did was let you teach Arun ForeFlight. Now he does all the flight planning. I'm just the driver."

She shook her head. "Lazy bastard."

5

———————

"Where're we going?" I breezed into the lounge in the Foundation hangar. A glass wall separated the comfortable waiting area from the big hangar where the Foundation's Piper Navajo crouched on her landing gear and showed us her tail feathers. Arun arranged his overnight bag, my overnight bag, and my flight bag at the door to the hangar.

"Everything is in your email, Will." Arun flashed a bright white smile in my direction, signaling the start of another game of *Persuade Will to Read His Email.*

"Great. Can I borrow your laptop?" I volleyed his serve. Arun allows no one to touch his laptop.

"I would be delighted to set up email access on your phone." His British accent laced the offer with a side of biscuits.

"No way. The last thing I want on my phone is my email. Then I'd have to read the stuff."

"When exactly—and how—do you read your email?"

"When I borrow somebody's computer."

"What about your iPad? You carry it for flight planning, for access to weather information, and you use it in the cockpit. Why not set up your email?"

"Because it's way easier if you just tell me things."

Arun shook his head. "It was supposed to be Memphis. The trip you've been inquiring about."

"Alright." I clapped my hands. "Memphis barbecue."

I knew about the trip to Memphis. Maybe I don't read every word of his emails, but I do peek.

"Wait," I said. "You made it sound like past tense. *Supposed to be Memphis?*"

"Memphis has been postponed. I substituted the trip to Peoria. What you call an 'out and back' trip."

Arun disappeared into his office, then called to me. "Read your emails."

6

———————

Andy told me when I returned home that night that the car made two passes before pulling into our driveway. We don't get much traffic on the road in front of the farmhouse. Ours is the only habitat with humanity on the one-mile stretch. Farm fields dominate the rest of the landscape. It's safe to assume that a vehicle navigating the narrow asphalt is either farm equipment or has business with us.

Two passes put Andy on alert.

My police detective wife is far from afraid to be at home alone when I'm off plowing through the sky. She's nevertheless pragmatic about variables that can send a situation south. Instead of meeting the driver at the mudroom door or on the front porch, she took up a post in the dining room where a bay window overlooks the driveway. The vantage point affords a view of the visitor and places the gun safe in the downstairs closet within a few short steps.

Andy told herself she would exercise the same vigilance if she wasn't pregnant, yet the added exposure she felt with our child nesting in her abdomen compounded her caution.

She watched the seven- or eight-year-old Chevy Malibu roll to a halt. The sedan looked familiar in a way that tickled her memory but not familiar enough to shake the information loose. Dark blue with a red pinstripe across the door shoulders and fenders; she'd seen it somewhere before. The sensation made her think she would know the driver when he or she—

She.

"Holly?" Andy asked the silent dining room.

As if hearing her, the young woman stepped out of the car, paused to examine the farmhouse and spotted Andy in the dining room window. She turned an elfish face upward and waved a cheery greeting, then pointed at the back seat and pantomimed bringing something into the house. Andy waved back.

Holiday Bennett, no middle initial, dropped into our lives last Christmas with the irony of her name standing out like a neon sign. On the night before the night before Christmas, I caught up to Holly and her children at a remote park after the desperate young woman stuffed a garden hose into the exhaust pipe of a decaying Dodge Caravan and then fed the other end into the cold minivan cabin. To this day, she doesn't know it was me posing as The Unseen Angel Gabriel who sidetracked her murder/suicide attempt and carried her and her children to a Christmas church service and potluck dinner. The dirty and disheveled little family contrasted sharply with the celebratory finery worn by the congregation that gathered in candlelight on that Holy Night. She and her children smelled bad after living for who knows how long in that dying minivan.

I braced for hypocrisy from every judgmental eye that landed on the small family. Truthfully, I might have been looking for a fight.

Instead of trafficking in criticisms and cruel comments, the congregation warmly offered assistance and kindness. Before the evening was over, volunteers conjured up shelter for Holly and her children, food and clothing, and a tow for her minivan. (I had to hurry to the scene ahead of the tow truck to retrieve my Toyota Corolla and make a certain garden hose disappear.) In the weeks that followed, temporary shelter turned into an apartment paid for by an extra offering plate passed during the Sunday service.

Despite the charity, the crimes Holly attempted did not go unnoticed by Detective Andrea Stewart. Andy could not dismiss the danger to the children. However, instead of arresting Holly for attempted murder and suicide, Andy placed her in the care of the county social worker, who reached out to a family services psychologist. After a week of awkward suicide watch thinly veiled as friendly visits by a rotation of volunteers, therapy sessions were arranged, first to assess the danger, then later to help Holly adjust to staying alive.

The therapy sessions did not reveal a psychological defect. Holly did not suffer from depression or suicidal tendencies. She didn't share the drug and alcohol habits of the men in her past life. She didn't smoke, tobacco or otherwise. She had no taste for hard liquor. She paired her beer intake with bowling. Her frank answers to the therapist and social worker, both in confidence and in casual conversation, revealed that the most banal of evils led to Holly's final desperate act. A girl raised in poverty and a broken home. An education system that dusted her under its rug. Validation found in bad relationships with bad boys and bad men. Pregnancies from two different baby daddies who bolted when money for drink, drugs, or smoke got diverted to formula and diapers. No family to turn to. Impossible to get work as the single parent of two small children. Eviction from an apartment in Racine after months of missing rent. A winter road trip punctuated by placing a garden hose in an exhaust pipe on a silent night. She selected Essex because the gas in the minivan's tank wouldn't last much longer. She couldn't afford to run out before she and the children escaped into carbon-monoxide sleep.

A simple story full of simple cruelties.

For each new detail peeled from Holly, a new kindness blossomed from the community. Donated clothing piled up in her tiny apartment. Furnishings, food, and toys for Casey appeared at the church. A daycare center run by a pair of church women found openings for the baby and Casey, which freed Holly for a job at the Piggly Wiggly. Paychecks landed in Holly's purse and in an account at the Farmers and Merchants Bank of Essex. The job gave purpose to Holly's days as much as it did money in her pocket.

My cynical assertion that the noble Christians at Andy's church merely talk a good game took a beating.

"TAKE THE DAY OFF, your Holiday is here."

Holly laughed at her customary greeting when she climbed the steps to our mudroom. She held a plastic Post Office carton in both hands. "Oh, dear. Look at that belly. Time to lay off the beer."

Andy pecked the young woman on the cheek and ushered her into our home. Holly slid the carton onto the kitchen table and tugged off a blue wool watch cap that covered her light brown shoulder-length hair. Her bright eyes darted about to gather impressions of a warm, comfortable kitchen and an enviable home.

"Gosh, you guys have a nice place here," Holly blurted. She looked around like a kid on her first trip to Disney World.

"Thank you," Andy said. She gestured at the box on the table. "What's all this?"

"Remember you said you were going to stop by because I said you could have some of Toby Leo's onesies?" Andy remembered, but she had hoped that Holly had forgotten. "He's growing so fast, and I've got a ton of stuff from the church ladies. Remember I said you could have these?" Holly plucked a blue onesie bearing an embroidered red fire truck from the pile. She held it up with an eagerness to please that Andy found both charming and awkward.

"You shouldn't have, sweetie," Andy protested. Noting a flicker of disappointment in Holly, she quickly added, "but these will go to good use. I promise. Thank you. It's very sweet of you."

"Heck, I just—I was out and about. Thought I'd save you a trip." Holly rummaged through the basket. "I know this is all boy stuff, but hey—you have a fifty-fifty shot, right? Did you know they can tell the sex now? I never knew the sex with my kids. Then again, they were both super big surprises."

Andy took the onesie from Holly. She held it up and tried not to notice the frayed edges or the stains that didn't wash out. The hand-me-down had been handed down before. She said firmly, "Works either way. I have no problem with a daughter of mine wanting to drive firetrucks."

"Right?"

"Holly, you didn't have to come all the way out here."

"It's no trouble. Gosh, I haven't seen you for a while."

Andy felt a sting in Holly's words. "I know. I'm sorry. We've just been so busy getting the nursery ready and—"

"Can I see?" Holly bounced on the balls of her feet.

"I would love to show you, but it's a work in progress and Will and I don't want to unveil it until it's finished."

"Oh, yeah. I get it. Totally." There it was again. A tiny sting. "But you'll show me when it's finished, right? Promise?"

"Of course. You must come and see it and meet the little one."

Holly brightened. "Yeah. Totally. Your baby won't be much younger than Toby Leo. We can do play dates."

Andy folded the onesie and placed it back in the basket. "I can't even imagine what it will be like to have a baby that's able to sit up and play."

"And I can't wait." Holly grinned.

"Say, I hope I'm not prying, but may I ask a question?"

"Shoot."

"That's a nice car. Whose is it?"

Holly lowered her eyes slightly.

"Oh, that's mine. I just got it. I traded in the van, that old rust bucket. I got a super-good trade-in on it and a super-good price on this. I think it's a lot safer for the kids. Don't you think so? This has airbags. I don't think the van had airbags, at least not any that worked. We banged into plenty, and they never inflated."

The light blinked on for Andy.

The blue Malibu had been on Al Raymond's used car lot when Andy canvassed for stolen VINs. The sedan disappeared for a while, then returned with a fresh set of *"LOW LOW LOW!"* lettering painted in fluorescent colors on the windshield. She'd seen it parked in the front row several times.

"I didn't even have to give a downpayment," Holly added proudly. "How great is that?"

Andy knew why the car kept returning to the weedy gravel lot. "Are you making payments to Mr. Raymond? Weekly payments?"

"Uh-huh. I'm getting extra hours at the Pig. They're going to make me a cashier in another month or two. That's an extra dollar an hour."

And you're probably paying thirty percent interest with penalty clauses that will jack up the payments until repo is inevitable. Jesus, Holly. Andy bit her tongue. She was all too familiar with Al Raymond and his Buy-Here-Pay-Here franchise. The blue Malibu had been in and out of the lot with a string of owners who could not afford the car and who lost it as soon as they missed a weekly payment. Each repo put the car back on Raymond's for-sale line and left the former owner with no equity or consideration for the money already paid in.

She should have talked to me, Andy thought, then just as quickly thought, *And how does that help? To be babied and told at every turn that you're not grown up or capable of handling simple functions in life?*

Andy reminded herself that Holly came from a place where no one had faith in her, no one had answers for her, and no one would care when she was gone. Now here she stood, beaming. Proud of a bucket of hand-me-downs. Proud of the Chevy key in her purse.

Who am I, Andy asked herself, *to step on that?*

"Cashier, eh? You are moving up in the world, Miss Holiday. Good for you."

Andy's approval supercharged the smile on Holly's face.

7

———————

Half an hour after Holly drove away in her new blue Malibu, Andy picked up her phone. She scrolled down her list of contacts until she found the one Lydia had dictated to her. She touched the entry, then the phone number under the listing for Caroline Gaffney.

It rang. And rang. And diverted to voicemail instructions from the U.S. Cellular female robot.

Andy ended the call, then tapped out a text message.

Hi, Caroline. I'm Lydia Davis's sister Andrea. She asked me to call you regarding your daughter.

She added her phone number to the text, then set her phone aside.

An hour later she tried again.

It rang. Then stopped ringing.

"Caroline?" Andy asked the open connection. "This is Andrea Stewart, Lydia's sister."

"Oh, hi. Yes. Of course. Lydia. How is your sister? We were such good friends back in New York."

"Lydia's fine. She has a new baby girl. Well…not so new. You probably knew about that."

"Yes. Of course. Grace, right?"

Andy held the phone to her ear and her eyes on a thousand-yard gaze through the kitchen window and across the corn field behind the house. She didn't know she did it, but I would have seen the way her eyes crept into a squint. Wheels turning. Listening to nuances of tone, hesitation, word choices.

"She's a darling," Andy said in a light, airy voice that had no kinship with her serious stare. "Listen, Lydia suggested I give you a call. She mentioned that you had concerns about your daughter. I'm sorry, but Lydia didn't tell me her name."

"Baxter. My husband was a misogynist. He insisted we name her Baxter so that she could make partnership five years faster than the Tiffanys and Barbies at her future law firm."

"Well, I used Andy with a 'y' just to see the look on the other cops' faces when we met face to face."

Andy heard a laugh. Forced. But a laugh.

"How is your daughter doing?"

"Oh, she's fine. You know how girls can be at that age. On fire about injustice one minute. Screaming at her mother the next. Do you have kids?"

Andy touched the beached whale.

"I will in about fifteen weeks," she replied. "Our first."

"That's wonderful. I envy you that first experience. So many extremes culminating in something wonderful."

"And Baxter? She's well?"

"Sugar and spice and everything nice, with a touch of arsenic if you're not careful. She's in her first semester at college. Please tell Lydia not to be concerned. I may have painted an exaggerated picture the last time we spoke. The rollercoaster ride of having a teenaged daughter. Tell her I hope we can get together again. Perhaps meet in Chicago like we used to and see who's first to crash the credit card limit."

"I will," Andy said. "It was nice meeting you."

"It was nice meeting you, too, Allison."

The call ended. Andy lowered her squint to the screen of her phone and the time recorded for the call. 01:49.

Short, but plenty of time for the lies Andy detected.

8

———————

Tuesday

My preferred method of saying *I told you so* is supercilious silence. On rare occasions when I prove to be right about something, I like to savor it. Radiate it. Maybe squeeze out a tight-lipped smile.

"I told you so," I repeated to Andy after shutting down the Navajo engines on the Three Lakes Airport ramp.

"You do realize that you're digging yourself a very deep hole, my love." Andy lifted off her headset and laid it on the seat facing her. She chose a seat in the Navajo cabin for the short ride from Essex to Three Lakes because maneuvering into the copilot's seat up front posed a challenge. The last time she rode up front with me our little peanut was the size of a peanut. Not so much anymore.

"I know. But these opportunities are so rare."

"You mean being right?"

"Absolutely."

The subject at hand was Andy's decision to travel to Three Lakes. Andy gets credit for trying to steer clear. After the curious phone conversation with Caroline Gaffney, she called the Town of Three Lakes Police Department. She asked for and spoke to the chief. She made contact as one professional to another, giving a carefully measured description of Lydia's secondhand concerns about her friend's daughter. She described her own interaction with the woman. Perhaps the chief could have one of his officers perform a wellness check, she suggested. No problem, she was told. One of the department's patrol officers would swing by during the next shift. The chief promised a callback.

Andy put it out of her mind for the rest of Monday afternoon. I checked in with her at midday to let her know Arun had concluded his business in Peoria and we would be departing soon. I told her I would be home in time to take her out to dinner.

9

———————

"And?" I asked after we were seated at our favorite table at Los Lobos, our favorite Mexican restaurant in Essex. A server arrived to take a drink order before Andy could answer. She stayed with the water already placed on the table. I ordered an iced tea as a gesture of pregnancy solidarity.

"She wasn't home." Andy gazed longingly at her favorites on the paper menu. "Do you suppose I can get the enchilada with a side of Pepcid Complete?"

"She wasn't home, or she didn't answer the door?"

Andy nodded to credit me with points for the distinction. "The officer called her number. It went to voicemail. He left a message that the department had received reports of a sick raccoon—possibly distemper, which is not all that uncommon—in the area and that he had stopped by to look around."

"Clever cover," I said.

"Actually, that part was true. It's been a problem. Anyway, her car was gone, but there was no sign of any trouble. The visiting officer asked her to contact the department."

"Ah! Good idea. Then when she doesn't call—"

"She did call. Said she was out running errands. Said she hadn't seen any raccoons—sick or otherwise—and that everything was peachy."

"What about the missing daughter?"

"She gave the officer the same story she gave me."

40

"Maybe it's true."

"No. She was lying," Andy said flatly. "She lied to the officer just like she lied to me. Everything she said to the officer and to me was contrary to what she told Lydia last week."

"Maybe the situation changed. Maybe she was BS-ing Lydia."

"I don't think so. I don't think a week ago her daughter was missing after spending the summer at a therapy camp, and then miraculously off enjoying her first semester at college. I just…"

"What?"

Andy hesitated. She propped one elbow on the table and absently twirled a strand of her hair around one finger. "When I spoke to her, she sounded… scripted. Like she was telling me something she had been told to say. And don't forget she called me Allison."

"An honest mistake; you just met her."

"She called me Allison. At the end. Like she meant to make the mistake. She also said she and Lydia should go shopping in Chicago."

"And that's bad because…?"

"Lydia has never been to Chicago with Caroline. They used to burn through credit cards in New York."

"Huh. Why would she say that?"

"A message."

"Or, like misstating your name, a simple mistake. Are you going to follow up with the police chief?"

"And tell him what?" Andy tightened the strand of hair around her finger. "She lied. She lied to me. She lied to the police. I could understand if she had second thoughts about talking to me. But not the police. Something's not right." Andy picked up the menu which we knew by heart. "What are you having?"

"There's nothing booked for tomorrow," I said. "It's a short hop to Eagle River. There's a nice airport."

"What are you having?"

10

While Andy used the Eagle River Airport restroom, I let the airport manager know that we didn't plan to stay long and didn't require fuel. He watched me sign in and then handed me a beat-up key fob that belonged to a gunmetal gray Toyota Camry. The crew car's musty smell hit Andy the wrong way. She quickly rolled down the window and ordered me to do the same. Andy suffered bouts of morning sickness in her first trimester, and although the affliction seemed to have passed, occasional ambushes by random scents cause her to reconsider her most recent meal.

She concentrated on breathing and managed our navigation needs using my iPad. The blue route line showed us through Eagle River, then down Highway 45 toward the small town of Three Lakes. Before reaching the Three Lakes city limit, we turned onto a narrow, forest-lined road that wound its way toward Planting Ground Lake. Pretty scenery and occasional glimpses of sparkling blue water explained the area's appeal.

Even with help from my iPad and a moving map that guided us on a winding wooded path, we nearly missed the driveway entrance to Caroline Gaffney's home. The wooded gravel track between two berms had a small mailbox with no number affixed to it.

I braked to make the turn, but Andy intervened.

"Don't stop," she ordered. "Keep going."

We drove another quarter of a mile. A broad driveway appeared on our left.

"Turn in here," she said. I obeyed. "Switch places with me and make yourself scarce."

"I'm not going in with you?" I hadn't seen this as a situation requiring me to vanish.

"Pregnant lady all by herself is about as non-threatening as it gets. Big strong handsome man in tow changes the dynamic."

"What happens if she invites you in?"

"I'll go in and have a chat with her. You check out the property. If everything is cool you can go back and wait in the car." She read the concerned expression I wore. "I'll be fine. And I'm sorry. I didn't mean to dictate."

"Yes, you did. Don't worry. You had me at handsome." I popped the transmission in Park and hopped out. She did the same. We swapped places.

Andy snapped her seatbelt and reached for the shifter.

"Hang on a sec."

I reached behind the driver's seat and unzipped a flight bag pocket, then extracted a pair of tubular rechargeable battery packs. Resembling the flashlights they once were, the devices had been modified to contain a small electric motor with a shaft extending from one end. From the same pocket, I grabbed two six-inch carbon fiber model airplane propellers. Nothing to trifle with, the blades had square tips and sharp edges.

I pocketed one of the battery packs and propellers. I snapped the other prop onto the shaft of the second tube.

Andy waited patiently.

In passing, I asked, "Want to hear my new name for—?"

"No thank you." She looked at me. "Ready?"

I visualized two control levers and closed an imaginary hand on the ball tops of the levers. Pausing long enough to lift a loving gaze to meet Andy's gold-flecked green eyes, I smiled and shoved the levers forward to the stops.

Fwooomp!

I vanished. Gravity released me. My butt grew light on the cloth car seat. The seatbelt held me in place.

Andy put the car in reverse and released the brake. She backed onto the narrow lake road and retraced our path. She pulled into the driveway and wove a path through dense woods until we pulled onto a broad parking area beside a beautiful wooden structure. High peaked roofs and a confusing array of angles gave the rustic house a creative architectural character that strongly suggested that something small had grown over time. New casement windows betrayed recent renovation. Tall pines populated a rolling landscape. A thick layer of pine needles carpeted the ground. The house occupied the highest ground on the lot. If another property bordered this one, it was hidden by the trees.

Andy parked the car near a freestanding four car garage and paused, pretending to look over the property and acting uncertain about getting out of the car. I released the seatbelt, grabbed the passenger assist grip, and pulled myself out the open side window.

"Clear," I whispered just loud enough for her to hear.

She gathered her shoulder bag and stepped out of the car. I noticed exaggeration in her movements. She emphasized the pregnancy for anyone who might be watching. An extra bend of the back. A stroke of the baby bump beneath her long, loose sweater.

She walked around the front of the car. On her way past the garage, she lifted herself on her toes to look through dark garage windows.

I thanked the weather gods for a windless day and used short, light pulses of power to pull me along above and behind her. She climbed stone steps leading to the left side of the house. Additional steps lifted her to a stone terrace that continued around the side of the house. We faced a formal double entry made of fine varnished wood. Beveled frosted glass panels decorated both sides of a solid door.

Andy paused to take in the marquee feature of the property. A steep slope began immediately below the stone terrace. More inlaid stone slabs formed a stair that dropped roughly fifty feet to a dock indenting the brilliant blue lake. Pristine woodland lined the shore. A red and white speed boat nudged the dock. At a distance the boat looked like a sleek bathtub toy. The scene belonged on a postcard.

"If the lake side of this house isn't all windows, the designer should be shot," I muttered to Andy.

"Mmm-hmmm," she hummed without moving her lips, a precaution induced by the doorbell camera. She pressed a button mounted in the frame. The high-tech sentry sang an electronic ditty.

Andy waited. Mid-morning sunlight reflecting off the lake's surface populated the trees above and around the house with wiggling light fairies.

No hint of movement or sound of steps came from inside the house. Andy tried again.

I gripped an ornate carriage lamp on Andy's right, one of two bracketing the entrance.

Andy hit the bell a third time. Rude, but also a signal that we weren't going away. I made a mental guess at Andy's intent. With the police already having shown interest, the option to not answer the door lost credibility. The *pregnant lady alone* gambit increased the chances of Caroline Gaffney responding.

Movement inside stayed Andy's thumb from pressing the doorbell a fourth time. The inner door opened.

A fit-looking forty-something blonde woman wearing a dark red sweater over tan pants peered past the edge of the inner door. A flash of recognition replaced her initially guarded expression. Without hesitation, brilliant white teeth accented a broad smile. She hurried through the small entrance to unlock and open the outer door.

Before Andy could utter a word Caroline Gaffney launched an effusive greeting.

"Oh, my God, Cindy! I completely forgot!" She swung open the door and filled the frame. She pressed one hand against a startled look pasted on her face. "The brownies I promised! I totally forgot! I'm so sorry!"

Andy didn't miss a beat. "Oh, no, it's my fault. I should have called."

"I feel so bad. I don't have any ingredients here. Ach! And I won't be able to run to the store until tomorrow. I don't have a car."

"What happened to your car?" Andy's concern bordered on theatrical.

"Oh, nothing really. Something about the thingy that runs the dohickey. A bunch of stupid lights came on and it had to be towed. I just—I feel so bad about letting you down!"

"Don't worry about it." Andy closed a compassionate grip on Caroline's forearm. "You know there will be far too much bakery as it is. I made extra. I've got you covered." Andy delivered the last four words in a measured tone accompanied by direct eye contact.

I had no idea why the two women engaged in this strange theater until the inner door swung wide open behind Caroline Gaffney. A very tall man leaned into the frame. A tight shimmering athletic shirt showed off sculpted chest muscles, broad shoulders, and powerful arms. He wore long hair tied in a fist-sized man bun. His clean-shaved face could have been sculpted with a chisel. He flashed a smile at Andy. The smile did not share warmth with his hostile eyes.

"Who's this, honey?" he asked.

"Cindy came to pick up the brownies I was supposed to make for the Lake Association fundraiser. I'm such an airhead. I completely forgot. Darling, would you get my purse from the kitchen table? I want to send some money to make up for this."

"No need." He pulled a gold money clip from the hip pocket of tight trousers. He peeled off a fifty-dollar bill and handed it to Caroline. She took it from his fingers as if it had been fished from a toilet. She handed the money to Andy. "My husband Rob to the rescue."

"We haven't met," the man leaned forward and extended a hand. Andy shook it. "Rob Gaffney."

"Cindy Pepper." Andy held the fifty up by the edges. "I can't take this. It's too much."

"Please," Caroline insisted. "I'm super embarrassed to have biffed this. How does that look for the new kid on the block? And I can't be there this afternoon to help sort everything. Please. Take it. A donation."

Andy reluctantly pressed the bill into a sweater pocket. She waved at the man. "Thank you, Rob! Good to meet you!"

"You, too, Cindy."

"Say hi to Dennis and the kids!" Caroline chirped.

"I will."

Under the man's watchful eye, Caroline closed the door. Andy waved again. The man ushered Caroline Gaffney into a dark hallway. He closed the inner door behind him.

Andy performed an amplified pregnant lady shuffle back to the Camry and lowered herself into the driver's seat. She made a show of pulling a small wallet from her shoulder bag and folding the currency inside. The act gave me time to maneuver to the open passenger window. I grabbed the roof and poked my legs through. I twisted my body and shoved myself down, bumping the dash, hitting my head, and bashing my shin. I jammed my hands against the roof to stabilize.

"Good to go."

Andy spoke out of the side of her mouth. "Stay hidden. Until I tell you."

Andy started the car, then took one more look up through the windshield at the house. She tossed off a cheery wave, then backed up and started down the winding driveway.

11

"She had marks on her wrists." Andy turned the Camry onto the narrow road. "Possibly handcuffs. Or zip ties."

"Who the hell was King Kong?"

"Not the husband she just divorced. That much is certain."

"That guy looked like a pro wrestling wannabe, wouldn't you say… Cindy?"

"That was quick thinking. She recognized me."

I was about to ask how but then remembered Lydia's role in this unfolding drama. Caroline Gaffney would have taken one look at Andy and recognized her as Lydia Davis's sister, her *police detective* sister.

"Dee, why aren't we stopping?"

"Just stay the way you are." She glanced at the mirrors. "I want to drive away solo in case anyone is watching."

The house was already well out of sight. I peered into the trees on either side of the road. "You think someone is hiding in the woods and watching?"

"Or they set up cameras."

"Cameras? That's a little overboard, don't you think?"

"Did you see his clothes? He wasn't wearing off-the-rack workout sweats from Dick's Sporting Goods. Italian would be my guess. His shoes were worth more than I spent at Kohl's Department Store last year. I don't know why he's there, but something about this feels…I don't know…professional. If I'm right, setting up cameras to monitor the road using his phone would be a basic security protocol. Just like getting rid of her car."

"Wait…what? Getting rid of her car?"

"No car means whoever is doing this can play the 'she's not home' card if, for example, a cop came snooping around."

As usual with my wife, I hurried to catch up.

"Where are we going?"

"Where do you think?"

She fixed a grim stare at the road ahead. Her hands gripped the wheel at 9 and 3 like they teach it now that airbags blast into your face from the steering wheel. The ribbon of road scrolled out beneath us. After an interval of silence, Andy tossed a pronounced nod at the empty passenger seat.

Fwooomp!

I reappeared and dropped onto the seat cushion.

"The cops?" I asked.

"Of course."

We approached the junction where the narrow road ended at Highway 45. She eased off the accelerator. A right turn would take us back to Eagle River and the airport. A left would take us into the town of Three Lakes.

I checked the road behind us. Empty.

"Stop," I said.

"What?"

"Just…stop for a second."

Andy braked and let the car idle. I hurried to assemble loose thoughts.

"I get it," I said. "No question. Bringing the police in is the right thing to do."

"But…?"

I spoke slowly, carefully. "Whatever is going on there has been going on at a minimum since yesterday when the police performed their wellness check. It's been going on since before you called. *Despite* your call and the cop visit, Caroline Gaffney has not been moved."

"Yes…so…?"

"This isn't an abduction, and I don't think she's a hostage. I think she has a babysitter."

A minute squint compressed her eyes. It told me that Andy added this factor to the equation in her head.

"Okay…" she said slowly, "Let's say that's true. We now have a babysitter who just got spooked because I showed up at the door."

"No," I countered. "He didn't. The police didn't spook him yesterday. The pregnant woman from the bake sale didn't spook him today."

"Based on what?"

"Think about the way he handled it. He bet on deception, not evasion or force. He could have not answered the door, but I think he read you as someone who knew she would be home."

"Either way, he undoubtedly got on the phone and reported my visit to someone higher on his food chain. King Kong is not acting alone."

"Based on what?" I echoed back to her.

"How did he get there? He has no car. And how did Caroline's car go away? He's not alone."

"Huh."

"And the fact that he's not alone is all the more reason to bring in the proper authorities."

"Maybe…but…Dee…you need to ask yourself a question."

"I do?"

"Yes."

She thought about it. She nodded. "Fine. If he *or they* meant her harm, why hasn't it already been done?"

"Exactly. I mean…did she look like she's been assaulted?"

"Except for the marks on her wrists, no." Andy would know. She'd seen enough women who have known the attention of violent men.

"He isn't there to hurt her. He's there to keep her under control. Which begs the next question."

"Which is?"

I touched my toe to the landmine.

"If this has to do with the missing daughter, does bringing the police to the door help? Or does it trigger a bad outcome for the mother and the daughter?"

I held my breath and waited. At times like this it's best to give Andy thinking space. I checked to see if we were still alone on the road. Solitary individual traffic crossed in front of us on Highway 45. Nothing approached from behind.

Andy stared into the distance. When she spoke, the words came softly, as much to herself as to me.

"Caroline Gaffney didn't say no when Lydia offered my help. The help of a police officer."

"The *off the record* help of a police officer."

"She wants help…just not official help."

"Affirmative."

"Will, that's not her call to make."

"Isn't it? You know better than anyone that a situation gains an entirely different aspect once the official gong is rung. A menu of potentially more subtle options is instantly off the table."

"A menu of *real world* options is brought to the table by the police." I got *the look*. "I don't like what you're suggesting."

"You shouldn't. You came here to offer the woman law enforcement guidance. You planned to assess the situation and either persuade her to go to the police or explain why they can't help her—and have us home by dinner time."

She said nothing.

"Now you have intel that paints a darker picture."

"Exactly why this has to go to the authorities," she insisted.

"Dee, if the police knock on the door again—*and you know sending a patrol officer out here again is the first protocol*—Caroline will lie through her teeth, just like she did when you came to the door. That's if she answers the door at all. In both cases, the police have limited options."

Andy shook her head. "Not after I report this."

"Report what? A stranger, an outsider, waltzes into the station with a weird story about a local resident—*a recent divorcée*—with a man who is not her husband in the house. Sounds pretty basic to me. But take it a step further. Who is this stranger reporting the non-crime? Oh, let's see… someone who has never even met the woman. Even with your credentials, they'll assign equal if not more suspicion to the person making the report."

"I can get past all that."

"Probably. Let's say your badge gets you traction. Let's say they take you seriously. Three Lakes has …what? A chief and four full-time officers? Five? Shift rotations put only one, possibly two, officers on duty at any given time. The Oneida County Sheriff's Department might add support, but nobody's going to commit to a full-on tactical situation just because a resident who does not appear to be home fails to answer the door."

She frowned.

"Any option they have will only escalate the situation."

She said nothing. I waited a minute, then opened my mouth to press my case. She put her hand up between us.

"Don't oversell this, Will."

I bit my tongue. She drummed her fingers on the steering wheel.

"I suppose you have a suggestion," she said. "Something along unofficial lines."

"Unofficial is my middle name."

She resumed a stony silence. I understood why. This was hard for her. She had her rules and her deep faith in the badge she carried. Andy does not like to color outside the lines defined by the job that defines her.

She abruptly looked both ways, then accelerated onto the empty stretch of Highway 45, taking the left toward Three Lakes.

I did a double take. "I thought we were going back."

"We are," Andy said. "But we just created a stir. A benign stir. My gut tells me the pregnant bake sale lady wasn't enough to disrupt the status quo. We can give it a little time, which serves two purposes. One…sitting on a hostage can be boring and we want things to become boring again."

"What's the other purpose?"

"I need a bathroom."

12

———————

A short drive took us to the small town of Three Lakes. Light traffic and available parking reminded me that this was the off season. Several storefronts displayed *Closed* signs in harmony with the deserted sidewalks. I made a guess that the population of Three Lakes tripled in the summer.

We passed a blue municipal sign with white letters listing the Three Lakes Police Department above an arrow pointing down a side street. Andy noted the sign but drove on.

At a three-way intersection, she pulled into a Shell station and parked at the curb fronting a convenience store.

She lifted herself from the car. I hopped out and followed. Inside, I split off to buy coffee. A few minutes later I pressed a plastic cover on a cup and stepped back outside to wait for Andy. She stepped into the sunshine looking both radiant and visibly relieved. Showing no hurry to get behind the wheel again, she leaned against the Camry fender beside me.

"I want my bladder back."

I held the cup up for her to inhale a dose. She closed her eyes and issued a grateful and satisfied hum. "I now know it's possible to love you and hate you at the same time." A dimple poked the corner of lips she pinched against smiling. "Okay," she said. "I have an unofficial thought or two of my own."

"Really? I mean—yes, of course you do."

"Did you see the boat? At the dock?"

"Yeah."

"Grab your iPad and see if you can find an aerial view of the lake."

13

F *wooomp!*

The sound I hear each time I vanish seemed amplified by thick silence in the dense woods all around us. Andy had parked and killed the Camry's engine half a mile from Caroline Gaffney's driveway as a precaution against surveillance or cameras, a worry I didn't share but also didn't argue.

I released my seatbelt and began to float. Able to better straighten my leg, I pulled a BLASTER and carbon-fiber propeller from one of the cargo pockets. I snapped the prop on the power unit shaft and gave the slide control a nudge. The unseen prop spun, creating a whirring sound and sending air down my arm. Two more units sat in a pocket in my flight bag, but I knew the batteries for the unit in hand were fully charged and didn't see a need for a spare.

"Keep the line open," she reminded me. Through a connection between her phone and my Bluetooth earpiece I heard her in-person voice repeated by her phone voice on a delay.

"Affirmative." The reverse delay played my voice through her phone speaker.

"Handle it the way we discussed, Will. I mean it. Keep this simple. No unnecessary risks. And *no exposure.*"

My wife does not trust me with improvisation. I can't imagine why.

"Got it."

I grabbed the steering wheel and pulled myself across the Camry's console. I planted a kiss on Andy's lips. She issued a startled squeak, then reached up and found the back of my head. She pulled me in for more.

"There's another option," I said when we parted.

"What?"

"We bag this business with Caroline Gaffney and just make out here in the car."

I looked for a smile. The opposite coursed her face. She reached for and found my arm and closed a grip. Like dark clouds reflected on smooth water, fear and worry surfaced on her smooth skin.

"What?"

Unable to see me, she lowered her eyes.

"Dee, what is it?"

She spoke without looking up. "This trip. You knew I'd stick my nose in it—not just for Lydia—but like you said, because I needed something. Something …more."

I closed my hand over hers. "I know you."

"Yeah." Her tone soured slightly. "That's the problem. I know you, too. Will, you can be amazing with this…*thing*…but it's getting out of hand. With Lewko. With New York. With treating those kids in Evermore. It's getting scary. All those media people calling after they found out who I was in New York—it took months for that to settle down."

Fwooomp! I reappeared. It felt wrong to sit there vanished. I could have found better times to have this conversation but kept the thought to myself.

"They only came after you because you stole the spotlight from Lonnie Penn," I said playfully. She ignored the compliment. "Hey, we got through it together. That's the deal. We get through it together. And yeah, I knew you'd want to help Lydia. I knew you'd want to bite into this and shake it."

She chuckled involuntarily. "Oh, so now I'm a terrier?"

"Sometimes. But the point is, I'm all in for you. Whatever you want. Even if that includes picking out gender neutral baby blankets." A recent activity I might not have handled perfectly.

She shook her head. "That's the problem. I don't want you all in. Not on this thing with Lydia and her friend and her friend's daughter. I don't want you throwing caution to the wind."

"I'm not, I'm just—"

"But you will. I know you. You'll take chances. You're getting cavalier about this *thing*. You've done it several times now. Just popping in and out of sight and saying, 'What difference does it make? People won't believe what they see. Who are they going to tell?"

"Who's really going to believe they saw an in—"

"That's what I mean! I have news for you; a *lot of people.* The top news story after New York was Spiro Lewko's Disappearing Act. Witnessed by *hundreds.* Stephen Colbert did a whole bit about it with Tom Hanks. YouTube is full of imitators and Facebook is flooded with memes. It's like an infection."

"That's why it's called vir—"

"You're not listening to me. If you go popping out of sight in front of King Kong, what's to say he isn't fully aware that this crazy technology exists? What's to say he doesn't put two and two together? It's part of the national conversation. *If we're not careful, you will be part of the national conversation, Will.* You can't pretend you don't know that."

"Are you saying we let this go?"

"No." She huffed a frustrated breath. "No. There's something bad going on at that house." Her eyes rose and met mine. "No. We do this. But here and now, promise me that you will not expose yourself. Not to King Kong. Not to Caroline. No matter what happens. Even if it puts Lydia's friend in a bad spot. You put us first. Promise me."

"That's an easy promise to make." I reached across the console and laid my hand on our baby's hiding place. "Us first. All three of us. I promise."

She slid her hand over mine and held it long enough for both of us to feel our unborn child kick a field goal. We both laughed.

"I guess that makes it unanimous."

She pushed out another deep breath, this one laden with relief.

"Let's do this," I said.

"Let's do this carefully."

14

———————

Andy enforced the police protocol of not generating the sound of a car door closing. She made me perform the window exit trick again. As before, the maneuver was awkward. I came close to hurting my back. When my feet cleared the opening, I called out.

"Clear."

She touched the power button and closed the window.

I aimed my BLASTER straight up at the gap between trees lining the road. Blue sky issued a wordless invitation. I thumbed the slide control forward. The prop spun and broadcast its sandpaper whine. Thrust pushed air down my arm and pulled me skyward. The Camry fell away. Tree crowns fell past me. A plateau of forest spread in every direction.

I indulged in the exhilarating ascent. One. Two. Three hundred feet. I neutralized the slide control and let myself continue upward, a reminder that without a functioning BLASTER and action on my part, nothing would stop me from rising to an altitude where hypoxia would kill me.

At roughly five hundred feet, with the roof of the gray Camry barely visible on the road below me, I added power and lowered my arm. The new thrust angle converted my trajectory to forward flight.

Lakes sprawled around me. Planting Ground Lake, one of the largest, lay at my feet, blue and shimmering. A land mass that didn't quite qualify as a peninsula nudged the blue water. The peaked roofs on the Gaffney property rose among the trees.

I flew a descending path over the lake, swung around in a wide loop, and lined up an approach to the house. At a safe distance, I killed the BLASTER and coasted between tall pines. Moments later, I pulsed quick shots of reverse thrust and came to a stop several inches above the stone terrace. I silenced the BLASTER and pocketed it, then anchored myself by gripping the corner of a patio table.

The designer of the house didn't fail his or her primary mandate. A wall of windows invited the lake view into multiple rooms. The largest, a rustic family room built around a huge stone fireplace, dominated the center of the house. Against a reflection that failed to include my own image, I peered through the glass.

Caroline Gaffney curled up in a fat leather recliner. She tucked her legs under her body and laid her head against the top cushion. Her left arm stretched across the arm of the chair. Black zip ties circled her wrist and secured her to the leg of an end table fashioned from a stone slab bearing a strong resemblance to the terrace and steps outside. I might have been able to move the table, but I doubted the woman would get far with it attached to her arm.

King Kong was nowhere to be seen.

His absence and her presence suggested that I might meet Andy's mandate to *keep it simple*. I pushed off the patio table and floated to a sliding door. I grabbed the handle, then planted my feet on the stone terrace. Using my free hand as counterpressure, I pulled.

The door moved. Not locked.

I scanned the interior one more time and then listened. Distant audio throbbed through the glass. I assigned the sound to a television in another room. I crossed mental fingers that SportsCenter absorbed King Kong's attention.

Fwooomp!

I reappeared and dropped my full weight on my feet. I slowly pushed the door open. The shush sound of wood sliding in the track brought Caroline Gaffney's head up off the recliner headrest. She threw a startled glance in my direction.

I lifted my index finger to my lips. She nodded and pointed in the direction of a hallway joining the far corner of the great room. I nodded back at her.

Leaving the sliding door open enough to pass through, I stepped onto plush carpeting. From a pocket I extracted my pilot survival knife. After unfolding the razor-sharp blade, I moved into position beside Caroline and pinched the zip tie. I carefully slid the blade under the plastic and tugged. The tie snapped open. She wiggled her arm free of the restraint and rubbed the skin on her wrist.

"*Who are you?*" she whispered.

"*You met my wife earlier. Let's go.*"

She lifted herself from the recliner trying hard not to let crinkling leather betray her movement. She pointed at her bare feet.

"*He took my shoes.*"

I shook my head and jerked a thumb at the exit. We crossed the carpeted floor in silence. She slipped through the patio door. I followed. I stopped long enough to slide the door shut again. No point in leaving a flashing sign that said, *They went this way.*

Caroline started on a path that would take her around the house to the parking lot. I grabbed her upper arm and pointed down the steps that descended to the dock.

"*This way,*" I whispered. I tugged her arm. She glanced back at the house, then followed my instructions.

We began down the steep stone steps. I checked over my shoulder. No pursuit.

Yet.

I glanced at my watch. 11:57.

Crap.

Whatever occupied King Kong's attention was about to reach the top of the hour. The lunch hour. Bad timing increased the odds that he would stroll through the house and find his prisoner gone.

We descended toward the lake. Thick pine trunks towered over us. I resisted hurrying. The stairway had no handrail, the angle was steep, and the stone steps were minutely uneven, adding a touch of instability to the descent.

I felt relief when we reached the foot of the dock. I thought Caroline would have figured it out by this point, but instead of trotting out to the boat, she stopped.

"Is someone picking us up?" she asked.

"No," I said. "Get in the boat."

"What?"

"We're taking the boat. That's the plan."

She landed her hands on her hips and attitude on her face.

"I don't suppose you have the key."

I looked at the outboard motor hanging from the back of the boat.

"That's not a pull start?"

She shook her head.

"What's going on, Will?" Andy's voice joined the conversation. I pointed at the earpiece and gestured for Caroline to stand fast for a moment.

"A little hiccup here," I said. "I don't have a key for the boat."

"You need a key for the boat," Andy said, not helping.

"It's in the kitchen," Caroline said.

"It's in the—" I repeated.

"I heard," Andy interrupted. The silence that followed berated me almost as much as I berated myself.

Andy's suggestion to use the boat had been brilliant. Largely because I didn't want Andy anywhere near this extraction if something went bad. I liked the idea of her waiting at the highway junction for my call. King Kong couldn't follow us on the water, and Caroline would know how to find a marina for a rendezvous with Andy.

"How did you not know the boat needs a key?" Caroline asked angrily.

"I fly airplanes. I don't drive boats."

Andy, thankfully, said nothing.

The rough shoreline on either side of the pier had no beach. Water lapped against a two to three-foot ledge of dirt tangled with tree roots. Hiking was out of the question without shoes. Swimming wouldn't get us anywhere that King Kong couldn't go on land.

"Does that thing have oars?"

"It's not a rowboat," she replied. I didn't care for her tone.

I hooked her upper arm and trotted out the white painted dock to the mooring. Just a small speed boat, probably capable of pulling a single skier, it had only two fixed seats and a bench on both sides of the rear well. I could not help myself; I looked at the dashboard. Yes, sure as hell, there was an ignition key slot for an electric starter. I looked at the engine to see if the woman with me simply didn't understand the concept of a pull start. She did. I looked for an oar but did not find one.

A balled-up light gray boat cover near the engine caught my eye.

"Get in," I ordered.

Caroline hesitated. I stepped on the bench seat and hopped down into the boat, which rocked under my weight. I turned and held out my hand.

"Get in and get under this boat cover." More hesitation. I held out my hand and said, "I'm going after the key."

"Why don't we just go back up and run for it?"

"Because you have no shoes, and he doesn't need to catch me. He only needs to catch you. Get in!"

She frowned but obeyed. A moment later she curled up on the rear deck. I threw the stiff canvas cover over her.

"It stinks," she said.

"Where's the key?"

"Kitchen. On a magnetic hook on the refrigerator. There's a yellow float attached. You can't miss it."

"Stay put. I'll be right back." I took several steps, then reversed. "Hey!"

"What?"

"This thing does work, right? Is there gas in it?"

"Fine time to ask," she snapped. "Yes."

"Okay. Be right back."

I reversed again and retreated down the dock. Andy's voice broke in my ear.

"Will, talk to me."

I gave her a quick update. Vanishing and launching would have been quicker, but I couldn't be sure Caroline wasn't peeking. I climbed the steps two at a time.

When I didn't answer Andy, she announced, "I'm coming."

"No! Stay where you are. I got this. Dee, I mean it. Please stay put." A tense moment of silence passed through the connection during which I mustered an argument invoking vivid images of Andy and our unborn child being manhandled by King Kong.

"Fine."

"Let me do this." I glanced back at the boat. Caroline stayed hidden. I pulled out a BLASTER as I climbed the stone steps. I snapped the prop on the electric motor shaft.

Halfway to the top, a split second away from vanishing, I stopped and realized my second major error.

"Oh, shit," I muttered.

"What is it?" Andy demanded.

I didn't answer.

15

K ing Kong stood on the terrace with his tree trunk arms folded across a huge chest. Looking up the stone stairs, the guy appeared even bigger than he had before.

"Where is she?"

"Who?" Stupid response, but the first that came to mind.

"Really?" He sounded tired and genuinely disappointed. "You're a fucking idiot."

He wasn't entirely wrong.

"She's gone," I said. "The cops picked her up at the road. They'll be here any second now."

"Wow, I would be in real trouble," he said, oozing sarcasm, "if that were true. And if she wasn't hiding under that boat cover."

"Well, if you knew that, why did you ask?"

The scowl forming on his face said he didn't care for impertinence.

I backed down a step. Then another. I cobbled together a plan involving a high-speed run to the pier, cutting the lines on the boat with my knife, shoving the boat as hard as possible out onto the lake, and leaping after it. In my head, the plan ended with the boat wallowing to a stop and this guy swimming out and beating the crap out of me unless I implemented the forbidden—vanishing and taking Caroline Gaffney with me.

I took another cautious backward step.

"Here's how this is going to go…" He matched my step with one of his own. "I'm coming down there to tear off one of your arms and beat you with

61

it until you tell me who you are and who that woman was this morning. And when you're done spilling your guts and begging me for your life, I'm going to crush your skull in my bare hands. How's that sound?"

"Impractical," I replied. I glanced at either side of the stairs. Pine trees populated the hillside. Many were old and mature. "I mean, you're a big guy, I grant you. But ripping an arm off? I dunno. There's bone and tendons. And I've been told skin can be tough."

"I'll manage." He made it sound like he's had practice. He took another step.

"What's your name?" I asked.

"Fuck you."

"Because I've been calling you King Kong in my head. Is it okay if I just go with Kong?" I took another step down. Roughly half of the stairs remained between us. I gauged the distance to the largest pine tree trunk on my left.

"How about if you answer my questions before you have your balls in your mouth and you find it difficult to speak?"

"Fire away."

"Who was the woman? Partner? Wife? Girlfriend?"

"Complete stranger. Met her at a monster truck show."

"Right. Is that your bun in her oven?"

I hated that he went straight to Andy's condition. Another reason to keep her away from all this. He knew it, too. He was baiting me.

I took a step down. Then another. I needed two more. I needed something else, too. A broken branch lay near the next step. Too small. A larger one lay on the slope beyond the first branch. I reached and scooped it up, then snapped off the weak end. The remaining portion, roughly the size and shape of a baseball bat, seemed solid enough for the task I had in mind.

He chuckled. "You do know I'm gonna ram that puny stick up your ass."

"Good thing it's puny."

One more step gained the best position I was going to get. He picked up the pace of his descent.

"Hey, look." I pointed at the house. "A baby osprey!"

I didn't wait to see if the silly line and clumsy ploy made a difference. I darted sideways off the stone step and onto the steep hillside. I nearly lost my footing. I scrambled to the nearest tree trunk, one of the largest. I drew myself erect and squeezed up against the tree so that he could not see me.

The inept attempt at distraction and absurd attempt to hide was intentionally idiotic—and more importantly, completely nonthreatening. I made myself thin behind the tree and got the response I hoped for.

He laughed. "Are you serious?"

More than you know.

I tucked my makeshift club against my chest and—

Fwooomp!

—I vanished.

Using the tree trunk for leverage, I shoved off. A brief glide carried me downhill and across the stone steps. I grabbed the nearest substantial tree trunk on the other side.

Kong trotted down the steps. He seemed to be in no hurry. Why would he? Hiding behind a tree was stupid. I had nowhere to go. And the woman hiding in the boat wasn't going anywhere. He had complete command of the situation.

I lowered myself into a crouch and shifted position with one arm around the tree. If this gambit failed, I intended to kick off the ground and regroup well out of reach.

Kong descended the steps at a light trot. For a man of his size and bulk, he managed to be light on his feet. He reached the tree I'd hidden behind and stopped.

"Come out, dumbass." He leaned back and forth to try and catch sight of me. A moment passed. "You're not going anywhere."

He hopped off the stairs and stepped across the slope to the tree. Up close now, he looked around the tree trunk. I was gone. Impossible. He searched behind the tree and the general area. He swung his formidable head from side to side, hunting for me on the slope.

He crouched slightly. His fingers curled into fists. His posture shifted to something tense and deadly.

"Nice try, asshole," he muttered, looking for a response.

I stayed silent.

"Go ahead." Bravado sharpened into anger. "Hide. We'll see if you want to come out when I start pounding on your lady friend."

He returned to the steps, constantly searching, hunting. Finding nothing, he hopped down the steps.

I watched his legs and feet, measuring his cadence. One. Two. One. Two. The stone slabs formed a steep stairway. One foot for each. I watched how his back leg swung for the next step as he approached.

He reached the slab nearest me. He planted his left foot. I thrust my unseen makeshift club out behind his calf like a fist-sized battering ram. His back leg swung the next step down but instead connected with the branch. His leg locked. Too late to adjust, he'd committed to the descent. His center of gravity carried his body over his locked-up legs. The branch whipped from my hands and snapped into view, but its purpose had been served.

He tripped.

Body mass threw him forward. His legs tangled in the branch. His arms flew out. He sailed forward and down. Splayed hands tried to break the fall. I heard a snap. He cried out, twisted and rolled. The roll made matters worse. One shoulder connected with a hard stone slab. He spun around. His legs sailed over his head and whipped down. I didn't see what happened, but I heard it. His left shin hit a stone edge. A muffled *crack* ignited a high-pitched scream. He performed another roll and skidded to a stop on his back with his head pointed downhill.

One leg folded under him. The other pointed uphill. Between the ankle and the knee, the bone formed an angle that did not belong to nature. My stomach rolled.

He squeezed his eyes tightly shut and howled.

Fwooomp!

I reappeared and emerged from my ambush.

Gasping, he opened his eyes. Through a curtain of pain, he spotted me standing a few yards uphill.

"Damn," I said. "That looks like it hurts."

16

"Will."

Andy's voice carried in the clear and then on delay in the Bluetooth earpiece. The duality of it confused me. I looked up the hill and saw her striding across the terrace. She descended several stone steps.

"Stop!" I shouted. The sight of her on the steep stone steps after watching someone trip and fall sent my heart rate through the roof. "Stop. Just…stay there. Better yet, go back up."

"Where's Caroline?"

I turned toward the boat and shouted. "Caroline! Come out!"

The stiff boat tarp shifted. Blonde hair and red sweater emerged. She tossed the canvas cover aside and wrinkled her nose at it. She sniffed her sweater and made a disgusted face that turned to astonishment when she saw Kong lying inverted, ten steps up from the bottom.

"Come," Andy instructed her. "We're leaving."

"Hey!" Kong cried out. "You can't leave me like this. You gotta help me."

"Well, tempting as that is," I said, "I'm more inclined to tear that leg off and beat you to death with it. How's that sound?"

"C'mon, man," He spoke through gritted teeth, "that was just trash talk. You gotta help me."

"We're leaving," Andy repeated. "We will send the police for you. They can call an ambulance."

"Although I honestly don't know who's gonna carry your ass up this hill," I muttered.

Caroline climbed the first half dozen steps then detoured onto the slope. She maintained a safe distance from Kong. Pine needles made the footing slippery. I carefully skidded down the hillside and reached for her. Lending an arm to grasp, I led her past the prostrate bodybuilder. She winced when sharp root edges and stones hurt her feet.

"Oh, Jesus," she whispered when she saw the compound leg fracture. She turned away. We rejoined the steps above Kong. Caroline finished the climb to Andy who waited on the terrace.

"Hi," Andy said. "I'm—"

"Andrea. I know." Caroline threw a hug around my wife. "I knew the instant I saw you. Thank you. Thank you for coming back."

"Go and get what you need from the house. We're leaving. We will take you somewhere safe. And then we'll talk. I promise. Move."

Andy's firm instructions grounded the woman. Caroline looked frightened and pale. She nodded and disappeared into the house.

"What's your name?" Andy called down to Kong.

"Fuck you," Kong snapped.

"Fine. Will," she called to me. I looked up at her. She dangled a pair of latex gloves in the air. "Put these on and take his wallet and phone."

I climbed the stairs to get the gloves. Returning to where Kong lay, I snapped the too-small gloves halfway over my fingers. Good enough.

"Phone and wallet," I ordered.

The big man let go of the wrist he'd been holding and shoved one hand in his pants pocket. He pulled out a knife. *Click!* A nasty blade snapped open.

"Come near me and I'll cut you. I mean it."

"No problem," I said calmly. I picked up the branch I had used to trip him. "Now, from what I know about a fracture like that, it is desperately important that you do not move and *do not* allow the bones to be damaged further or the whole question of whether you will ever walk again comes into question."

I planted my feet on the slope adjacent to his injury. Like a major leaguer stepping up to the plate, I adjusted a firm grip on the stick and took a couple practice swings over his leg.

"Alright! Alright! Jesus!" He dropped the knife and threw up both of his hands in surrender.

"Wallet," I said.

He squirmed until he was able to pull a thin wallet from his back pocket. He tossed it. Poorly. The leather flopped at my feet.

"Now your phone. Open it first."

He pulled a black plastic-cased smartphone from his pocket and tapped the screen to open it. He tossed it. I caught it despite the flopping latex fingers. I heaved the stick into the trees and climbed the steps to Andy. I handed her the phone which she took with one gloved hand. With her other hand, she used one knuckle to tap the screen and scroll.

I flipped open the wallet.

"He's got a California driver's license under the name Benjamin Everly," I said. "A couple of credit cards with the same name. A Wisconsin concealed carry permit—"

"Is he carrying? Did you check him?"

I hadn't, but his shirt and workout pants offered no concealment for a gun. "Not that I could see."

"Move back," Andy ordered me. She did the same. We edged out of Kong's line of sight just in case. I finished rifling through the wallet. "The carry permit is the same name. No cash, but he had that money clip. Nothing else."

"Nothing else? No Triple A card? Insurance cards?"

"Nope."

Andy held up the phone. The screen showed recent activity.

"He called someone four minutes ago. We need to go."

17

———————

Andy used her phone to snap pictures of the driver's license and the recent calls screen on Kong's phone. She left the phone and wallet on the patio table. We entered the house and gathered Caroline who found her shoes but not her purse or phone. The woman grew irate and then panicky until Andy firmly told her to leave both items. Andy assured Caroline she would be returning soon with the police.

We hustled from the house. Moments later Andy drove the Camry down the narrow curving blacktop at fifteen above the posted 25 mph speed limit.

"Does the name Benjamin Everly mean anything to you?" Andy asked our passenger.

Caroline, seated behind me, replied, "No." She sounded weak and winded. I glanced back. Strands of her hair hung askew. Her makeup stood out against pale skin. A smudge of mascara stained the corner of one eye.

Delayed trauma, I thought. Events caught up with her.

"Have you ever seen him before?" Andy asked.

"Never. He—he just showed up at the door. He pushed his way in. He tied my hands. I thought he—he might—you know. God, I never felt so—so utterly helpless. But he didn't do anything. He didn't touch me. He didn't take anything. He didn't say anything or ask me anything. He wouldn't answer any questions. He made me sit there while he watched TV. He did nothing. It was like that for three days."

"Did he speak to anyone on the phone?" Andy asked.

"Several times. He always left the room."

"Did he make the call? Or did someone call him?"

"I…uh…I'm not sure. He just—one minute he's just sitting there, and the next he's on the phone."

"Did he say anything to you about your daughter?" Andy asked.

"About Baxter? No…I don't think so. Why?"

"Why?" I interrupted. I twisted to face the back seat. "You do know that's the whole reason we're here." She held a blank stare. I pressed. "You told Lydia she was missing. Is that correct?"

"I guess so—"

"You guess so?"

"—I mean, yes."

"How are you not sure? Lydia said you said she disappeared from some camp. Is that true?" I asked.

"I don't know—I mean, yes. I think so."

"Christ, lady," I said. Andy threw a warning glance at the rising tension in my voice.

"I'm sorry…I didn't mean to…I mean, I'm glad you came. And yes, I'm worried about Baxter."

"Okay. What's the deal with this camp?" I asked.

"It's an isolation immersion. The opposite of an intervention. We—I— her parents—we're not supposed to interact with her until she's ready."

"Sounds a little 'culty' to me," I muttered.

"Oh, it's not," Caroline insisted with what sounded to me like the true belief of a cult member. She must have heard it in her own voice, because she quickly settled her tone. "Look. Wayne and I were at our wits' end. Baxter was going through all the issues and rebellion you'd expect from a teenaged girl but dialed up to 11. A dear friend in New York stepped in and persuaded her private therapist who's always booked out to eternity—absolute top of the profession—to help us. She worked with Baxter, and it was like a breath of fresh air. We had our daughter back. And when she recommended the Academy—Saint Martin Academy—it sounded ideal but impossible to get into. My friend helped. It *is* the very top of the line. The top."

"What about the gone missing part?" I asked, tightening my restraint. "Doesn't sound so 'top' if they lose the kids."

"I—I don't know."

"How can you not know? We came all the way up here—"

"Will," Andy said softly. She reached across the console and stroked my arm.

"I'm sorry," Caroline said. "Yes. No. I mean—I don't know."

Andy glanced at me. I rolled my eyes.

"Caroline," Andy said gently, "it's alright. Just tell us."

Caroline said, "This feels like the old pattern. Before she went into therapy, Baxter ran away several times. A few times she went to her friends' homes without telling us. Other times, we just didn't know. But she agreed to go to the camp—she was excited—but now this—I just—it feels different."

"Different how?"

"She sent a few post cards from the camp. Very basic. Neutral. Lukewarm apologies. I didn't know whether she meant it or if they made her write them. She runs hot and cold like that. Then in September, nothing. Three weeks ago, I got angry. I told them I was coming. They told me not to, but I said I wouldn't take no for an answer. That's when they told me she was no longer there. I blew up. Things got heated. They said I signed off on the policy when I enrolled her. Kids can come and go as they wish. It's not a prison. They said she's eighteen. She has legal rights. I was furious."

"That's when you spoke to Lydia?" I asked.

"Around that time, yes. Maybe I was angry. Maybe I colored the picture a little too—"

"So, it's more accurate to say she just took off," I said, "than to say she's 'missing.'"

"Did Everly—the big guy—did he say anything about Baxter?" Andy injected with a soft tone deployed as much to soothe Caroline as to send me a message to back off.

"No. Nothing about her. Except when you called."

"That thing about college?" Andy asked.

"Yes. He told me what to say. He made me practice. He warned me. He said a lot of very graphic things about what would happen to the boys if I spoke out of line."

Andy, eyes fixed on the road, asked, "He threatened the boys? Specifically the boys? Not Baxter?"

"Uh-huh."

"That stuff you said on the phone about Baxter being in college…did he emphasize it? Or was it an aside?"

"Um…just…he said to say that Baxter's in college and that everything is fine."

"Where are your boys?" I asked.

"They're with their dad in New York. He insisted that they finish school in the city. God! I need to call him. I need to know that they're alright." Caroline gripped the back of Andy's seat. "Please! Can I use your phone?"

I reached for mine when Andy stopped me.

"You can call when we get to the police station," Andy said. "There are good reasons not to make calls to your ex-husband from our phones."

"What do you mean?"

"I mean that we don't know if your ex- is involved, and if he is, whether having someone invade your home and hold you like that makes your ex-husband also a target or the perpetrator." Andy glanced at me and read the new question on my face. To me she said, "New York lawyer. Might be tangled up in something that made a client angry."

"Ah."

From the back seat, "That sonofabitch."

We reached the Highway 45 junction. This time Andy didn't stop and let the car idle. She turned left. Ten minutes later she selected a parking spot from a row of empty spaces facing the single-story Three Lakes Municipal Building and Police Department.

18

"What do I tell them?" Caroline leaned forward and looked through the windshield at the municipal building.

Andy twisted in the driver's seat. "Go slow. Tell them exactly what happened. Nothing more. No opinions. No guesses. No speculation. Be precise and don't omit anything. Not even the smallest detail. Okay?"

Caroline looked uncertain.

"I'll be there. I can fill in details in terms they will understand. I want to let them know about that man on your property. They need to dispatch an ambulance but have police present."

Caroline gripped her knees as if to steady them, or else to steady her hands.

I opened my door and slid into the cool sunshine. It might have been an aftereffect of the encounter with Kong, but my shoulders felt stiff and tense. The sensation ran contrary to my growing relief.

This trip began as a lark on Andy's part with backhanded encouragement from me—a break from the combined boredom of homelife and anxiety of the approaching childbirth. A way to get out of the house. But with things taking a dark turn, I fully agreed with Andy. The time had come to hand this off to the police.

My mind wandered to the Navajo waiting on the Eagle River Union Airport ramp. She didn't need fuel for the return trip to Essex. A quick preflight check and we would be on our way. The sky beckoned like a cleansing haven. Airborne, we would put Three Lakes and Caroline Gaffney in our wake.

Caroline opened her car door and stepped onto the pavement from the rear seat of the Camry. Bright sunshine did her no favors. She looked worn.

I heard it, but didn't immediately identify it. A snap. A muted tap. I'm not sure what to call it. I had no time to register the sound because something more immediate trapped my attention.

Caroline fainted. She collapsed where she stood.

I reached for her but couldn't get around her car door fast enough to catch her. She folded and dropped to the asphalt. Her upper body flopped backward. Her eyes drooped and her mouth went slack. Her head hit the pavement. Hard. Hard enough to bounce.

I dropped to my knees and shoved my hand under the back of her head. Her hair felt wet and slick. My fingers came away bloody.

"Andy! She faint—"

The word lodged in my throat like unchewed meat. Rigid and hurting.

The blood on my hand was nothing compared to the spreading stain in the center of Caroline's chest. Not just a spreading stain, but a gush. A stream. Blood saturated Caroline Gaffney's red sweater. Dark.

Blood shouldn't show on a red sweater like that.

"Jesus, Andy!" I called out. "Andy, I think she's b—"

I looked up through the open rear door of the Camry and froze.

Andy sat in the driver's seat with her head turned. She did not move. She faced me.

Her skin white.

Her eyelids fluttering.

Her mouth open but unable to speak.

I didn't understand. I'd never seen shock like that on her face, not on my police detective wife whose iceberg cool never ceases to astonish me.

"Wha—?" I started to ask.

She lifted her hand. Blood ran down her fingers.

"Will?"

She looked at me then down at her belly.

19

I threw open the driver's door. Andy blinked. Bewildered. Pale. Unable to speak. For the second time in as many minutes, I watched blood wick through the fabric of a sweater. A dark stain spread across Andy's abdomen, across the baby bump.

"Dee! Jesus!"

I tore the seatbelt free and threw the straps aside. My hands came away bloody. Andy slumped toward the passenger seat. I pulled her back and flattened my hand against the spreading blood, willing it to stop, begging it to go back where it belonged. Beneath the soaked fabric, I felt the rising curve of her belly. Our baby.

"I need help!" I shouted.

Sunshine and the quiet of a deserted off-season holiday town answered me with pitiless silence. I shouted again. And again.

Pressing the wound beneath Andy's right breast, I leaned my elbow against the car's steering wheel. The nasal horn sounded. I held it down. The car horn joined a stream of curses flowing from my lips.

How long I held that horn down, I have no idea.

I heard footsteps. Shouts.

Someone tapped my shoulder.

"Shot," I snapped. "She's been shot! My wife! She's been shot!"

"Move!" a woman scolded me. A hard grip closed on my shoulder and tugged me backward. I wanted to resist. I wanted to stay and press Andy's blood back into the wound, but the grip that pulled me away belonged to

74

someone strong, someone better qualified to do something—*anything*—than me.

A woman in a blue uniform leaned in over Andy.

I staggered backward. Electrocuted. Paralyzed. Numb.

The woman touched the radio mic button on her shoulder. She spoke. I caught key words.

Ambulance.

Gunshot victim.

Adult female. Appears to be pregnant.

A man in police blue pulled me backward. "Give her room."

A third uniformed body in blue ran past, rounded the car and dropped on the other side of the car where Caroline had fallen. He said, "This one is dead."

Dead.

Not dead—not dead—dead isn't possible—not possible—

The word didn't belong, couldn't belong, couldn't be anywhere near us, near Andy.

"I got a pulse!" the woman leaning over Andy announced.

"Help her," I begged. "Please!"

"Two minutes out!" the officer pushing me away said. "Help is two minutes out."

It might as well have been forever.

20

"Mother and baby are stable."

The man in scrubs said the only words I ever wanted to hear. He spoke from a distance, nearly the length of the sterile hallway. He showed mercy and made the critical announcement as soon as he saw me. I rose and hurried to meet him.

"Mother and baby are stable," he repeated, now close enough to take my arm in a firm grip. I must have looked unsteady.

My throat closed, trapping words. I could not answer to thank him. I could not speak.

His grip intensified.

"Come. Sit with me."

He led me back to the pale waiting room where desperation fidgets on plastic chairs and the floor is carpeted with dread.

THEY WOULD NOT LET me ride in the ambulance. An officer from the Three Lakes Police Department intervened when the EMTs loaded Andy into the boxy red and white vehicle.

"Let me go wi—" I begged.

"You can't. You'll just get in the way. Let them do their job."

"But—"

"You're with me." He led me to a black and white Three Lakes Police SUV angle parked behind the Camry. I didn't recall seeing it arrive. I saw nothing except Andy's pale, frightened face. She remained in the car seat while the woman in blue pressed a gauze pad against her wound. She kept up the pressure until the ambulance pulled into view, until the EMTs took over and carefully moved Andy to a stretcher that they quickly loaded into their unit.

We climbed in the police SUV and accelerated after the ambulance. Lights and sirens.

The officer asked my name. I gave it. He asked for Andy's name. I gave it. He could have asked for my Social Security number and the password for our online banking, and I would have given each because the words between us—none of them meant anything against the red and white strobe lights flashing on the back of an ambulance carrying my entire life up the road.

As he drove, he pulled a wet wipe from a packet lodged in a pocket in his door. He handed the alcohol-soaked sheet to me. The gesture confused me until I looked at my hands. Dried blood coated my fingers.

Andy's blood.

I took the sheet from his fingers and wiped my skin.

"Did you see the shooter?"

The shooter. I closed a mental fist around the idea that someone had committed this horror. A person. *A person whose days are now numbered.*

"No." I described arriving at the station. Getting out of the car. Hearing a *snap* sound. Seeing Caroline faint. Except she didn't faint.

The officer said the bullet struck Caroline in what shooters call *center mass*—the center of her chest as she stepped out of the car. Clean in and out. She dropped where she stood.

"My bet," he said, "the ME will find no bone strike. Straight through, else it wouldn't have hit your wife."

"I heard her head hit the pavement," I said distantly. A useless fact.

"I doubt she felt it," he asserted. "Did you see anyone? A parked car? A passing vehicle?"

Did you get the license plate? Andy's voice asked in my head. She always asks.

"No."

"Did you hear the shot?"

"No."

"Nothing? Not a *crack* type of sound?"

"No."

"Huh. Probably a subsonic round fired with a suppressor," the officer said. His matter-of-fact tone made me want to punch him. I wanted to scream. He mused on. "Somebody meant to avoid a gunshot and a sonic crack from the round. Plenty of energy, though. Went through the first woman and part of the car seat and, well…"

I lost him after that. His voice faded into white noise that I couldn't hear over the sound that the flashing ambulance lights made in my head. A sound like screaming.

"The bullet lost some energy." The doctor in scrubs sat down beside me. I tried to focus, to hear him over the five words ringing in my head—

Mother and baby are stable

"The bullet passed through the first victim and through a corner of the car seat—we found fabric in the wound—before it lodged in your wife. It hit her right vertebrochondral rib, number eight, at the junction of the costal cartilage." He touched himself on his right side. "Here. The strike shattered the number eight rib. Mr. Stewart, we removed the bullet, but your wife needs surgery to remove the bone fragments."

Bone fragments. Andy has gold flecks in her green eyes. She kisses with smooth soft lips. She sprouts dimples when I make a joke. *Why are we talking about bone fragments?*

"Mr. Stewart?" He tapped me on the knee.

"Sorry."

"That's alright. This is difficult. Let me repeat to you that the mother and baby are stable. Vital signs are good. She was awake and aware when she came in. There's been some blood loss but—"

"Wait. You said *was*?"

"We placed your wife in an induced coma. I'll get to that. As I was saying, there's been some blood loss but we're getting that under control. But now here's the thing…"

But…? No. There can't be any *buts*.

The ambulance took its own goddamned time.

Can't they go any faster? God, how far is it to the hospital? A ribbon of pale asphalt streamed under the hood of the police SUV.

"There was a guy," I said.

"What guy?" the officer asked.

"At Caroline Gaffney's house on the lake. The dead woman's house. There was a guy, a home invasion. He broke in and has been holding her for three days. My wife is a cop. She called you about it. You did a wellness check."

The officer didn't ask for the address or comment. I wondered if the half-assed wellness check had been performed by him. I had no doubt that everyone on the small department staff knew about Andy's call. A busybody call, a waste of time, they no doubt labeled it.

"Was this guy the shooter? Did you see him?"

"No."

"Back up." he said. "You know this how?"

I explained Caroline's connection to Andy through Lydia. I described our initial visit and the bake sale theatrics. I followed that with a sketchy version of spiriting Caroline out of the house. I told the officer that the guy—the home invader—thought we went for the lake, and that he followed and fell on the stairs.

"You'll find him there. He broke his leg. He's not going anywhere."

The officer radioed this new information to dispatch. The radio burst with busy chatter from officers keyed up by a shooting in their small town. The dispatcher diverted units to investigate. I considered telling my escort that they'd need at least half a dozen people to carry King Kong up the hill. Screw it. Let them find out on their own.

BUT NOW HERE'S THE thing...

"What is it?" I asked. Demanded, more like. The doctor took no offense. I wondered how often he held these tragic conferences. Should I count myself lucky because there were far worse talks to give to families?

Mother and baby are stable. What did he say to people when the patient wasn't stable? What did he say when the daughter pulled from a twisted wreck showed no brain activity? When the child lifted from a frozen river never resumed breathing?

Mother and baby are stable. Was I ungrateful because news like that was not enough—not by a long shot?

"The bullet, thankfully, remained intact, but the rib that it struck fragmented, and those fragments did some damage. They need to be removed surgically. Carefully." The doctor took a breath. "The good news is that by that time the bullet was nearly out of energy and the rib strike may have saved the baby. The bad news is that we think one fragment may have penetrated the amniotic sac. Right now, we do not detect any leakage. It's possible the fragment didn't break the sac. It's also possible that if it did, it's plugging the hole. We won't know until we go in."

"But you said the baby is stable."

"The baby is stable. For now. The baby was not harmed by the bullet or the impact or, again as far as we can tell, by any fragments. We are ninety-nine percent sure of that. But we won't know for certain until we're in."

He had kind eyes. I decided he had children of his own. Maybe grandchildren. His empathy ran deep, yet something in the tone of his voice thanked whatever deity he favored for the grace that he was not me. I held that against him.

"Mr. Stewart, the issue is that any breach of the sac presents potential for infection. Such a breach almost always triggers premature delivery. If the baby's environment becomes untenable, your wife will have no choice but to deliver. Your wife told us she's twenty-nine weeks pregnant. Infants can survive a premature birth as early as 22 weeks, but that doesn't mean the odds are much better at 29 weeks."

"Can it be repaired? The sac?"

He made a face that expressed thin hope. He said, "I don't want to give you any wrong impressions here. This is not a good situation. One more thing."

One more thing.

I imagined those words cut into marble on a headstone.

"What?"

"A surgical procedure this delicate requires the patient to be fully sedated. That adds risk. For both your wife and the baby. But there is a greater risk. Any movement of the fragment could tear the amniotic sac. Your wife had to be stabilized. This is what I said earlier. She was awake and responsive, but we've placed her in an induced coma to immobilize her."

I stared.

"The coma will keep her from making the slightest movement that could pose a threat," he said. "She needs specialized prenatal surgery, and we're not equipped for this. The best prenatal surgery in the state is at Children's in Milwaukee and at UW in Madison. My suggestion is Madison. I discussed this with your wife before we induced the coma and she agreed, but because sedation has been administered, we need your consent."

"Hell yes. Do it. Do whatever has to be done."

"I thought you might say that. I've already called for an air ambulance and notified UW. The helicopter launched out of Marshfield fifteen minutes ago and should be here shortly. She will be flown to Madison. Please believe me when I tell you it is the safest and fastest way to transport her."

"I get that."

Calculations burst through my head. Airspeeds. Distance. My Piper Navajo could easily outrun a helicopter, even the turbines flown by air ambulance services. But the Navajo cabin wasn't set up for a stretcher. Getting Andy in and out of the cabin would be jarring. Out of the question. On top of that, I would have to land at the Madison airport. A helicopter would save precious time by landing at the hospital with far less shifting, lifting, and jostling of Andy.

"Do it," I repeated. The words sounded like a prayer. "Can I see her?"

"Yes. Of course. You can wait with her, but she will be nonresponsive."

"Can I ride with her? To Madison?"

He shook his head. "They won't allow it. I'm sorry."

"Doesn't matter," I said grimly. "I'll get there ahead of them."

21

———————

*G*od, *I love this woman.*
     I leaned on the door frame feeling my guts ripped out and thrown on a fire. Feeling a gaping sinkhole yawn underfoot. Feeling myself swallowed by infinite darkness.

This can't be happening.

Andy lay still, silent, angelic. Her hair cascaded around her pale face. She slept, but the aura of her sleep wasn't peaceful or voluntary.

The baby bump rose prominently under the sheet. Larger than I remembered. Larger than yesterday. The child inside was ours, but at this moment belonged solely to Andy and the skill of strangers. One hand, the one with the IV line taped to her skin, lay on the dome formed by a thin sheet. She touched our child even when unconscious. To reassure. To protect.

The door frame pressed on my shoulder, holding me up. I wasn't sure I could take another step into the room. Not if taking a step made this real.

A thousand secret moments flew at me like bugs hitting a windshield on a summer night. Her touch. Her kisses. Her smiles and earnest attempts not to smile when I hatched a bad pun. We were improbable. We were never meant to be. We met only because she could not be swayed from owning something that had been taken from her. I joke that she dated me out of pure stubbornness. She jokes that it's true.

I never knew anyone like her.

And you never will again.

Losing her was not an option.

I took the four steps to her bedside without ever feeling the floor. I laid my hand on hers, on our child.

The sting in my throat and eyes intensified. My vision blurred.

"They're here," someone said. "You can't be in here."

Voices broke the silence behind me.

People in scrubs and masks hurried into the room. A small woman who looked like she wanted to administer a hug gently moved me out of the way.

A flurry of choreographed actions unfolded. The rapid-paced dance moved Andy from the bed to a gurney, the whole time keeping her motionless on the long, stiff board beneath her back. They wheeled her and our child from the room. Someone handed me her shoulder bag and a garbage bag containing her shoes and socks; the rest, bloodied, were gone. I did my best to keep up until someone put his hand on my chest and said I could not go "out there" where the helicopter blades spun and the light blanket covering my wife rippled in the rotor wash until they slid her into the air ambulance cabin.

Moments later the pilots powered up the rotors and lifted the ship through a brief hover into transitional lift and the bright blue sky.

I didn't watch the shrinking speck climb. I ran.

22

It never occurred to me that I had no way to get to the airport. I broke out of the small hospital entrance alone. A portico shaded me from the afternoon sun. I had no reason to think of the hospital as a hotel, but it disappointed me not to find a line of taxicabs.

Shit.

I pawed at my pants for my phone despite having no clue who to call. Did Eagle River have a taxi service? Uber?

The airport courtesy car remained at the Three Lakes Municipal Building and Police Department, probably surrounded by yellow plastic police tape. *Do Not Cross. Heinous Crime Scene.* I wondered how long they would keep the vehicle. The people at the airport would want to know what happened to their aging Camry.

More immediate concerns elbowed the question aside.

I needed to get to the airport. Fast.

I tapped the BLASTER in my thigh pocket and calculated the time and distance to the airport, and the remaining battery charge.

"They didn't find anyone."

For a moment I wasn't sure where the voice came from or if it meant to speak to me. I turned around. The police officer who drove me to the Aspirus Eagle River Hospital walked through the power front doors. Young and fit, he had short blonde hair and a square jaw. He probably played first base for his softball team. He carried two cups of coffee. I didn't want coffee but automatically accepted the offer.

"I'm sorry…what?"

"They didn't find anyone. At the Gaffney house. Nobody there. Nobody on the steps leading down to the lake. No big fella with a broken leg. Nada." He sipped and looked at me with just the right amount of skepticism.

"Seriously? The guy was there. Busted leg. Had to clock in at two-fifty or more."

He shrugged.

"No reason not to believe you. I guess he figured out a way to get up and walk off. We've got a call out. I'm hanging out here in case he shows up at the ER."

I glanced at the black and white SUV parked in the lot.

"Listen," I said, "I really need a favor."

23

H alfway to the airport I let out an expletive worthy of Pidge.

"What?" the officer asked, startled by my vehemence.

"My flight bag. It's in the back of the car at the crime scene. *Dammit.*"

He immediately checked his mirrors. "Want me to turn around?"

"No," I snapped. "God, no." I slapped my thigh and the cargo pants pocket where I *always, absolutely always* kept the airplane key. "No, keep going. I can fly without it. Our overnight bags are there, too. Can you...?"

"Sure." He drove on.

The trip from the hospital to the airport took three, maybe four minutes. It felt like hours. I spent the better part of the journey checking the sky through the rear side windows for a glimpse of the air ambulance. I saw nothing and soothed myself with the knowledge that Andy and the airborne EMTs were moving south fast.

The SUV had barely stopped in front of the FBO building before I threw open the door and piled out trailing a hasty "Thank you!"

I burst into the FBO and crossed my fingers that there would be no one at the desk. No one to greet. No one to make small talk. No one to ask where their courtesy car was. Luck stayed with me. I hurried past the office and through the warmly finished lounge. I exited quickly.

She waited for me at the far edge of the ramp. Ready. The speed in her lines made promises to me now. Twenty-one Tango Whiskey.

I'll get you there. Strap in.

Halfway to the airplane, I heard a jet engine whine. The familiar sound came from the south perimeter of the airport. Like many small airports, Eagle River Union has no parallel taxiways. Departing and arriving aircraft must back taxi using the active runway. The procedure is not dangerous if everyone uses common sense, diligence, and the standard traffic advisory frequency.

In the distance, a gleaming white executive jet sporting twin tail-mounted engines reached the end of the airport's longest runway. The engines spooled up as the jet made a tight one-eighty and lined up for takeoff into the northwest breeze.

I became aware of someone standing near the nearby gas pumps. A man paused whatever task he had at hand to watch the jet.

"Hey! Excuse me!" I called out. He glanced in my direction. "Any chance you can tell me who that is?"

He shrugged. "Not from around here."

The jet pilots applied power. Speed built slowly at first, then rapidly. In short order it raced past us, nose lifting, taking flight. True to form and function, it assumed a steep climb attitude and collected altitude quickly.

"Not local?" I called to the man watching the jet rise into the blue.

"Never seen it before."

I jogged closer to the fuel pumps as the jet roar died away.

"Can you tell me…did they drop off or pick up?"

"Picked up, I guess. They didn't even shut down. As soon as they were on the ramp, a guy asked for the gate to be opened, and a couple SUVs pulled out here."

"Did you see what they loaded?"

He looked at me, assessing the possibility that I was asking one too many questions and determining his liability for answering. He shook his head.

"Thanks!"

I bolted for the Navajo.

"Pidge." I pressed my phone to my ear. "Where are you?"

"Sitting in a crappy FBO hut in Iowa with my thumb up my ass. The goddamned passengers are taking their happy fucking time. Why?"

"I need help. Right now. Grab your iPad."

"Why?"

"Just do it. Open it to the map and drill down to Eagle River. Do you have traffic engaged?"

"Hang on. Don't lose your shit. I gotta…" I heard her grunt, then curse, then make something clatter. "Fucking stupid…who put that shit there?…okay…hang on…got it. Eagle River?"

"Eagle River. A private jet just took off on Runway 4. Left turnout. Probably eastbound now. Do you see it?"

"Gimme a sec." I knew what she meant. It takes a few cycles of internet Q&A for the traffic information to fill in. My heart hammered. "Are you gonna tell me WTF?"

"Find that jet first."

Holding the phone against my head, I opened the Navajo cabin door and climbed in. I didn't want to be caught standing on the ramp when the FBO manager realized who I was and that I was leaving without returning his car.

"Eastbound?" Pidge asked.

"Probably."

"I got one fast mover. A little south of Iron Mountain. Private. Climbing for the flight levels."

"Can you be sure it's the one I saw? Like, is it the only one in the area?"

"Looks that way. WTF, Stewart?"

"I need you to follow it. Don't lose it. I need to know where it goes."

"Shit, why can't you do this? Or do it on FlightAware. I got people who might show up here at any second."

I dropped into one of the passenger seats and squeezed my eyes shut. The sting in my throat expanded to a full choke hold.

"Listen," I said. My voice cracked. "Shit happened. Andy—she—she took a bullet. She—"

"THE—FUCK—YOU—SAY!"

"I don't have time to explain. She's on an air ambulance headed for UW Hospital in Madison. I'm about to fire up and chase after her. I gotta go. But I need to know where that jet winds up."

"Jesus Motherfucking Christ! How is she? How—Jesus, Will—the baby?"

"Stable. She and the baby are stable. The baby wasn't hit but Andy needs specialized surgery. I gotta go. Do this for me."

"On it."

A beep announced that Pidge ended the call.

SOME THINGS you should not rush. Launching a high-powered complex airplane is one of them.

I climbed in the cabin and secured the door. Dropping into the pilot's seat, I flipped switches with my left hand and set the prop and throttle with my right. I forgot the battery switch. I flipped it. Reaching for the starter, I forgot to run the mixture controls to full rich.

"Stop!" I froze and squeezed my eyes shut. "Just stop. Breathe."

I collected air, held it for a four count, then eased it out.

"You're not going to do Andy any good piling this into a crater or skidding down a runway with the gear up. Get your shit together."

I opened my eyes and shook the needles out of my fingertips. I let a calm, almost cool sensation flow down my neck and into the tight muscles of my arms. I carefully returned the switches and levers to the closed position. From atop the high instrument panel I lifted my half-size clipboard, the one I use to take notes and copy clearances from ATC. I turned it over and put my index finger on the first item of the Start checklist taped to the back.

I read the first item aloud. "Passenger Briefing – Check."

Fifty-two minutes later the wheels kissed the wide pavement of Madison's Runway 36. As I taxied to the ramp, I radioed the Wisconsin Aviation FBO desk to call a taxi for an urgent run to University Hospital.

The cab waited for me at the curb.

24

____

"What are you doing here?"

"What the fuck do you think?" Pidge dropped her flight bag on the floor and slid into the plush chair next to the one I had been warming for hours. "What's the word?"

I shook my head. "She's—they're in surgery. They didn't get her in for almost an hour after she got here. I guess they had to find the right surgeon. I mean—an hour—I guess they moved heaven and earth to get her in. That's…" I checked my watch. "…a while ago…"

"Mother…" Pidge heaved a heavy sigh. "They got any booze here?"

"There's all kinds of energy drinks, water and soda over there. A bunch of snacks. A whole kitchen." I pointed. "Seriously, what are you doing here? I thought you were on a charter in Iowa."

"I was. I ditched the passengers over at Wisconsin Aviation." She read the shock on my face. "Not like that. I know the owner. Great guy. He totally bent over backward to help. He lined up one of his guys to take the passengers up to Essex."

"What did you tell the paying customers?"

"Medical emergency. I told them I had to divert to fly a little girl with a bad kidney valve."

"Kidneys don't have valves."

"Fuck you. They tell you anything?"

"Nothing I didn't already know."

"You gonna tell me what happened? Jesus, Will, why was Andy running around getting in gunfights when she's about to pop a kid?"

"It wasn't like that," I said.

"Hang on," she said. She hopped out of the chair and trotted to the refrigerator in the plush lounge. I couldn't help but compare the amenities to the spare little waiting room in Eagle River. Plush furniture. A gas fireplace. A full kitchen. The room itself was the size of a small aircraft hangar. Plenty of space to allow worried families to cluster in privacy. I chose a leather recliner that commanded a view of the room entrance and the long hallway that led to the surgical suites.

Pidge returned. She pulled the tab on a can of Pepsi and flopped back in the chair beside me. Her leather flight jacket squeaked against the leather upholstery. She stuck out her lip and blew a lock of her short blonde hair away from her forehead, then fixed a hard glare on me.

"Take it from the top."

"You gotta be fucking kidding me." Pidge let her jaw hang, astonished, when I finished the movie pitch version. "That's insane."

"The worst of it is, I encouraged this. I thought it would make Andy feel, I dunno, better. Useful. She's been restless. She's a cop, for God's sake. Picking paint chips and buying baby stuff—I mean—she's into all that, and she is over the moon about being pregnant, but she breathes blue air."

"More than anybody I ever knew," Pidge agreed. "And you didn't see or hear anything? No gunshot? No car blasting off?"

"Nothing. And no, I did *not* get a license number."

"Oh, is your wife ever gonna be pissed."

I wanted nothing more at that moment.

"I got the dope on that jet outta Eagle River," Pidge said. She leaned forward and pulled up her iPad. "You think these guys are involved?"

"It's as good a guess as any. You sure it's the right aircraft?"

"Traffic wasn't exactly heavy at that moment. I picked him up right away. There was nothing plodding around Iron Mountain at the time. A couple DAL flights up in the thirties, but…what was it about this flight?"

"The airport manager said two SUVs loaded the jet, which rolled in, never shut down, and rolled right out again. He didn't see anybody with a broken leg, but I got the impression he didn't get a good look. King Kong was gone when the cops got there. He never showed up at the hospital. That means somebody came and got him. They had to take him somewhere." I gestured at the iPad. "Don't keep me in suspense. What have you got?"

She tapped the screen.

"Well," she said. "It wasn't easy. I had to keep checking every few minutes. It got a little dicey tracking it over Detroit because there's a shit ton of traffic and the airplane is registered as private. Luckily my human cargo showed up like two hours late, mother fu—."

"Pidge."

"Right. Rochester, New York. Oh, and the plane tracked as a Phenom 300E. Nice ride."

The private registry prevented the N-number from showing up on apps like FlightAware and ForeFlight, but not the aircraft type. Private or not, that detail matters to other pilots. Pidge tapped the screen and expanded a photo of a small business jet capable of single-pilot operation. The twin-engine jet from Brazil's Embraer had a solid footing in the business jet market, especially with small operations or owner-operated flight departments.

Pidge raised her iPad to show me a stock photo of a 300E.

"Did you happen to notice when it landed? The time?"

"This ain't fucking amateur hour. They dropped off the radar at the end of the runway in Rochester at 1521. Now all we gotta do is get our hands on a copy of the tower transmissions for today. I don't suppose you have any friends in high places at the FAA?"

"How about the FBI?"

25

"You got my message," I said.

"Is she okay?"

Special Agent Leslie Carson-Pelham insisted on using FaceTime. I held the phone up to see what I looked like in the tiny inset box. The image was too small to judge. Leslie looked the way she always does in her black t-shirt and black blazer beneath tousled boyish hair.

"For now."

"What happened?"

I recited a rapid-fire description of everything up to the minute.

"No word yet?"

"They sent a nurse out a little after they started. She said everything is going well, but that it could be another hour or two. That was two hours ago. She said not to worry. That Andy is getting—oh, hell." I froze.

"What?"

"I—I completely forgot about her family. Her sister. Her mom and dad. Dammit. I've been so—"

"Will!" Pidge snapped her fingers to get my attention. "Relax. I called Rosemary II. She's on it."

Mere mention of the name steadied me. Hearing that Rosemary II was up to speed had the effect of a cool breeze. No one else I've ever known blends a bottomless well of empathy with impeccable logistical skill. I didn't know what or who Rosemary II had called to spread the word, but it would be everyone who needed to know.

"Who's that with you?" Leslie asked. I swiveled the phone.

"Pidge is here. You remember Pidge."

"How could I forget? Hi, Pidge."

"Hi…uh…FBI."

"Leslie."

"Right." Pidge fidgeted in her seat. I turned the phone back to my face, freeing Pidge to glare at me.

"I need a favor," I said. "I need a copy of the tower tapes for Rochester International Airport between 4 and 6 p.m. Eastern time."

Leslie didn't show surprise. "What are we looking for?"

I liked the *we* of that.

26

"Mr. Stewart?" The nurse I'd seen earlier walked partway into the lounge area. I shot to my feet. She offered a smile that I could not interpret. "Would you come with me?"

Pidge looked up at me and flared her eyes, then made *Go!* gestures with her hands. I hurried to fall in step with the nurse.

"You wife is out of surgery. She's doing well. The doctor would like a word with you." She looked back at the lounge. "Do you have someone who can be with you?"

"Uh…"

"It's good to have someone with you when the doctor explains everything. There's a lot to take in."

That didn't sound good. I waved for Pidge to join us. She caught on and caught up.

The nurse led us down a long hallway, then used her ID badge on the security box beside a pair of huge wooden doors. A latch snapped loudly. The doors swung wide enough to grant passage to a full hospital bed on wheels. We continued into a maze of hallways and patient rooms. I missed whatever signage identified this area as the ICU but sensed a higher pitch of activity. We stopped at a nursing station and were handed surgical masks and paper hospital gowns.

"We need you to wear these to maintain a sterile environment. I'm going to ask you not to approach the bed where your wife is resting, Mr. Stewart. This is a critical time. We want to avoid all possibility of infection. Miss…?"

"Page."

"Miss Page, I'm going to ask you to not enter. If you stand at the door, you will be able to hear the doctor. Are you okay with that?"

"Affirmative," Pidge answered from beneath the mask. We slipped on the paper gowns and followed the nurse down a new hallway. Halfway to the end, she gestured for me to enter an open door and for Pidge to wait. Full darkness had fallen outside a bank of windows. The room had subtle lighting, like a romantic restaurant, most of which came from LEDs adorning a riot of equipment and monitors. Steady beeping affirmed the presence of precious life. A screen painted Andy's heartbeat in bright digital colors.

A doctor stood at the foot of the bed in full mask, gloves and paper hat.

Andy lay immobile, wrapped tightly on a backboard, her head only slightly elevated by pillows. An oxygen mask covered her nose and mouth. Her long hair puffed out a paper hat. Tubes dangled from an IV stand at her bedside. Monitor wires ran under the hem of a sadly flower-patterned hospital gown. So many wires and tubes.

At the sight of it, my breathing grew labored. My chest grew tight.

She slept. This time, she did not rest her hand on her belly. Both hands lay at her side, wrapped by and hidden under the blanket.

"Mr. Stewart, I'm Dr. Narendra Maharashtra, how do you do?"

"Could be better." It came out coarse and dry. I took a step. The nurse closed a grip on my arm. I nodded to accept the limitation. Her eyes smiled over her mask.

"Understandable. Completely understandable." Dr. Maharashtra spoke English with more Indian accent than my ear was trained for. I worried that I might fail to catch vital words. "Let me begin by saying that the surgery went exceedingly well. This was a very difficult situation, but your wife is strong, and she is stable, and the baby is stable as well. There is every reason to have confidence in a good outcome for both mother and child."

A sharp breath shot from me, chased by a shudder. For a moment I doubted the structural integrity of my knees.

"Thank you," I whispered.

I could not take my eyes off Andy's face. I've seen my wife sleep. I've stared and marveled at her serenity. This was not that. She lay still, but beneath the surface, if it was possible, a current of worry ran like a riptide. Worry or fear.

Or maybe that was just me.

The doctor's words, most of them, flowed at a steady clip.

"...know, of course, that she has been placed in a medically induced coma. We're using thiopental which...considerations for the fetus. For now, your wife's respiratory function is strong, as you can see, but there are systemic adverse effects…respiratory drive that could require ventilation, something we are watching closely…not concerned about cerebral perfusion pressure since this is not a matter of brain injury…Were you told why we have employed this treatment?"

I stared at Andy's face. She consumed me. The nurse gripped and gently shook my arm.

"I'm sorry. What?"

"Your wife must remain completely immobile. Her injury resulted from a bullet that shattered the right vertebrochondral rib, number eight, at the junction of the costal cartilage. We removed fragments from the base of her right lung and the lining around her stomach which was not penetrated. One fragment, however, penetrated the amniotic sac, what we call pPROM or preterm prenatal rupture of the membrane."

"Yes, that's what they told me," I said, struggling to demonstrate that I was not completely overwhelmed.

"Yes, indeed. This fragment, it's like a tiny spear or arrowhead, but fortunately it is smooth. pPROM almost always results in terminating the pregnancy by delivery. Risk of infection to the fetus such as fetal inflammatory syndrome…severe neonatal morbidity with respiratory distress… neonatal sepsis, pneumonia…and maternal complications…"

His list of horrors washed over me, mixed with words I did not understand and did not want to know.

He continued. "It is generally thought that rupture of the membrane is an irreversible event because most women begin labor spontaneously within several days. A small number, however, remain undelivered thanks to spontaneous sealing of the membranes."

"Spontaneous sealing? It heals itself?" I swiped at small hope.

"No. That will not be the case here. A foreign object caused the pPROM. However, despite the penetration, the fragment itself plugged the hole it created. Had it not done so, the amniotic sac would have drained causing the problems I have already outlined as well as internal fluid buildup and premature delivery of the baby. Like many such injuries, the worst thing you can do is remove the projectile which would be rather like pulling the plug on a bath. Do you see?"

"Yes."

"Until recently, this circumstance inevitably induced delivery, but we have deployed a new technology. In simple terms, Mr. Stewart, what we did was create a mesh to lay over the wound and micro stitch the mesh to the sac, drawing the sac itself tight against the bone fragment, like the drawstring of a garbage bag—forgive the analogy. Do you see? Like this." He held up one thumb, then made a loop with the thumb and forefinger of his other hand. He closed the loop around his thumb and drew it tight.

"That's…"

"That's fucking clever," Pidge said.

"Yes, thank you, yes, it is. But it means that the fragment must remain in place. Do you see? It must remain in place to prevent the hole from allowing the fluid to escape. This, of course, increases the risk of infection that I have outlined. Do you see?"

I nodded.

"Now, I must discuss with you the need to keep your wife stable and immobile. A medically induced coma carries high risk, not just for your wife, but for the fetus…something we cannot use indefinitely to sustain immobility…adhere to ABCDEF Bundle protocols and PADIS guidelines, of course, which…unnecessary sedation and that is why, of course, ICU teams try to keep patients awake and as mobile as possible…"

He droned on. The words fell on me like cold rain.

"…in this case with the pregnancy, which will come to term in, I believe, 15 weeks…and of course avoiding the risk of your wife suffering from post-ICU syndrome…the protection of the fetus and her viability at birth…will be removing your wife from the induced coma as soon as we can be assured that the self-deploying micro sutures and mesh will hold. Do you see?"

I stared at the woman I love. The droning ceased.

"Will?" Pidge prompted me.

The nurse squeezed my arm.

"Yes," I said. "I see. How soon?"

"We feel it best to bring your wife out of the induced coma after no more than twenty-four hours. We will be monitoring her closely. The primary use of such treatment is to reduce brain swelling, which is not a factor in this case. Our intention is to reduce the medication over the next twenty-four hours. You can see that we have applied light restraints and will continue to do so during the waking process to ensure that there is no movement that will cause harm. Do you have any questions?"

"Can I stay with her?"

"We prefer not. It is critical to avoid infection. Our staff will keep you closely apprised of any changes or issues. Know that she is resting comfortably, and that the fetus is unharmed."

"What happens to the fragment?"

"I'm afraid it must remain. For the full term of the pregnancy. It is a plug, you see. If it comes out for any reason, the term of the pregnancy will end."

"Can the kid kick it?" Pidge asked. "The bone plug thingy?"

"Very unlikely, but another reason to keep the mother as immobile as possible."

"And then what?" I asked. *Andy's favorite question.*

"Then we wait for delivery. Caesarian may be indicated, but that remains to be seen depending on whether she makes it to full term or not. The plug is tiny, Mr. Stewart. We speak of it as if it is a spear or arrow, but it is tiny and if the mesh holds to full term, the fragment will be delivered with the placenta and normal afterbirth. Do you see?"

"I see," I said. "Thank you."

Dr. Maharashtra stepped to the door. As he passed, he landed a hand on my shoulder. "She is a strong woman, Mr. Stewart. Very strong." He slipped past Pidge.

The nurse let me stare for a minute before ushering us into the hallway.

"I suggest you get some rest. We can set you up with a patient room if you like. The kitchen is open until ten. You can also have food delivered to the lounge."

I nodded and instantly forgot everything she said.

She led us to the nurses' station where we removed and disposed of the masks and gowns. In short order we were back in the luxuriously appointed and depressing as hell lounge. I landed in the same chair as before. Pidge dropped in the one beside me.

"She's got this," Pidge said. "She's not a pussy like you. She's got this in spades."

"Yeah." *God, I hoped she was right.*

27

———————

Wednesday

"Hey," Andy rasped. Her voice was dry and hoarse. She licked her lips. "Hey," I said through the mask. "They don't want me too close. They said I had to keep one hand on the door handle." I lifted my gloved free hand and waved, an awkward substitution for the hug aching in my arms. The paper gown rustled. She looked at me, then down at the baby bump which prompted me to add, "They tell me that Little Ethel is okay."

"Not calling..." A crystalline tear rolled from the corner of her eye. "They…yes…baby's fine…they told me."

"They've been good about that. No TV drama—you know—dragging it out until after the commercial."

"We're not…" she swallowed, "…we're not calling her Ethel,"

"True. She could be a boy. Hor—"

"No." She squinted at the blue sky high in the window. "What time…?"

"Wednesday. Almost noon. They've been working you up out of the induced coma all morning. I was in earlier, but you were loopy—which was nice. I got you to tell me about all your old boyfriends."

"No worry," she said. "They're all dead. I saw to that."

An old joke of hers. Reviving it felt good, felt like relief.

"Did you know you're on TV?"

She blinked, bewildered.

"They put a stent through the wound that runs a fiber-optic line down to a microscopic camera aimed at a section of the repair so they can monitor the fix. Groundbreaking stuff. The camera has its own light. When they turn it on, you can see it through your skin. You've got a landing light, dear."

"Don't…don't make me laugh."

"Could be helpful for all those bathroom trips at night."

"Please stop."

"One more," I said. "You could say it's the light of my wife."

Dimples seeded a smile.

"Now I'm done. Did they tell you what they did down there?" I asked.

"Before you came in," she whispered. She looked around. "Water?"

"There's a tube. Turn your head…the other way." She turned away from me and found the tube rigged near her head. "It only gives out a little at a time. I guess they didn't want you lifting a cup of ice chips."

She sipped.

I wondered how much she had been told. I wondered if Dr. Maharashtra performed his terrifying monologue on fetal inflammatory syndrome and severe neonatal morbidity and respiratory distress and neonatal sepsis, pneumonia and maternal complications. Turns out I had been listening.

In a full, if weak, voice she said, "I get to turn my head. Nothing else. It's that or go back into a coma which is not good for the baby."

"Yeah. No movement…um…" I felt a need to speak so that she wouldn't. "What they did is pretty cool. Did they tell you? They threw a tiny net over everything, and it has these micro robot claws lodged in the fibers, and they sent a signal that activated the claws and pulled it all tight." She nodded. "You're making medical history, Dee. There's about a hundred scientists down in the parking lot watching your insides on a jumbotron."

Dimples reappeared. "I told you not to make me laugh."

"On it."

"Tell me something serious."

"I love you." My damned throat tightened and nearly cut off the third word. I wanted to say more but couldn't. I wanted to take my hand off the door handle and scoop her into my arms but couldn't.

"You, too," she whispered. "Will…for a moment I thought…"

I nodded. *So did I…so did I.*

We traded deep and meaningful silence. A fresh tear crawled down her cheek. I rubbed mine away before they drained into the mask.

"Did you…?" she whispered, barely audible. I leaned closer. She licked her lips and tried again. "Did you get a license number?"

28

A nurse who looked like she wanted to administer a medicinal hug ushered me back to the central nursing station.

"She needs her rest," I was told. "She will still be feeling the effects of the coma medication off and on. She will want to shut her eyes, and she shouldn't feel a need to fight it. You should go and get some lunch. We'll take you to see her again this afternoon."

I ditched my third paper gown, hat, gloves and booties and returned to the vast lounge. Pidge sprawled in a leather chair with one leg hooked over the arm. She thumbed her phone.

"She's awake," I said.

"How's the baby?"

"They say the baby is fine."

"I bet," she said. "Probably went on a wild drug trip during the last twenty-four hours. Andy's okay?"

"As much as she can be. She's not supposed to move."

"Sucks. Did you hear from your FBI pal?"

"Not yet." I triple-checked my phone. No missed call or message from Leslie. I looked over the list of notifications.

"You should get some food. Have you eaten since yesterday?"

"What are you…channeling Rosemary II?"

"I'll channel the scolding she will paste on me if you don't eat something."

"What about you?"

She extended her leg and pointed a shoe toe at a can of Pepsi. "Charter pilot breakfast."

"Right. I'll get something in a minute. Got a couple calls to answer." I stood. Pidge and I had become the sole occupants of the lounge. A small family shared the space briefly during the morning. Their kids woke me from the second of two hours of sleep I managed; the young mother and father were deeply apologetic.

I wandered toward the kitchen to put some distance between me and Pidge. It wasn't that I had anything to hide from her. I just didn't need a second opinion.

I scrolled and poked the contact list on my phone. Tom Ceeves answered my call before it rang on my end.

"What's the word, Will?"

"On Andy or from the beginning?"

"Andrea first. Then take it from the top. Before you do…have you heard from Bobbi Emmett?"

"Who's he?"

"She's the chief in Three Lakes. She's the one shoved you outta the way to give Andrea first aid."

"Oh. Please tell her thanks. And no, I haven't talked to her."

"I know Bobbi. She's got a temper. She wasn't happy you took off, but I smoothed her feathers. She wants to talk to you. Along with a couple of guys from the sheriff's department. Let's chat, and then conference her in. Okay?"

"Yeah, sure."

I explained Andy's current condition, the medical miracles of the last 24 hours, and the sequence of events that began with rolling into a parking spot at the Three Lakes Police Department. After that, I recounted Andy's involvement, beginning with Lydia's afternoon of leisure. Tom listened without comment. When I finished, he let the line hang silent long enough for me to wonder if I just told the whole story to myself.

"This kid, this girl…you think she's the MacGuffin?"

"What? No, her name is Gaffney. She's the daughter of the woman who was shot." It frustrated me that Tom had listened poorly. I didn't think I could have been clearer.

"I know all that," Tom said. "MacGuffin. Alfred Hitchcock. You never heard the term?"

"Hell, no. What's it supposed to mean?"

"Never mind. I'm asking if you think this girl is the reason for the home invasion and the reason that woman was shot."

"Maybe…or not…I don't know."

"Well, somebody didn't want the mother talking to the police. Somebody preferred a murder investigation to a missing person investigation. I can only think of one reason why that would be."

It's bad enough when my wife quizzes me on her police work. I didn't need her boss doing it, too.

"I give up."

"Because they think they can get away with it. They think there's no chance the Three Lakes Police Department and the Oneida County Sheriff has the resources or the skill to catch them."

"That's some arrogance."

"Maybe. Or maybe they have their shit locked down. Listen, stay on the line. I'll conference in Chief Emmett. She's going to want to hear everything you just told me. Hang on."

THE CONFERENCE CALL swallowed up another half hour. It was joined not only by Chief Bobbi Emmett but by two detectives from the Oneida Sheriff's department. I'm acquainted enough with my wife's profession that being made to tell and re-tell the story and answer the same questions from four different angles didn't surprise or irritate me. My interrogators doled out sympathy when they ran out of things to ask me. They offered heartfelt good wishes for a sister in blue. Everyone on the line expressed gratitude that Andy and the baby were not hurt worse than they were. When the crime scene cops clicked off the line, Tom remained.

"I assume you're gonna hang around there for a while," he said.

"Until I know she's safe, yeah."

"Uh-huh. Well…tell your wife…tell her I…well, you know."

"Sure, Tom. You and me both."

29

Pidge ambushed me when I sat down beside her. She dropped her leg and spun to face me.

"Why didn't you fucking tell them about the jet? And Rochester?"

"Nothing to tell," I said without returning the eye contact she used like a hammer. "Not until I hear from Leslie."

"Bullshit." Anger mixed with mischief on her pixie features. "You don't want to share. Does this mean what I think it means?"

"I doubt it."

"Fuck, yes. It does. I want in."

"In on what? There's nothing to be in on."

"No?" She laughed. "You just told the cops a story about some humongous dickhead with a compound fracture who magically disappeared, but you left out the key piece of information suggesting where he might have gone. And I know why."

I stood up, hoping to end this conversation. "Do me a favor." I plucked the Navajo keys from my pocket. "Run out to the airport and get me Andy's shoulder bag. There's a garbage bag with some bloody clothes. Leave that. Also, she carries a Glock in her bag. Leave that in the copilot seat pocket. Make sure you bring her phone."

I tossed the keys. She swiped them out of the air.

"That proves it. You're leaving. That's why you want her to have her phone."

"I'm not leaving. I'm going to find the cafeteria and get some food so that you can report back to Rosemary II that I have taken nourishment."

"Bullshit."

"I'll be *goddamned* if I'm going to leave her side."

"Bullshit," Pidge repeated. "Even if you don't leave, she's gonna kick you out. And then…"

"And then what?"

"Then you and me are gonna go fuck somebody up."

PART II

30

———————

When they let me back in to see Andy, the backboard was gone. The head of her bed slanted to a medium-upright position. Andy's knees and legs were elevated. The new posture created a cradle for the baby bump and probably also served to reduce Andy's ability to move. The clever water tube repositioned itself with the movement of the bed. A nose canula replaced Andy's oxygen mask. A web of tubes and wires ran to multiple monitors and served as reminders of my wife's critical condition.

As if the pale shade of her skin didn't cover it.

Andy lay with her eyes closed. Her chest rose and fell beneath a thin blanket. I counted each breath. The monitor at the head of the bed kept a tally, but all I cared about was the next, and the next after that.

I noticed something I hadn't seen before. A second monitor displayed rows of digital data. A heartbeat line crawled across one small window at a rate higher than Andy's.

It hit me. *That's our baby.* Our child. There with us. In the room.

Andy has frequently guided my hand to the baby's movements and kicks, but in those tender moments I was not touching the child, I was touching Andy, Andy's pregnancy. This was different. The monitor's graphic interpretation of life gave the little creature independence. It had its own heartbeat. Its own struggle. Was there pain? Did it feel Andy's terror when the bullet struck? Would the event plant seeds of memory without words or images? Vague feelings that the growing boy or girl could never explain? Nightmares?

Andy rolled her head to face me with half open eyes. I smiled.

"I'd offer to make out with you, but..." I gestured at my gloved grip on the door handle. "My old Sunday school teacher used this technique for teens at parties."

"I'd take that offer," she whispered.

She winced.

"Does it hurt?" I asked.

"Like a bitch." She grimaced. "It hurts when I breathe. It hurts when I move. It hurts when I think."

"Well...don't move, don't think, but keep breathing. That's medical advice, you know, because I'm dressed like a doctor."

"You're dressed like a bag of microwave popcorn." She smiled, shuddered, and winced again. "Ouch."

"Pidge is here. She says hi, along with a few other choice words. They won't let her in. I got the golden ticket. Everybody sends their love. You have the support of a coven of witch doctors."

"Witch doctors?"

"Yeah. They're back in Essex performing dark rituals on your behalf."

Curiosity tinted her face. "What?"

I wanted to kiss that face. I tightened my grip on the door handle.

"Earl's marching around attempting to *anger* away any infection. Tom's using his size and that annoying silence-thing he does to ward off bad juju. Pidge is down in the lounge mother-effing this and mother-effing that. She says it's cleansing. I happen to know it's also how she cleans her apartment."

The joke raised a smile but stayed below the laugh threshold.

"Rosemary II is broadcasting love and well wishes—so much that it's showing up on radar and interfering with IFR traffic over Essex. The radar screen looks like one of those psychedelic sixty's cartoons. All flowers and rainbows. And Lane wants me to send her a video feed from that camera inside the wound."

"You talked to Lane?"

"God, yes, for about an hour." Rosemary II's teenaged daughter cut her fifth period class to call me for an update. "She picked my brain until it hurt."

"Nobody gets a video feed of my insides," Andy declared. "God. I'm sorry to make those dear people worry."

"Those people love you. I—" There it was again. The sting in the throat. The blur fogging my eyes. "I get it."

Andy rested both of her hands on our child's igloo. She closed her eyes.

She squeezed her lips tightly against abrupt emotion because emotion meant crying and crying caused movement.

"Hey," I said quickly. "Wanna talk some cop shop?"

She sniffled several times and nodded, relieved.

"Remember King Kong?" Another nod. "Well, on the way up to the Eagle River hospital, I told one of the Three Lakes PD guys about Kong. Guess what? They went out to the lake house, and he was gone."

"On that leg?"

"Yup. No sign of him."

Andy's eyes narrowed to the squint she often employed while on duty. "Remember the call he made? Four minutes before we looked at his phone?"

"I remember."

"Somebody came and got him."

"It would have to be a crew of at least three or four."

Andy looked around. "Where did my phone go?"

"It's in with your clothes in the Navajo. I sent Pidge to fetch your bag."

"Don't let her bring the—"

"Nope. Already told her. Just your bag and your phone."

"I should—" She swallowed then spoke hoarsely. "Dry mouth." She took a sip from the tube.

"I know what you're going to say. You think you should call the investigating team in Three Lakes. I already did."

"The pictures…"

"I'll send the pictures as soon as I have your phone."

"The DL and that—"

"Recent call screen. Yeah. Slow down there, Detective," I held up both hands. "I just got a stern lecture on the evils of getting you agitated. Promise me you're not going to start making conference calls to a murder investigation."

"Will, I—"

"No, I want a promise. Or I'm not giving you your phone. I already told Three Lakes PD and a couple guys from county everything that happened."

She settled on her pillow. "God, this sucks. What did the doctor tell you?"

"Doc says you're looking at maybe two weeks of staying absolutely stationary. He and all the scientists down in the parking lot are rooting for the amniotic sac to kick in and try to heal itself, which will reinforce the mesh holding the fragment plug in place. But he said we can't count on that."

"*Two weeks?*" She looked stricken.

"Swear to God. I just talked to him. He'll be in to see you this evening, so I'm sure he will tell you all about it. But yeah. Two weeks."

"And then what?"

I shrugged. "He wouldn't commit. Probably bedrest for the rest of the pregnancy. Just a guess. I'm not a real doctor. I only dress as a bag of microwave popcorn."

"Bedrest at home?"

"Maybe. If you're a good girl. I have no idea."

She locked her jaw, which caused her lower lip to gain slight prominence. I learned early in our marriage to read that as a warning sign.

"Dee," I said cautiously, trying to head off the storm clouds, "your number one priority is to keep that breach of the amniotic sac from opening. That means sitting still. For however long it takes. That means not getting agitated over a murder investigation in Oneida County. Remember, you're not an investigator, you're a victim."

Andy deploys silence when I'm right about something she opposes. I got an earful of nothing.

I let her simmer for a moment, then broke the rules. I released the door handle and moved to the side of the bed. I picked up her hand and held it in mine.

"Listen," I spoke quietly, "your job is to heal and keep Little Ethel or Horatio comfortable."

"My job..." She huffed an angry breath that caused a shot of pain that made her wince again. "My job should also be to help track down the sonofabitch that did this."

"Don't think that's not happening."

She rolled her eyes. "You need to—"

"Call Leslie. I did." I lowered my voice. "Look, you're right. Somebody picked up King Kong and I think I know where he went." I explained about the jet and how Pidge tracked its flight path. "I told Leslie to talk to the tower crew and get an ID on the plane. With that maybe she can work out where they took the big ape to repair the broken leg. It's being handled."

She looked at me like a suspect.

"What?"

"What's the flight time from Madison to Rochester?" she asked.

"How would I know?"

"Will...?"

"Two hours and twenty-one minutes with the current winds aloft," I replied. "Just off the top of my head. But I am not leaving your side, Dee. Wild horses could not drag me from—"

"Really. You're going to stand here and watch me lie still for two weeks?"

"If they let me. I love staring at you. We can work on baby names. Horatio. Balto. Sigmund, if it's a boy. We already have Ethel for a girl."

"Go and help Leslie."

"What?"

"You heard me." She said nothing for a long moment, undeniably her most potent argument. "Don't lie. You know you want to."

"Maybe." I shuffled my feet. "I admit, I wouldn't mind having a chat with Mr. Kong. One of *those* chats."

I expected the lecture. The one about due process and law and a citizen's rights, spiced with warnings about exposing myself and using *the other thing* to scare the living daylights out of people.

The lecture didn't come.

"Go," she said. "Please. But get me my phone and promise to keep me up to date."

"Are you sure?"

"Will, the only reason for you to be here is if something bad happens. Why don't we block the odds of that by not having you here."

"I'm sure that makes sense in your mind."

"Go. I'll be fine. I don't intend to let anything bad happen."

She is a strong woman, Mr. Stewart. Very strong. Dr. Maharashtra's assessment wasn't wrong.

I squeezed her hand. She reciprocated.

"Only if you're absolutely sure. Because I'm happy to stay here and think up more baby names."

"You could," she said, "but neither of us can afford the divorce."

31

I swiped to answer my phone in the hallway outside of Andy's room.

"Took you long enough."

"It's a law firm," Leslie said. "The jet's registered to a law firm. How's Andrea?"

"Holding steady. They're talking about having her lie still for two weeks."

"How still?"

"On her back, in a bed, and they told me not to make jokes, so she doesn't laugh and jiggle the bone fragment. That kind of still."

"I wouldn't worry. Your jokes are no threat. What's the long view?"

I explained the outside chance that the amniotic sac would self-heal. Hearing a touch of excitement as the words come from my mouth made me wonder if I was trying to convince myself.

"That's some crazy tech."

"Tell me more about this law firm. Caroline Gaffney's husband is a lawyer. Is it his firm? Because you know what they say. It's always the husband."

"Wayne Gaffney works for one of the most exclusive firms in Manhattan."

"How exclusive?"

"Oh, let's just say his firm might reject your pal Lewko for not having enough money. It's that kind of exclusive. But...no. The firm that owns and operates the airplane you tracked is not the husband's firm. Quite the opposite."

My train of thought derailed for a moment. Reject Spiro Lewko? The man had more money than God. How could anyone be richer?

"You still there?" Leslie asked.

"Sorry. What do you mean *opposite*?"

"Well, they may operate a private jet, but this law office is a one-room month-to-month rental in a not-so-exclusive part of Rochester, New York. From what I can tell the firm uses an answering service and employs a single licensed lawyer. They appear to specialize in personal injury cases involving commercial trucking…or motorcycles…or anything that looks like a payday."

"Business must be good."

"My guess is that the lawyer fronting for this 'firm' collects a paycheck and a percentage and doesn't even know about the jet. Or the yacht. Or the villa. Or whatever else they're hiding from the IRS on the books of the holding company that owns the holding company that owns the law firm. I've seen this setup before, Will. I have friends in the intelligence game that use law firm fronts like this."

"Why law firms?"

"Overblown claims of confidentiality. Hiding behind privilege. That sort of thing. If someone gets too inquisitive, they roll out threats of lawsuits, injunctions, etc. If pushed, they tie you up in court. The good ones—the well-funded ones—keep a friendly judge in their pocket to throw weight around. It discourages anyone from looking too closely."

"Are you saying there's a spy connection to this?"

"That's a very theatrical word, Will. I wouldn't go that far."

I drifted toward the nursing station and tugged off the paper gown as I walked and talked.

"No? Someone assassinated a woman in the parking lot of a police station using a silenced weapon. The same people scooped up a guy with a compound leg fracture who had been holding the targeted woman prisoner in her own home. And they have a secret jet. What does all that tell you?"

"I'm not disagreeing that this has polished touches. I'm just not ready to jump to the CIA or the Mossad or the Russian Federation. Nor am I dismissing Wayne Gaffney's firm. They roll with the highest rollers. That kind of money buys all kinds of former operators. Hell, Bezos's security team has a bigger budget than the Secret Service Presidential Detail."

"Bezos might have more enemies. What about medical treatment of the big guy? Does this ambulance chaser have any connections to a hospital or clinic? They had to have a reason for flying him to Rochester."

"Working on it."

"Can you look into something else?" I told Leslie what little I knew about Baxter Gaffney going missing, if she was in fact missing.

"Sounds like mother-daughter teenaged drama, Will. And missing persons is not really my bailiwick."

"What is? Seriously, what are you doing these days?"

"Keeping an eye on you," she replied. She let it hang long enough to worry me that she meant it. "But mostly keeping my head down. Things have not gone well in the halls of power since the attack on the capital. In a lot of ways, it's only gotten worse."

"Politics," I said sourly. "Leave me out of it."

"You wish. But yeah, that's what I'm doing these days. Keeping Will Stewart out of it. They're still looking for the pilot that dumped that airplane on the Arlington Bridge."

"When you're not babysitting me, do you think you can find Broken Leg Guy?"

"I can find Broken Leg Guy. But first tell me why."

"*Are you serious? Why?* Because *some piece of shit pulled a trigger and —dammit—*" I stopped myself. A black fury boiled up on the fresh memory of blood on my hands. Andy's blood.

"Will…"

"*What?*"

She paused, then said, "You see…that's what I'm worried about." She added slowly, deliberately, "Andrea was not the target. Do you understand that?"

"*That doesn't change the—*" I stopped myself again.

I took a deep breath. I counted to ten.

"Leslie…" I said calmly, "I just want to ask the gentleman in the nicest possible way who fired the shot that killed Caroline Gaffney and then struck my pregnant wife. I'll be cordial. I'll be friendly. We'll have tea. I'll appeal to his decency and humanity. Okay?"

"Right. What's your ETA for Rochester?"

32

I had two problems with flying to Rochester.

First, I was operating on two hours of sleep. A fatigued flight across black expanses of The Great Lakes sounded a lot like something from an accident report.

Second, I needed to ditch Pidge.

As much as I shared her desire to find and *fuck somebody up,* I did not want her tagging along. Pidge's idea of messing with somebody didn't stretch beyond a scrappy bar fight or cutting the stems off someone's tires after said bar fight.

I had far worse in mind. Pidge would only get in the way.

"Okay," I said to Pidge when I returned to the lounge. "Here's the plan. Andy's kicking me out, just like you said. I'm going after the broken leg guy. Leslie is tracking down the details. I'm too tired to make the flight tonight, though. And the truth is, I don't want to leave Andy just yet. The nurse said she would give me something to help me sleep. I'm going to sack out in a room here and launch in the morning after I see her again."

"We," she said, as expected. "*We* will launch in the morning."

"No. You're going to leave now and get the Baron back up to Essex or else Earl will have both our heads. Go home. Get some sleep. Go in tomorrow morning and clean up the schedule for the next couple days. Get Dave in to cover. I'll pick you up on the way to Rochester."

No dummy, she looked at me with all the suspicion I deserved.

"You know I'm right," I argued. "Earl's out of his mind with worry about

Andy, but life goes on and he's going to start tossing grenades if you leave one of his airplanes sitting idle in Madison and blow up his charter schedule. Sort it out."

Pidge may be the better pilot, but as her original instructor I will always wield authority over her.

That didn't stop her from doling out side-eye.

"It's gotta be this way," I insisted.

"Fine." She handed me Andy's shoulder bag. "Her phone's inside. And hey…"

"What?"

"Don't fuck me over, Stewart."

"When you get to the ramp, do me a favor and leave your iPad in the Navajo for me. Mine's in my flight bag up in Three Lakes. In the morning, you can bring a spare from the flight school."

"Don't delete any of my porn," she warned. "It's a carefully curated collection."

33

Thursday

I broke through the top of the clouds at the same time as the rising sun. I took a shot of bright morning light directly in the face. Cleared to my cruising altitude of 9,000 feet, I let the autopilot do the work as the fully fueled and lightly loaded airplane locked on the purple GPS line between Madison and Rochester. The flight route did not include the stop in Essex I had promised Pidge. Halfway across Lake Michigan my phone vibrated. Considering the message Pidge texted, I'm surprised the device didn't spontaneously shatter.

Andy had been awake when I slipped in to see her shortly after 5 a.m. She didn't admit it, but a night of restless sleep merged with suppressed pain on her face.

I hung her bag on the bed's guardrail, then made an elaborate show of using a paper towel and hand sanitizer to clean off her phone before I handed it over contingent on a promise that she would leave the Three Lakes Police Department to their own devices.

"I can't," she said. "They're going to want to talk to me."

"Fine but keep your distance. Let them do their jobs."

"They're not going to find anything," she stated.

"Yeah...well...I might have overlooked telling them about the jet and Rochester."

I got *the look*, and for a split second felt a molecule of gratitude that she was confined to the bed.

"It's probably a wild goose chase," I hurried to say. "Look at it this way. It gives you something to tell them. Just don't blow up their phones."

"If I blow up anybody's phone, it will be Leslie's."

I tried to pout. "Not mine?"

"Are you saying I blow up your phone when you're away?"

"Okay. I walked right into that one." I hesitated. I asked, "Are you sure about this?"

"Go. Just...just keep me posted. Don't stay away long. You know where to find me when you get back." She paused, then touched the biodome housing our child. "We'll be fine."

We.

Andy and I traded airborne kisses and promises of love, then I slipped out feeling ghost hooks in my back with taut lines tugging me back to my wife and unborn child.

Despite the part of me screaming not to leave her, taking action felt good. The tiny yellow pill and comfortable bed that the night nurse provided put me out for almost seven hours. I woke up refreshed and ready to fly.

A little under three hours after takeoff, I rolled to a stop on the ramp at Frederick Douglass Greater Rochester International Airport where a cold drizzle painted tiny diamonds on the windshield and the FBI waited for me in the private jet terminal.

34

"I found it," Leslie said after we climbed in a car that she had either rented or else driven all the way from Washington, D.C. She threw the small sedan in gear and weaved through the parking lot onto an airport access road.

"Found what? King Kong?"

She glanced at me for as long as busy traffic would allow.

"Who?"

"Broken leg guy," I explained. "Oh, that's right. You haven't seen him yet, have you. He looks like a pro wrestler. I call him King Kong, Kong for short."

"Well, that's not his name and neither is Benjamin Everly. The Benjamin Everly on that driver's license you sent me exists…and doesn't exist."

"Neat trick. How does that work?"

"Benjamin Everly has a legit license, a job, a Social, probably a wife and three children in some suburb of Sacramento, but it's all a legend. A good one, though. A damned good one."

"Spies?" I asked.

She scrunched her face. "Really don't like throwing that word around. Makes it sound like some silly two-dimensional thriller plot. Buying into that crap makes people in my job lower their guard, and that's a bad idea because the real world can bite you in the ass."

"Huh?"

"Everly. I did a deep dive on the guy. He's not real. If this is a government agency's legend, then it's pretty good. If it's private enterprise, then it is top notch work that speaks to something very different and potentially dangerous."

"Go back to the headline. You found Kong?"

"I found a clinic. A mall walk-in storefront pop-up urgent care clinic owned by the same law firm that owns that lovely executive jet."

Leslie ignored the red sequencing light on a freeway ramp and accelerated rapidly. When the car ahead elected to merge at 38 miles per hour, she cut around it on the right, kicking up accumulated road dust in the breakdown lane. We merged at the appropriate 75 mph suggested by the 55-mph speed limit.

"Why do I suspect that a storefront urgent care clinic is a perfect fit with a month-to-month rental law firm that specializes in the kind of vague injuries that make a good case in court?"

Leslie tapped her nose. "Probably a pill mill, too."

"Is he there?"

She shrugged.

"What?" I asked. "You're not sure?"

"Do I need to be? The connection seems clear. And if he's not, we'll find him. How far can a guy get on a broken leg?"

35

"We do not have a patient by that name," the girl with purple streaks in her reddish hair and makeup inspired by Elizabeth Taylor's turn as Cleopatra said without referring to the monitor on her desk.

"And…you know this…how?" Leslie asked.

"Because we don't have patients here." She slipped a little snark between syllables. "We're not a hospital. We are an urgent care treatment center meeting the needs of people who are experiencing illness, minor injury, or other non-critical health conditions."

"Right out of the brochure," Leslie said. She turned around and looked at the empty waiting room wedged between a nail salon and a pizza place. When we pulled up, I noted that the pizza place opened at 11, just twenty minutes hence. My thoughts slipped to a pepperoni slice or a nice hot calzone if the timing worked out right.

"What's down there?" Leslie pointed at the hallway extending deeper into the building.

"I don't see why I have to…answer…your…"

Leslie held up her badge wallet, taken from the inside pocket of her black blazer in a way that—oops—showed the butt of a weapon tucked in a shoulder holster. The girl dropped her jaw.

"Let's try this another way, miss. What's down there? How many people are down there? And who are they?"

The girl rattled off her reply. Examination rooms. Two people. One part-time nursing assistant and a man she didn't know.

"Broken leg?" Leslie asked.

The girl, now looking genuinely frightened, shook her head emphatically. "I don't go in the rooms. I just answer phones, okay? And the pay here sucks and I'm hoping my application at Target totally goes through. And like as soon as I save up enough money I'm going back to school."

"What are you studying?"

"Criminal psychology."

Leslie suppressed a smile. "You'll be fine," she said kindly. "Just keep doing what you do and don't touch the intercom or text anyone or do anything else while we go down there and have a look for ourselves. Got it?"

Red and purple hair bobbed obedience.

Leslie slipped around the end of the reception counter and entered the hallway. Four doors, two on each side, wore number tabs near the top of each doorframe. All four rooms were open and unlit. A bare bones examination table and small desk occupied each room. Two of the rooms also had plastic chairs. Only one of the rooms had an occupant—the nursing assistant who sat at the small desk. She glanced up but showed no interest in us.

We passed a digital scale in the hallway. Leslie led me into the open door at the end of the hall. A large room, twice the size of the small examination rooms, it held what looked like an operating table. Round lights hung on articulating arms over the table, which had a disposable paper covering. White cabinets, a sink, and a few rolling IV stands shared the space.

The feature that caught our immediate attention occupied a plastic chair next to a small desk identical to those in the exam rooms. A man in a white shirt, tie, and black fleece watched us enter with an air of detached interest. One arm rested on the desk. One leg crossed the other.

"And you are?" Leslie asked.

"You first." He did not move. I guessed him to be in his mid-forties, about four inches shorter than me, but wiry, fit and probably strong. His clothes were neat, his shoes expensive looking. His gym membership probably accounted for a thousand dollars-worth of apparel in his wardrobe.

Leslie took her time examining the room. I did the same but had no idea what I was looking for other than the obvious fact that a nearly 300-pound man with a broken leg was not present. I crossed my fingers that Leslie would later reveal the clue that said Kong had been here and had been treated. A particular wrapping in the waste bin. A shred of gauze on the floor. Plaster dust from a cast.

"Are you a patient here?" Leslie asked.

"No."

"A doctor?"

"No." The man made no attempt to fill in the blank.

"Then who are you?" Leslie asked.

"I thought I made it clear. You first."

I couldn't help but give the guy points for keeping his cool. The word *spy* zipped through my mind. Maybe the FBI was about to meet the CIA, and the plot would take a sharp turn.

I watch too many movies.

"Federal Bureau of Investigation," Leslie said.

Leslie reprised her wallet extraction and held up her FBI identification. With one smooth move, the man produced a phone that had been in his hand the whole time. He lifted the phone, snapped a photo of the ID, then before I could blink, swung the phone, aimed and shot a photo of me. All without uncrossing his leg.

"What's your name?" Leslie asked.

"Excuse me one minute," the man said. He thumbed his phone screen. After a few seconds, he tapped a button, then palmed the phone again and waited.

Leslie grew stern. "Show me some identification."

The man smiled and made a casual *just a sec* gesture with his free hand. "This will only take a moment."

I pulled out my phone and quickly located the Benjamin Everly driver's license image I sent to myself from Andy's phone. I took an aggressive step and held up the screen.

"Hey," I said sharply. "Recognize this guy?"

The man looked at the image but said nothing.

"Benjamin Everly," I blurted. "Where is he?"

No response.

Leslie's phone rang. She cocked her head and stared at the man in the chair.

"I wouldn't ignore that," he said.

The ringing did not stop.

Leslie plucked the phone from the inside front pocket of her blazer. She gave the screen a glance then swiped the button to answer.

"Leslie here," she said. She held the phone to her ear. Silence in the room made the voice in the tiny speaker audible, though the words were not distinguishable. The man in the chair did not change his expression. He and I listened to Leslie's side of the conversation.

"Yes, sir."

"Yes, sir."

"I'm sorry sir, but my authority comes from Director Simm—" A subtle shock rippled through her composure.

"He—what? When?"

The voice on the other end delivered a thirty-second monologue. Two or three times, Leslie opened her mouth to speak but cut herself off.

The distant voice ended what had become a tirade with *Do you understand?*

Leslie stared coldly at the man in the chair whose expression showed neither triumph nor contempt.

Do you understand?

Leslie swallowed. She found words and pried them loose.

"Yes. Sir."

The call ended. No one spoke. I felt like a kid caught in cold silence punctuating an argument between mom and dad.

Leslie reversed her phone and snapped a photo of the man. If the move caused irritation, he concealed it perfectly.

"I believe you were just leaving," he said without moving.

Leslie said nothing. She turned and walked out, incorrectly assuming I would follow.

36

Fwooomp!

I vanished. Leslie, marching on an angry stride, plowed past the front desk without looking back or at the girl with the streaked hair. I grabbed one of the exam room doors and pulled myself into the frame. Wedged there, I waited.

In part, I thought I might hear something useful. A phone call made to a superior might provide a clue, especially after the small triumph of thwarting a probe by the FBI.

No sound came from the end of the hall.

I waited, and began to fear that Leslie might realize what I'd done and return to interfere. She did not appear, but neither had I heard the clinic front door open and close.

Footsteps put an end to my speculation. The man in the shirt and tie appeared. He walked down the hallway with a blank expression on his face and purpose in his stride.

I waited for him to pass, then wedged one foot against the door frame and reached out and grabbed both arms at the elbows. His muscles flexed immediately and would have jerked free if I had not shoved the levers in my head hard against the stops and extended *the other thing* to his whole body.

FWOOOMP!

He vanished. I lifted. His feet parted with the floor. Mine planted. I heaved him backward, over my head. He jerked and flailed. The muscles in his arms became cured concrete, validating my assumption about that gym membership. He kicked, too, but without leverage or inertia, he gained no advantage. It would not take long, however.

I hurled him over my head and released. An electric snap bit my hands.

Fwooomp!

He reappeared somewhere near the acoustic ceiling tiles. Gravity took charge. He instantly dropped to the floor. He attempted to brace but hit hard.

I rotated and—

Fwooomp!

—reappeared facing him.

"Benjamin Everly," I snapped at him. "Where is he?"

The tidy shirt and tie man on the floor looked a mess now. Blood appeared beneath his nose. His tie hung askew. His fleece wormed its way up his torso, exposing a shirt that had come untucked.

I stepped over him and leaned down to ask again, "Everly! Where is he?"

My mistake.

He moved fast, too fast for me to try and figure out how he did it, but one second, I stood dominant over him and the next I crashed to my knees with my left arm twisted high against my back and my shoulder screaming in pain. Not satisfied with that, he swung around behind me and shoved my face to the floor. I turned my head in time to avoid the same nose injury he'd suffered.

He said nothing and I could not speak. A knee landed on my back, shoving all the air from my lungs.

"Let him go," Leslie said from somewhere. I hoped she issued the order from behind the barrel of her gun. I hoped she would shoot him and relieve the horrible pain in my left shoulder joint. "Now."

She did not shout. Nor did she shoot the sonofabitch.

He released the grip on my wrist. The fire in my shoulder went out, leaving embers to burn for the next several days. His knee left my back. I assume he stood to face Leslie. I could only crawl forward hoping to escape his reach.

When I finally looked, I saw him tidying his fleece and shirt. He resumed his stroll down the hall and passed Leslie without sparing a glance. I heard the clinic's front door open and close.

Leslie looked down at me as I swung around to face her.

She said nothing, which felt worse than any comment she might have made.

"Did I mention I'm no good in a bar fight?"

37

———————

"What the hell was that?" Leslie asked.

"Not now." I heaved myself to my feet. "I can catch up to him. His car. I can foll—"

"Forget it," she said.

"No," I insisted. I started for the exit. "He could lead us to—"

"Forget it," she repeated. She gripped my arm. "He's not going to lead you anywhere and certainly not to your friend Kong. Come with me."

She pulled me toward the pizza place next door.

"Not hungry," I said. I lied.

"I am, but that's not why we're stopping here."

She opened the door and gestured for me to enter a pizza restaurant called Lenny's. Black and white checkerboard floor tile accented red, white, and green tiles running halfway up the walls. A long counter fronted the working heart of the place, a pair of stacked pizza ovens. The owner or top chef stood at the far end twirling a disc of pizza dough in the air. Leslie chose a table for two near the storefront windows and insisted I sit.

"What are you having?" She waited. I saw no point in resisting.

"I'll take a slice of pepperoni and a Coke or Pepsi, whichever they have."

She went to the counter and ordered. A minute later she slid a tall soft drink across the table at me and sat down with a glass of water for herself.

"What the hell, Leslie?" I demanded. "I had him right where he wanted me."

129

She laughed.

"He wasn't going to tell you anything, Will. That was a childish move. And you could have gotten hurt. How would that help Andy?"

"Fine. Add insult to insult. But, Jesus, Leslie…he knows. He knows where they stashed Kong. He probably knows who the shooter was. He probably knows a ton."

"I have no doubt. But you weren't going to beat it out of him."

"I suppose you have a better idea?"

"I always have a better idea."

She turned her head. Her momentary humor faded. Her face shifted to a dark expression matching the gray clouds and steady drizzle outside at the windows.

"Bill Simmons is out," she said.

I knew the name. I also knew the implication.

Leslie knows about *the other thing*. On her own initiative, she assumed the role of ally. As far as Andy and I can tell, she has not taken her knowledge to the FBI as an institution. Her former boss, Mitchell Lindsay, learned about me after Andy and I approached him. After Lindsay's murder, Leslie appeared in our lives. She kept the secret. She never shared how, but Leslie operated with what seemed like very loose supervision, most recently under the Director himself, William Simmons.

Andy and I believe that Leslie never formally explained *the other thing* to Director Simmons. All we knew was that he freed Leslie from a burdensome chain of command and a suffocating bureaucracy. For as long as we've known her, Leslie worked as a free agent.

Such arrangements can create enemies within your own agency.

"Gone? Simmons is gone?"

"The White House has been on a tear. They're gutting DOJ and they have had a hard-on for the FBI. Simmons stood in the way. He has powerful allies on The Hill. Or had. Something happened last night."

She fished out her phone and tapped through several screens. A CNN headline confirmed the news. *FBI Director William Simmons has resigned.*

"That guy knew. Who was that guy?"

"I don't know."

"Well, he seemed to know you."

"No…I don't think so. But one thing is certain. He has friends in the new regime. He sent them my ID to identify me and get me off his back. And it worked."

"Who called you?"

"Acting Assistant Director Roger Conners."

"Wait…Conners? Roger 'Big Rog' Conners? The home furnishings guy on the internet? He's not in the FBI."

"He is now. By order of the President of the United States, he's now the Acting Assistant Director under the new Acting Director."

"Who would that be? Beavis or Butthead?"

One of the guys behind the counter produced a paper plate and muttered, "Slice of pepperoni and a veggie calzone." I liked the bare bones approach to customer service. It felt like value.

I fetched the food and sat down again.

"Leslie, what's the rest of it?"

"Pardon?"

"What's the rest of it?"

"Oh," she faked levity, "you mean my new assignment. I'm to report back to the office in D.C. for assignment evaluation."

"What does that mean?"

"It means they look for the worst bullshit assignment they can find and 'Big Rog' the Furniture Sale Guy offers it to me."

"Or?"

"Or I submit my resignation."

I uttered Pidge's favorite response to bad news.

We sat without exchanging words for a long minute.

She broke the silence. "Simmons never said he knew about you, and he never asked. I didn't tell him, but the man didn't have a stupid bone in his body. I have no doubt he put it together or that Lindsay left him a dead man's switch letter. Pretending not to know and giving me a free hand gave him plausible deniability. But that's not all. I think he wanted you and Andrea as allies. I think he understood that he has enemies capable of doing a lot of damage if they got their hands on you. Keeping you unofficial was one way of preventing that."

"Great."

"My point, Will, is that even if he's out, he won't leave your secret behind. And I won't either. You have my word."

"Eat it," I said. She blinked, mildly stunned. "My slice, I mean. It's yours. I gotta go." I pointed at the parking lot. The man from the walk-in clinic strolled across the pavement. I could only assume that he had stopped somewhere, perhaps to make the phone call I hoped to hear in the hallway. Or to clean up his bloodied nose. The taillights on a boxy Land Rover acknowledged his approach when he used his remote to unlock the vehicle.

I hurried to the door. The restaurant's only occupied table contained Leslie and our uneaten lunch. The crew behind the counter had thinned out to just the guy tossing dough in the air. He watched his work, not the front door.

I pulled a BLASTER from my flight jacket pocket and snapped a prop on the shaft extending from the end of the device. A pulse of the slide control mounted on the side of the cylinder caused the prop to spin. Good to go.

Leslie called after me. "He's not going to lead you anywhere or tell you anything, and I've got—"

I didn't wait to hear the rest.

Halfway through the front door, I turned to Leslie.

"I'll call you."

I pushed the levers in my head all the way to the stops and—

Fwooomp!

—I vanished.

38

Rain doesn't reach my skin when I vanish. A cool sensation wraps around me. I have no idea what it is or how it works, but it insulates me from rain, from heat, from cold, and I think on one or two occasions, from toxins in the air. Rain, however, does have an impact on my body, the same as wind resistance or a solid wall. Rain drives me down.

From the door of Lenny's Pizza, I took a calculated half-leap. In clear air such a leap would have no end. Without input from a BLASTER, I would simply sail out of the earth's atmosphere. In rain, however, the line of such a leap becomes an arc.

The Land Rover backed out of its parking space.

I sailed across open pavement, first rising, then descending toward the rear of the vehicle. I engaged the BLASTER and adjusted the trajectory. Short bursts of prop wash blew down my outstretched arm. I sailed toward the top of the SUV. The timing was tight. The Land Rover backed into the open traffic lane, stopped, and lurched forward just as I closed a grip on the luggage rack. The vehicle jerked me forward. Drizzle turned to a horizontal spray as the vehicle gained speed. Ignoring a stop sign, the driver turned onto the small access road fronting the strip mall. He accelerated quickly.

I let my grip on the right-side luggage rack slip until my hand reached the rear of the bar. I hung like a flag in the wind off the back corner of the vehicle. I pulled my legs forward. My toes found the bumper. I crouched, letting the vehicle block the rain and the spray from other vehicles.

The gamble in this carried little risk. I've been here and done this before. The easiest way to follow someone was to simply go with them. Leslie didn't have faith, but I reasoned that if Shirt and Tie Guy drove somewhere that pointed at Kong's location, the gamble would pay off.

Or he could be on his way to get an iced latte at his favorite coffee shop.

39

A little under an hour after getting hauled through Rochester by the Land Rover, I found a comfortable chair in the lobby of the Hyatt Regency Hotel and called Leslie.

"It's something called the—"

"Granite Building," Leslie interrupted over the phone line.

I looked up at the name carved in stone on the impressive façade. The monument to brick, stone and steel held down a corner of downtown Rochester. Halfway up the building, stone columns rose into recessed arches. The building looked good for its age, probably owing to renovation and restoration at some point. A tech company dominated the first-floor corner windows.

Shirt and Tie Guy disappeared into an entrance under brown cloth awnings after snatching a lucky parking space directly in front of the neighboring building of blue glass. I used the BLASTER and a few maneuvering tricks to follow him into the Granite Building lobby where he called for and boarded an elevator that I was not able to reach in time. I watched the elevator rise directly to the 8th floor, a reasonable guess for his destination since he was the sole occupant, and the elevator returned directly to the lobby when I called it.

I scanned the empty lobby and nearly pulled the levers to make myself reappear when I spotted the inevitable security camera.

Live your life as if someone is always watching, Andy likes to say. More and more she's correct.

Instead of popping into sight on camera, I pushed off a wall and drifted to a directory mounted on a pedestal near the entrance.

8th floor. There were four listings. Only one made sense.

My immediate impulse was to explore the 8th floor offices and see if I could catch a conversation or eavesdrop on a phone call that would give away Kong's location. A persistent version of Andy's voice in my head said calling Leslie would be smarter. To make a call required me to reappear, something I was not inclined to do in or around the Granite Building lobby.

I used the entrance to a parking garage across the street for cover, reappeared, and walked to the Hyatt Regency lobby, which faced the Granite Building. I found a gray chair in the gray lobby and made the call.

"Yeah," I said to Leslie, "something called—"

"Gallica Security Services," she said, making no effort to suppress a tone of superiority.

In my mind, Andy gave me one of her *Told you* looks.

"Right," I said. "Anything else you care to lord over me?"

"First off, the pepperoni slice was amazing. It's going to give me heartburn tonight, but it was so totally worth it. Second, if you had shown a little patience instead of running off like that, I could have told you all this using my phone and, oh, I don't know—the resources of the FBI."

"Do you still work for the FBI?"

"That's the nice thing about having no one to report to. Makes it harder for them to fire me. Anyway…and third, it's technically Legio III Gallica Security Services, named after one of the most famous Roman legions, apparently Caesar's favorite before they voted him out of office abruptly."

"Oh. For a minute there, I thought it was an old school video game. How did you know about Gallica and this location?"

"I told you. FBI. I took a picture of your sparring partner. His name is Deland Hollis. He's the managing partner for Gallica Security's Rochester New York office."

"Bingo. I'm betting this outfit is who Kong works for."

"Hold that thought. Where are you now?"

"Across the street from Gallica at the Hyatt. I was thinking you should join me and then we'd poke around up there. I know a shortcut."

"If you mean going up the side of the building, that's a hard no. Also, I have a better idea. If you want to poke around a law office, I suggest Winston Karl & Cardinal in New York City."

I waited. She waited me out.

"Okay. I give up. Who are they?"

"If you cross-check the social media pages of both Gallica Security and

Winston Karl, you will see some interesting convergences. A Venn diagram sort of approach."

She lost me and I wasn't afraid to admit it. "What does that mean?"

"It means that Lucas Winston, second-generation namesake of said law firm, can be seen at the Met Gala and other *beau monde* events rubbing elbows with Chesterton Poyne, the owner and founder of the preeminent worldwide high-level personal protection firm. I give you…Gallica Security."

"This is starting to sound like word salad, Leslie. Or name salad."

"Guess what law firm Caroline Gaffney's husband works for."

"Oh."

"Exactly. Now go back to your thought about who Kong works for."

40

―――――――

Leslie convinced me there was no point in floating around in the Gallica offices in Rochester. They weren't going to hide Kong there, and Hollis wasn't going to hold open conversations about the big man's location. Nor could we reasonably expect to find invoices for ambulance services or secret medical clinics lying exposed on desktops. She told me that she still had friends at the Bureau willing to help her by slipping small tasks into other open investigations, and that a search of area ambulance services was already underway. She also suggested looking into orthopedic surgeons in the Rochester area, possibly with connections to Gallica Security. She estimated arriving to pick me up in less than 20 minutes.

I ducked into a coffee shop and used the time to call Andy and dry out my flight jacket.

"Did I wake you?"

"No. They just came and took away the lunch tray."

"Something delicious?"

"I have my choice of Jell-O colors."

"Nothing solid?"

"Liquids for now. A matter of movement, if you get my drift."

I put two and two together and stepped to the precipice of making a joke about her wearing an adult garment, then remembered her comment about not being able to afford the divorce.

"Gotcha. Has the doc been in?"

"He's coming in this afternoon, they think around four."

"And how are you doing?"

"Well, I am roughly 30 or 40 endless hours into sitting here motionless, and I can tell you the precise length of every single minute of it. We will never again talk about a vacation that involves sitting on a beach."

I winced. "Sorry. I wish there was something I could do."

"Lydia's here," Andy said. "She brought my Kindle. She said she loaded up the entire Louise Penny collection for me, but those are cop stories, so…"

"Try them. Give them a chance. There's probably a lot more to it than police procedural stuff that's just going to make you mad. I think they take place in Canada. You can pretend they do cop stuff differently up there."

"Where are you?"

"Rochester, still." I weighed the pros and cons of sharing and decided that the overwhelming con was that she would not let it go until I brought her up to speed. I explained the events since my rendezvous with Leslie. I concluded with, "It's always the husband."

"Maybe." Her doubt surprised me. "If he wanted to get rid of her, why was he holding her against her will?"

"I give up. Why?"

"I also wonder what the end game was. How long did they plan to keep her?"

"Why does that matter?"

"It might not. Or it might mean that there's some event or process defining the duration of her imprisonment. See what I mean?"

"Some clock ticking? And then what? Kill her? Or release her?"

"I don't know."

I liked the extra energy I heard in her voice. The medical staff had warned against talking about the case with her. Knowing Andy as I did, not talking about the situation struck me as a worse idea.

"Tom said something interesting about the shooting. He said somebody preferred a murder investigation to a missing person investigation."

Andy remained silent for a moment. I waited, knowing that she stayed physically connected to the phone but had ventured into a mental room full of white boards and pinned photos and the weird obsessive yarn strings you see in movies when they find the basement lair of a serial killer. I can't help it, that's how I see the inside of my wife's often brilliant mind.

When she returned, she asked, "Has anything more come up about the daughter?"

"I don't think so. But I'll ask. That's our next stop."

"Do something for me when you see the father."

"If I can."

"Ask to see if she's posted anything on social media. Ask Leslie to check into that as well."

"Okay, although Leslie's skeptical about the daughter having anything to do with her mother's murder. What time did you say the doc is coming in?"

"Around 4."

"Can you call me as soon as possible after?"

"Yes." She paused, then said, "Will?"

"Yes?"

"This isn't about someone coming after me. You know that. This wasn't an attack on us."

I didn't answer because I can't lie to my wife. Not to her face and not over the phone. What she suggested was that I should accept whims of fate that put people in the wrong place at the wrong time and that I should pretend that the harm that follows senseless violence has no point of origin, no credible intent. And that the black murder lurking in shadow corners of my heart, looking for an outlet, thirsting for blood, should be politely told *this is no one's fault; it just happened.*

I could not and would not say that to her.

This wasn't an attack on us. Like hell. A finger put enough pressure on a trigger to send a bullet into *my wife, my child.* That finger belonged to someone who does not know that every time they look at a clock they are seeing a countdown.

"You understand what I'm telling you," she insisted.

"I understand."

And she understood what I wasn't saying.

"Leslie's here. I gotta go. Call me after you see the doc, okay?"

"I will. I love you."

"Love you, too."

"Be careful."

"I can't," I said. "Tuesdays and Thursdays are 'Be Careful' days this week."

"Today is Thursday."

41

Leslie suggested I leave the Navajo in Rochester, and that we take a commercial flight nonstop to LaGuardia. I argued for a direct flight in the Navajo to Republic Airport on Long Island. She laughed the idea off saying it would take us forever to get into the city and that cab or uber fares would add up to what we would pay to fly via commercial airline. I silently conceded that ramp and tie-down fees would skyrocket the costs, but that's as far as any argument went. Whatever we learned from a foray into Manhattan, I was convinced it would lead us back to Rochester and Kong.

I let Leslie win. The Navajo remained in Rochester. Delta 5343 touched its wheels to Runway 13 at LaGuardia shortly after 6 p.m. I halfheartedly grumped that in the time it took to taxi to the gate we could have driven into the city from Republic Airport. During the long slow ride, I noted a missed call from Andy. I decided not to call back while sitting within close earshot of a plane full of people.

Just landed NYC. Call you as soon as I can. I sent the text and pocketed my phone. At the same time, Leslie scrolled screens on her phone.

"What are you looking for?" I asked.

"Hotel on Lexington. Someplace near or around Gaffney's office."

"Why?"

Leslie lowered her voice. "I want to make a visit tonight. To his office, and if he's not there, to his home."

"Tonight?"

"Element of surprise."

42

We had no bags to collect. Halfway to the terminal exit I told Leslie I needed to make a check-in call with Andy. I diverted into an empty gate area. Leslie pointed at a small coffee shop and said she'd wait there.

"Hey," I replied when Andy greeted me. "Sorry for the delay. I didn't account for being airborne."

"Did you fly into New York?"

"I let Delta do the flying. Got us to LaGuardia which is…well, you know. You've been here. Leslie booked rooms at the Hilton Midtown."

"I'm jealous. I mean this is nice and everything, first class, but not quite a luxury hotel."

"I promise not to use the spa. Solidarity, babe. Did the doc come in?"

"He did."

"What did he say?"

"Doctor Obvious? He said I got shot. That it hurts. That they'd rather not give me anything for the pain except Tylenol which is useless. And that I should sit still." Andy's report used a matter-of-fact tone. I easily detected her seeping frustration. She added, "Oh, and he also went into a twenty-minute lecture on oligohydramnios and polyhydramnios, and the need for an amniocentesis."

"The needle thing?"

"Yeah."

"Why does he want that? I thought we were already dealing with a punctured whatchamacallit."

"They want to monitor the amniotic fluid. It provides a lot of data on the health of the baby. And it's critical now, with a possible infection in the mix."

"Okay." I had no clue, but it seemed to make sense.

"He said the issue of infection is slightly mitigated by the fact that it was a bone fragment, and not the bullet itself, that penetrated. Less contamination. He still wants to monitor the fluid." She paused. "Will, he asked if we want to know the sex of the child."

"What did you tell him?" I wondered if events changed Andy's mind. Up to this point, we adopted the old school approach, waiting to be surprised.

"What do you want to do?"

I tried and failed to read between the lines. "I want to do what you want to do."

"I don't know. I feel like…if something goes wrong…"

"Nothing is going to go wrong." I said quickly. "We already decided that. Nothing is allowed to go wrong."

"Tell that to Caroline Gaffney," Andy said darkly. "Sorry. Tell me about Everly. Did you and Leslie find him? Have you heard anything from Three Lakes?"

I gave Andy the update. She seemed grateful to pocket the medical discussion and shift to cop mode.

"Did Leslie run the identity of this Hollis person? And what's the background on Gallica Protective Services? God, I wish I had my laptop. I bet I could get Tom to do a deep dive into—"

"You do *not* need your laptop, and you do not need to sic Tom on anybody. You need to chill and relax and meditate and count the holes in the ceiling tiles."

"Well, that su—*ouch*." I swear I felt the pain with her. She said nothing for a few seconds.

"I shouldn't be stirring you up like this," I said, thinking I should end the call.

"Darling, if you want to stir me up, come back here and stroll around the room wearing that sexy paper costume. I've had a taste for popcorn all day."

"Plain or buttered?"

She laughed then winced and said in a tight voice, "Don't do that."

"I rest my case."

She released a loud sigh. "This is intolerable, Will. Oh, and Lydia showed up again. This time she brought me a stack of fashion magazines. Seriously?"

This time I laughed. "That could have been you, dear."

"Gak. Shoot me now. And of course, the cover of *Vogue* features a gorgeous pregnant celebrity. It's terrible," she whispered into the phone, "but I resent her for flaunting it for a camera while I have to lay here."

"Okay. I get that. When I get the flu, I hate anyone who isn't nursing a triple-digit temperature and body aches."

"Well, that explains it."

"Just remember, this comes from love. She's there because she cares."

"I suppose. Thank God Mom and Dad are in Paris. Liddy talked them out of rushing to the airport when she called them with the news. We're arranging a FaceTime tonight. Gee. That should be fun."

"Again. They care. Also, by showing up on FaceTime you stand a far better chance of preventing them from showing up at the door."

"See," she said, "this is why I love you. This and the sexy paper outfit."

We did the momentary silence thing again. With anyone else, it would have been awkward. With Andy it feels like stroking her back when she rests her head on my chest. Or taking each other's hand when we're walking.

I interrupted the moment.

"Would you do me a favor when you see Lydia?" I asked.

"Of course."

"Ask her if Caroline Gaffney ever talked about therapists or treatment for her daughter."

"Why?"

"The camp thing. I was wondering who referred Caroline to the camp. I'll tell Leslie to ask the husband the same thing when she interviews him."

"You're not going to be there?"

"Oh, yes, I will be. Just not part of the conversation."

43

The clerk at the Hilton looked askance at me when we checked in. Leslie had a roller bag. I didn't.

"The airline lost my luggage," I lied. "Can you bring it up to the room when it gets here. It's tagged."

"Certainly, Mr. Stewart. How many room keys would you like?"

"Tw—uh—just the one." A pang of something sharp went through my chest, thinking of Andy, thinking of how much I would have preferred to have her standing beside me. I've done more than my share of hotel and motel stays alone and we managed, often because she was busy with work or choir practice or any of a dozen ways she dissipates energy. This felt different.

Leslie and I rode the elevator to the 14th floor, found our rooms, and agreed to rendezvous in the lobby near the check-in desk in twenty minutes. The arrangement gave me 19 minutes with nothing to do in an empty room. I checked out the view, which overlooked West 54th Street. City lights sparkled to infinity. Ten thousand busy lives rushed by on foot and in vehicles below. The vaguely ziggurat architecture of The Luxury Collection Hotel dominated the next block, its face lit by spotlights. Our cab passed it before depositing us in front of the Hilton. Before that we passed the glittering marquee for Stephen Colbert's Late Show. Down to the smallest food cart everything and everyone seemed absorbed in purpose.

Snap. Sharp and yet dull at the same time. The sound of the bullet striking Caroline Gaffney played on repeat in my head. The sound connected to a weapon which connected to a person. A person who, tonight, walked and talked and laughed somewhere. He or she might even be there on the busy street below my Hilton Hotel room.

That person was my purpose.

I closed the room curtains and finished the wait for Leslie in the lobby.

"It's always the husband." I looked up at the stone scrollwork and flag-draped 45th Street entrance. Granite markers bearing the 450 engraving flanked the recessed brass-trimmed doors. "If he works here, it's definitely the husband. This place looks evil."

"It's a post office. Grand Central Post Office."

"Yup. Evil."

"They built the office tower on top of the post office." Leslie pointed at the modern, diamond-topped structure above. "Come on. We're going up."

We entered the building and navigated a gray marble path to the office tower elevators. A directory noted a floor listing one tenant.

"Humphry Patrick Alison," I pointed at the brass placard beside the elevator button. "They may get their own floor, but they don't get an ampersand."

Leslie didn't comment. She pulled a pair of black-framed glasses from her shoulder bag and slipped them on. When she caught me staring, she said, "Makes me look like some junior agent from archives or some such."

The elevator doors opened on the law firm's lobby. The space had the dimensions of a small gymnasium. Glossy wood paneling, high ceilings, and recessed lighting surrounded randomly spaced sofas and chairs for those who waited. The firm's name glistened in gold letters on wood paneling behind a counter-height reception desk. Three mesh-back chairs lined up at three workstations. All three chairs were empty and the workstations bare. The absence of a receptionist did not surprise me, given the late hour. What surprised me was the full lighting and the degree of activity beyond glass walls on both ends of the lobby area. Half a dozen people worked in partitioned glass cubicles, some with heads hovering over documents spread on desks, some with eyes focused on screens or clustered in two- and three-person conferences. Young staffers, men in shirts and ties, women in light blouses and skirts, hurried up and down channels between the glass walls.

"Kinda busy for close to 8 p.m. wouldn't you say?" I muttered to Leslie.

She shrugged. "Maybe this is a normal workday. These places can be intense. Hours are still billable after five. *Excuse me!*" She waved down a young woman passing through the lobby area carrying a box of documents.

The carton appeared heavy. The woman did not look like she wanted to chat. She glanced at the empty seats behind the counter.

"Someone will be here in a…well, shortly," she said.

"Yeah, that's not going to cut it." Leslie produced her badge wallet. "FBI. We'd like to speak to one of your junior partners, Wayne Gaffney. Is he still in the building?"

The woman's face changed instantly from annoyance to interest. She swerved and dropped the box on the top of the counter.

"Is this about his wife?" she asked breathlessly. "My God, we just heard about that this afternoon. Terrible. Just terrible."

"I realize it's late. Is Mr. Gaffney here?"

"He is," she replied glancing at a minimalist curving staircase that faced the elevator. "Partner offices are one floor up. I think he's meeting with the security people and a few of the seniors. I can call up to his assistant if you—"

"Thank you, no, we'll see ourselves up. It's a tragic time for Mr. Gaffney. We'd rather not make a fuss."

Leslie didn't wait for a reply. She pivoted and crossed the lobby, then took the stair steps by twos. I fell in behind her.

"Do you want me to… you know?" I asked when we reached the top.

"Not yet." She flicked her gaze at a black bulb mounted in the ceiling. Security camera. She did not break stride, but marched through a second reception area, smaller and cozier than the one below but equally empty. From there, we entered a wide hallway between offices that featured opaque walls for privacy. I noticed that the size of the offices grew as we approached the end of the building.

"Do you know where you're going?" I asked quietly.

"No clue."

A young woman stepped out of an office and hurried in our direction.

"Excuse me," Leslie flagged her down as we approached. "We might have gotten turned around. They sent us to Wayne Gaffney's office…?" Leslie raised her eyebrows and waved her badge again.

The young woman adopted a sad expression. "Of course," she said quickly. "God, it's so awful. Mr. Gaffney is in his office. Go to the end, go left, go left again and as you come back in this direction his office will be second on the right."

Second from the corner. I calculated the stature his office real estate represented.

We walked to the end of the hall, turned left, traversed a short hallway, then turned left again. Leslie stopped abruptly and examined the space. She studied the ceiling in both directions. I saw no black bulbs.

"This is good." She snugged her grip on her shoulder bag and turned away from me. "Grab my shoulder strap and do it."

I closed a fist on the strap just below her armpit. She pushed down on her bag to make the leather rigid.

Fwooomp!

The cool sensation enveloped me. My feet lost touch with the carpet. Leslie glanced back, shook her head, and started walking. I floated in trail with a close-up view of her short black hair.

A moment later she opened a closed office door and leaned in.

"Who are you?" One of two seated men facing a large desk asked sharply. A third man, looking tired and drawn, looked at us from behind the desk.

Leslie treated the challenge as a friendly invitation. She pushed the door wide open and walked confidently into the office where she held up her ID for the third time in as many minutes. I released my grip and traded it for a hold on the edge of the door.

"Special Agent Leslie Carson-Pelham. I'm with the FBI and I was sent to follow up with Mr. Gaffney. I assume you heard from our office today, sir?" She moved quickly to the desk and held out a hand which Gaffney took and shook automatically.

Gaffney looked confused, "I…uh…I heard from—"

"The investigative team in Wisconsin. Yes, I understand. I'm not with the investigative team. I'm a liaison with the FBI Counsel's Office. They sent me over to open a channel in case there are any questions tangent to client confidentiality, or that require confirmation of privileged information or a special master."

"Special master? Nobody said anything about a special master." One of the two men facing Gaffney rose to his feet. "I think there's been a misunderstanding here."

"And you are?"

"Greg Pollum, Senior Partner. Agent Carson, you are wildly ahead of yourself and I'm going to inform you right now that for this conversation I represent Mr. Gaffney, and he won't be answering questions."

Leslie feigned surprise. "I wasn't sent to ask questions, sir. In that sense, I think you're right, Mr. Pollum, there has been a misunderstanding. Mr. Gaffney has just lost his wife—"

"Ex-wife," Gaffney said firmly.

"I beg your pardon, and I am so sorry for your loss," Leslie said. She leaned across the desk and scooped up Gaffney's hand again. She held it the way a mother would hold a child's hand. "You've just lost the mother of your three children in a violent incident five states away. There's nothing to suggest involvement by you sir."

"Then I don't see a purpose to your presence here, Agent Carson," Pollum said.

"Which is not really my concern. And who are you, sir?" Leslie turned to the second man who remained seated. Cold eyes looked up at her. He made no move to rise, or to take the hand she extended toward him. Leslie did not falter. "You must be with the security firm. Gallica, is it? This might be a stroke of good luck. The authorities in Wisconsin sent me this photo…" She pulled out her phone, stroked the screen, tapped, and held up the device. "Do you recognize this man?"

Pollum intervened. "I thought you said you weren't here to ask questions."

"Never miss an opportunity to clarify and confirm available data."

No response. Leslie showed Pollum, then Gaffney.

"Anyone?"

"Who is he?" Gaffney asked, drawing a sharp look from Pollum.

"A person of interest, Mr. Gaffney. Someone who was last seen with your wi—your ex-wife. His name is Everly, although that may not be his real name."

No one spoke.

Leslie put away the phone. "Gentlemen, I'm just a messenger. Someone sent to show the flag and let you know that the Bureau will make every effort to tread lightly where any of your—let's just say—high-profile clients are concerned."

Pollum abruptly generated a smile. The word *greasy* popped into my head.

"Please, Agent Carson, forgive us. This news came as a shock. And frankly, we were not aware of FBI involvement in the case. I have friends at the Bureau and I'm sure I can clear up any of the communication issues you mentioned. It was kind of you to come in person."

Leslie cut off Pollum's gesture for the door.

"Is this your family, Mr. Gaffney?" She stepped lightly around the desk and picked up a framed photograph from Gaffney's credenza. A studio shot, the image showed Caroline Gaffney with her husband, two boys, and a pretty blonde in her upper teens. "Have you been contacted regarding a protective detail? Again, it's not my role, but under the circumstances, until we can clarify the motive behind the crime, it would be a wise precaution. I can make a call. Are your children in school?"

"At this hour, my boys are at home with the sitter. My daughter is away at college."

"Have you been able to reach her? Does she know?"

"I'm—I think—she's been notified. She's in her first semester at Penn State."

"I don't mean to intrude on your grief, but would you mind if I take a picture of this picture? I'd like to pass it along to the investigating team. It would be very helpful if they deem it necessary to engage a protective detail."

"I don't see any reason for that," Pollum said.

"I'm sure we can find this photograph online, sir." She lifted her phone, pointed it at the framed photo, and snapped the picture. "This will save us time, sir. Thank you."

Gaffney blinked. Pollum turned a shade of red and opened his mouth to protest but was cut off.

"We will manage protection of Mr. Gaffney and his family," said the man who had remained silent. I heard excellent English over a hint of accent. "In fact, it's already been seen to."

Leslie turned slowly. Her dark eyes lost the warmth they wore a moment ago. They settled on the seated man.

"That's so kind of you," she said. "Are you with Gallica?"

"I work for the firm."

Leslie waited. He matched her.

Pollum stepped between them. "Agent Carson, we appreciate you stopping by. I'll be in touch with your superiors, of course. As you can see, our colleague is dealing with grief and a difficult situation for his children. Now is not the best time. If you would please excuse us."

He reached for her arm but thought better of it when she fired a searing glance at his hand. He stepped back and waved at the door.

Leslie turned once more to Gaffney. "The Bureau extends its condolences, Mr. Gaffney, to you and your beautiful children. Let me assure you that we will do everything we can to aid in the investigation and see justice prevail."

Gaffney stared at the empty surface of his desk.

Leslie walked as far as the door.

"Oh—sir, one more question if you don't mind. The investigative team in Wisconsin spoke to a witness who mentioned a camp your daughter attended this past summer. Do you happen to know the name of the camp?"

Gaffney glanced at Pollum, who shook his head.

"Was Baxter referred there by your daughter's therapist or doctor?"

Gaffney said, "That would be Doct—"

Pollum stepped between Leslie and Gaffney. "Agent Carson, I thought I made it clear that any questions you have should be channeled through me. Do I need to speak to your superior?"

Leslie smiled.

"You assume I have a superior."

She closed the door behind her.

I hung in the air at the opposite end of the room.

44

———————

None of the men spoke, as if the air stirred by Leslie's wake might catch the conversation and carry it to her.

Pollum took his seat and pulled out his phone.

"Go home, Wayne. Go be with your boys." The words sounded sympathetic, but the tone carried no warmth.

Gaffney appeared shellshocked. Early gray at the temples put him in his late forties or early fifties, but his pallor and the lines etching his face added a decade. For someone who hated his wife, he seemed genuinely devastated by her death.

He lifted himself to his feet and stood for a moment, as if uncertain about what to do next. The nearly silent third man stood and escorted him to the door.

"Gris," Pollum said without looking, "find out how she got in here." The order had the ring of a threat.

Gris nodded, and at that moment I saw in him the same stoic confidence as the man at the walk-in clinic, Hollis—the same falsely benign and unassuming quality that belied a dangerous, coiled capability. I learned that the hard way with Hollis. The man called Gris promised the same lesson. He escorted Gaffney into the hall and closed the door behind them.

Pollum leaned back in his chair, tapped his phone, and held it to his ear.

I pushed off the wall. The action set me in motion across the carpet. A small sitting room area drifted past on my right. I gripped the top of a sofa and edged closer to Pollum, who sat with his back to me. Reaching the end of the furniture, I curled my body into a cannonball and pulled myself down until my head became level with Pollum's. A gentle push sent me across the last span of carpet to the back of his chair. I closed a light fingertip grip on each side of the chairback and eased to a stop.

I turned my head to position my ear for the best reception. Someone spoke to Pollum. I missed the first part.

"—may I direct your call?"

"Get her on the line, Sissy," Pollum ordered.

"Uh—the doctor is in a group session at—"

"I'm sorry. Is there a problem with this connection? Or are you stupid? Get her on the fucking line."

"One moment, sir."

Pollum drummed the fingers of his free hand on the leather arm of the chair. His breath came in impatient huffs, growing louder as each counted off the seconds he was being made to wait.

"What is it, Leonard?"

"It's time for you to take a vacation. A 31-week vacation."

"Don't be ridiculous. I have patients, a schedule. I'm speaking at the Women's Conf—"

"Caroline Gaffney is dead."

An audible gasp hissed through the line.

"What—how? Was it—?"

"*A…terrible…fucking…tragedy*, Mina. Read between the goddamned lines. As I see it you have two choices. I am not going to spell them out to you on an open cellular line. Make the right choice or someone way over my head is going to make a choice for you and you will not like it. Do you understand?"

The woman did not speak for a moment, then said, "How long have I got?"

"Yesterday."

"Leonard, that's out of the question. I can't just—"

"The FBI showed up here a few minutes ago. Does that put a little goose in your step, Mina? Some pencil pusher who said she was from the Office of the Legal Counsel. I'm not worried about the fucking FBI, Mina. But you need to be damned worried about what some people will do to clean house if the FBI is poking around…"

As Pollum spoke, I leaned away, turned my head, and examined his grip on the phone. He held it in his left hand, but not in his palm. Only his thumb and forefinger secured a grip—a light one—on the device. An idea blossomed.

"…This agent tried to make her visit sound routine, but there's something about the little bitch that I don't trust…"

I released the left side of the chair and reached for the top of Pollum's phone. This would be crazy. Stupid. Andy would have none of it.

"…Gris was here. He *heard* her ask about you. Do you get that? When—"

I pinched the phone and jerked it from his fingers. My plan was to toss it over my shoulder and across the carpet, then push off and skim over it to read the contact name on the screen before he could pick it up.

Fortune occasionally favors the clumsy because my pinch-grip on the phone immediately slipped. The device tumbled from my control. It bounced on the top of the leather chair back and spun to the floor. I had just long enough to think *Heads or Tails* before it hit the carpet, bounced and flipped, and thankfully landed screen side up.

Mina Macallan. New York area code. 456 then the same first three numbers as the code box on the Foundation hangar. Ends in lucky 7.

"What the—?" Pollum twisted in his seat. He checked for the phone on the chair.

212

456

Hangar Code

7

Pollum stretched and looked over the chair back at the phone on the floor. If he wondered what nefarious force jerked the device out of his fingers, he dismissed the question with a grunt. He heaved himself to his feet and stepped halfway around the chair, leaned down, and scooped up the phone.

"You there?" he asked.

I no longer heard the response.

"Dropped my phone. Which is timely because this conversation is over. You heard what I said. Do it."

He lowered the phone and tapped the screen. I decided that the chances he would take in the view were slim and pushed myself in the direction of the office windows. It was a good call. Pollum marched to the door and departed.

212

456

Hangar Code

7

I didn't stay for the view either.

45

Fifteen minutes of slow, sometimes awkward maneuvering passed while I retraced the path to the elevators, called for a car, had to let it pass because of the way people were arranged across the interior, called for another, and then had to plaster myself against the ceiling when the damned thing filled up. Who works this late? Worse, when it arrived at the ground floor and emptied out, a cluster of new riders filed in, blocking my exit. I had to ride up and back down again. This time, the elevator car remained empty. Mindful of a camera, I elected not to reappear in the elevator. I pulled myself out at the top of the door and deployed my BLASTER with which I flew around the Grand Central Post Office until I found a short hallway where I was able to reappear out of public view.

"Where are you?" I asked Leslie when she picked up my call.

"Parking garage entrance off Park. That security guy just escorted Gaffney inside. I want to see if I can get a vehicle plate. Did anything good happen after I left?"

I explained what I heard and saw.

"Did you see how Pollum got a little touchy when I asked about the daughter? You said her mother told you she was at this camp thing? And that she bolted? But dad seems to think she's at Penn State."

"It's a divorce. It's messy. I think we need to find that doctor. Quick. She's about to make a run for it."

"Agreed. I'd love to know what would scare someone into doing that."

And I'd love to scare her into telling me who shot Caroline Gaffney and my wife.

"Which way is Park Avenue?" I asked.

"We entered off Lexington. Stay there. I'll find you. Meanwhile, give me that name and phone number. I'll see if I can find this doctor."

46

I checked my watch. Almost 8:45, yet the sidewalks remained hazardous with people. If this had been a theater district or an avenue lined with restaurants, I would have understood. Half of the people hustling past me emptied out of the office towers all around. Working late. Hurrying home. Maybe picking up carryout on the way. Most held a phone to their ears.

Leslie jogged through pedestrian traffic and found me standing at the corner of the Grand Central Post Office building where Lexington and 45th crossed each other. A little out of breath, she pushed me back against the building when I started toward her.

"Dr. Mina Macallen specializes in family therapy. She has a midtown office and she lives on the upper east side. *Whooh*!" Leslie bent over and rested her hands on her knees, gulping air.

"You know, I could have come to you."

"You'd get lost."

"How do you know all this?"

She laughed. "Ever been vaccinated?"

"Yes."

"Well, the chip Bill Gates put inside you feeds your precise location, your scholastic history, your bank records and your TV viewing habits directly to Microsoft and the FBI. We know everything about everyone."

"Right. Sorry I asked."

"Google, dumbass. People bitch about the FBI collecting data, but then they turn around and hand their lives to Google. What exactly did Pollum say to her?"

I repeated the conversation as I remembered it. Her expression darkened.

"We need to find her before someone else does."

I looked at the tall buildings all around us. "You said her office was in midtown? That's around here, right?"

Leslie shook her head. "You said she was in a session when he called. If she was, it's either been interrupted or it's ended by now. If she's going to rabbit, she'll stop at home. We need to go there." She searched the street. "It's going to be a bitch getting a cab at this hour."

"Cab?" I said archly and with a horrible accent. "We do'n need no stinkin' cab!"

47

———————

What we needed was a Walgreens, I quickly came to realize.

Leslie led me a short distance down the sidewalk beside the post office. We ducked into the first of three public entrance portals, all joining a common inner entrance. Instead of entering the building, we slipped behind the first wall. A channel above our heads provided for what I assumed to be after-hours security curtains. I considered slipping behind one, but space was limited and exiting would be problematic. Huddled in limited privacy, Leslie pulled out her phone and opened the map application. She tapped in the doctor's residential address. I watched the blue dot land on the grid of streets lining Manhattan's upper east side.

"Do you know where this is?" I asked.

"Roughly."

"Okay. You're the navigator. Memorize the route, because when we're not visible, neither is the screen. We can stop at intervals if we need to consult the map."

I pulled the power unit from my pocket, snapped the prop on the shaft, and held it up. "BLASTER."

"You do realize that the only thing worse than what you're about to do to me is calling it that."

"That's what Andy says. I'm working on a much more *brillianter* name. Come around to this side and take my left arm." Leslie stepped into position. "Easy. You don't need to cut off the circulation."

We peered past the edge of the entrance and gauged the pedestrian traffic, the street traffic, and the windows across the street. If one thing could be called consistent about New Yorkers, it's that they travel the streets fully absorbed in their own business. Few people lifted their heads or looked from side to side. Most shared their travel time with a device.

"You may feel like you might fall but you don't have any weight while you maintain contact. Ready?"

"Thanks, captain, but we've done this bef—"

Fwooomp! Sometimes it's better to surprise people. Leslie uttered a startled squeak. We vanished.

I tugged the corner of the wall and lined up on the momentarily empty entrance. A tap of my toes and short burst of power launched us toward the stone scrollwork well above the heads of any passing pedestrians. We passed under the stone artistry and into the space above the busy sidewalk.

Despite my instructions, Leslie's fingers dug into my arm.

<h1 style="text-align:center">48</h1>

Reduced power immediately became evident in the BLASTER, but my first concern as we emerged from the post office entrance hung over our heads. Wires ran to and from the traffic lights governing the intersection of Lexington and 45th, sparking worry that more cables were strung between the buildings lining these streets. The only reason I could think of for prohibiting lines between buildings was the Thanksgiving Day parade route. Beyond that, I had no idea what if any ordinances allowed or denied stringing wires. Against the night sky, wires would be impossible to spot.

I hoped for the best and aimed the power unit straight up. We climbed until the highest building in our vicinity fell away. Over my right shoulder the layered crown of the Chrysler Building ruled the skyline. I leveled off even with its curved apex.

"Did you have to go so high?" Leslie asked in a loud voice.

"You don't have to shout. It's just us birds up here. And yes, we did. I'm worried about wires." I lowered my arm and pushed the slide control on the power unit. The prop buzzed, unseen. Air rushed up my arm. We surged forward. A good start, but I knew the signs. The rechargeable batteries in the power unit were losing their charge. The tiny map Leslie had consulted made the distance to our destination seem easily covered. Yet, I knew this feeling from piloting an airplane. The needles on the fuel tanks nudged the bottom quarter with nothing but horizon ahead.

New York sprawled in every direction. Manhattan flowed beneath us. Towers of stone and glass reached for our feet. An endless sea of lights winked and sometimes glared at us. Had we been an intruding aircraft, our belly would have been lit well enough for a maintenance inspection.

"Stay on Lexington," Leslie instructed. She moved. I think she reflexively pointed. "All the way to the park."

Ahead, a flat rectangular span of black broke the pattern of city lights. Central Park was like an airport in a major city, one of the few areas not sprinkled with street and city lights.

Reachable, I thought, feeling the faintly diminished vibration of the electric motor and spinning prop. The batteries inside were rechargeable but the battery charger was in my flight bag. I needed two new C cell batteries. I watched the streets below for a Walgreens or one of those riotous electronics stores.

Wind made our eyes water. I keep a set of ski goggles in my flight bag for precisely this condition. No help to me now. Between the relative wind making it hard to see and a sense that I should conserve power, I backed off to about 65 percent of full power.

Leslie sensed the change. "Are you slowing down?"

"We might have a fuel issue. Battery fuel."

"Don't you have a spare?"

"I have many spares. There are two in my flight bag in Three Lakes, and half a dozen charging in my mudroom in Essex. I also keep a supply of extra batteries at Walgreens on virtually every corner of every town in America. If you see one, let me know. We might need to make a stop."

"What happens if we run out of power."

I shrugged so that she could feel it. "We keep going on the line we are currently following. The problem is that the Earth curves, and we will eventually climb into the upper atmosphere."

"What?"

"Oh, don't worry. We'll pass out from lack of oxygen long before we get to space and freeze solid."

She said nothing for a block or two, then muttered, "You're a real buzzkill."

49

———

The power unit, despite rapidly losing charge, did not fail us. Leslie counted off the streets she knew. Central Park eased past on our left like a great raft of darkness floating on a sea of light. After calling out a small pond named Conservatory Waters and then the Central Park Boathouse, Leslie excitedly told me to, "Turn right on 75th!" More pointless pointing followed, but I got the gist of it when she said, "By that school."

Descending, we passed over canyon neighborhoods of short and tall apartment buildings. Vehicles crammed themselves bumper to bumper at both curbs of the one-way street below. I worried about wires again.

I contemplated the landing approach, and the question of confronting Macallen. I estimated that we had a fifty-fifty chance of arriving at her address ahead of her, thinking that it all depended on how seriously she took Pollum's warning. Or threat. Or if she showed up at all.

Playing out possible scenarios of ambush or intrusion while gradually descending, I spotted the red and blue twinkle of emergency lights painting the trees and building edges and reflecting in windows.

"Is that…?"

"Her block," Leslie answered. "Can we make a pass overhead?"

"Yeah."

I changed the angle of my wrist. We leveled off roughly 200 feet above the centerline of 75th street. Traveling several blocks under power, I stopped the prop when we crossed an intersection where two police SUVs angled across the pavement as a barrier. We rode momentum the length of the block looking down through tree branches at an array of emergency vehicles including an ambulance. The crew of the ambulance stood outside their unit in a cluster, killing time. Not needed.

A woman lay twisted on the pavement, surrounded by police officers in uniform and in plain clothes. One of them pointed a camera. A powerful flash added lightning to the awful scene. With each flash, the spray of blood under and around the woman's body marked her death scene in glossy fresh red. Blood painted a streak on the pavement, telling a tale of a body dragged.

"Christ, that's her," Leslie whispered. *"Take me down."*

"In a few seconds," I replied, not wanting to startle police officers below with the sound of a drone over their heads. We drifted to the end of the block.

"Whoever they are, they didn't waste any time," Leslie muttered.

Curious onlookers populated the narrow sidewalks near the scene. Many of the windows on each side of the street showed silhouettes. Lots of eyes but nearly all of them were focused on the tragedy in the middle of the block.

I used a short burst of power to stop our forward movement, then carefully lowered us between the trees on the next block. The sidewalk, windows, and porch spaces were empty. The incident happened a block away, too far to see anything meaningful through a window. A few people hurried up the sidewalk for a look. I steered toward a minivan that nudged the curb near the center of the block. Confirming no vehicle traffic, I lowered us to the pavement and shook my arm to signal Leslie to release.

Fwooomp!

An electric snap coursed the length of my arm. Leslie reappeared matching her stride to our forward movement. Without hesitation, she slipped around the front of the van and joined the sidewalk on a light jog that carried her to the corner where she paused long enough to show her badge to a patrol officer holding the perimeter of the crime scene. From there, she angled her way to the cluster around the body.

I ascended back up through the tree branches. Leveling off even with the roofline, I followed Leslie at a slow glide over the scene by pulsing the waning BLASTER power.

Leslie used her badge and elbows to pass through the cordon of police and EMTs. She moved toward the body with a purpose.

Macallen lay in the street, twisted and abused by the ton or more of motor vehicle that hunted her down. Her face pressed the unforgiving pavement. Her arms were spread as if to hug the earth. One arm turned palm up, bent at the elbow in a way that suggested a broken doll rather than a person. My stomach rolled. I looked away as I passed.

I spotted a young woman hugging her knees on the steps to a nearby apartment building. A police blanket draped her shoulders. Sobs wracked her body. She buried her face in her hands, perhaps to keep her eyes from the magnetic pull of the horror in the street. Short, dark hair draped her cheeks. A policewoman sat beside her, pen and pad in hand, asking questions. Answers came in nods and shakes of the head.

I stopped, reversed, then hovered overhead, catching a word or two, most of them coming from the interrogating officer. When the officer spoke the young woman's name, I searched for Leslie. I found her engaged in somber conversation with two plainclothes officers.

I rotated, pulsed the BLASTER, and drifted over her. I descended until I was able to tap her shoulder firmly. She turned to respond, saw no one there, then pretended to brush the fabric of her black jacket.

"Excuse me one sec," she said to the officers. She stepped away and found space on the sidewalk several long strides from the next nearest person. She pulled out her phone, waved her fingers over the screen, then pretended to engage in a call.

Forced to use minimal and nearly silent power, a minute or two passed before I maneuvered to a position directly above her.

"The girl on the steps," I said quietly. "Her name is Sissy. That's Macallen's receptionist. She took the call from Pollum. She came here with Macallen."

"Got it."

"I'm running out of battery."

"Go find a bodega," Leslie commanded. "Then meet me at the hotel bar. I'm going to talk to Sissy."

She pocketed her phone and weaved a path through the police toward the apartment building steps.

50

My landing consumed the batteries' last gasp. A few feet from the light shining through a bodega's product-crammed window, I used shadow and the edge of the building for cover. An exposed pipe provided a grip. I swung around the corner and—

Fwooomp!

—reappeared as if I'd just made the turn on the sidewalk. Pedestrian traffic had thinned but was by no means gone. No one seemed to notice or care when I passed into the shop window's light. The narrow establishment promised batteries and almost anything else a person could think of, but I had a higher priority.

I pulled out my phone.

Andy answered quickly.

"Hi lover." The cheerful note in her voice sent an electric throb down my chest. "I've got some news."

"Lemme have it."

"Uh-uh. You first. What's happening?"

I strolled along the grated glass front of the corner shop. Noting that six out of ten New Yorkers held phones to their ears or in front of their faces as they walked, I fit right in.

I paced the sidewalk and recounted the evening's events. Andy listened without comment or question. My tale ended with the apparent hit and run death of Dr. Mina Macallen and speculation that circumstances caused Leslie to join forces with the New York City Police Department, channeling our unofficial activities and everything we knew into an official investigation. Saying it aloud, I realized that despite my strong desire for a private moment with Kong, the idea of stepping away from this tangled and frustrating mess had an appeal.

Pangs of homesickness for Andy mixed with growling hunger in my gut.

Andy slipped effortlessly into detective mode.

"How sure are you that this doctor knew Caroline Gaffney?"

"I'm not sure of anything, but Pollum told her about Caroline's murder, so there's that. Her name came up when Leslie pushed the dad with questions about the daughter. If I had to guess…I'd say that the doctor was the girl's therapist or whatever and that she played a role in sending the girl away. But I could be all wrong because the dad says the girl is at college."

"Caroline never said anything about college."

"Well, her ex-husband seemed convinced. Listen, I'm tired. I'm hungry. And I miss you. Your turn. What's the news? And hold the medical jargon. Give me the high school graduate version, please."

"There is a chance—*an outside chance*—they could send me home on Saturday."

I blinked. My feet froze to the spot they occupied on the concrete. I stared at a busy New York street without seeing a thing.

"Are you kidding me? How is that possible?"

"It's healing. The doctor says the amniotic sac is healing itself with the help of the mesh. My body is literally growing over the mesh and appears to be sealing against the fragment. You should have seen the man. He was positively giddy. He's probably partying with all your scientist pals down in the parking lot."

"Dee…I…I don't know what to say."

"Don't get your hopes up. This is great news in theory—but Will—I don't know about going home. There are so many considerations."

"Such as?"

"He said he will only release me if I remain immobile."

"We can do that. We can set up the living room like we did back when I had the pelvic break."

"He wants me in an articulating hospital bed so I can lift the legs and head."

"I'll get Arun on that right away."

"He wants a full biometric connection. He wants monitors that feed real time data. And he wants that video feed—but I think that's just because he's so giddy about his new tech working."

"We have internet."

"He's not willing to let me make the trip on the ground. Too risky."

"What is he thinking?"

"Helicopter."

"That's perfect. They can land on the road right in front of the house."

"There's more. He wants someone with me 24 hours a day. He doesn't want me lifting a finger for anything. *Anything.*"

"Dee, *this is all doable*. Seriously."

"Darling, the cost of something like this is insane. And he's talking about the full term. *Fifteen weeks.*"

"Did you have other plans? Look, we can make this work. We can. If the medical issues are not a deal breaker. What about the risk of early delivery?"

"Still a factor. He said they will regularly monitor the amniotic fluid, which was not pleasant, I have to say. By the way, the test they did today was all good. No infection or contamination."

"Thank God."

"He said every day that I don't cause the sac to breach is one day closer to a normal delivery. But if something happens, if something causes early delivery, we're still looking at a high-risk premature birth."

"Are you worried about the facilities in Essex?"

"No. Not really. It's a good hospital with a good neonatal care unit. But…"

"If he says it's safe, then we can do this."

"I know…but…"

"But what?"

"Will, *the cost*. We're already underwater with whatever this is costing. Insurance isn't going to cover a private helicopter ride or 24-hour home care. And before you say a word—*don't!*"

"Don't what?"

"I know what you're thinking."

No surprise there. "The Foundation." I confirmed her mind reading.

"That money—the Foundation's money—that's not meant for us."

As much for us as anyone.

One hundred million dollars created the Christine and Paulette Paulesky Education Foundation when I put a gun to the head of diseased, amoral billionaire. The money wasn't donated in good faith or willingly or with any expectation of charitable use. The bullet in the chamber of the gun I held wasn't asking for philanthropy. Neither I nor Andy ever imagined using the funds personally, but this wasn't about taking a luxury vacation or buying a vanity automobile. Andy keenly understood the shortfalls in our finances. After my accident, the only reason we had health insurance at all was

Andy's job. I didn't need a calculator to know that the medical bills for this incident had already crushed our deductible less than a year after we paid off the last one.

"Dee, do you think Spiro Lewko or Gates or Bezos pay for health insurance? Hell, no. People at that level get sick and buy a hospital. Neither one of us ever imagined touching the Foundation money, but I'll be damned if we put you and the baby at risk for lack of funds. I will burn through every penny the Foundation has if that's what it takes. And you know that Sandy and Earl and Arun will back me on this."

I recognized the sudden silence at the other end of the call. I also recognized the black fury powering the words I spoke. *Murder* stirred deep beneath that black fury. Unbidden, the image of a finger on a trigger flashed in my mind. Someone pulled that trigger. Someone sent a bullet into Caroline Gaffney that found its way to Andy. Standing on a New York City sidewalk, I may not have been any closer to finding that someone, but no shred of doubt existed that I would, and dues would be collected.

Sudden realization blindsided me.

"Dee, what did he say about the healing? The doc."

"What do you mean?"

"Did he describe a rate? Did he measure it against expectations? What's making him giddy?"

"Um…it's just…it seems like it's going much faster than they had any reason to hope. They didn't think there would be *any* healing, let alone at the pace it's gone in 24 hours. He called me a bit of a wond—oh."

She fell silent.

I waited, knowing that Andy had collided with the same conclusion I had.

"Will. Do you think…?"

"I don't know."

How many times? How many times have I lifted her in my arms and made us vanish?

How many times? I religiously avoided making her vanish once the pregnancy was confirmed. Andy harbored fears of how *the other thing* might affect the developing fetus and I honored and respected those fears. But before that…

How many times?

How many times did I slip into hospital rooms where children fought cancer? How many times did the curative property of *the other thing* produce a miracle? Whole wards full of miracles. Not long ago, a busload of miracles.

Was *the other thing* a healing factor for Andy? Did it build up in her? Did the times I enveloped her in *the other thing* infect her with something? Like a virus? A benign or benevolent virus, a healing virus, but something alien nevertheless.

My head spun.

"*Ohmigod, Will,*" she whispered. "It's healing the amniotic sac."

"Dee. You can't know that. Everything up to this point has been normal," I spoke slowly, firmly. "Every checkup. Every scan. This could be *your* body, *your* strength. Or that mesh thingy. We don't know."

"But—"

"*And* it's *good* news, right?"

"Is it?"

51

"Where've you been?" Leslie charged past me and into my hotel room. "I've been calling you."

"Oh shit." I reflexively pulled my phone from my hip pocket. Missed call notifications littered the screen. "Sorry. I keep it muted when…you know…"

"Have you eaten anything today?" She looked around the room. She may have been looking for incriminating pizza boxes or fast-food wrappers.

"I had a slice on the walk back here. What happened? Did you talk to the receptionist?"

"I haven't eaten a thing. Let's go downstairs and see if we can get something. Or a drink. Wait. You walked back here?"

On the elevator ride to the lobby, I explained my pitstop for batteries, and my decision to walk the dozen or so blocks back to the hotel after a jarring phone call with Andy.

"She had news," I said.

"What's wrong?" Leslie read the abbreviated version on my face. "Is she okay?"

"Yeah, she's fine. A little too fine."

I explained the issue. We walked out of the elevator and into the bar. We each took a seat on a leather stool facing the glossy black bar under an oval of recessed overhead lighting.

"Interesting," Leslie said when I finished. I gaped at her.

"Interesting? What…like the Chinese proverb 'interesting'?"

"No. Well…maybe. Listen, let me ask you a question? Have you been sick since…you know?" She lifted her hands and made an absurd fluttering motion that forced an involuntary chuckle from me.

I imitated the fluttering motion.

"What's this supposed to be?"

"The thing. You. You doing *the thing*." She repeated the gesture.

"That looks like something out of a Monty Python skit mocking a Vatican ceremony." I did it again.

"Screw you. Answer my question."

"Have I been sick? Like how? You mean the flu? A cold?" I hadn't thought about it, although I did sometimes consider that my odds against contracting cancer ought to be low. "Not really. Not that I can recall. I don't usually get that stuff, but I don't think you can make a connection. The broken pelvis took its own good time to heal. And it still hurts when it rains. What about you? You've been…I mean, we've done…you know…" I wiggled my fingers in the air.

Leslie shrugged. "I had a cold a few weeks ago. And I feel like crap right now, but that's because I'm on my period." She caught the look on my face. "What?"

"Nothing," I blurted as the heat in my cheeks ignited a sudden blush.

"Spit it out, Stewart."

"I just…I didn't expect you to mention…"

"Good God."

"Hey, I don't have a prob—"

She spun on me. "Why should fifty-one percent of the population be expected to stay mute about a physiological event that happens every freaking 28 days just because you men can't handle the subject? Lord, if one of you tweaks a knee or pulls a hammy playing sports, we never hear the end of it."

"Totally fine with me. I hope it goes well…or whatever it's supposed to do." That didn't help. "Want me to…you know?"

I raised both hands and performed the fluttering motion.

She looked disgusted and waved for the bartender's attention.

"I can't believe you're still married."

52

———

Leslie ordered Pino Grigio. I asked for my usual.

"Sissy—Miss Trudy Wilkerson—was with Dr. Macallen when it happened. They were crossing the street. She said a black car or SUV—she wasn't sure—pulled out of a parking spot and drove into the doctor. Like—drove into her from a stop, you know? Wasn't moving fast—a slow-motion hit and run. That's why the victim was dragged. The vehicle didn't throw her into the air or over the hood but instead knocked her down. The driver kept going. She got pulled under and rolled up."

I raised my hand in a Stop gesture. I didn't need the graphic description.

"Doesn't sound like there's any question about it being intentional."

Leslie shook her head. "Sissy Wilkerson said the car just missed her. Lying in wait. That makes it first degree intentional homicide. Just like Caroline Gaffney."

"And Pollum knows who's behind this. He said so—kinda. You should arrest him and beat it out of him."

"Right," Leslie huffed derision. "What's my probable cause?"

"He practically warned Macallen to beat feet and get out of Dodge," I said, my voice and emphasis rising. "He said she should make the right choice or someone else would—"

Leslie looked at me pointedly.

"Oh. Right." I knew what her perturbed expression meant.

"Yeah," she said. "How is it that I heard a phone conversation between Pollum and the victim just before she was murdered?"

173

"I get it."

"I do have something else, however. Sissy opened Macallen's apartment for the NYPD guys. They let me in. I got a look around and took some pictures. Here." She drew her phone from her shoulder bag and fingered through a gallery of photos. She found what she was looking for, a photo of a framed photo. She handed me the phone. "There's a bunch of them."

I held the device and swiped.

Macallen with the mayor of New York.

Macallen in evening wear on a red carpet with a Marvel movie actor.

Macallen in different evening wear surrounded by men.

Macallen with Spiro Lewko and two other billionaires I recognized. I tossed Leslie a raised-eyebrow glance.

"Yeah. That's your pal. Keep going," she said.

Macallen with the Gaffney family.

"That's Caroline Gaffney and her husband and children in happier days, I presume."

"Actually, that's recent. See how the daughter is taller than her mother?"

She was. She had the *18 going on 30* look.

The next showed Macallen and Caroline Gaffney and her husband and—

"Holy shit, is that—whatzisname?"

"Bindle Foss. Yes."

Bindle Foss. Lately you couldn't throw a rock at a newsstand without hitting a picture of the up-and-coming master of the universe, Bindle Foss. His movie-poster face populated magazine covers from *Wired* to *Forbes.*

"Is he still nipping at Musk's heels for the title?" I asked.

"Some estimates put him ahead. He makes your pal Lewko look middle class. Bindle Foss owns a majority share of the largest investment brokerage house on Wall Street. His tech investments are being called 'second-generation Elon' because the second generation of tech either gobbles up the first or leaves it on the trash heap. People put up memes that calculate how many millennia it would take to spend all of Foss's money. Yeah. That's him."

"Wow. Macallen and the Gaffney family ran with some people in the rare air. How recent is this?"

"That was taken last June at an exclusive black-tie kickoff to the Museum Mile Festival—right before they would have shipped the girl off to camp. It's interesting that the doctor was socializing with the parents of one of her patients. And yes, I was able to get Sissy Wilkerson to confirm that Macallen was treating Baxter Gaffney for all the usual rich-teen issues. Apparently, she's been in therapy for several years."

"Who's socializing with whom here?" I asked. "Specifically, is Foss in this picture with Gaffney as a client?"

"Foss? I doubt it. Foss owns his own law firm."

"It's not…"

Leslie laughed. "Ambulance chaser from Rochester? No way. He has an army of lawyers on salary. The man's been sued over 3,400 times and counting. I don't think there's any connection other than a photo op at a charity event. Donate ten grand and get your picture taken with a guy who has more money than the national treasure of the bottom twenty percent of the world's sovereign nations combined. That kind of thing."

"Where did you get these?"

"Macallen had a zillion of these photos in her apartment. Framed all over. She liked her celebrity selfies. She's got pictures of herself with Tom Hanks and Rita Wilson, Ryan Reynolds and Blake Lively, Taylor Swift and that football guy she was dating. Lots more."

"So, what's the significance? What are the chances that hanging out with one of these people got Caroline Gaffney and Mina Macallen killed?"

I handed back the phone. Leslie closed the screen.

"Beats me. Tom Hanks doesn't seem like the murderous type." She put away her phone. "Sissy was tight-lipped about Macallen's doctor-patient relationship with the girl—patient confidentiality and all that—except she did confirm that Macallen had her enroll Gaffney's daughter in a very private, very exclusive, very hush-hush teen counseling camp for girls."

"Nothing new. That's what Caroline Gaffney told us."

"Except that Sissy's recollection was that this place didn't take anyone who wasn't born on a diamond-studded umbilical cord. She was surprised that the Gaffney girl got in."

"Any idea where?"

"How would you like to fly me to the Straits of Mackinac?"

"Mackinac Island? Really?" I studied Leslie. She had been close to Assistant Director Mitchell Lindsay. If mentioning the location of her former boss's murder brought up bad memories, Leslie hid it well.

"No. Another island."

Another island. Another day away from Andy.

I touched the ache that had been simmering in my chest and said, "If we're not any closer to finding King Kong, then I'd rather fly home to Andy. Besides, my airplane is in Rochester."

"Which is why we have two seats on the 8:15 flight out. Once we get to Rochester, you can fly home to your lovely wife. The island is practically on the way."

53

I was tired.

We ate a room service meal at the hotel bar. Except for a disappointing slice of sidewalk pizza, the food was the first of the day and the first hot meal I'd had in two. Between the cheeseburger and a cold Corona, my body threw in the towel. I sagged where I sat. Leslie picked up the tab and I excused myself from her company. Upstairs, I peeled off the same clothes I'd been wearing from Essex to Three Lakes to Rochester to New York. A hot shower took the last rebar out of my bones. I tapped out a late *I love you see you tomorrow* message to Andy, not wanting to call and potentially wake her.

A few seconds after pulling the crisp white linen over my naked shoulder and dropping my head to the pillow I was gone. That kind of exhaustion should have taken me through until the alarm, set for 5:00 a.m. on my phone, shook me awake.

It didn't.

The intruder showed up at the foot of the bed outlined by slivers of inevitable light that seeped around the edges of the curtains. Not tall or muscled like Kong. But compact and capable, like Hollis. He wore all black and made no move toward me. He had no face. I froze, barely breathing, thinking that he did not see me and would not see me if I remained rigid.

He moved to the windows and lifted the rifle to his shoulder. Sighting through a scope mounted atop the weapon, he found his target. Caroline Gaffney, standing on the other side of the Camry car door where I now found myself standing. This time I knew the shot was coming. This time I knew the shot would penetrate Caroline, the car seat, and Andy where she sat behind the wheel.

If I could shove the car door across his line of fire, it might divert the bullet. Automobile steel is not bulletproof, but it can send a round off the target line. I pushed. I leaned into it. The damned door was as rigid as the car body to which it was connected.

Standing at the hotel room window, he fired. No sound. I knew that he fired by the swing of his finger against the trigger.

I still had time. The bullet had to travel. I threw my body into the car door to stop it. I tried to scream. I tried to save Caroline Gaffney, but the door refused to move. *Snap!* She dropped in a heap.

From inside the car, Andy looked up at me with blood on her hands and I screamed.

Or tried. Nothing came from my throat.

The man at the window turned to me and shouldered his sophisticated rifle. He spoke. His voice had the quality of glass ground between stones.

"I'll run down the doctor with my car. Saves a bullet."

I fought off the sheets and leaped from the bed, forsaking flight for a fight.

No good. I stood alone in the room.

1:17 a.m.

I did not go back to sleep.

54

Friday

I refused to fly Leslie to an island in the Straits of Mackinac. When we met in the hotel lobby, I told Leslie I didn't see the point. We could expect little or no cooperation. The rich hide their imperfections and bury their embarrassments. At best, we might receive a cursory tour prompted by Leslie's FBI badge. At worst, they would refuse us at the gates, backed up by threats and lawyers. That wouldn't stop me, but I wasn't in the mood to float around among empty cabins or risk collisions in a busy dining hall.

Leslie responded to my refusal with an understanding that I did not expect. Leslie is a driven woman who will pursue her cause to its roots with argument, pleading, even bribery. I did not expect her to throw me an awkward hug and tell me to go. *Go home to your wife. With my best wishes.*

"And what are you going to do?"

"I don't know. Don't forget, I think I'm fired. I've been dodging calls from Big Rog the Furniture Sale Guy. Maybe I'll take a long drive out to Penn State to see what the Nittany Lions are up to these days. What the hell is a Nittany Lion, anyway?"

I didn't know. I was just glad she didn't insist on a pointless trip to the girl's camp. Leslie said she would hedge her bets and make a few calls to see if anyone at the camp knew anything.

The hotel room nightmare clung to me like spider webs you inadvertently collect in an old barn, but it changed nothing. If anything, my resolve tightened. I would still find the finger connected to the hand connected to the murderer who stood at my hotel window in the night, the soulless prick who nearly took everything from me without a second thought.

But I'd been away from Andy for too long. Returning to her closed a grip on me. The murder in my heart sank below the surface of whatever black bog hosts it.

AFTER A SHORT COMMERCIAL flight from LaGuardia to Rochester, I filed a flight plan and flew the Navajo back to Madison where I parked at Wisconsin Aviation and caught a cab to University Hospital. I arrived in Andy's hospital room shortly before noon. The staff insisted on maintaining the visitation protocols—I still had to wear the microwave popcorn costume, a mask and gloves—but I was allowed to approach Andy, to kiss her, to touch the soft dome where our child slept under the watchful eyes of a video stent and biometric monitors.

"You need a shower," Andy said when we broke our lip lock. "You have a hint of wet dog about you."

"I got caught in the rain. If I take a shower and throw away my clothes, can we make out?"

The gold flecks in her green eyes sparkled. Her smile stopped short of a chuckle that would have caused her to wince.

The nurses needlessly fussed over my arrival, repeating rules I already knew, feigning horror at the idea that I might crawl in bed with her, although when I offered to join Andy nude, I caught one nurse casting a speculative eye in my direction.

Andy's passions were less intimate. "Fill me in. What did you find?"

Detailing the events of the last two days took less than ten minutes. Speculating about the case occupied the next hour. Andy fell sound asleep while I droned on about connections I saw between the law firm of Humphry Patrick Alison, Gallica Protective Services, and the murder of Caroline Gaffney and her daughter's therapist. I shared a low opinion of Wayne Gaffney with my wife.

"It's always the husband," Andy said as the lids of her eyes dropped a curtain on both her attention and her consciousness. I had been warned that because she continued to endure pain and she shunned anything but Tylenol, that pain left her exhausted.

I stopped talking. Simply staring at her filled a void I'd been feeling.

Dr. Maharashtra appeared late in the afternoon to grant guarded approval for Andy to be moved, but only after we assured him of preparations on the scale of a land invasion. Armed with his approval, I began making calls.

Arun Dewar swung into action when I asked him to see if he could not only find but install a fully articulating hospital bed in my farmhouse living room. When he asked what to do with our furniture, I told him I didn't care if he tossed it on the lawn and had a bonfire. He proposed to slide our sofa against a wall and find room in the garage for the rest.

Tom Ceeves promised to have an EMT team from the Essex Fire Department on hand to transfer Andy from the air ambulance to the house, and police units ready to close the road in front of our house as a landing pad for the helicopter.

Rosemary II joined the effort with energetic promises of prepared meals. Minutes after hanging up with Rosemary II, her daughter Lane called my phone full of excitement about setting up Wi-Fi boosters all over the house and connecting a device called a Roku to our television. I said Yes to whatever tech plans she hatched; the girl knows far more than I do.

Sandy Stone, audibly weary from a long day as a kindergarten teacher, applied instant energy to the task of hiring a visiting nurse, setting up a schedule and managing the billing arrangements. She dismissed any question of payment that did not have the Foundation writing the checks, exactly as I predicted she would.

As each of these calls ended, a knot tied itself in my throat.

At the center of the storm, Andy lay against a pillow, sometimes dozing, sometimes compulsively pushing around strands of hair and apologizing because she claimed she looked frightening. I saw only a goddess, somehow glowing even when she bit down on shards of pain.

Light conversation waned in the early evening when her eyes grew heavy again. Against mild *pro forma* argument, I turned off the lights, kissed the woman I loved, and insisted she sleep. She protested, arguing that she wasn't the least bit tired.

I paused at the door to pantomime a kiss only to see that her eyelids had fallen again.

This time, it was not the knot in my throat that rose up inside. Seeing her face framed on the pillow by a cascade of hair, where her hands rested on our unborn child, knowing how close we had come, knowing that the person who did this blithely ate carryout or watched a movie or sipped a glass of cabernet...

Something black and determined rose from infinite depths.

55

Saturday

I beat the helicopter back to Essex and to the house by about twelve minutes. After half a day of waiting for several doctors to visit and assess her condition, and then enduring the slow paperwork process of discharge, half a dozen nurses, aides, and even Dr. Maharashtra joined in carefully disconnecting Andy from her leads and monitors, then supervised the air ambulance crew in transferring Andy from the hospital bed to a wheeled stretcher. They wheeled her through the halls and into an oversized elevator. The elevator took her to the top floor where they exited the hospital and rolled her onto the helipad. Under the supervision of the flight nurse, they lifted her inside a waiting helicopter. The flight nurse stabilized her and closed the doors. I stayed long enough to see the helicopter take off, then I raced to the airport, skimped on a proper preflight, hopped in the Navajo and flew at full throttle to Essex County Airport. The traffic display on my iPad showed me overtaking the slower helicopter. I passed the air ambulance with several miles and several thousand feet of separation as I began my descent. I landed and parked the airplane on the ramp in front of the Foundation hangar and jumped in my car. Arriving on the narrow east-west county road that fronts our rented farmhouse, I was astonished to see a line of parked cars extending in both directions. Anger sparked my first thoughts; clearly plans had gone awry. Thanks to the traffic jam, the helicopter crew would be forced to land in the cornfield across the road, adding to the distance and rough ground over which Andy would have to be carried. I quickly realized that Essex PD angle-parked across the road at both edges of our property, blocking off a span of smooth open pavement as a landing pad.

The fire department's boxy rescue squad unit filled our driveway. Half a dozen EMTs in blue uniforms waited beside their unit. More blue uniforms, the police, kept a small crowd clear of the path between the road and our porch entrance. Officers wearing county sheriff's brown strolled on the road outside of the helipad roadblocks, directing cars to park and arriving visitors to cross the lawn near the barn, well clear of the landing site. Two fire trucks idled on the pavement as well. Firemen sat on top of their units watching the skies. I questioned the need for fire trucks until I realized that the crews made up most of the softball team that rivaled Andy's police department team in games that took no prisoners. These men and women knew Andy as a fierce rival, and a dear colleague.

In the milling crowd I saw Tom Ceeves, Pidge, Arun, Earl and half the flight instruction and charter pilots from Essex County Air Service. Andy's church choir clustered by the porch along with the flock's pastor. I wondered if they planned to sing. Holly Bennett held baby Toby Leo in her arms while her daughter Casey shyly hid behind her mother's blue jeans and studied the only other humans her size, my nemeses Harriet and Elise. Lydia waited on the steps leading up to our porch. She energetically chatted with Sam Morrissey, my favorite ER doctor, who wore a light jacket over his scrubs. Two similarly clad nurses sat on the steps. Mae Earnhardt and the junior dispatch trainee whose name I can never remember loitered like children beside the monolith that is Chief Ceeves.

Walking into this carnival after I parked at the end of the line of guest cars, I received an earful of choice words from Pidge. She concluded with, "Real nice, Stewart. Way to leave me hanging."

I shrugged it off. "Didn't find anybody to eff up, so it would have been a wasted trip. Maybe you'll still get a chance."

She scowled at me and muttered, "Hope springs eternal."

Earl consulted an iPad that he held in the gnarled claws he passes off as hands. I wondered how the touchscreen functioned given his scars and callouses.

"Twelve minutes out," he barked at everyone around him. A few who didn't know him took surreptitious steps to gain distance from the man with the gargoyle countenance.

"This is kinda insane," I said to Pidge.

"We're just glad to have Andrea home and well." Beside Pidge, Arun gazed at the cloudless blue sky. I spotted a glitter of dampness in his eye.

The beat of rotor blades ended casual conversation and ignited urgent calls. People pointed at a spot low on the south-southwest horizon. The spec grew larger. Radio exchanges between the units on the road and the arriving helicopter carried through police unit speakers—the snap and crackle of terse professional communications. Someone reported wind direction and speed to the flight crew.

Rosemary II appeared out of nowhere. She threaded her arm inside mine, then tugged me close, patting and holding my hand. She smelled of bakery and her smile dazzled.

I've never seen an aircraft settle so gently onto the earth. It was nearly impossible to tell when the helicopter ceased downward motion. Someone had briefed the flight crew well. I reminded myself to thank them. The chance came when the blades swung to a stop and the clamshell doors at the back of the aircraft opened, prompting the entire cadre of Essex FD EMTs to form two lines under the tail boom.

Knowing enough to stay out of the way, I strolled to the front of the aircraft where the left-seat pilot popped open a vent window.

"Nice landing," I said. "Thanks."

"Are we down yet? I can't tell. You must be Stewart."

"All day."

"She's been the perfect passenger. Hope we never see her again."

"You and me both, brother."

I flashed a thumbs-up and left them to their cockpit duties. I hopped the ditch by the mailbox and found an out-of-the-way spot on the lawn.

It struck me darkly that the EMTs looked like pallbearers as the stretcher bearing Andy emerged from the back of the ship. A flight nurse hurried from the cabin and quietly issued crisp instructions. The EMTs flanked the stretcher in two lines of four. As if gliding on air, Andy was carried from the helicopter to the house, up the steps, through the porch and through the French doors into our living room. As she passed, a round of applause rose from people who called out to my wife. Covered in a blanket with only her face exposed, she could only offer a smile in return.

The ballet continued when the crew lined up her stretcher beside the hospital bed. With hands everywhere for support, she remained stationary while the stretcher dropped away and was pulled clear. Then without jarring her in the slightest, the team slid her onto the fresh sheets of the hospital bed. Still holding her, the crew waited as Dr. Morrissey adjusted the bed to receive her. She could have been a vial of nitroglycerin considering the delicate handling she received. The nurses accompanying Morrissey fussed on either side of the bed, hooking up electronic leads to monitor pads, adjusting blankets, asking if she was comfortable. One of them helped her arrange her hair.

I saw Andy wince once or twice during the transfer, but she fought to keep a smile on her face. When the nurses finished their work, I was allowed to approach.

"No gown or gloves?" I asked.

A nurse produced a bottle of hand sanitizer and squirted clear cleanser into my palm. "Keep this nearby," she said. She put the bottle on a tray table beside the bed. I noticed the furnishings that accessorized the hospital bed. A tray table, several free-standing monitors, an IV stand and an oxygen system joined our living room décor.

Dr. Morrissey gestured at the sanitizer. "Use that when you're around her or handling anything she uses or touches. Stay away if you have the slightest hint of a cold coming on. Keep the room ventilated, and…" he turned to the crowd that had formed around the perimeter of the room "…everybody OUT."

"Thank you!" Andy called out. "Thank you all so much!"

The EMTs and a few others issued well wishes and blessings and made jokes as they filed back out through the porch onto the front lawn.

I heard a rap on the window at the side of the house. A small face appeared, held high by unseen hands. Casey Bennett smiled and waved. Andy waved back, which widened the little girl's smile.

"She waved at me! Mommy!" The cute face and blonde curls sank beneath the sash.

I looked down at Andy. She looked up at me. We said the words in unison.

"Holy crap."

56

The helicopter, rescue squad, fire trucks and police vehicle departed along with nearly all the well-wishers. Rosemary II fetched a hairbrush, a small mirror, and a makeup case for Andy and told me to make myself scarce. Lane Franklin hovered in the dining room with a pair of remotes in her hands.

I congregated with Chief Ceeves, Earl, Pidge and Arun in the kitchen where a cloud of something savory filled the air. The wall clock said a cold Corona would not be judged harshly. I was about to offer a round when a tired-looking Ford sedan rolled up the driveway. Two men disembarked and walked to the front of the house where they mounted the porch steps. I paused my bartending duties and went to meet them. They peered cautiously into the living room.

"Is this the scene of the crime?" the older of the two men asked. Sporting a beer belly, a crew cut and looking like John Wayne in his final films, Deputy Chief Don Schultz of the Milwaukee Police Department grinned at me and put out his fleshy hand, which I took and shook heartily.

The man beside him—smaller, wiry, with dark features and a heavy black beard—waved.

"Oh my God!" Andy cried out happily. "Chief Schultz! Greg! You didn't have to come all the way up here.

"We brought you a six pack," Schultz lifted a cardboard carton of Spotted Cow in the air. "Or most of one."

"Please tell me you didn't let him drive, Greg," I said, taking and shaking the hand of the younger man.

"God, no. Or I wouldn't have come. How are you, Will?"

"Happy to have my girl back home."

"Is it okay to come in?" Schultz asked. "We got a stern warning from a nurse outside."

"Slather some hand sanitizer and don't get too close." I handed over the pump bottle.

Rosemary II appeared under the arch leading to the dining room, drawn by the commotion.

Andy said, "Amanda, you remember Deputy Chief Schultz and Detective Greg LeMore from the Milwaukee Po—"

She got no further. Rosemary II rushed the two men and threw her arms around them.

"Of course, I know these fine men!" She cried. "Of course!"

Lane ventured into the room.

"And look at you!" Schultz exclaimed upon spotting the girl who had once mobilized his entire department. "Holy cow!"

A blush blossomed beneath Lane's milk chocolate complexion.

"Hi, Lane!" Greg LeMore waved cheerfully. "Good to see you again."

If the memory of her abduction intruded on the moment, Lane did not show it. She smiled brightly and said to two of the MPD officers, "I remember you. I remember you both."

"Let's not get all gushy here." Schultz shifted his attention to Andy. "How's the lady of the hour?"

"Sore," Andy replied. "But I couldn't be more pleased to see you. How have you been?"

Schultz handed me the six pack after plucking one more from the carton. Three of the remaining five were empty. He grinned and pried the cap off with his bare hand. He jerked a thumb at LeMore.

"Well, for starters, you may now address his highness as 'Lieutenant LeMore.' Got a nice ring to it, wouldn't you say?"

"Congratulations!" Andy's smile certified her sentiment.

LeMore shrugged off the attention. "No big deal."

"Oh, hell yes, it is," Schultz said, "Now you can't bitch about the brass because you're one of 'em." He lifted his beer in a toast to LeMore.

"Can you stay for dinner?" Rosemary II asked.

"Please say yes," I intervened. "There's way too much food."

"Got any more beer?" Schultz asked.

We did.

57

Rosemary II served an extravagant buffet style meal. Andy's diet was supervised by the nurse who remained behind when Morrissey departed. A gentle offering of light fruits, yogurt and some juice. I said it wasn't much for a pregnant woman until Andy told me they were feeding her six times a day.

The rest of us were treated to a variety of steamed vegetables, an amazing chicken curry dish, and fresh baked rolls. And beer. Deputy Chief Schultz's habits had not changed since I'd last seen him. At least this time he didn't have the car keys. He polished off another of the Spotted Cows while I opted for a Corona with a wedge of lime. LeMore asked for and received coffee which Rosemary II brewed using our pot, our coffee, our filters, and yet managed to make it smell and taste amazing. My conviction that the woman used witchcraft strengthened.

Everyone kept their distance from Andy. Lane helped me set up a ring of dining room and folding chairs. We did our best not to make Andy laugh, although Schultz's larger than life personality prompted a few giggles and everyone seemed fueled by joy over having her alive and at home. We talked about life in general, pried a few words out of Lane about school, and studiously avoided discussion of the shooting in Three Lakes.

That worked for me.

When we finished eating (too much) Rosemary II and Lane collected plates. Andy prompted me to help, but I was instantly booted from the kitchen. Pidge and Arun called out their goodbyes from the dining room, then departed. Chief Ceeves found a chair and traded acquaintance cross-checks with Chief Schultz. Was this guy still in blue? What happened to old so-and-so? Did this or that idiot finally retire?

LeMore caught my eye and tipped his head toward the porch. We slipped out and closed the French doors behind us.

"Heard anything from Three Lakes?" he asked.

"I don't know that I will, but I've got a friend in the FBI who let me tag along on some leads."

"Do tell."

I cleared room for LeMore to take a seat in one of the wicker chairs where Andy's accumulated Madison hospital souvenirs had been dumped. There were cards. Someone sent flowers. Someone bought a stuffed bear holding tiny mylar balloons, momentarily making me feel like I should have gotten her a gift. I shifted the debris to the floor, then scooped up the magazines Lydia dropped off. When I stood, I found LeMore wide-eyed and pale.

"Jesus, Greg, you look like you've seen a ghost."

He pulled the topmost magazine out of my hand and rotated the cover for a closer look. His mouth hung slack.

"Fuck," he said softly. He stared at the celebrity image on the cover. "That's Jane Doe the Girl of the Lake."

"Who?"

He held the magazine up in front of my face. I scanned the glossy *Vogue* cover and felt a version of whatever electric jolt LeMore had just experienced.

"No, it's not," I said. "That's Baxter Gaffney."

PART III

58

"Excuse me!" Andy called out. I hopped to the French doors and split them open.

"What can I do for you, sweetheart?"

"You can stop talking about me and my case out there with Greg while his partner here tries to distract me with small talk." She cast an accusatory glance at Chief Schultz.

"Who me?" Schultz muttered. He gulped his Spotted Cow and pasted a poor facsimile of innocence on his face.

"Bring it in here," Andy ordered. "What were you saying about Baxter Gaffney?"

"Who's Baxter Gaffney?" Greg asked for the second or third time.

"Who's the Jane Doe of the whatever it was you said?" Andy asked. "I could hear you through the doors."

LeMore and I filed back into the living room-turned hospital room and stood at the foot of Andy's bed. I held up the magazine.

"Who's this?"

"That's Chaney Foss," Andy said. "Lydia gave me a pile of magazines I would never read. That's her on the cover of *Vogue*. What does she have to do with anything?"

"Whoa, back up the truck." LeMore pointed at the glossy cover. "You know this woman?"

"Of course not. Not personally," Andy said. "She's Bindle Foss's wife.

Vogue is doing a running feature on her like she's the first woman ever to have children. It was gooey." She made a face. "Okay, fine. I did read it."

"Bindle Foss…the billionaire?" Chief Schultz asked. "Stupidest name I ever heard. Lemme see that."

I handed over the magazine. He stared at the cover, then looked up at LeMore, who nodded to confirm the realization they shared.

"Sonofabitch…" Schultz said. "But…can't be…"

"Okay," Andy said sharply. "Sit. Everyone. I'll conduct the interview. Start with you, Greg. What are you talking about?"

LeMore lowered himself onto a folding chair.

"Jane Doe the Girl in the Lake. Couple-three-four years ago, we got bulletins from…what was it, Chief?"

"Sault St. Marie, I think. One of them UP places."

"About a body found in the lake," LeMore continued. "Would've been Superior where she was found, but the bulletin reached as far south as Gary and, well, really any city on the water around the central part of the Great Lakes. It was spring, and the water was super cold, so the body was well preserved. That's why they thought she might have come from just about anywhere. I think somebody contacted one of the universities to see if they could get a study on currents—maybe get a fix on where she came from. I never heard what resulted. Long story short, she was a Jane Doe with no ID, and the Sault St. Marie police took a shot at checking to see if we had any reported missing that matched. Anybody who fell offa' some yacht or other. I remember her because she had no sign of drug use, no sign of physical harm, and—"

"No, that's not what it was. She was beat up," Schultz recalled.

"Oh, yeah. Right." LeMore stroked his dense beard. "Broken bones. Like she'd been beaten or maybe took a fall, only she didn't have the kind of impact damage you see in a body hitting the sidewalk."

"And the coroner up there said she had just given birth. Like right before she died," Schultz interjected.

"Yeah. That. It prompted a search for…you know," LeMore suddenly struggled, looking at Andy.

"A child," she said. "A newborn." Her hand moved to her belly.

"Yeah. Nothing came up."

Schultz held up the magazine for everyone. "I could be wrong. It's been a few years. But sonofabitch—this woman is the spitting image of the composites we were sent of that Jane Doe. You know? They did some photo magic to show what she would have looked like alive. She would have looked like this."

"How old?" Andy asked.

"Late teens," LeMore answered.

"That woman is in her thirties," I said. "Mid-thirties."

"She's thirty-five," Andy said. "I read the article. She's thirty-five and carrying her second child. That was one of the angles on the story. Did you know that a birth after thirty-five is considered a *geriatric* birth?"

"I'll give you one guess whether it was a man or woman came up with that term," Rosemary II chimed in with no effort to hide her disgust.

"Coincidence," I said despite Andy's feelings about coincidence in law enforcement. "Not the geriatric thing. I mean, the photo. That lady on the cover is married to Bindle Foss. If she wasn't she wouldn't be on the cover of *Vogue* showing off—what is that?—about four months? Five?"

"Four," Andy said. "She's barely showing, but that was the fashion angle to the article. *Vogue* is covering how her body changes prompt new looks as she goes through the pregnancy. A whole new wardrobe every few weeks. Apparently Chaney Foss has granted exclusive access to *Vogue* and they'll be covering her fashion decisions right up to the birthing suite. The editors say they want to celebrate the female form as it is 'sculpted by pregnancy.'"

"Yikes." I fake-smiled at Andy. "Do you feel sculpted, dear?"

"With a garden trowel, love." Andy fake-smiled back.

"When did that come out?" LeMore asked.

Schultz examined the cover. "Huh. Last week."

"My turn," LeMore said. "Who's Baxter Gaffney?"

Andy looked at me, but I waved her off. "Go ahead. You tell it."

"She's the reason I'm in this bed for the next fifteen weeks."

59

"Hold on," Schultz held up a commanding hand. "Hold the goddamned horses a minute. You got a missing girl who looks like a found dead girl who was dragged out of Lake Superior—what?—four years ago who looks like a billionaire's wife who's pregnant the same as the found girl was and—are you kidding me?—you got the FBI involved in this?"

"Yes and no," I said. "Leslie might be fired at this point."

"The Bureau is a dumpster fire for sure. Did you see who they just named Acting Director? Motherf—" Schultz bit his tongue but shook his head.

LeMore held up a hand. "Will, you said the guy in Rochester took a picture of her ID—"

"Cool as a cucumber," I interjected.

"—and then made a call, and a few minutes later she gets reamed out by that asshat from the furniture business?"

"Yup."

Schultz glanced at LeMore, then pointed at me with his beer bottle. "Connect the dots."

"I don't get it."

"I do," Andy said. She got an admiring nod from Schultz. "It would take some serious juice for a private party to reach into the Bureau and get a senior Assistant Director to turn on a dime like that. Who has that kind of power?"

"You said the FBI saw photos of this girl's family with whatshisname, right?" LeMore held up the magazine. "Foss?"

"Yeah," I replied, "but they were just red carpet photos, and the focal point was the therapist. And she was also in photos with Tom Hanks and a dozen other celebrities."

"I never trusted that Hanks," Schultz muttered.

"Six degrees of separation," Chief Ceeves muttered. "And none of it explains an intentional homicide up in Three Lakes."

Nobody answered.

Andy pushed herself up on her pillow, a move that made her wince, but she covered it with an energized look on her face. "We need to connect the dots, Chief, but from the other direction. I went into this hoping to help a mother out with her missing daughter and the thread now goes through the intentional homicide in Three Lakes and in New York. The line starts at the other end. Not with the daughter. We should—"

"We should all give Andrea the rest she needs," Rosemary II interrupted.

Morrissey's nurse, who had been in the kitchen, appeared on cue.

"I second that. Gentlemen, it's time to stop playing Masterpiece Mystery and let Ms. Stewart settle in." The nurse looked at Andy's monitors. "You've got her pulse and blood pressure up. Enough is enough."

Everyone stood. The cops in the room looked a little sheepish. LeMore laid the copy of *Vogue* on his chair.

"Take that with you," Andy pleaded.

"I can pick up a copy. Don't worry. I will."

Andy looked up at her guests. "I could kiss you both for coming."

"I'll take a rain check on that," Schultz said.

"No, you won't," I said. "Everybody out."

60

I knew better than to move the investigation to the front lawn. It only would have agitated Andy to know the discussion continued without her. LeMore mouthed *I'll look into this* on his way out. Goodbyes were said. Car doors thumped in the early darkness. Headlights swept past the porch windows as cars backed onto the road. I waved to everyone from the porch steps, then returned to find the nurse waiting beside Andy.

"We have business to conduct," Andy told me. "Make yourself scarce."

"I'll get some pillows and blankets and set up on the couch."

"No, you won't," Andy said.

"I'm here all night," the nurse informed me. "I work third shift. I've got knitting and she will need attention during the night."

"Can I get you anything?" I asked the nurse.

"I'm fine. Now do as your wife tells you. Scoot."

This wasn't how I wanted the day to end. I had hoped to dim the lights and stay with Andy until she slept. I hadn't considered other needs imposed by Andy's forced immobility.

"C'mere, you." Andy beckoned with her hands. The nurse, sensing the coming moment, went to look for something in the kitchen.

I leaned close, drew in her scent, and dove into the green and gold pools of her eyes. The knot snuck up on my throat, screwing up the nice little speech I was about to give.

"I know," she said. Always a step ahead of me.

We kissed goodnight.

61

Sunday

The night should have invited my black-clad faceless assassin into my dreams, but a quick shower and most of a sleepless week conspired with the comfort of my own bed to knock the stuffing out of me for almost nine uninterrupted hours. Sunlight pried my eyes open.

That and an incredible scent rising in the house.

"What's going on?" I asked Andy after pulling on pants and a shirt and hurrying downstairs.

We traded a good-morning kiss.

"Amanda's in the kitchen." Andy drew in a savory sniff. "God, that smells good."

"I know. What is that? Bacon? Cinnamon? Coffee?"

"They said I could have solid food today. I'm starving."

"Lemme go see," I gave Andy another kiss, then added one on her belly for Little Ethel.

The nurse who had stayed the night sat at our kitchen table cradling a cup of coffee.

"Good morning," I greeted her and pointed at the cup and then at Rosemary II. "Did she make that?"

"It's sooooo good. I normally don't drink coffee at the end of a shift. You know, to try and sleep during the day is hard enough. But Oh My God."

"Good morning, Will. Did you sleep well?" Rosemary II hovered over the stovetop, busy with cooking.

"Like Andrew Jackson." She looked at me funny. "He's dead. What's all this? When did you get here…three a.m.?"

"Nonsense. Just a few things. Andrea needs some real food." Rosemary II glanced at the nurse who began gathering her travel bag and coat. "Are you sure you can't stay?"

"I would love to, but that's my ride." She pointed at a car pulling into the driveway. "I'm tag-teaming with Cynthia. We're roommates so it works out nicely. She'll take the next shift and I'll be back this evening. Bye!" She hurried out the door.

"I'm glad she's being looked after," I said. "I'll be here all day, too."

"No, you won't!" Andy called from the living room.

I mouthed to Rosemary II, *Does she have bat ears?*

"Tell him, Amanda, please," Andy said.

"Go," Rosemary II ordered. "Sit down. I'll bring your breakfast in."

"WHAT DO YOU MEAN, I can't stay?" I asked after seating myself at one of the two place settings at the dining room table. I was glad to see that Rosemary II planned to join in the lavish breakfast she had prepared. Eating at the table alone would have been uncomfortable. After loading a plate for Andy, Rosemary II sat down beside me.

"You'll drive me batty," Andy said between mouthfuls of the first real food she'd eaten in days.

"What are you talking about? There's nothing on the books for the Foundation. I can help."

This brought a laugh from both women, and a subsequent grimace for the pain from Andy.

"I have you booked out on a parts run," Rosemary II informed me.

Parts runs were the simplest, easiest air charter operations on Earl Jackson's schedule, usually flown VFR by junior pilots in the single-engine Piper Arrow or Earl's Cessna 182 workhorse. That said, I always enjoyed the trips because it involved picking up mining equipment parts in Milwaukee or Rockford and rushing them to Upper Michigan where some broken small gear or motor or electronic control prevented giant mining machinery from running. Hauling parts and pieces had the advantage of not carrying human cargo that needed attention and tended to mess up schedules.

Still, I wanted to protest. My plan for the day had been to stay with Andy and meet her every need.

Cynthia, the day nurse, chimed in. "I was told to have you ready for a video conference with Dr. Maharashtra and his team at ten a.m."

"See? I've got a busy schedule," Andy said. "Video conference. Sponge bath. Magazine reading. The day is jammed, Will. Not to mention certain activities for which you absolutely positively may not be present."

"The pickup is in Rockford. Dropoff in Ironwood. They said the load would be ready at 11." Rosemary II put the issue to rest.

The plan wasn't terrible. I figured I would easily make it home for dinner with Andy and whoever else happened to be on hand. The prospect of Rosemary II's cooking had an appeal of its own.

"Fine. But I'm taking the Navajo. The Foundation can underwrite the difference for billing."

FORTY MINUTES later I sat down at the old desk in the hangar. I pulled out my iPad and began flight planning for the parts run. Clear weather blessed the operation with a comfortable simplicity. All I really needed to do was figure out the timing for a run down to Rockford to ensure arrival by 11 a.m.

My mind wandered to the exchange with Schultz and LeMore. To the pieces floating at random in Three Lakes, Rochester, and New York. A mix of photographs and a mystery of three young women who looked almost identical. I once met a man on a charter flight who would not stop talking about how he lived in Jonesboro, Arkansas next door to a man who he thought was me. Or my twin brother. He swore we were identical. Clones, perhaps. He could not get over it. I finally told him it probably wasn't the marvel he thought it was, given that there are billions of humans on the planet and only one basic design. He said it was funny that I was not speaking with a southern accent.

The memory of it made me wonder if similarities between Baxter Gaffney and a dead girl and a *Vogue* celebrity were a distraction.

In the middle of that thought, my phone rang.

"Where are you?" Leslie sounded winded.

"Essex. Where are you?"

"Coming to you. I'll be there in…dammit." She went silent for a full thirty seconds. I heard a loud car horn go by with a strong Doppler shift. "Yeah…I shouldn't do this while I'm driving. I'll be there in about six hours."

"I'll be gone. I've got a flight." I explained the run.

"Rockford? Really? How hard would it be for you to meet me in Chicago?"

"Hard."

"Yeah, okay. I get it. O'Hare. All that. What about South Bend?"

"Hang on." I tapped the map screen and laid down a pair of course lines, then checked the flight time for each. "How about Elkhart, Indiana? Can you be there in an hour and fifteen minutes?"

"Sure."

"Don't screw with me on the timing. I need to be in Rockford at precisely 11 a.m. to pick up a whatchamacallit and then fly it to Ironwood as fast as possible. What about your car?"

"It's an FBI rental. Fuck 'em. I can be there in an hour and fifteen minutes and Ironwood, that's way up north, right?"

"Uh-huh."

"Well, that's perfect."

"Why?"

"Because Baxter Gaffney isn't at Penn State. So, after you dump your cargo in Ironwood, you and I are going to hop over to an island in the Straits of Mackinac."

62

———————

Leslie took the copilot's seat and donned the headset that hung from a hook on the cabin partition. I asked her to wait until I had switched over to Chicago Center who, exactly as I expected, directed us to an intersection southwest of the Class B airspace around O'Hare. Well southwest.

"How about if we cancel IFR and go over the top at 12-5?" I asked the controller. "Can I get flight following?"

I knew the answer and gave the young woman at the other end of the radio connection time to reach the same conclusion.

"I think we can take you through on a more direct route. Stand by."

I grinned at Leslie, who had no idea why.

A few minutes later we were cleared through the busy airspace, although they requested that I climb to 12,000.

Lake Michigan sparkled in the mid-morning sun to our right. Level at 12,000 feet, I set up the power and mixture for cruise, then spoke to Leslie through the intercom.

"Okay. Tell me. But if you hear voices on the line, hold up."

"Right. I went to Penn State and waved my badge around. Yes, they said. Of course she's enrolled. Of course, she's here. Attending classes. They got an administrator to look at their system and he said she's posting grades. You should have seen the look on his face."

"What?"

"Her grades. They suck."

"Fits everything I've heard so far about this girl. She's got issues."

"Not the way you think. Finding her on campus was next to impossible. The university had her listed in a dorm, standard for incoming freshmen, but she wasn't where she was supposed to be. I found an RA who recognized the name but couldn't recall ever meeting her. I found some girls who thought she was supposed to be on their floor, only they never saw her, but then—"

I threw up my hand to cut her off. A transmission from Center went out to another aircraft.

"Go on but cut to the chase."

"Four stops later I came to a room she was assigned to but the roomie there said she moved off campus a week into the semester. But that's not the weird part."

"Yeah?"

Leslie held up her phone with one of the photos she'd taken in Dr. Macallen's apartment. She pinch-zoomed in on the girl.

"That's Baxter Gaffney."

"Okay." This was nothing new. Leslie swiped the photo away and held up a new photo. This showed a picture of a picture on another phone. She pinch-zoomed in on the blonde girl in the image.

"That's the Baxter Gaffney who's enrolled at Penn State," she said.

The autopilot had command of the Navajo, so I lifted Leslie's phone from her fingers and did my own zoom in on the pretty blonde in the picture, caught in a moment with her new roomie at college.

I studied the image for a moment, then handed back the phone.

"That's not the same girl. Who is it?"

Leslie put away her phone.

"No idea. I went back to Admin and had them look up her student ID." She swiped her phone again, this time producing a photo of a Penn State Student ID. "That's the girl that's on the Baxter Gaffney student ID. That's the girl that has been attending classes...rather poorly. That's the girl who checked into the dorm for about a week, then ditched her roommate."

"Is she the one who's been texting with Wayne Gaffney? I'm at school, daddy. Having a ball. Hate the food."

Leslie shrugged. "Maybe. Weird, right?"

"Oh," I said, "I don't know. You want to hear weird?"

I told her about the magazine cover.

63

I worried about Andy and called her while we waited in Rockford for the van to arrive with the vital geegaw that would save the mining industry in Upper Michigan. They were late, as was often the case.

"I'm fine," Andy assured me when I called from the ramp.

"How did your video conference go?"

"Crazy. There were like nine people on the call, and they watched video from that stent. Will, it's just amazing to be able to see in there."

"Isn't it all, like gunky? The lens?"

"It's not optical. It's…I don't know…infrared? Radar? Whatever they're doing, they can see the mesh and the fragment and the way the amniotic sac has healed over the mesh. It's getting stronger."

"I bet the science geeks love that."

"Over the moon. I feel a little bad."

"Why?"

She lowered her voice. I wondered if the nurse hovered nearby. "These results might be misleading. If you know what I mean."

"Of course, I know what you mean. I have an idea. Let's not debate this right now, okay? This might be a conversation best had with Stephenson. I have news. I picked up Leslie."

"How?"

"She was just out there by the airway hitchhiking." I told her what Leslie found at Penn State. "We're going to hop over to the mystery camp after we make the drop in Ironwood."

"That sounds like an episode of Scooby Doo. You and Leslie, sneaking around the mysterious camp on the mysterious island. Don't expect a haunted house. I looked up the place. It's nothing like that, although the online presence is a little vague."

"What is it like?"

"Exactly what you'd expect from mega-money. Modern. Super-well equipped. Like some kind of west coast spa or a cult retreat put up by some mega-church, if you ask me. Somebody threw a ton of money into the place, which means it probably costs a ton of money to send your kid there."

"Leave it to the rich to figure out how to make money off mental issues. Um…this might mean I'll be late getting home. I hate not being there for you. I mean, I know the nurse is there, but there's a lot more to do around the place."

She laughed—as if I had a clue.

"Funny you should mention that. Hang on. I'm putting you on speaker." I waited for something to go wrong and the connection to break, but a moment later Andy's voice gained the room's ambiance. "Say Hi to Holly, Will."

"Hi, Mr. Stewart!" a cheerful voice chimed in.

"Hey, Holly. What's up?"

Andy said, "This was Sandy's idea. She thought Holly might make a good daytime companion for the next fifteen weeks."

"I quit my job at the Pig," Holly said. "I told them what was going on and they said they would take me back after the baby comes."

"Uh…that sounds great." I wasn't sure, one way or the other.

"Holly's taking over the laundry, the household chores, she's amazing," Andy said. I tried to gauge whether she truly meant it or not. "Oh, and she's going to finish painting that last wall in the nursery."

"I love that idea," I said. I'd nearly run out of excuses for not finishing the project. I pictured myself coming home after Andy's labor and the birth of our child and then staying up all night to finish painting the room the child would occupy.

"Cool!" Holly chirped.

"Lydia has offered to help with childcare now that Holly's daughter has met the royal princesses, and they have become buds. Grace is almost out of diapers anyway, and my sister has a thing for babies so she's already in love with Toby Leo. That way Holly can stay late on nights when you're not here."

I had to admit, I felt a touch of relief. However noble I planned to be about staying by Andy's side, in less than 24 hours I began to see flaws in that plan.

"I'll still be around," I said. "Arun said he would modify the flight schedule for the rest of the term."

"I don't think that's going to be a problem."

"Listen," I said, "I gotta go. The van is here. I'll call you—uh—when I call you. Love you!"

"Bye, Mr. Stewart!"

"Love you, too," Andy added.

64

———————

"Any idea where we can hire a boat?" Leslie asked the ramp rat at St. Ignace airport as he pulled a long length of fuel hose from the reel on his truck. The flight from Ironwood to Mackinac County Airport in St. Ignace on the north end of the Mackinac Bridge took under an hour.

"Kinda boat?"

"One that floats," Leslie said. "We're not here for fishing. We just want to take a ride over to one of the islands."

"There's ferries still running. They run 'til the ice comes."

"No, not to Mackinac Island. A different island."

He tugged the hose to the wing and removed the cap for the inboard fuel tank. Careful to align the heavy metal nozzle to avoid splash back, he squeezed the trigger and began sending aviation fuel into the tank.

"Maybe a fishing charter but not for fishing? Something like that? Somebody who wants to make a few bucks?" I offered.

To his credit, the kid concentrated on his fueling duties. As the tank neared full, he backed off the flow, gently topping the tank before pulling back the nozzle and capping the tank.

"I guess there might be somebody at the marina, 'cept those are mostly private-owned boats. There's a few fishing charters run outta the docks between Shepler's and Star Line—er—Mackinac Island Ferry Company. Usta be Star Line. You could try there."

I pulled a ten dollar bill from my wallet, folded it and handed it to the kid who blinked at it and gained fresh enthusiasm for helping. "You know, come to think of it, there's Walter. He's got a boat there by the ferry lines."

"Give me Walter's info, please." Leslie pulled a pen and notebook from her shoulder bag.

65

We strolled the length of the wooden dock. Our heels sounded loud against the deep quiet of the small bay. Except for seagull cries and the whisper of water lapping against stone, almost no sound rose into the afternoon air. I considered the number of hours of daylight remaining and estimated the distance across the Strait to the small island Leslie had shown me on Google Maps during a cab ride from the airport to the dock.

"That's Big Saint Martin Island. This is Saint Martin Island." She pointed at two green blobs against blue on my iPad map screen. "And this is Little Saint Martin Island. That's where Saint Martin Academy for Excellence was built. The website says it was a camping destination back in the day. Mackinac took away some of the appeal, what with an actual town and ferry service and that cool fort. Things dried up for camping in the twenties, died completely during The Depression, and was largely ignored until the sixties. A bunch of hippies tried to make it into a little piece of heaven but didn't account for the absolute bitch of a winter they have up here. I guess the Coast Guard had to come in and rescue them before they started eating each other."

"Why is there anything there now?"

"Somebody threw a bunch of money into it. Look at these photos." She held up her phone and scrolled through a handful of screen captures.

Newly constructed buildings full of warmly lit windows, wooden decks, peaked roofs and stone fireplaces constituted the Academy structures. Shots of chlorine green pools and smooth tennis courts and stone campfire rings suggested a level of camping on par with a fine hotel. Not shown, however, were people.

"No glamour shots of the happy residents."

"Privacy. This place is all about privacy. From what I've been able to find, they'll run your tab at around ten thousand dollars a day."

"*A day?* Christ, I'm in the wrong business."

One of the photos showed a small fleet of sailboats docked against a thirty- or forty-foot cabin cruiser—the reason the island didn't need ferry service.

"I assume they close for the winter season," I said. "I mean, these waters often freeze solid."

Leslie shrugged. "No idea."

WALTER SMITH INTRODUCED himself on the dock beside a trim and tidy fishing charter boat. Hardware for the fishing equipment gave away the boat's purpose, but no rods or reels currently took up space.

The captain of this vessel was a solid looking man in his upper sixties or early seventies. He looked strong and moved confidently on his deck and on the dock. He had a round face, wiry eyebrows and a matching white moustache beneath a receding line of short white hair. He wore wire rimmed aviator sunglasses with a medium yellow tint that gave away friendly eyes. Flannel over jeans with thick black suspenders finished off the fisherman look that could have also passed as a logger or a truck driver. He instantly struck me as a man comfortable in whatever elements he found himself.

"Chuck called me from the airport to say you were coming," he said, extending a hand. "Said you want to go to Little Saint Martin."

"You know the place?"

"Never been there, but yeah, everybody around here knows the place. They spent a ton of money building some kinda academy, I guess, something like five years ago. Operated it as a camp or academy for a year or two. Then shut it down. Then they opened it up again last spring. And now they shut it down again. How do you run a business like that?"

"It's closed?" I asked.

He studied his boots for a moment and nodded. "Yup. Could'a saved you a trip over here if they'd'a called sooner. Closed except for a few guys they hired to keep an eye on the place. Keep squatters out. You know. Caretakers, they tell me."

I glanced at Leslie. It seemed like there was little point in making the trip.

"Can you get us there?" she asked.

He leveled a shrewd look at her. "Sounds to me like they don't want visitors."

She reached inside her shoulder bag and pulled out her FBI wallet. "We're not visitors."

He studied the ID and shrugged. We took that as a yes.

66

"I don't like boats," I said to Leslie. We sat in a pair of chairs meant for people who purchased an expensive fishing experience. "I get seasick."

"Cut it out."

"Seriously. I do. I used to get carsick when I was a little kid. I can't go on any of those rides at Six Flags or Universal. I puke my guts out."

"You're a pilot, for God's sake!"

"I know. It scares the hell out of the passengers when I start puking out the side window and then I gotta go lay down in the back."

Leslie gawked at me while the wind generated by the boat's forward speed ruffled her short black hair. I grinned back at her.

The ride to Little Saint Martin skimmed a glass surface. Walter's boat had substantial power beneath the deck, if the sound of the engines gave any indication. He did not spare the horses. We cut a distinctive wake in the Straits of Mackinac. St. Ignace shrank to a dark line on the glossy surface as the sun backlit the Michigan coast. South of the town, the towers of the magnificent Mackinac Bridge rose five hundred feet above the water, dominating the horizon. Even from miles away, its giant sweeping cable lines challenged the idea that such a thing had been crafted by human hands.

Walter estimated the distance to Little Saint Martin at 6.7 nautical miles, a guess that seemed strikingly precise, which told me he didn't join the enterprise casually. At close to thirty knots, he predicted the crossing to take less than fifteen minutes.

I climbed out of the fisherman's chair when I heard the engine sound change. Joining Walter on the boat's simple bridge, I looked ahead at three unassuming islands. On each, green pines and a sprinkle of deciduous trees marched all the way to the waterline. The smallest of the three had a substantial dock; no other sign of civilization could be seen from the water. I found that unusual. A view of the water in any resort sells reservations.

"Those caretakers you mentioned," I said. "Are they out here now?"

"Don't know."

"You live here all your life?"

"Oh, no. Just a couple years."

"Running fishing charters somewhere else before?"

"Nope. Trucking. Before that, mining in South America."

I glanced at him. "Seriously? Then why fishing?"

"Seemed like it might be fun. It was here or Washington. Mollie—that's my wife—she let me flip a coin. Here we are. Although I think one more winter will do it. She's got her eye on the Oregon coast."

"What do you know about this place?"

"I heard a few stories."

"Like?"

Walter glanced back at Leslie. "She really FBI?"

"Down to the Glock in her bag."

"And you?"

I shook my head. "I'm just the pilot."

He studied me like he wasn't buying it. "I don't want to talk outta school if things are going to get official."

"I wouldn't worry about that."

"Okay." He adjusted the power for our approach. "Like I told you, the town thought this was gonna be a resort. A spinoff from the main island, you know? Touristy. When I tell you they spent a lot of money, I'm talking boat-loads. Buying the island. Building. Construction. The building materials had to be brought in by ship. And it went up in a hurry. Months, not years. Takes money to grease that track, lemme tell you."

"Who's the builder? The owner?"

He shrugged. "A fella on the town council said all they ever dealt with was lawyers and project supervisors. Said the owners were listed as some offshore company owned by a company owned by a company owned by a shell company. Etcetera. Said the excuse for all the privacy was to keep competitors from tipping to what they had planned. A lot of baloney. Because in the end, they all went away and then all we heard was that it was turned into this Academy."

"That's what we heard."

"Thing is…" He gazed over the bow, but not at the dock or the island. "Thing is, they had to hire staff. You know. Cooks and such. Janitors. This is where the stories and rumors spread. They hired from town. Young men. Early twenties. Late teens. Strong backs and weak minds."

"What's wrong with that?"

I got a dose of side eye. "Did I mention it was an all-girls academy? Teenaged girls? Word was, this had been made into some kind of treatment camp for troubled girls. Now, what sense does it make to hire a bunch of hormone volcanoes to work at an all-girl camp?"

"Doesn't sound like the best judgment, I guess."

He chuckled. "Gasoline on hot embers, is what. The kids they hired were sworn to secrecy, but rumors got out about parties. Right there under the noses of whoever was running the place. And you can guess what that meant. Mostly, the local hires kept their mouths shut because they didn't want to put a good thing like that in Dutch. A couple stories leaked because some of the local girlfriends got wind. But can you imagine? And it wasn't just them. There were visitors to the island. Coming and going."

"You think they were running some kind of brothel? Trafficking?"

He shook his head. "No. Nothing like that. Just…I guess after a hard week of intensive study or therapy or whatever they had those girls up there for, they decided to feed them some meat on Friday nights, if you get my drift. Not like any therapy I ever heard of."

He powered down the boat and cranked the wheel as we approached the dock. With a deft hand and calibrated eye, he eased the vessel against the dock, kissing the rubber bumpers so lightly I didn't feel the boat stop.

"I can't guarantee you won't get a negative reception," Walter said, killing the engine. He directed me to hop onto the dock, then tossed me a line which he then followed and tied to a cleat. Moving like a man thirty years younger, he fetched another line at the back of the boat and repeated the process. "I should have asked. You want me to wait for you, doncha?"

"Affirmative."

Leslie joined me on the crisp, white dock. We contemplated a cobblestone path that rose from the dock and entered the woods.

"Hold up, there," Walter said, closing a grip on my arm. He pointed. "Didn't notice that before. Somebody's here ahead of you."

I followed the line begun by Walter's extended arm and pointed finger. Far down the shoreline where it began to curve out of sight, a familiar shape hung over the water. The tail of an aircraft, a seaplane.

"Well, well," Leslie said.

"After you, Scooby," I said.

67

———————

The dock was just that. A dock. There was no beach. No beach house. Tidy white planks gave way to poured concrete. Tire marks on a concrete pad betrayed the presence of vehicles. The setup would have allowed vessels larger than Walter's to tie up, perhaps to unload supplies. The tire marks might have belonged to forklifts or other heavy loaders.

Joining the concrete, a beautifully laid cobblestone road rose into the woods, looking quaint and welcoming. Utterly impractical, it spoke to appearances rather than purpose.

We followed the cobblestones. Late afternoon sunlight angled down through the trees. Above average temperatures caused by the abundant sunlight dropped noticeably in the shadows cast by trees. The woods reminded me of something similar I'd seen on Mackinac Island one night while a fire raged. This time the shadows didn't wiggle and dance at the whim of flames consuming a big old house.

We didn't have far to go before we saw structures. I expected cabins, possibly made of log construction, or faux log. The structures that emerged from among the trees were made of wood and meant to feel rustic, but at the same time were modern, loaded with glass and comfy decks, and skirted by meticulously trimmed gardens. I stopped counting at eight. They spread out in a rough circle around a central building that looked more like a corporate meeting center, the kind used for what executives like to call a 'retreat.' A spiderweb of sidewalks made of decorative slate joined the surrounding buildings to the central hub.

"He wasn't kidding," Leslie muttered.

"What?"

"I overheard your conversation with the captain. He wasn't kidding about the money. Jesus, do you know what it takes to build something like this in a place like this? No roads. Everything shipped in by boat. Must've been a fortune."

"And they did it in a hurry. That costs money."

Leslie stopped before we reached the edge of the tree line. "Wanna know something funny? I looked at this island on Google Maps. This place isn't there."

"Seriously?"

She reached in her shoulder bag and pulled out a compact set of high-quality binoculars. Lifting them to her eyes, she scanned each of the structures.

"Seriously. If you look at Google images, there's nothing on this island. The other two islands are restricted for conservation and the same. This is the only one that's privately held. What do you suppose it takes to get Google to fudge the photos from space?"

"A shit ton of money or else the government."

"It's not government. And here's another funny: Take a look." She handed me the binoculars. "This place is empty. Stone cold empty. No campers. No counselors. Nobody."

I didn't see signs of life either. "Maybe they're out hiking."

"Doubt it. Look at the back buildings."

"I see. Plywood on the windows."

"There's a stack of plywood sheets by that utility shed on the far side of the property. They're sealing up the buildings for winter." I handed her the binoculars. She returned them to her bag. "Did you bring your toys with you?"

"Don't leave home without 'em." I patted the pair of power units in my thigh pocket.

"It looks empty, but I have a feeling somebody is waiting for us. Let's do this like the lawyer's office. I want you to turn around and head back toward the dock. When you get to where you think you can do it without being seen…"

I lifted my hands and made the silly fluttering motion. She frowned at me.

"Whatever," she said sourly.

"See you."

I turned and started back into the woods at a brisk pace. After covering twenty or thirty yards I angled to the edge of the cobblestone track to where a tall, thick tree trunk rooted itself close to the road. I trotted off the pavement, took a few steps to the tree and swung behind it in case someone watched from a distance. Passing close behind the tree trunk—

Fwooomp!

—I vanished.

68

Leslie isn't as small as Pidge, but she also isn't a tall woman. From two hundred feet up she was a diminutive figure. She approached the central hub at a steady, purposeful pace.

I used light BLASTER power to pace myself above her and to match her track against a gentle westerly crosswind. I could barely hear the whine of the electric motor or whisper of the prop pulling air through its blades, making the sound impossible to hear from the ground.

As Leslie approached the central building, I reduced my altitude, anticipating that she would enter the building, and I might need to drop down and join her.

Less than thirty feet from a set of stone steps that rose to a wide porch, everything changed with a jolt. A shot cracked the silence. Leslie froze and for an instant I thought I would see her topple. She thought the same. Her hands automatically slapped her chest, her torso, feeling for the bullet strike.

"Stand still, Agent Pelham," a voice shouted.

Sonofabitch. I knew that voice.

Hollis, the unassumingly dangerous Gallica man from the Rochester clinic, stepped into the light from the shadow cast by the porch overhang. He held a pistol high and with his eye carefully aligned to the sight. This was not some casual gunplay. His finger rested on the trigger and his aiming stance suggested that the next shot would not miss, even at a distance.

Without taking the line of fire that connected to Leslie's center mass, he carefully descended the steps, closing the distance, increasing the accuracy of the semiautomatic pistol in his hands.

Leslie eased her hands away from her body and spread her fingers.

I twisted my wrist so that the steady pull of the BLASTER put me on an elevator descent line directly toward Hollis.

"Agent Pelham, I'm going to give you one chance to live. Tell me precisely why you're here and what you're looking for and who knows of your mission and then I will let you live. Choose silence or to bullshit me, and I will end your life where you stand. Go."

"That's a sweet offer, but you're going to kill me anyway."

"True." Hollis nodded his head just enough to keep his aim.

Ten feet above him—

Fwooomp!

—I reappeared. Gravity clawed me downward. I had time to line up one foot with his outstretched arm. The rest came to chance.

I hit him with all 185 pounds I brought to the party. My right foot caught his forearm. The back of my left thigh hit the top of his head. His forearm dropped and the pistol fired. Something sparked on the pavement less than five feet away. His head took a jolt that I thought might snap his neck. The rest became a tangle of bulk and body that ended with a hard jolt on the pavement. He broke my fall, but not by much. I hit hard on top of him. My left wrist took an electric jolt. My right knee tried to take a bite out of the pavement. The shoulder Hollis had stung in Rochester let me know it remained sore. Hollis slammed into my guts and blew the air out of my lungs for the second time since I met this prick.

I rolled onto the arm that had held the gun and felt him try to jerk free. The weapon was somewhere behind my right elbow. I tossed aside the blaster thinking I might be able to get a grip on his weapon before he could bring it free. But he was fast and a blow to my left side stunned me. He began to pull his arm out from under my body. I knew he would fire the weapon in the process, directly into my torso, when—

"Don't—fucking—move."

Leslie towered over both of us, her weapon drawn and held in a professional two-handed grip, the black hole of the barrel hovering over Hollis's right eye.

All motion beneath me stopped.

69

———————

"This place is empty. Cleaned out," Leslie reported.

We stood in the beautifully rustic lobby of the central building. A two-story fieldstone fireplace towered behind us. Comfortable padded chairs and sofas trimmed with varnished wood spread around us. On one side, the lobby opened on a broad dining hall, not with cafeteria tables, but with individual round tables attended by nice chairs. Tall windows let the last rays of evening sun paint the wood in the room a warm gold color.

Opposite the dining hall, a reception desk faced the lobby. Behind that, Leslie found offices. Empty offices. Empty desks. Empty filing cabinets.

"They knew what they were doing," she added. "It's not like it was abandoned. It's spotlessly clean. Tidy. Even the wastebaskets are empty."

"Any computers?"

She shook her head. "A few docking stations, but no CPUs or external drives. That, however—" she pointed at the camera bulbs mounted in the ceiling "—is very much present and alive and working. I'm certain we were being watched from somewhere."

"Were?"

"I found the security office. The system is up and running and recording, but there are no archive recordings. There might be a central hard drive, but I doubt it's local. There's a satellite link setup, so I think it's feeding the cloud. Or was. I might have accidentally cut the line to the satellite modem." A devious grin suggested it was anything but accidental.

Her sabotage came too late. Her image and mine were already on someone's screen somewhere.

"Did he say anything?" She pointed at Hollis who sat in a chair with his hands bound by the zip ties Leslie, like my wife, apparently carries wherever she goes.

"Not a word."

Leslie walked to Hollis and sat down facing him. She picked up the small wallet the man carried and pulled out the plastic-sealed driver's license.

"Nevada. Benjamin Everly."

"That's the same ID that—"

Leslie nodded quickly. She already knew.

Hollis did not move, react or respond. He reminded me of the nameless, faceless government types that populate superhero movies when villains need to rack up a body count. The bookish appearance, I knew, masked something far quicker and more dangerous.

Leslie tossed the wallet and ID on the coffee table.

"You guys all carry the same fake ID?"

Hollis said nothing.

"Deland Hollis, I will be charging you with assaulting a federal officer, with attempted murder, and with a dozen different offenses." Leslie caught Hollis smirking. "What?"

"That will be a neat trick," Hollis said. "Considering that you have no authority here. Or anywhere. Moreover, before the sun rises, you and your friend here will be named in civil litigation for the bodily harm you have caused me during trespass on private property that you committed *as private citizens with no legal standing.*"

Leslie sighed. "A variation on the 'do you know who you're dealing with' and the 'I'll have your badge' speech I keep hearing whenever I arrest some corrupt blowhard. Maybe save us having to read the subpoena…who are we dealing with here? Clearly you think they have some power. They obviously have a ton of money."

"You don't have a badge. Not anymore."

Hollis dimmed his smirk and returned to statue mode.

Leslie, recognizing an impasse, flopped back in her chair.

"I have two questions. One for you, Leslie. Do you know how to do that thing where you cut off the blood to his brain and cause him to pass out? That chokehold?"

"The one that's illegal for law enforcement to use? That chokehold?"

"Yeah."

She flexed her eyebrows. I took that as a Yes. "What's your other question?"

I stepped directly in front of Hollis and crouched. Eye to eye, I looked at him for a moment. He held his stone face. I got the sense that he took pride in it. Pride in knowing he would never break under interrogation. Torture, maybe, but not under pressures applied like mild sleep deprivation or other semi-legitimate attempts at breaking him down. But there was a chance…

We held eye contact for a long, long moment. I concentrated on the tight little circle of his pupils. He didn't blink. Tough guy.

"Are you afraid of heights?" I asked.

He said nothing. But his pupils spoke.

70

As is often the case where the waters of three Great Lakes converge, changes in the weather come without notice. In fall, the Straits can be unpredictable.

That's how Captain Walter put it as we motored away from Little Saint Martin Island. I took one more look along the shore to the east to see if I could spot the seaplane—maybe even get a tail number using Leslie's binoculars—

Did you get the license number?

—but the veil of fog moving in on shifting winds obscured that part of the island. Things were changing fast.

"He's gone," Walter told me when I gave up looking. "The seaplane. Took off when the shooting started. I was considering it myself."

"A misunderstanding," I said.

"Right."

Walter didn't lift an eyebrow when we returned to his boat with a prisoner. Leslie and I walked a solid ten feet behind Hollis. We'd already seen his capabilities. Hollis, for his part, exhibited confidence in the forces that he claimed would turn Leslie's arrest into a charge of false imprisonment and would spark litigation that would last for years and cost her hundreds of thousands of dollars. He came peacefully.

"We best be moving," Walter suggested when we approached. Lit by the sun, the approaching fog gave off an orange glow, a tidal wave of cotton candy drifting over calm waters.

We boarded and cast off. Walter did not spare the horses again. Despite the speed he applied, the fog overtook us halfway back to St. Ignace around the time the sun dipped below the horizon. Things got dark quickly. Walter turned on the boat's running lights and reduced the throttle. He consulted equipment mounted on his command station dashboard, including an iPad with a moving map app. I had no concerns about finding the port in what had become visibility measured in hundreds of yards.

Hollis occupied one of the deck chairs with his hands bound together and then bound to the back of the chair. He wasn't going anywhere.

"This happens a lot in fall," Walter explained. "Warm, moist air comes in over the cooler water. Sometimes you can see the water currents by where the fog forms. Look at that." He pointed.

The layer of fog on the water was dense, but above it, the last glow of sunset lit the sky. Although the land had gone dark, the high towers of the Mackinac Bridge remained in the final rays of sunlight. Both towers looked aflame, but only for a few minutes. Then gray enveloped us.

"Never gets old," Walter mused.

I gave him credit for not asking questions. Not even when we docked, and Leslie took him aside.

"What do we owe you captain?"

"Whaddya got? 'Cause I didn't have plans this afternoon and you folks made my day interesting. Feel like I owe you."

"Does this cover it?" Leslie produced currency from her shoulder bag. She pressed a small roll of bills into Walter's hand. He didn't glance at it.

"If it gets me and Mollie out for a nice dinner, it more than covers it."

"I have one more favor to ask," Leslie said, glancing at Hollis, still bound to the chair. "How about if you go enjoy a beer before you come back to secure the boat or whatever you do at the end of a day?"

Walter fixed a friendly gaze on Leslie. He did not look at Hollis. He did not ask questions. Instead, he held out a hand.

"Nice meetin' you, Agent—"

"Leslie. Call me Leslie."

"A pleasure, Leslie."

<h1 style="text-align:center">71</h1>

L eslie stepped behind Hollis.

"You might as well cut me loose now," he said. "Or we can do it at whatever police station you plan to surrender yourself to as a *former* member of law enforcement."

"Does this really work?" I asked Leslie, ignoring Hollis. Ignoring him caused an uptick in tension in the man. He tugged on the restraint.

"If it doesn't kill him," Leslie replied. "That's why it's been banned. Apply it too vigorously, and—" She made a cutthroat gesture.

"This isn't necessary. I have no reason to resist you," Hollis insisted, exaggerating a casual tone.

"How often does it kill someone?" I asked.

"Usually when applied by an amateur. I've had training."

Leslie drew up close behind Hollis and swung her arm around his neck. Bright panic flashed in his eyes.

"I'm telling you—you don't need to do this."

"Hush. Sleep tight," Leslie whispered. She leveraged one arm against the other and pulled. Hollis jerked and stiffened, but she had him tightly in her control. Her head touched his and her rigid arms prevented him from moving. "Hush," Leslie repeated as Hollis protested.

He struggled, gasped and grew wide-eyed. His skin took on a purple hue. She wore a terrifyingly calm expression. Her eyes closed. Her face grew serene yet beneath all that, she looked as if every muscle in her upper body had turned to stone.

Hollis struggled until he didn't. When he went slack, she held the grip for a moment for certainty. When she released, he slumped. She touched her fingers to his neck and held them for a moment.

"Is he dead?" I asked.

"Nope." She moved around the chair and tightened a zip tie around his ankles.

"How much time do I have?"

"No idea." She produced a knife identical to the survival knife I carry in a jacket pocket. She sliced the zip ties that bound Hollis to the chair, but not the ones that held his wrists and feet. "Don't kill him."

"No guarantees," I said coldly. I closed a grip on his neck from behind. *FWOOOMP!*

72

Hollis moved. Thank God. It felt like half an hour had passed.

Took him long enough, I thought.

Touches of twilight remained in the sky above us. A world of white spread below us. Land peeked through the fog layer on the south end of the Mackinac Bridge and the top of Mackinac Island. Strange eddies and patterns imprinted the layer in the Straits. I thought about Captain Walter's mention of how the fog can be governed by currents in the water.

"I wouldn't get too frisky if I were you," I warned him.

He tested his arms and found them still bound. He kicked his feet, registering that they, too, had been tied. He blinked and took in the view. And there it was. Ragged panic.

"Around five percent of the population suffers from genuine acrophobia. Fear of heights. If you were one of those five percent, you'd be paralyzed right now. Roughly one third of the population suffers from Visual Height Intolerance. Those are the folks who are not paralyzed by height, but don't go out in that glass horror chamber on top of the Willis Tower in Chicago—used to be the Sears Tower."

Hollis stared, absorbing the impossible.

"You're on the North Tower of the Mackinac Bridge 550 feet above the Straits," I said. "You're outside the cable line, which crosses over your head up there. This shoulder of the tower sticks out a few feet on the side. Nobody goes here. That's why there's no handrail like there is up on top. There's no

226

access—except maybe by helicopter or belay line from above. Like I said. I wouldn't move if I were you."

He squeezed himself against the concrete wall at his back. The wall rose a few feet to where channels swept up to the cable mounts on top of the tower. At the top, a guardrail protected a small platform. Someone not frozen by fear or bound hand and foot might climb to the top. Hollis didn't qualify.

In both directions, the massive steel-encased cables for the suspension bridge swept downward until they disappeared into the mist. We were in clear air above the fog. Visibility in any direction touched on the infinite. But evening fell rapidly, and darkness closed in. The red warning lights on top of the bridge towers flashed and gave the scene a hellish touch.

"It's a nightmare," I said. I hung in the air above Hollis anchored by one hand on one of the concrete channels leading to the cable mount. The other clutched a BLASTER. "If you had acrophobia, you'd be catatonic. For someone with VHI, your guts clench. Your muscles turn to water. I bet you couldn't stand up if that platform caught fire. Your knees would melt. You'd probably go over the side."

Hollis pressed harder against the concrete. He stared at the edge.

"It's only a couple seconds until it's over. You hit that water at 120 miles per hour and it might as well be concrete. It'll break every bone you have, and your guts will explode, but that won't matter because you'll be dead. It sounds quick, but I bet you'd spend an eternity in those four or five seconds, thinking at light speed about all the ways you wish this wasn't happening. Am I right?"

"WHAA--?" he blurted. "What the fu—"

"Language, Deland. May I call you Del?"

"WHO ARE YOU?"

"No need to shout, Del. I have a perfectly clear connection to you. Amazing tech. And no, I'm not going to tell you how you got here. Give me what I want, and you might live to ask if there's an elevator when some-one…maybe…comes and gets you."

The pace of his breathing increased. I wasn't sure what I'd do if he hyperventilated.

"Del. Pay attention to me. If it helps, close your eyes."

He raised himself to a seated position with his back to the tower. It prob-ably didn't help. If I were in his shoes, I'd curl up into a fetal ball and squeeze my eyes shut until I either died of hunger or thirst or someone saved me. But that's just me.

"You—*you can't do this!*"

"Oh, yes, I can. I've done it before. It's remarkably effective. I caught just a hint of reaction when I asked if you had a fear of heights, so this was a done deal. I mean—come on—it's the Mackinac Bridge. Now you can tick this off your bucket list."

"What do you want?!" He did as I suggested and squeezed his eyes shut. He spoke through gritted teeth.

"Who do you work for?" I asked.

He did not answer. I chalked it up to good training. An automatic response to interrogation.

"I'm going to guess you are ex-military. Maybe ex-special forces, or at least you claim to be on whatever resume you gave Gallica or when you pick up women in bars. You've had training. You can resist threats and even torture, so those are off the table. Maybe you think you can fake your way out of this with lies. Let's save some time. Here's what's going to happen. I will ask all the usual questions. You are free not to answer. You are free to lie. Or you can tell me the truth. Doesn't matter. Regardless of how you respond, I'm leaving you up here. You will stay up here, and no one will hear you screaming and no one will come for you, and in a couple days when delirium sets in from thirst—assuming it doesn't rain—you will think you can climb this wall behind you, but you can't, being all tied up like that. The point is, no matter what you tell me, I'm leaving you here tonight. But—!"

I let the statement hang. Dead silence cloaked the top of this tower, interrupted only by the occasional exhaust bellow emitted by a heavy truck on the fog-bound roadbed below.

"But what?"

"But…in a day or two, after I have a chance to determine if what you tell me tonight is true, I may place an anonymous call to the Michigan Department of Transportation. 'Hey, I just happened to fly over the Mackinac Bridge and there's a guy out on the ledge at the top of the north tower. Check it out.' Think you can hold out a day or two?"

"What do you want?"

"Who shot Caroline Gaffney?"

Hollis steadied his breathing. I recognized the technique. Breath in. Count four. Breath out. Repeat. After a moment, he said as calmly as he was able, "I don't know any Caroline Gaffney."

"Did I mention that *all* of your answers must prove to be true. Fuck with me on any one and you'll rot up here or decide to end it quick. Once more. Who shot Caroline Gaffney?"

"I don't know a Caroline Gaffney. You need to understand how it works. We're not some fucking rent-a-cop organization."

"Right. Special forces."

"Fuck you. All you know about special forces is what you see in movies. Me and the people I work with are the real deal. And that means we operate in the real world. And that means we compartmentalize. We operate on need to know. I didn't need to know anything about anyone named Caroline Gaffney."

I gave him credit. He kept his eyes closed. The VHI held its grip on him. But he managed to remain coherent.

"What about a girl named Baxter Gaffney?"

"Same answer."

"Your ID says you're Benjamin Everly. I saw the same ID on a guy in Wisconsin. Explain."

"Standard issue. We all carry one like that. They're real as shit to local LEOs who get in the way."

"Tell me where I can find a Benjamin Everly who looks like a pro wrestler and just got his leg broke on an assignment in Three Lakes, Wisconsin."

"I don—" He bit off the rest. He hesitated. "Fine. His name is Lew Portis. The company flew him to Rochester, just like you thought. To that clinic, just like you thought. He got treatment and was moved right before you arrived. That's where I came in."

"Moved where?"

"Safe house."

"Where? Don't bullshit me, because you were in charge there. It was painted all over your face."

He huffed in frustration. "Yes. I was local AIC."

"Where's the safe house?"

"It's a penthouse. Condo building in Rochester. The Willows. Look it up."

"Does Kong—er—Portis know who would have been the shooter in Wisconsin?"

"If a shot was authorized, it would have been someone on his team. We work in teams."

"Who's we? Gallica Protective Services?"

"Yes."

I felt my blood heating up. "Is assassination part of the package?"

"We don't—" More hesitation. "We don't *sanction* unless it's absolutely necessary to protect the primary."

What exactly makes it necessary to put a bullet in the belly of a pregnant woman, Del?

It would be so easy. Just make him vanish, pick him up, and make him fly. Give him those four seconds to wonder what could make someone mad enough to do that. *Maybe tell him just before you let go.*

"Is that your job? To sanction? Have you sanctioned someone for the convenience of your employer?" Black hatred seeped into each word.

"C'mon, man. I'm giving you everything here. Everything I told you will check out. But if you make me tell you something like that, then there's nothing for me even if they do come and get me. I might as well throw myself off the edge."

The fog had thickened. Traffic slowed on the roadway beneath us. Lights moved through the mist like luminous bugs.

"Who's the primary?"

"Unknown. Seriously. Look, I may have been in charge, but I work at the operator level. I'm not admin. I—*don't*—*know*—and for good reason. We do what we're told, go where we're told, see and hear only what we're told to see and hear. That's it. Gallica is top of the fucking line security. Better than POTUS gets. Better than Putin gets. The reputation sticks because there are rules. Rule number one is Need to Know. Period. Next question."

I said nothing.

He spoke breathlessly. "I mean it. We have guys who make Seal Team Six look like a bunch of pussies. Guys who do their tours and when they get out of the shit they can't get the shit out of their veins. People like that don't just retire to some fucking suburb. Gallica takes only the best. Training and discipline is in the DNA. *Need to Fucking Know!*"

I said nothing. The silence agitated him.

"Hey!"

Good. Let him stew.

"Hey! Are you listening? I told you what you wanted, now get me the fuck down from here!"

I released my handhold. The steady breeze instantly pushed me away from the tower. Nearly blinding, the red light on top of the tower blinked its relentless warning to low-flying aircraft.

"GODDAMMIT! ANSWER ME!"

Not far away, the lights of St. Ignace glowed up through the fog, gaining luminance as night blackened the sky.

Hollis continued to cry out, growing faint as I rode the breeze along the line of the bridge. When I finally pushed the power slide on the BLASTER forward, the electric motor hum and prop noise drowned out the last of his pleas.

73

"We're going to Rochester," I told Leslie as soon as I walked into the FBO office at St. Ignace Airport. She waited on a sofa with a copy of *AOPA Pilot* spread on her knees, a Coke on the end table, and a bag of Fritos at her side. Put Ray Ban Aviators on her and she could be any charter pilot.

"Again?"

"Hollis gave up King Kong." I stopped at the desk. The same young man that fueled the Navajo earlier and who connected us to Walter sat on a stool behind the counter thumbing his phone. He glanced up at me and hopped to his feet. I had settled the fuel bill earlier. "Do I owe you for the tie-down?"

"No, sir," he replied brightly.

I glanced at the clock and the dark, foggy ramp. From my wallet, I pulled a twenty-dollar bill and slid it across the desk.

"Thanks for staying open for us. Appreciate it."

"Thank you!"

"He gave up Kong?" Leslie asked as we marched through the mist toward the Navajo. The airplane glistened under a ramp light that cast a cone-shaped veil on its wings.

"Yup."

"Can I ask a question?"

"You just did."

"Can we take off in this fog? I mean, is it safe?"

"Hell, no, it's not safe. But yes, we can. And we're about to. Go untie that rope under the wing."

WITHOUT EXPLAINING the technique involved in a zero-zero takeoff, when the ceiling and visibility are nil, I told Leslie that the fog was not very thick, that we would lift off at flying speed, that the airplane would naturally climb and in a flash, we would be in the clear air above the fog. I explained that the unsafe part of the operation was that if anything went wrong, we would be screwed if we needed to get back down, but that I knew there were airports to the south and west of us that were not fogged in should an emergency arise.

She took it all on faith, and in short order we climbed to a cruising altitude. An hour and forty minutes later, after a pleasant ride through Canada's airspace, we descended for landing at Rochester's Frederick Douglass International Airport.

74

The Willows, according to research Leslie conducted during the ride to Rochester, might top the chart for exclusive urban living in Rochester. The high-rise built in the center of the financial district opened to great fanfare and boasted 100 percent presale occupancy. Views of the Genesee River, the Saint Paul Quarter, and the Charles Carroll Plaza all upped the price of entry, according to Leslie. None of it meant anything to me except the part about it being exclusive, with 24-hour on-site security.

"What do you bet Gallica contracts for the security?" I asked after she read me the Zillow stats and other trivia.

"No bet," she said. "The project has been hailed as a masterpiece of urban renewal planning, on-time and under-budget construction, and a contribution to the aesthetic design of the skyline. Everybody loves the place."

"Just curious. Who owns it?"

"Well, it's condos, so technically the buyers own their interior walls, but the builder was…lemme see…"

Lemme see turned into fifteen minutes of silence from Leslie while we cruised over the black landscape of Ontario. I listened to the generally mute air traffic control frequency while she thumbed her phone.

"It's interesting," she finally said. "The original builders sold the project midway through construction to someone who sold it again after completion, and it has changed hands multiple times since. My guess, however, is that it's all in the family, because these companies all belong to other companies that belong to other companies. It's all rather incestuous."

"Is there a bottom line?"

"Not that I can find with my phone at 20,000 feet."

"We're cruising at 9,000 feet."

"Whatever."

"You'd be unconscious if we were at 20,000 feet. So, why is such a success story treated like the illegal hideout of a mob boss?"

"Taxes. I bet this financial shell game means there's been zero paid in taxes. That's how it works. The world is ruled by accountants."

"Speaking of the world rule…have you talked to Bad Bob the Sales Guy?"

"You mean Big Rog, the Furniture Sale Guy? Also, Assistant Director of the FBI? No. Why?"

"I don't want to be indelicate, but Hollis sure made it sound like you no longer work for the Bureau."

Leslie shrugged. "He's probably right. This is that scene in the crappy buddy cop movie. '*Gimme your badge and your gun! You're a loose cannon. You're fired!*' That shit is the worst."

Yeah. Until it happens. I didn't press the question. I had a feeling Leslie was aware of her status with the Federal Bureau of Investigation and either wasn't saying or wasn't facing it.

Change of subject.

"Are we going after this guy tonight?" I asked.

"I don't see why not."

"And how are we supposed to find him?"

"First, ask the security guard in the lobby. If that doesn't work, try your Peeping Tom approach."

75

"It's been a while since I've done this," I said. I gazed up at the silver and glass tower, guessing it to be thirty stories. Hollis said it was the penthouse. Nice digs for a safe house, but I understood the play. They weren't kidding about the 24-hour security. Not one but two armed guards manned a station in the lobby, with one of them leaving at random intervals to walk the full perimeter footprint of the building, including a stretch along the river that seemed popular with pedestrians. Leslie pointed out half a dozen cameras ringing the plaza opposite the river side of the structure. There were, no doubt, many more.

We abandoned the frontal assault approach in which Leslie charged the lobby waving her badge and demanding access to the penthouse floor. Even if granted, which was unlikely without a warrant, a warning would reach the top before she did.

That left me. I remembered the last time I took on one of these buildings in Chicago. Getting inside had been a problem that was ultimately solved by flying at a floor-to-ceiling glass window with a giant piece of concrete.

"Balcony," Leslie pointed out when we did our reconnaissance, strolling along the river walk with her arm hooked inside mine. I didn't wonder what Andy would think of such theater. In any imaginary love triangle, Leslie was a greater threat to me than to Andy.

"I see." Each floor offered the owner a lovely balcony on the side facing the river. Solid polished steel substituted for railing, which might have reduced the view from inside, but it enhanced the aesthetic of the outside.

The usual sliding doors offered access to the condos. Easy enough for me, I decided.

"Shall we?" Leslie asked after our walk took us a couple hundred yards past the building.

I looked at my watch and at my surroundings. After 11 p.m. and still too many people.

"Over there." I pointed.

A set of steps descended to a dock at river level. The dock was empty. Descending the steps put us below the eye line of the pedestrians on the river walk.

Fwooomp! I made us vanish when we reached the bottom step.

"*Jesus,*" Leslie whispered, "*a little warning, please.*"

I laughed.

Using BLASTER number two for the evening, I launched us from the pier, flew a curved arc over the placid waterway, then angled back toward The Willows. We rose steadily until we reached eye level with the top floor.

Below the penthouse, balconies alternated in a checkerboard pattern up the side of the building. At penthouse level, the balcony ran the width of the building.

"I did one of these once before I knew how to make BLASTERs," I told Leslie as we approached. "Went up the side like Spiderman. Scared the crap out of me." Not to mention having a broken pelvis at the time.

"Now you know how I feel. Can you just get us on solid ground, please?"

"Recon, first."

I set up a slow cruise along the side of the building about twenty feet out over nothing. Leslie tightened her grip.

The penthouse, it turned out, occupied two floors at the top of the building. In some places, the windows showed stacked rooms. In others, the windows rose floor-to-ceiling on two-story spaces. One of the spaces looked like a ballroom.

"Jesus, this is where they hide a guy with a broken leg?" I muttered.

"Why not? You've got staff coming and going. Maybe even events. Parties. Bringing in medical personnel is easy with that kind of cover."

"I guess."

We rounded a corner. More windows. More rooms. A few people moved in and out of light and shadows inside. In one room, a television blazed SportsCenter to an empty space. I momentarily hoped to find Kong there, given his viewing habits at Caroline Gaffney's home. No such luck.

"Are you really going to leave that guy up on the bridge?" Leslie asked as we turned another corner, now traversing the side of the building opposite the river.

I wanted to say Yes. I wanted to think he deserved to die up there or perish hitting the water at 120 miles per hour, the two being roughly the same. He wasn't the owner of the hand that pulled the trigger that shot Caroline Gaffney and nearly killed Andy. But he could have been. He would have accepted the order without question.

So, yes, I wanted to say I planned to leave Hollis to rot.

I would have, too, if Andy's face didn't rush to my mind.

"We'll see," I said. "His intel has to prove out first."

And at that moment, it did.

76

———————

"That's him," I said.

"You weren't kidding. He's huge."

"No shit."

Kong lay on a hospital bed that might have been the equal of the one Andy occupied, but he made it look like it belonged to a child. A complex rig of steel bars and cables suspended the white log of a leg cast above the foot of the bed. He had the head of the bed cranked up to more than a 45-degree angle as he watched a television mounted on the wall. I couldn't see the screen, but I could guess what channel he had on.

A sofa and several chairs gave the otherwise empty room a small suite effect. The suite connected to a bar area. A small kitchen with a refrigerator and sink added conveniences.

Medical supplies lay strewn on a table near the bed. Discarded boxes. Pill bottles. A plastic bag of cotton swabs. A tray with assorted tools and a few hypodermic needles suggested that some of Kong's treatment took place in this room.

"That must have hurt," I muttered.

"What?"

"Never mind. Let's go around to the other side. That's our point of entry."

<h1 style="text-align:center">77</h1>

———————

I caught the latch when it fell from the locked sliding door, preventing it from dropping to the balcony floor and making noise. The sprawling living room on the other side of the glass had no occupants, but it was lit up like a party. Lamps and recessed lighting warmed the space. Expensive carpeting supplemented by even more expensive decorative rugs covered the floor. A selection of modernist paintings hung tastefully along the walls. Sculptures that made no sense to me filled corner spaces and the odd table.

Money oozed from every dimension.

I slid the door aside. Leslie remained hooked to my arm. I had to rotate and slip in sideways. With Leslie clear of the doorway, I told her to grip the frame, giving me leverage to pull the door shut.

We ventured forward a foot or so above the carpet.

Getting to the other side of the penthouse took us through the ballroom, through a game room, and up an elaborate spiral staircase to the second floor. Luck stayed with us. We heard voices and a television, but we saw no one. My sense of direction guided us until we found a broad open archway that entered Kong's makeshift hospital room. It was even bigger on the inside.

"*I got this*," Leslie whispered. She tugged her arm free. An electric snap bit my skin when she reappeared and dropped to the carpet.

"*Wait—what?*"

"*He knows you. He doesn't know me.*"

She barely finished saying the words before she marched into the room as if she owned the place.

Kong blinked at her, then ran his eyes up and down her full height. There was no mistaking the assessment, making me wonder what else he was being provided with.

"Mr. Everly," Leslie said officiously. "I'm Linda Himmel from Gallica corporate in New York, how do you do?"

"What? Uh—fine. Who are you again?"

"Himmel. Gallica. New York. They didn't tell you I was coming because there was no reason to tell you. After all," Leslie spread her hands and gestured at the hospital rig, "it's not like you're going anywhere."

"It's not Everly, it's Por—"

"I am aware of your name, sir. I am also aware that for the purpose of this discussion, you are Mr. Everly. I really don't think you want me using your birth name."

"What's this about? I already talked to Rivers."

"Yes, well, that's the problem." Leslie circled the foot of the bed.

"What do you mean, 'problem?' What problem?"

"If you would give me a moment, I'll explain. One moment." She lifted her shoulder bag and laid it on a nearby chair, freeing her hands. Looking around, she selected a dark, polished statue roughly eighteen inches tall. To my uneducated eye it resembled something from an island culture. A woman, smooth, with abundant hips and breasts. Leslie lifted it from the table it adorned. She tested the heft and nodded to herself.

The move made Kong noticeably uneasy.

"Rivers never said there was a problem. Lemme call him—" Kong picked up his phone from the table adjacent to the bed.

"Put your phone down, Mr. Everly. Rivers no longer works for Gallica. Rivers has been…*removed*."

Kong stared. Leslie stared back as she moved, strolling on an arc around the foot of the bed until her path brought her to face the cast-bound leg.

"Mr. Everly, let me explain my instructions to you. May I?"

He nodded.

"My instructions are to come here and review the Gaffney exercise, identify fault for it turning into a huge clusterfuck, and render judgment on those responsible. We thought it best to begin with the team leader."

"I was team leader."

Leslie tipped a tiny bow in Kong's direction. "I am aware. And the team under your command?"

"If you are who you say you are, you know very well who my team was." Anger added grit to his words. I recognized the tone. "Lady, I don't know you. I don—"

"I think I may have left out one key element of my instructions, Mr. Everly."

"Portis. It's fucking Portis. Or didn't you know that?"

"Lew Portis. I know your name, your DOB, your Social, your mother's nickname in high school—I know everything about you down to the girth of your penis, asshole. Here's something you didn't know. I also have clear instructions to enter this room, find something heavy, and beat that cast until it shatters and whatever screws are holding your leg together fly out like popcorn. I have instructions to continue beating that leg until the bottom half literally hangs from this traction rig all by itself. That is, of course, if you do not cooperate with me."

Kong went pale. He glanced at his leg, then at Leslie. She smiled.

I drifted slowly into the room.

"Team, please."

"Ray Killian, driver. Jack Rudder and Paul Entilles on perimeter. Trace Murphy on overwatch."

"Who ordered Trace Murphy to carry out the sanction?"

"Rivers. He told you that, right? He should have told you that."

"He said you called it."

"That's bullshit! That's total bullshit! I called Rivers in Chicago as soon as—when I went down with *this*." Kong stabbed the air with one of his huge hands, pointing at the cast. "Rivers made the call. All the way. He made that call."

"To you or directly to Murphy?"

"By the book. To me. Then I alerted Murphy. What the fuck is this all about? We handled it by the book."

Kong used his elbows to thrust himself away from the mattress. It caused his leg to tug against the cables that held it suspended above the bed, which caused him to grimace.

"Who are you?" A woman's voice startled me. It came from behind.

Before I could rotate, I took a sharp jab in the back. The force of it shot me across the carpet to the bottom of the bed where I grabbed the traction frame. A clatter followed me. When I looked back, I saw a woman sprawled on the floor among the contents of a tray full of food that had splashed and spattered in every direction. She had run right into me.

Hitting the traction frame caused it to jolt, which caused Kong to shriek. Leslie blinked and stepped back. She reached for her shoulder bag.

"*We gotta go,*" I whispered to her, hoping Kong was too consumed by pain to hear.

I jerked the traction rig. The log of plaster swayed sharply. Kong shrieked again. The move sent me to Leslie where I grabbed her arm and used it to plant my feet on the floor.

"*Gimme that,*" I whispered. She held out the statue.

Then I alerted Murphy. The words rang in my ears. Kong alerted Murphy. To do what overwatch does. Take the shot. Take out the woman.

I lifted the statue from Leslie's grasp. It pressed me to the floor. I let go of Leslie and turned.

"Fuck you, Kong," I said loud enough to draw a startled glance. In horror, he watched the statue rise in the air, then swing down on its own, smashing into the plaster cast, crushing and breaking it and the leg within into two angled segments still chained to the traction frame.

He screamed.

78

————————

"We need a room for the night. Cash. No credit cards." I landed us several blocks away from The Willows. In shadow between two buildings, we reappeared. I stowed the BLASTER, noting that the batteries were starting to fade.

I felt…cleansed. I also felt the murder in my heart grinning up at me from its black depths. It had a name.

Then I alerted Murphy.

"I don't have that much cash." I pushed aside dark thoughts.

"Me either. Can you get us near the airport? We can try one of the cheaper motels there."

"I think so, but it will burn the last of the batteries. I have spares in the flight bag, but for tonight, this is it."

"Just get us to a Hampton Inn or Holiday Inn Express for the night. Off the grid. We'll get some sleep and head out in the morning."

"For?"

"First, for Indiana. I want to get that car back. Then, I believe there's someone named Rivers at the Gallica Protective Services Chicago office that we need to chat with, wouldn't you say?"

I liked her thinking, but several things worried me about the plan.

"Whoever he is, he's going to be alerted. By now they will have figured a few things out. First, Hollis disappearing when he was supposed to be killing you. Second, the attack on Kong was obviously you. And third, what do we do about our phones?"

"You make a good point about our phones, or at least mine. I'll pull the battery and card. Your phone should be okay because nobody knows who you are. A nice side effect of…" She wiggled her fingers in the air.

"That looks stupid."

"I know." She smiled. "Let's go."

THE LAST AVAILABLE room at the Holiday Inn Express consumed most of our cash and offered a single king bed. I wanted to keep looking. Leslie shoved the cash at the clerk and said we'd take it.

"You want me to sleep on the floor?" I asked when we entered the room sans luggage.

"Do what you want. I have no problem sleeping in the same bed with you." She tossed her shoulder bag on the desk and shook off her black blazer. "The bed is huge."

"Doesn't bother me if it doesn't bother you." I matched her casual bravado. "You have nothing to fear. I'll be thinking about my beautiful wife."

"So will I," she said. "And you're right." She pulled her pistol from her bag and checked the magazine, then the cylinder. "I have nothing to fear."

79

"**I**'m sleeping with another woman tonight."

"Have fun."

I felt the stupid grin on my face fade. Andy deftly parried the joke. I heard a chuckle on the phone line, then a muted *Ouch.*

"Nice try," she said. "Leslie texted me half an hour ago. I think she wanted my approval."

"I think she values your friendship more than mine."

"Can you blame her?" Another light chuckle. This time she hid the pain it induced. "As a matter of fact, I'm sleeping with another woman tonight, too."

"Okay, this has gone off the rails."

"Holly's staying over tonight."

"With the kids?"

"Good God, no. It's bad enough she has one helpless infant to deal with. No, Casey is on a sleepover with Lydia's girls and Toby Leo is the new crown prince of the Davis household."

"That will not sit well with the Infant King Alex. Beware regicide." Since becoming a widow two steps ahead of divorcing her philandering husband, Andy's sister Lydia seemed to thrive around infants. Her own, Princess Grace, and the simultaneously gestated Alex, the son of Lydia's teenaged Nanny by way of Lydia's cheating husband. The children filled Lydia's household with a blend of joy and chaos.

"The children are too taken with another new baby to notice the plotting. Speaking of which—for God's sake, fill me in."

I explained the trip to St. Ignace and the information gained from Hollis and then from Kong. I may have glossed over the parts about the Mackinac Bridge and the buxom fertility statue.

"This Rivers…who is he?"

"I was hoping you might poke around the internet and see what you can find. He seems to be middle management at the Chicago branch of Gallica Protective Services. You know…in the 'Go Ahead and Kill Her' department. But if he's middle management, he might show up on the 'About Our Team' page of their website. You could get lucky."

"Isn't that something Leslie might be better suited to do? I mean, I'm happy to see what I can find via department resources, but she can get more from the FBI, maybe from their Chicago office."

I glanced at the closed bathroom door. The shower drummed against the Fiberglas bathtub. Even so, I lowered my voice.

"I'm not sure where Leslie's status with the Bureau lies right now. She's showing hints of giving the whole organization the flying finger."

"That business with Big Bob?"

"Yes. The truth is, I don't think she's touched base with her office since she got that call. I'm not sure she still has a job."

I could feel Andy's frown through the phone. "It wouldn't be surprising. The news hasn't been good. There's a purge underway and the sad truth is that they're targeting certain people. Certain people like Leslie. I'll get into my laptop and see what I can find. Do you have a first name?"

"Just Rivers." I didn't mention the name of Trace Murphy. That one belonged to me. I may not be able to lie directly to her, but I can occasionally pull off omission.

"If he's middle management, he might show up in a press release. I'll see what I can find." I heard the energized note in her voice—the same note inspired by Lydia's story about her friend's missing daughter exactly one week ago. "Which reminds me," she continued, "did Leslie find anything more on the girl at Penn State? The Baxter Gaffney who isn't Baxter Gaffney?"

"I don't know. Like I said, she doesn't seem to be trading information with home base."

"I'll text her and ask her to send me the image from the student ID. Maybe I can find something."

"Don't piss off Tom. And while you're not pissing people off, include all the doctors and nurses who are telling you to stay still and not get agitated."

"Ha. Tom already has me running searches from bed. He hates that stuff. He's always trying to get me to handle his keyboard work at the office. Now he thinks he has a captive computer servant. That or he thinks it's a good way to keep me busy."

Clever boss, I thought.

She continued. "And so far, sitting here with my laptop has not offended my caregivers, although they might be under the impression that I'm surfing shopping sites for baby clothes."

"Well, listen, we've both got other women to sleep with, so I'm going to say goodnight."

"I love you."

"Oh sure. If I had a nickel for every time—"

"Shut up and kiss me."

80

Monday

The Holiday Inn Express includes a free breakfast with the room. Casual travelers may disdain the menu, but seasoned road warriors recognize easy refueling when they see it. And coffee. Sometimes the coffee prepared by minimum wage night clerks is better used in asphalt, and sometimes it can be pretty good.

I held a mug of pretty good in both hands while Leslie loaded a plate with mixed fruit and a croissant.

"No eggs or bacon?" I asked when she joined me. She glanced at the load on my plate.

"You're going to have a heart attack before you're fifty."

"Not me. All that plaque in the arteries is what keeps the men in my lineage upright. Even after death they can't get us to lie down in the coffin."

We ate first, then talked.

"Here," Leslie said. "I sent pictures to Andrea. She sent this back sometime in the night." She slid her phone across to me. "I don't think she's sleeping well."

"Hardly. Between the busted rib and little Ethel kicking field goals and a bladder the size of a penny…"

"Are you guys having a girl?" Leslie blinked at my use of the name. "And tell me you're not naming her Ethel."

"Ethel's a perfectly solid Wisconsin farm name."

"Maybe a hundred years ago."

"No idea if it's a girl or boy. We're going old school on not knowing the gender. What am I looking at?"

I held her phone in my hand. Onscreen, the display showed a playbill for a show called *She Told Her Story.* The artwork tried for modern and feminine but came off looking like a fourth grader's potato stamp project.

"That's the playbill for an off-Broadway show. One and done, I think. Swipe it."

I flicked the image away. A new image slid into place, a black and white head shot, the kind actors carry around for casting directors. The girl in the shot had an elegant look, a touch of film noir aided by a slight homage to 1940s hair styling and maybe a little soft focus. I recognized her immediately.

"That's the Baxter Gaffney on the Penn State student ID."

"Marion Hollister. She's twenty. Wants to be an actor. Had a small role in the off-Broadway production of *She Told Her Story* and several bits as a teen actor in television commercials. Currently appearing in the role of Baxter Gaffney, Penn State University student."

"Andy found this?"

"I sent her the student ID images. She managed the facial recognition search with her office resources, then pieced it together."

"What's an actress—?"

"Actor. Nobody says actress anymore."

"Thank you, Lonnie Penn. What's an actor doing playing the real-life role of a missing girl under the nose of the real girl's father who ought to be able to tell the difference?"

Leslie sipped her coffee and leaned back in her chair.

"Let me unpack that complex question. First answer, for money. My guess is that somebody found Miss Hollister between paychecks and offered her the role. She probably took the moral high ground and said no, but when the money offered rose above the moral high ground, she took the job. Easy cash. She spends a week in a dorm, establishes presence, goes to enough classes to clock in, then switches to off-campus housing to ride out the contract, however long it is supposed to be. She looks enough like the missing girl to make it work. Maybe they told her that the real Baxter was sorting out some health issues and just needed a couple weeks, and didn't want to lose her place at Penn. Second answer, either the dad knows what's going on, or he's been duped."

"Duped? Not recognizing his own daughter?"

"Estranged daughter. Troubled kid. I could see it. Hard to connect with in the first place, then shipped off to a camp, then shipped off to a university. Might be some hardcore separation between them. Dad's a lawyer. He may have dug in, especially given the divorce. Daughter says she never wants to speak to him again after what he did to mommy. It's plausible. Or he's flat out in on the plot."

"Okay. So, what the hell is the plot? Is she missing? Is she hiding? Is she a runaway who said screw you to her dad and now dad's paying someone to keep the kid's slot at Penn open? What the hell is this?"

"My guess? None of the above. I think someone preferred a murder investigation to a missing girl investigation."

"Huh," I said. "That's exactly what Tom said."

"Don't forget the Girl of the Lake. Another Baxter, if looks don't deceive."

"Have you done anything with those names we picked up from Kong? What does the Bureau's Skynet computer tell us about Killian, Elliston and Murphy?"

"The Bureau has replaced intelligence with 'artificial' intelligence in the form of Big Rog the Furniture Sale Guy. That's as artificial as intelligence gets. No. Not yet. I need to tread lightly at the Funny Business Institute."

I didn't press.

"What about Hollis?" she asked, studying the surface of her coffee. "Are you leaving him up there?"

"I expected you to override me and called Michigan DOT by now."

"Nope. That's your call. The bullet hit your wife. I won't get in front of you on that. Not with Hollis. Not with Murphy, either."

She lifted her eyes from her coffee to mine and held an unblinking and intense stare for a moment.

"I appreciate that." I pulled out my phone and checked the ForeFlight app. "Temperature in the low thirties last night in Upper Michigan. It got cold out on that slab of concrete. Bet he's thirsty, too."

I put my phone away. She said nothing. We ate in silence for a few minutes. When I finished, I asked, "Where do we go from here?"

"Well," Leslie said, "I'd be grateful if you flew me back to Indiana so I can retrieve that Bureau rental car. Then I'll drive up to Chicago and see if I can arrange a meeting with Mr. Rivers of Gallica Protective Services."

"Happy to drop you off. I'll meet you in Chicago. You might get deeper into the bowels of Gallica Protective Services if we operate as a team."

She chuckled. "Right. Abbott and Costello Meet the In—"

"Hey," I interrupted, "if you're going with the film classics, it's Martin and Lewis."

"And let me guess. You're—"

"That's right."

81

Peeps from the B
I checked my phone near the end of the hour-long cab ride from Palwaukee Airport to the Hyatt Regency in downtown Chicago, simultaneously uttering a curse on the former mayor of Chicago for destroying the incredibly convenient Meigs Field. Leslie's text read like the kind of cryptic communication Andy exchanged with Lane Franklin, a high school sophomore who spoke fluent emoji. I decided this wasn't that. This was a short-burst message. Something she thumbed out in a hurry.

Peeps from the B
People from the Bureau.

After the death of Assistant Director Mitchell Lindsay, Leslie worked with a blessing from Director Simmons. With Simmons gone and the Federal Bureau of Investigation being gutted by an administration looking for servitude and loyalty that had nothing to do with law enforcement, I feared Leslie had pushed things too far. This message suggested trouble.

I should have seen it. Hollis, as much as I hated the man, displayed no arrogance when, facing an FBI field agent, he simply hit speed dial and moments later a senior albeit amateur FBI official instructed Leslie to stand down.

Hollis performed an act of sheer power. No need to pull a gun. No need to make threats or pound his chest. He played cards neither Leslie nor I held.

Peeps from the B
They intercepted her in Elkhart, Indiana. What was it she had been

ordered to do? Report back to D.C. for evaluation. Instead, she threw her hat in the ring with me and Andy, committing to insubordination that could not, and did not go unpunished.

Her text meant the guy in the foxhole beside me just took a hit. I was on my own.

The cab dropped me at the Hyatt Regency, a comfortable choice for its familiarity. I chose it also because nearby, in a steel and glass office building, Gallica Protective Services - Chicago leased a floor or two or three. Somewhere inside, a middle-management dweeb named Rivers shuffled his papers, juggled his personnel assignments, authorized murder, and probably drank too much coffee.

"Looks like it's just me coming for you, asshole." I deleted Leslie's text message and wondered if the building had roof access.

82

"Hi, Mr. Stewart, this is Holly." A not-Andy voice answered my call, speaking softly but with a smile I could hear on the line. "I answered because Mrs. Stewart is sleeping."

"Oh," I said. "Good." My watch said eleven-fifteen.

"We keep the phone on vibrate for her naps. She had a rough night last night. I tried not to notice but she was up a lot on her computer."

"Right. Your sleepover. I'm sorry you didn't get much rest but thank you for staying with her."

"I'm fine. I have a baby at home. This is like a vacation for me."

I sipped my second coffee of the morning and leaned closer to the window of the small, corner shop. The view included the entrance to the Mid-Atlantic Building, an inappropriately named office tower on the edge of the Chicago River. Something called Mid-Atlantic Insurance accounted for the geographic misnomer. Nothing on the outside of the building indicated the presence of Gallica Protective Services. I got the address from Google.

"How's our girl doing?" I asked Holly.

"Good, really good. Margie—she's the day nurse—she gave her a sponge bath this morning and we had a good breakfast with some solid foods." She laughed. "I sound like I'm talking about my kids."

"What about the wound? Did the nurse have anything to say?"

"Oh, Mrs. Stewart did a FaceTime with Dr. Maserati this morning." I laughed silently. Holly continued, "I couldn't understand everything he was saying, but he was like kinda bubbly. I guess that things are healing better than anyone expected. I did hear them say that there was no sign of infection. They did another one of those needle tests. I couldn't watch."

"That's good. Did they talk at all about removing that stent? The thing with the video feed?"

"I wanted to give them privacy, but Mrs. Stewart—"

"You need to call her Andy, Holly."

"Oh. Okay. Um…I told Andy I could go upstairs while she was on the call, but she told me to stay. I read some of her magazines. Wow. Did you see the one with the pregnant lady on the cover?"

"Yes."

"Holy cow, that lady is rich. But Mrs. Stew—Andy—is way more pregnant. Like, that lady is like only something like 14 or 16 weeks or something. Anyway, um, that thing you asked about."

"The stent."

"They want to keep it another few days. M—er—Andy made a face like she didn't like that, but she didn't put up a fight about it."

"And she still stays immobile. Right?"

"Like a statue, Dr. Maserati told her."

"You're a sweetheart, Holly, for staying with her. Do you know how to play poker?"

"Omaha, Texas Hold 'Em, Seven Card Stud, or Five Card Draw?"

"You should be able to talk her into a game of Five Card Draw. There are a couple decks of cards and some chips in the bureau in the dining room. Top drawer. Get whatshername, the nurse—"

"Margie."

"Get her to join in. Andy will protest, but she loves to play."

"That's great, Mr. St—"

"Will. I'm Will. She's Andy." Something we told Holly a dozen times before.

"Okay."

I heard a voice in the background. "Is that Will?"

"Here," Holly said. "She's awake now. Goodbye, Mr. Stewart!"

83

───────────

"This is going to drive me insane," Andy said when Holly handed her the phone.

"I hear you talked to Dr. Maserati."

"Who?"

"That's what Holly called him. That's what I'm going to call him from now on."

"No, you're not. And yes, I spoke to him this morning. And the thing we talked about is doing the thing we talked about."

"Good."

"Is it? I mean—yes—it's great that it's healing the way it is. He said if this continues and they feel the fragment has been neutralized, I might be able to get up and move in a *very limited fashion.* His words. I asked him to define limited and be sure to include the toilet. He said I should balance a fine crystal wine glass on my nose when I walk. And he said that might not happen for at least three to four weeks. He's not in the optimism business."

"I may have lost Leslie," I said, hoping to avoid deeper discussion about the possible healing properties of *the other thing.*

"Okay. Whiplash. What?"

I explained the cryptic text in the context of the call she received from the Acting Assistant Director for the Furniture Bargains Institute.

"You don't think they arrested her?" Andy asked a little breathlessly. "That would be a travesty. Look at what she did on the Arlington Bridge, for God's sake. That woman is a national hero."

"Apparently so are the hundreds arrested from an armed mob that tried to attack the capital, according to some pundits. Let's not get off track here. Ever since Leslie got that warning shot across the bow in Rochester, she's been cagey about contact with the Bureau. Even for things like running a name or background. I think she's in much hotter water than we knew."

Andy took a moment to think. "You don't imagine she would throw you under the bus…would she?"

"Never. But I may be on my own here."

"Come home. Forget about—I don't even remember what you're doing there. What are you doing?"

"Rivers. He authorized the shot that killed Caroline and—"

It hit me again. Dead center in the throat. That knot. I drew and released a full breath.

"Come home, Will," she said softly. "Let the…"

"What? What were you going to say? *Let the authorities handle this?* The authorities just sidelined the one person working hardest. The authorities want the opposite of answers. Somebody wants this buried."

She didn't answer and I felt bad for snapping. I looked for an out.

"Did you hear anything more from Greg?"

"He dug up the old notice. It's as he said. The composites of the girl found in the lake resemble Baxter Gaffney and Chaney Foss, but think about it, Will. That's all nonsense. Exactly the kind of backward evidence chain that only muddies up an investigation."

"Probably. But both Tom and Leslie said the same thing. Someone is less concerned about a murder investigation than they are about a missing person. I think that someone has an office up the street here and I'd like to have a word."

"No. You can't. You—"

"What's that, Dee? You're breaking up. I'm going through a tunnel. And there's an airplane taking off. Right here in the tunnel. And a train. A freight train. Wow. Man, it's a long one. I'm going to have to call you back."

"Stop it. Just…be careful."

"I'll check the calendar. Love you."

84

I joke with Andy that I only need to be careful every other day. She keeps a different calendar in her head. In her mind, *every* day is a Be Careful day, something I toss back at her when she's headed out the door with a badge and police service weapon in her bag and I'm headed out the door to navigate pop-up thunderstorms or ice in the clouds. As old and moldy as the joke has become, she is reassured that I will do as I am told if the day of the week ends in Y.

When my call to her ended she laid the phone on what had quickly become a cluttered bedside table. Holly—who had done her best to avoid listening to our conversation by bringing a fresh glass of water from the pitcher in the refrigerator—returned to Andy's bedside and sat down.

"Is he flying today?" she asked. "I guess I assumed he is, but is that what you meant? Be careful?"

"Will is a superb pilot. He's always careful. I would trust him—I have trusted him—with my life. With *our* lives." She rubbed the bump. "I always ask, and he always says yes, and the thing is, I don't have to ask. He is the most careful pilot you could ever meet."

Holly gazed at Andy and for a moment Andy could not read the expression on her face. Confusion? Clarity? A distant thought percolating to the surface? Andy was about to prompt her when Holly lowered her eyes as if embarrassed. She started to speak, then stopped.

Andy asked, "What is it, Holly?"

Holly shrugged. Andy thought she might brush the moment aside. She didn't.

"It was Mr. St—Will. It was Will, wasn't it. He was the angel."

Holly's stark realization gave Andy a jolt. Calculations of who knew what and when raced through her mind along with a stern *This is getting out of hand!* Worse, on the heels of her own admonition, Andy felt sharp anger rise. This was an imposition. Now she had a duty. A fire to put out. Now she must warn or threaten Holly, or beg her collaboration, or explain things she did not want to explain. She needed to swear Holly to secrecy. She needed—

"At the hardware store. That night." Holly's gaze probed a great distance, the kind reached across a landscape of memory. "It was him."

The tumult that rose inside Andy washed away just as quickly as it had boiled.

A sad smile creased the corners of Holly's lips.

"I wanted to buy Casey a candy cane. So that she would have something. Just something. But I didn't have enough. And there was this angel. I'm sorry."

"For what?"

"He—um—Will, he paid for the candy cane. But I never looked at him. I couldn't. I'm sorry. I just couldn't. It was Will. I should tell him I'm sorry. Shouldn't I?"

Andy reached for and took Holly's hand.

"Don't do any such thing. The last thing he would want is for you to ever mention it. But yes, honey. It was him. He can be an angel at times."

"A careful angel."

Holly's smile widened.

85

———

I wasn't careful. I was an idiot. If Leslie had been present, I would not have made a colossal mistake. She would have understood the terrain, properly estimated the adversary, and calculated the capabilities of an international security company that I missed completely. The same for Andy. My wife never would have let me blow things so badly.

Before stopping at the coffee shop for my amateur surveillance of the building, I prechecked my bags at the hotel. From my flight bag, I kept a hat and two fully charged BLASTERs. I wore my Air Force flight jacket because it has pockets everywhere, and in the left shoulder pocket, I slipped the slim survival knife I usually carry in the flight bag.

Satisfied, I finished my coffee and set out on the busy streets of Chicago thinking I was just another pedestrian hurrying after his own affairs.

I could not have looked more like Will Stewart, pilot, from Essex County, husband of Detective Andrea Stewart, witness to and victim of Caroline Gaffney's murder, if I had hung a sign around my neck.

Ignorant of my failure, I walked purposefully up the sidewalk in front of the Mid-Atlantic Building like any of the hundreds of pedestrians on the windblown downtown Chicago streets. Having every right to enter a public building, I walked through the double door entry and cruised across the glossy brown and gold marble-lined lobby. I pulled up at a directory embedded in a pedestal near the elevator bank. I kept my head lowered, using the brim of the hat to shield my face from the obvious cameras mounted in high corners of the lobby. Like anyone with business in the building, I ran my finger down the glass surface of the directory, intentionally passing the listing for *Gallica Protective Services – Floor 15* and instead tapping something called *Media Management* on the fourth floor. I called for and boarded an elevator and rode it to the fourth floor, then entered a door with *Media Management* lettered on a frosted glass door.

Inside a modest office with gray walls, gray carpeting, and a gray atmosphere overall, I lifted my phone from my pocket and stared at it with what I hoped was a confused look on my face.

A woman behind a high reception counter greeted me with a lackluster, "Can I help you?"

"I think I'm beyond help. This clearly isn't Shapiro Orthodonture." I looked around as if there was one last chance an orthodontist would miraculously appear.

She smiled. "I think you want the third floor."

"Damn. One of these days I have *got to* learn to operate an elevator. All those buttons. Thanks. Have a good day."

I left, called the elevator, and then departed the building feeling satisfied and successful.

Maybe they saw me on cameras that I didn't spot. Maybe they stationed people on the street after confirming that I landed the Navajo at Palwaukee. Maybe they had illegal access to my credit card information and saw the booking at the Hyatt. I told myself such a privacy breach should have been next to impossible but the same applied to prompting an Assistant Director of the FBI to derail Leslie. Maybe it was because they'd already seen me once in Rochester and a second time entering Wayne Gaffney's law firm.

Or it could have been the *Essex County Air Service* logo and type embroidered on my hat.

Idiot.

PART IV

86

Monday Night

F loating naked above the carpet, I assessed the damage. No clothes. No overnight bag. No flight bag. No phone. No room keys. No wallet.
No airplane keys.
And only one screaming thought in my head.
"I'm giving them a green light."
"Andy…!"

PHONE. At any given moment, depending on location, there could be hundreds of phones around me. Everybody has one. Picking someone's pocket or purse didn't pose a huge challenge. Getting through a facial recognition or security code screen did.

The realization that I had screwed up, that I had been a rank amateur playing in a pro league, hit me. With Leslie gone, my big plan had been to break into the Gallica offices and then find an office or desk belonging to someone named Rivers. Maybe rifle through his drawers. Maybe call the building security and report the break-in, luring the man back after hours for a chat, perhaps on the roof. Or something. I didn't know. I thought I could wing it.

Idiot.

They saw me coming, probably all the way from Rochester. Tracking the plane required nothing more than internet access and the tail number thanks to public dissemination of ADS-B data. Identifying me in the lobby of their Chicago headquarters—well that was just stupid on my part. I handed myself to them on a silver platter.

The team in Essex is in position.

I needed to warn Andy, and I needed to do it five minutes ago.

The simplest way would be to grab a towel, wrap up my privates, and then streak through the lobby to the main desk. They had phones. Police emergency, I would tell them. Call the police. Not the Chicago Police, the City of Essex Police.

Calm down, sir.

You want us to do what?

If you would please relax, we'll get someone here to help you in a moment.

Here's an officer now...

I saw myself in handcuffs without anyone listening to desperate warnings from the naked man in public.

I had to steal a phone or find a desk phone with no one nearby.

I PUSHED off the suite's sofa on a vector for the entry hall and door. Halfway there, I stopped. I checked the closet for a big fluffy robe. If they had a camera in the suite, a ghost was about to shrug into a robe. No such luck. Nothing hung in the closet but empty hangers and a dry-cleaning bag.

Passing the bathroom, I contemplated the towels folded and stacked on a shelf near the shower. Easy to grab one and wrap it around my hips.

Except I'd tie up one hand holding the damned thing. Probably drop it.

To hell with it. I planned to either remain vanished or not give a damn what people saw.

At the door, I had no choice. I had to open the door, even if it was being watched. The suite didn't offer windows that opened or a balcony from which to launch. Like one of the intruders said, there's only one way in or out.

I pressed my hand against the wall for leverage and pulled the door open just enough to slide through. The door snapped shut behind me with terrible finality. Alone in the hotel hallway without a stitch of clothing, the enormity of my task took shape. I prepared to evade if someone came running, but the hall remained empty.

I pushed off the wall and sailed across the hallway carpet. The path took me to the next door on the opposite side. I used the corners and door handle to adjust my flight path. I crossed the carpet to another doorway. And then again. And again.

My final vector took me into the small elevator lobby. A table with faux flowers and a mirror faced the elevator doors. I floated to the table. Just as I hit, the elevator issued a loud *ding*. Seconds later, the doors opened. Voices and laughter accompanied a cluster of four people, three men and one woman, who walked through the elevator lobby and then dispersed in both directions.

I didn't wait. I pushed off the table and glided through the closing elevator doors. Hitting the back wall of the car, I grabbed the midriff-height handrail and rotated to face the control panel.

My feet hit the car floor when the car suddenly went up.

Wrong way!

I maneuvered myself to the control panel and pushed the button with the embossed star marking the main lobby.

Nothing happened.

I pushed again. Same result. I senselessly pushed the button half a dozen times and irrationally imagined that something about being vanished prevented the button from accepting instructions—

—until I saw the key card scanner hanging below the button panel. Without a key card, I wasn't going to tell this elevator anything. I needed the stairwell.

Matters descended from bad to worse when the panel announced floor 32 and the door opened to a group of six people, all chatting and laughing and ready for a night out in Chicago. With the exit blocked, I kicked the floor with my bare feet and shot up, twisting and rotating until my back and butt bumped into the metal roof of the car just as the last of the six boarded. I placed both hands on the car wall and stretched until my feet met the opposite wall, wedging myself in position.

Naked.

The only thing that kept me from freaking out over being naked was the ticking clock in my head.

The team in Essex is in position.

I searched the group below for a purse or pocket with an accessible phone. Or better, someone holding a phone that I could snatch—

Oh, crap.

They didn't press the button for the lobby. They pressed the button for the parking garage beneath the hotel.

The car descended, building speed. The trip became an express run. Digits marking the floors flashed on the wall panel. The elevator sank past the second-floor check-in level, the first-floor lobby, and ultimately stopped at the parking garage where it emptied.

Decision time.

Sooner or later, someone would call this car to the lobby or check-in level. I didn't care which. I only knew that my best chance of finding a phone lay on those two levels. I needed sooner; I could not afford later.

I could grab the top of the door and swing out into the parking garage, then work my way up to the hotel entrance. This meant going outdoors, and that stopped me.

My failed reconnaissance in the afternoon had been on foot in downtown Chicago, a city living up to its nickname with winds gusting to twenty-five miles per hour. Braving that kind of wind in the vanished state would require my every move to be hand over hand. At no point could I reliably push off and expect to glide across open space without the possibility of being swept away.

I stayed in the elevator car. The doors closed. The car rose. I crossed mental fingers, held my breath and said a prayer.

The car stopped at the first-floor lobby.

Growing more desperate by the minute, I nearly kicked a man in the head when I hooked my hands on the top of the open door and pulled myself out of the elevator car. The move was a gamble because it sent me into the open air of the lobby without a targeted destination.

The Hyatt Regency's first-floor lobby is a huge open space. A portion of the second-floor check-in area overlooks an array of spaces containing tables, a bar, seating, and more. Hanging steel frameworks lend coziness to multiple spaces beneath a high ceiling.

I shot directly at one of those flat gray lattices. Huge beams crisscrossed above café tables and a U-shaped bar. As I approached, I saw that I was high. I rotated, pointed my feet skyward and reached. My fingertips brushed the steel frame.

"Dammit!" I cried in frustration. Faces at the bar glanced around, then returned to their conversation or their drinks.

I continued sailing, rising higher. I crossed over the lattice and then over another until I collided with the wall beside a huge sculpture of bent metal forming an impression of Lake Michigan waves—at least to my eye. I recovered to an upright attitude before hitting the wall, catching myself with my hands and feet. Without something to clutch, contact like that is nothing but a bounce. If I didn't act fast, I would merely ricochet off the wall into empty air, losing speed and drifting helplessly.

I planted flat palms on the wall and pushed sideways like someone trying to rub wax on a car hood. I added a little downward English to the shot. It worked. Although I bounced off the wall, the maneuver controlled the next vector.

I sailed into the glass barrier on the edge of the second-floor check-in area. Four block-like desks lined one wall ahead of floor-to-ceiling windows draped with vertical blinds. Each of the blocks contained two to three workstations marked by thin-screen monitors. Only two of the workstations were manned. Only one had a customer. While a Hyatt desk clerk worked his keyboard, the customer swiped her screen. Except for bobbed blonde hair, she reminded me of Leslie. Trim. Athletic. Self-assured. A messenger bag hung from one shoulder, probably containing a laptop. A black roller bag sat near her feet like an obedient labrador.

The phone in her hand caught my eye. She held it with her right hand and swiped with her left. Grabbing a phone out of someone's hand carried high risk. I pushed the idea to Plan B and heaved myself over the glass railing. A smooth glide took me across the unattended beige marble to the desk on the farthest right.

I hit the front of the desk, grabbed hold, and heaved myself over, flipping in the air over the workstation and landing behind the desk. My feet slapped the marble floor.

Perfect. Except no phone.

How do you run a hotel without phones? I could not imagine it until I heard the digital ring of a phone at one of the desks down the line. A second clerk appeared and picked up a mobile device docked to one of the workstations.

No land lines.

The workstation at my fingertips had the same docking station, but no phone. Nor could I see a house phone, once a common fixture in hotel lobbies. And I could not remember the last pay phone I'd seen.

Plan B.

The woman waiting for her room continued tapping and swiping while the clerk behind the desk worked his keyboard. Looking for something. Looking but not finding, if the mild frustration tinting his expression told the tale.

"This will only take a minute," he assured the woman.

I pushed myself sideways down the line of workstations. At the second-from-last, I gripped the end and laid out a shot that would take me directly over the patient customer's head.

At any second, the clerk would announce success, and the woman would tuck her phone in her bag and finish the check-in process.

Go!

I pulled myself forward and upward. Shooting toward her I once more cringed at the idea that she could somehow see me, full frontal, coming at her.

I passed over her head, reached down, pinched the phone, and plucked it from her fingers. She happened to be looking at the clerk at that instant. A tug and sudden emptiness in her hand startled her into a clipped shriek. I slapped the phone against my chest and felt a snap as it vanished.

The clerk looked up. She looked down.

"My phone," she said, hardly believing herself. "It's—it's gone. I had it a second ago. It—"

"Did you drop it?" The clerk leaned over the desk.

"I don't—I don't know. I—"

"Maybe it fell in a pocket...?"

She patted her pockets and searched for the phone on the floor. I sailed away, hitting the wall and once again using one hand and two feet to change the vector. Like a banked billiard shot, I bounced back to the railing overlooking the first floor.

This was no place to reappear, nor was this spot a good place to operate a phone that appeared to float in thin air—not with the phone's owner searching this immediate area.

I pushed hard against the railing and skimmed just above the floor to the wall and a door marked MEN'S. Without pockets, I had to clutch the phone between my naked thighs while I pried open a door that could have simply been pushed by someone anchored to gravity.

I slipped inside. The restroom was empty. I entered a stall and locked it.

Fwooomp!

Now visible, my nakedness startled me. Except for an episode of interrupted skinny dipping, I'd never been naked in public before.

The phone screen had gone dark. I touched it.

And bit down on a scream.

Enter Passcode

87

I pulled open the MEN'S room door so hard it slammed the wall, setting off a gunshot sound that drew eyes from every direction. Everyone looking got an eyeful. I didn't care. Clutching a handful of coarse paper towel over my genitals with one hand and the stolen phone in the other, I marched toward the woman who had stopped searching the floor for her phone thanks to the naked man in the lobby.

"I need your passcode."

She gasped. Behind her the eyes of the desk clerk grew to saucers.

"I need your passcode. The passcode. What is it!"

"That's my phone!" She took an involuntary step backward.

"Yes. I found it. And I have an emergency. I need to call 911."

"Fuck yes," the clerk said deadpan. He lifted his own phone and dialed.

"Give me my phone back," the woman demanded, still backing up as I approached.

"You don't understand. My pregnant wife is at home, in a bed, unable to move, and very bad people are breaking into my house." I held out the phone. "ENTER—YOUR—PASSCODE!"

She stared at my hand with a glance or two spared for the rest of the package.

"Please," I begged. "She's alone. She can't move."

I thought she might scream, but instead, using both hands, one to steady, one to touch, she tapped the screen four times. The phone opened.

"Thank you." I stepped back and hit the telephone icon on the screen, counting off the seconds before some oversized and underpaid security guard tackled me from behind. I brought up the keypad and dialed Andy's number.

"Pick up pick up pick up pick up *please*."

It rang until it didn't. *You've reached Detective Andrea Stewart. Leave a message.*

I waited for the beep. Andy always checks voicemail.

"Dee! Get out! Hide! They're in Essex and they're coming for you! I'm calling Tom!"

I hit the red button and glanced at my surroundings. Here he came. Security. Big, as predicted. Uniformed. Red-faced and ready to flatten me.

I turned to the woman who continued staring at me, or at least parts of me. I held up the phone and spoke calmy and clearly. "I swear on my unborn child I will return this to you."

"Uh…okay…"

I dropped the paper towel and bolted. My feet slapped the marble. My parts did what such things do at a full gallop. I felt a million eyes on my skin. I aimed for the glass railing at the edge of the check-in area. The security guard altered his track and broke into a run to intercept. I was fast. He was clumsy and heavy. Still, geometry made the race close. I hit the railing before he hit me. Burdened with the phone and no pockets, I used one hand to grab the railing.

I leaped over. My grip brought me around and down. Before full gravity could pull me down at a speed that would injure me—

FWOOOMP!

—I snapped out of sight. Gravity lost the battle. I dropped to the first floor at a reasonable rate, landing on both feet.

FWOOOMP!

I reappeared, drawing startled gasps from the dozen or so guests at the bar and at the café tables. I didn't give them time to look. I ran for the doors that opened on the arrival and departure lanes. A uniformed bellman automatically opened the doors for me, did a double take, and uttered a few words as I passed.

The next cab in line had the rear door open as a well-dressed couple prepared to board. I leaped past them, jumped inside and slammed the door after me.

"What the—?"

"DRIVE!"

"Get outta my fucking cab!" The driver twisted in his seat, glaring at the naked man in the back. I tapped the phone screen to keep it active.

"An extra hundred if you pull away now. NOW!" The bellman at the hotel door made no move to be a hero. The couple whose cab I had stolen stopped and gawked. Inside, the security guard hit the stairs in pursuit.

"Fuck no! Get out!"

"Two hundred!"

He hesitated. "What exactly do you plan to pay me with?"

I rattled off sixteen digits and an expiration date. He stared. "Go! I memorized the goddamned card, so DRIVE!"

The security guard hauled his weight down the stairs, hit bottom, and broke into a run, yelling at the bellman to *Stop that sonofabitch!*

"Okay," the driver turned back to his steering wheel, "but just don't get the idea that I never seen this before. Happens all the time."

He threw the car in gear.

I tapped the phone call icon.

88

"9 11, what is your emergency?"

"Someone is on their way to kill my wife. I need you to connect me with the City of Essex Police Department, Chief Tom Ceeves. Right now!"

"What is your location, sir?"

"My location doesn't matter. Connect me to the City of Essex PD RIGHT NOW!"

"Sir, there is no City of Essex in the Chicago area. What is the nature of the emergency?"

I hung up.

"Dude, is that real?" the driver asked. "And secondly, where are we going?"

"Palwaukee Airport. And shut up."

I dialed again. The direct line to Andy's office. With her on leave, I prayed someone else would pick up.

It rang.

"City of Essex Police Department, how can I help you?"

The voice belonged to—

"Alicia!" I remembered her name, the young dispatcher. It surprised me to hear her voice during an evening shift. Nights belonged to the senior dispatcher, Mae Earnhardt. "This is Will Stewart."

"Oh, hi Mr. Stewart, how's Detec—"

"In deep trouble. I need you to send every active unit to my house right now. Tell them to make as much noise as possible. Some very bad, very well-armed people are on their way to kill my wife. Do it now."

"Uh—yes, sir!"

"And get the Chief out to my house!"

"Yes, sir!"

The line went quiet. I wasn't sure if she put me on hold. I waited. Seconds turned into minutes. My heart hammered in my chest.

This took too long. I jerked the phone away from my ear and ended the call. I tapped Andy's number again.

"Hello?" Her voice. *Thank God in Heaven*, her voice.

"Dee! Why didn't you pick up?"

"Whose phone is this? I didn't recognize the number."

"Later. The team that hit Caroline Gaffney is coming for you. They're in position and coming. I already called dispatch. She's sending everybody to you, loud with lights. You need to lock up and lay low."

"This is real?"

"This is real. Go."

She ended the call.

<h1 style="text-align:center">89</h1>

"Dude, are you kidding me?" the driver asked. His English was excellent with a slight accent. The ID mounted under Plexiglas said his name was Mohammad al Rashid. The eyes glancing at me in the mirror were dark brown verging on black.

"Just get me to Palwaukee Airport. Fast. Speed if you can, but don't stop. Don't stop for anybody. Not the cops. Anybody." I looked through the rear window at the traffic. Headlights jockeyed for position in the busy lanes behind us. They could have been couples out dating or teams from Gallica that had witnessed the bizarre scene in the hotel lobby. There was no way to tell. I leaned closer to the divider. "There's a damned good chance the people I'm talking about are coming after me, too. They were at the hotel."

The driver stomped on the gas and ran a yellow, then red, light.

"Follow me now, assholes!" he shouted at his mirror.

I dialed a new number. It rang, then went to voicemail. I didn't bother leaving a message. Pidge never listens to her voicemail. I tapped out a text.

Pick up. It's Will. I added four digits to the message, then hit send, then dialed again. The stolen phone was an iPhone like mine, but the woman had personalized it with some kind of weird cartoon motif. It annoyed me. The phone rang.

"Come on, Pidge. Pick up." More rings.

"What the fuck?"

"I need you to come and get me. Right now. Grab anything that has gas and come and get me. Fast."

"Where?"

"Palwaukee. Pull up to Signature but don't shut down, don't stop."

"Is that code for real?"

"Real. The people who shot Andy are coming back for another try."

"Jesus, Will! Call the—!"

"I already did. God willing, they're already there. I need to get there, too, and the Navajo is down. Come and get me. Signature at Palwaukee. Hurry."

"See you when I get there."

She ended the call.

I sat shaken, bare skin against bare leather with nothing in my hands but the phone and my terrified thoughts.

I dialed Andy again.

No answer.

90

Hell is a waiting room.

Hell is sitting naked in a cab on a thirty-seven-minute drive through Chicago traffic with a madman at the wheel with no idea if Andy lived or died at the hands of the Gallica team.

Hell is gripping a section of security fence at Palwaukee Airport at night with a phone that locked because you forgot to keep tapping the screen to prevent it from locking and no passcode to get back in.

Hell is what your imagination hands you in those moments.

PIDGE PULLED up in the E-55 Baron that Earl keeps on hand for small charter runs. I was glad she chose the airplane. It's a hotrod thanks to Beechcraft mounting the -58 model's bigger engines on the -55 model. She taxied onto the ramp, selected a corner away from the Signature building, and used differential engine power to swing the airplane into position to depart as quickly as she had arrived. She let the engines run.

I had no choice. The cabin door for the E-55 opens over the right wing. With the spinning prop and engine several feet away, there was no way for me to glide over the wing in the vanished state. The propwash would have blown me into the next county.

Fwooomp!

I reappeared beside the Signature Aviation Services FBO building and ran. Every twig and bit of gravel between the fence and the ramp bit into my bare feet. The ramp was much better, but I picked up painful bits all the way to the rear of the Baron's right wing. I hopped on the step and stretched my stride to avoid planting my foot and weight on the flap.

I popped the door latch and dropped into the seat beside Pidge. I slammed the door and latched it.

Pidge looked over my naked body. I expected the worst. Beating her to the punch, I reached across her and grabbed the aircraft checklist which I spread across my lap.

"Shut up. Go. Get us out of here." I pulled on a headset.

I thought she might make a joke or call for a clearance but instead she sat on her seat cushion and stared at me. I wasn't in the mood for her jokes. I turned to snap at her and bit my tongue.

She wore pain on her face. Deep and dark.

"What?" I asked as soon as the earphones settled, and I could hear her through the intercom. "What is it?"

"It's—Rosemary II texted me from your place."

"How did she…?"

"Don't be stupid. Everybody knows by now. Even Earl. You know how that goes." Pidge held up her phone. "It's—it's not good."

I read the words.

"Oh Christ, no."

91

Andy and I have discussed this. If either one of us ever calls and declares an emergency, immediate action follows with no questions asked. Act first. Sort it out later.

At the end of my clipped call to her, she stared at the phone for a moment, not in disbelief. She stared just long enough to organize her thoughts.

"It's your turn," Holly reminded her. The hand she would lay down in the interrupted game of Five Card Draw was a good one. When Andy didn't reply, Holly looked up from her cards. "What is it?"

"That was Will. Holly, please go and lock the back door. Then check the porch door." She looked at Margie, the nurse. A woman in her early twenties had confessed that this was her first nursing job—which probably accounted for her being assigned the long night shift. She enjoyed it, she said. Especially the company in this assignment. She developed an instant rapport with Andy, who told Margie she was pretty in a classic movie sense. A handsome face with styled hair that would look good in a picture with Humphrey Bogart or John Wayne.

The sudden shift to stark seriousness alerted Margie. "Is everything okay?"

"Margie, listen. Something bad is about to happen. The people who did this to me are coming back."

"What people?"

"The people that shot me." Margie's eyes flared. Andy knew when shock had a value and how to use it. "Listen carefully to me and do as I say. I want you to go upstairs—listen to me!" She saw Margie's attention shift to the bed, to her patient, driven by her instinct to protect her patient. "You said you wanted to work in the ER someday. Well, this is an emergency. We need to think and act on our feet, okay? Do you understand me?"

She nodded.

"I want you to go upstairs. Go to the last bedroom on the left. Get in the closet. There's a pile of linens in there. Pull as much of it over you as you can and be still."

"No. I can't leave you."

"Yes. You can. If you don't take care of yourself, you can't take care of me. People are coming. Bad people. I will need you when this is over."

"What about you?"

"I'm a cop. I'll be fine. Now, GO!"

"Come with me," Margie said. "I can help you up the stairs."

"They'll search until they find me. If I'm here, they won't search. Go."

Margie moved for the stairs. Holly returned.

"I locked the porch door."

"Holly, go in the dining room and open the closet door. Go."

Holly hurried to the adjacent dining room. Andy heard the door open.

"Whoa," Holly declared.

"Put the fingers of your right hand on the four finger slots on the gun safe and push the buttons I tell you to push."

"Okay."

Andy touched her belly and closed her eyes.

"Pinky."

She heard a beep.

"Index."

"Which one is that?"

"Number one."

Beep.

"Number three."

Beep.

"Fuck you finger."

Beep.

"And now the index—er—number one again."

Beep. Click. The gun safe lock released.

"Open it, Holly. Bring me the handgun second from the left on the top shelf."

"The Beretta M.92?"

Andy broke a weak smile. "Yeah. That one. There's a magazine in the gun and a round in the chamber, so be careful. There's also a magazine beside it. Bring that, too."

Holly took too long. Andy asked, "Are you finding everything?"

"Is this a Remington Fieldmaster 12-gauge?"

"Yes, Holly, but I can't use that. Just bring me the Beretta."

Holly hurried back to Andy carrying the handgun, carefully pointing the barrel at the floor. She handed Andy the weapon and the extra magazine.

"My grampa had a Fieldmaster," Holly said.

"Run back and get my vest. My ballistic vest. It's on the lower shelf."

Holly ran the errand and handed Andy the slab-like black vest. Andy positioned it over the baby bump and tried to press it all around our child. She reconsidered. No one would be shooting at her from the ceiling. She used the bed's power control and raised her feet and knees until they were almost level with her eyes, then shifted the vest to under her bottom. She considered the line of fire. A bullet entering from the front of the house would hit two layers of vest beneath her thighs.

Please God let it not hit our child.

"Holly, now listen. You heard what I told Margie. I want you to do the same. Go upstairs and hide."

Holly shook her head. "I'm staying with you."

"No," Andy said sharply. "I can't have you here. I can't have you in the line of fire. The police are coming. I can't have you mistaken for an intruder. I can't be worried about you. Go upstairs."

Andy had no time to argue against the stubborn resolve forming on Holly's face.

The lights went out.

"They killed the power. They're close," Andy whispered. *"Holly, do as I tell you. Go upstairs and hide!"*

To Andy's relief, the black shape that had been Holly at Andy's bedside melted away.

One more task. Andy held down the buttons on her phone until the Slide To Power Off control appeared. She swiped and watched the phone screen go black, then slid the phone under her pillows.

I can't take your call now, love, she thought. *And I can't have that thing lighting up and making noise.*

Andy closed her eyes. She slipped the Beretta M.92 semiautomatic handgun under the blanket with her right hand. With her left, she slid the extra magazine under her left butt cheek.

Breathe in. Count four. Breathe out.

Repeat.

She heard a door latch snap. It came from the dining room. Or was it the kitchen? Were they inside already? She held her eyes tightly closed and listened. The sound did not repeat. No new sounds joined it. The house lay still and silent.

Breathe in. Count four. Breathe out.

She opened her eyes and hoped that the few minutes of rest she'd given them improved her night vision. Around the room, windows took shape. Light from a full moon peeking from behind a partly cloudy sky gave the yard a gray tone broken by ebony shapes and shadows. Moonlight sloped into the house and cast geometric shapes on the floor.

Andy gripped the Beretta and thumbed off the safety. She slipped her finger into the trigger guard and waited. Her hand wanted to shake. She willed it into submission. She gritted her teeth and repeated the breathing exercise.

She waited.

Time ticked by. She imagined seconds like water dripping in a metal downspout after a rain. Silence. Then, drip. Silence. Drip.

Maybe they wouldn't come, she allowed herself to wish. Then she scolded herself for wishing for the best. The best never happens. Plan for the worst. That's what happens. Always the worst.

What's the worst that can happen?

She remembered asking Will that fraught question when she argued for pursuing Lydia's concerns about her friend's daughter.

"*I guess we know,*" Andy whispered to herself, the words barely surpassing the sound of her own breath.

Will said he called Tom. If so, they're coming. Loud and with lights. The right call. Make all the noise in the world, she thought, assessing the tactical picture. Don't sneak up on well-armed professionals who are willing to kill. Make noise. Drive them away. You're not going to make any arrests tonight. Not these people. Come at them like a circus parade and make them disappear.

Any minute now.

Any minute now she would hear the wail and warble of the east side night patrol. They would be fastest to respond. Denny White or Jean Harris. Good officers, both. One or the other would come like gangbusters and the people Will warned her about would take off. That would be best. No shooting. No firefight. *Just go like you were never here, for the love of God.*

Darkness moved across the front porch window.

Someone tested the knob. Locked. Good girl, Holly.

Andy lowered her eyes. She knew her night vision improved in the periphery. She stared at her unborn child and registered movement at the fringes.

There. Motion. Slow. Slow doesn't catch the eye. *These guys are pros.* The thought sent ice down her spine.

B-BANG! Not gunfire. A sharp hammer blow. Was it one or two? From the front or back? Or both? Something metallic clattered to the porch floor.

They punched the lock. Probably an air piston device built to knock deadbolt locks out of wooden doors.

Tactics changed. The signature shriek of the porch screen door opening confirmed that stealth had been discarded. The intruder didn't care if she heard him coming. He knew he faced a soft target. An immobile target.

She slid the Beretta out from under the covers but held it below the sight line of the intruder. Darkness had been his play, a sign that the intruder employed night vision equipment. He would see the gun if she held it high. Keeping the muzzle below the line of the bent mattress, she aimed at the French doors.

Human-shaped blackness crossed through the muntin bars on the French doors. She heard the knob turn. The latch release. The door swung. She steadied her aim. The first shots would go through the mattress and couldn't be relied on to fly true. She would empty the clip after raising the weapon clear of the mattress.

She closed the space between her finger and the trigger.

"Drop it." The voice came from a second intruder in the dining room—as black as the void from which it rose.

There are two!

"I said, drop—"

BANG!

Light and sound exploded. Caught in the flash for only an instant, a man in the dining room stood with both hands gripping a weapon aimed at Andy. Frozen in light for a split second, the right side of his head turned to mist.

BANG-BANG!

Double muzzle flashes overwhelmed Andy's night vision for the second time in as many seconds. These came from the French doors and for a horrifying instant Andy expected bullets to penetrate her bed. But the flashes exposed the intruder at the French doors. He aimed at the dining room.

At his own man? She barely had time to consider her luck before muscle memory and training brought the Beretta up and her trigger finger took over.

She aimed high. At the head. She wasn't the only one with a vest. She counted seven shots before freezing her trigger finger.

Against deafening silence, she heard the thump of bodies dropping to the hardwood floor.

Two intruders down.

Two?

It hit Andy. The latch click she heard just after the lights went out. It wasn't someone entering. It had been the gun safe closet.

"Holly? Holly, are you there?"

"I'm here."

Is this a Remington Fieldmaster 12-gauge?

"Was that you? Did you fire?"

From the black of the dining room, deeper now that her night vision had been ruined by flashes and afterimages, Holly replied.

"My grampa taught me."

"Jesus, Holly."

"Yeah."

She sounded winded. Small wonder. Then Andy remembered the double-tap shot by the intruder at the French doors.

"Holly are you okay?"

"I think…"

The double-tap. Holly shot first. Then two flashes. Two shots. Oh, no…

"Holly? Holly, did he shoot you? Are you bleeding?"

Holly said nothing at first, then weakly: "I liked that…that part…about being pregnant."

She's in shock.

"What part?" Andy asked, desperate to sustain her attention.

"No bleeding. No visits from the Red Baron. Getting my period. Mine is always on the full moon, like tonight. I get bad cramps."

"Holly? Holly, are you bleeding?" No answer. "Just stay where you are. Don't move. Help is coming."

It could have been the ringing in her ears, but Andy thought she heard the first faint shriek of a police siren in the distance. She reached down for the phone and squeezed the button to bring it to life, then in a near panic shoved it back under the pillow.

Overwatch. The Gaffney shooter.

"Holly, stay still. Don't move," Andy whispered.

"Okay." She sounded clearheaded, but weak. Compliant. She had to be in shock. Hiding in a closet and then blasting half of a man's head from his body might have that effect. So would being hit by a bullet.

Andy switched the Beretta from her right hand to her left. She adjusted the ballistic vest, aligning it with the porch windows. Hunkering down as far as possible, she stretched her left hand over the side of the bed.

"*Holly,*" she whispered, "*I'm going to fire again. There might be one more out there. Be ready.*"

"*Okay,*" Holly whispered. She sounded better.

Andy awkwardly held the Beretta with her thumb in the trigger guard. She didn't aim. She pointed.

She fired. Twice. Then she jerked her hand back.

Metal and glass exploded beside the bed. Hammer blows hit the medical monitor and shattered it. Three shots. Shards of glass flew at Andy. She covered her head and her eyes and instinctively, her belly.

Sniper. Overwatch. In the corn field across the road.

During the first round of firing, Andy's muzzle flashes were blocked by the intruder that came through the porch. Now, in the clear, the third man fired at center mass where the muzzle flashes originated.

The shots she fired inside the house created close-strike thunder. The shots fired outside had been silent. Suppressed. She froze, fearing he might shift his aim. If he had thermal imaging, if he had infrared…

Uneasy silence and acrid gun smoke filled the air.

Overwatch is overwatch, Andy told herself. *He won't come in. His team is down. As soon as he hears sirens, he'll book it.*"

"What would she think?" Holly's full voice broke the silence.

"*Hush, Holly!*" Andy cringed in the darkness.

"*What would she think?*" Holly repeated using an obedient whisper.

"*Who?*"

"*The lady in the magazine with all the money. What would she think of me? I couldn't even buy my baby a candy cane at Christmas. What would someone like that think of me?*"

"*She wouldn't. She doesn't. Hush, Holly. Be still.*"

Andy held her breath and listened.

Holly sighed loudly.

"*She would hate me. I think. It's all she can do…because…*"

Andy heard an engine rev. Tires bit gravel. A car raced away in the night as the sound of sirens grew clearer. In another moment, winking red and blue painted the moonlit landscape. She breathed again. Holly had gone silent.

"*Because?*" Andy prompted her.

"*Because I am.*"

92

———

If I hadn't been nearly catatonic with fear and rage and horror, I would
have noticed that Pidge was still doing almost 200 knots a mile out on
final for landing on Runway 31 at Essex County Airport, yet she deftly bled
off the speed, dropped the landing gear and flaps, and slipped the wheels
onto the surface with a tender touch. She left the brakes alone and rolled the
length of the runway, taking the last turn onto the ramp and shutting down
on the roll. I popped the door open and climbed onto the wing before she
came to a stop.

"Call me when you can," she shouted after me when I dropped to the
asphalt and sprinted for the Foundation hangar.

Taking only enough time to jump into a pair of greasy coveralls I keep in
the hangar utility cabinet, I burst out of the hangar and into my car.

It's bad. Hurry.

Rosemary II's text to Pidge said more. Not a lot more. But enough.

I didn't worry about speeding. There was no chance of getting caught.
Every police and sheriff's unit in the county was at my house.

I skidded into the driveway and onto the lawn. The car had hardly
stopped before I leaped from the driver's door and raced to the porch,
passing a cluster of cops and deputy sheriffs who knew better than to try and
stop me.

I burst into the living room where Tom Ceeves and Rosemary II stood
beside Andy's bed. There were others there. Uniforms. People. Equipment.
A blur.

All I saw was Andy.

She lay where I last saw her. Rosemary II held Andy's hands. Andy spoke to Tom. Focused. Determined. Reciting facts in sequence. She wore her professional face; one I'd seen her wear when taking statements or making reports. She was in cop mode, unflappable, precise. I saw why. Bodies covered by silver blankets littered my home. Officers took photographs and stepped around the bodies and puddles of blood.

From under one of the silver blankets in the dining room, a small hand extended. A woman's hand. Andy's shotgun lay nearby. A braided strand of bracelet circled the wrist. Something made by a child. I knew which child.

It's bad. Hurry.

Andy occupied the eye of the storm, calm, doing the duty embedded in every bone in her body.

Until she took one look at me.

Her eyes filled. Her lips quivered. She fought the tidal wave, but it came.

I felt my own eyes flood with tears.

I pushed past anything and everyone and found a way to wrap my wife in my arms. She shook against my grip. Between broken sobs she whispered a single word.

"Holly."

93

Most of the Fire Department showed up. Many of them rushed to help wearing civilian clothes. One of the EMTs, Jeanie Halder, erected a curtain around Andy's bed. She produced a folding chair for me to sit on. Rosemary II shifted into mother mode and tried to tidy up until Tom snapped at her not to pick up shell casings. He instantly apologized for his tone and politely asked her to see about some coffee in the kitchen. Undaunted, she scooped a clutter of playing cards from the floor before slipping out of sight.

Andy and I held each other. Then held hands. We did not speak. Voices in the room dropped to inaudible levels. We heard heavy plastic unfold and spread out, thumps and thuds, and whispered commands as bodies were lifted and removed. All three of them.

A short time later, Tom Ceeves leaned in between the temporary curtain halves and pointed a finger at me.

"A word?"

Andy nodded her blessing. I slipped out. Tom led me through the kitchen and into the mudroom at the back door, which took us out of the line of sight that included the dining room where a Jackson Pollock painting of blood and brains adorned one wall.

"She tell you what happened?"

"Not so much."

Tom shuffled his feet and studied the floor. "Andrea got your warning. Good on you for that. She had Holly fetch her weapon from the gun safe. She sent Margie upstairs to hide, and Holly, too, but Holly went into the gun safe closet. It looks like the two men came in simultaneously. Andrea thought there was only one. The second got the drop on her. Holly popped out with the shotgun and got Prick Number Two. When Holly fired, Prick Number One fired at Holly—so Andrea took him out but not before he fired two shots. One missed. One clipped Holly. Femoral artery.”

“Jesus.”

Tom huffed a hard breath. “Holly was gone in a couple minutes. It was dark. Andrea didn’t know. Holly wouldn’t tell her. And even if Andrea knew, and she could have gotten to her…” He shook his head. “There’s nothing—” He could not finish the sentence.

I sniffled loudly.

Tom shook it off and continued. “We got IDs off the dead guys. They’re both—”

“Benjamin Everly.”

Tom eyed me. “Like that guy in Three Lakes. Gonna explain that?”

I told him who they worked for. There was no doubt in my mind at this point. The certainty turned wheels in my head.

At that moment, and for the last time in my life, I thought about Hollis.

Tom said. “There was a third guy. Andrea said he was on overwatch. Hiding in the corn field across the road with a long gun and a scope. She drew his fire before he took off.”

“She told me that part.”

“Any idea who that might be?”

He waited.

I said nothing.

“Come on, Will. You know it doesn’t work that way. Your wife doesn’t work that way.”

“Andy? Maybe not. Are we done here?” I didn’t mean for anger to infect my tone. Tom let it pass.

“Not quite. I just got a call from Earl Jackson. He’s out at the airport. He says he’s got something you need to see. He knows what happened here but he insists. I pushed, but he doubled down. Said you’d be able to tell me what it meant after you saw it, whatever *it* is.”

“Now?”

“He sounded pissed.”

“He always sounds pissed.”

“Urgent pissed, then.”

94

Andy and I kissed. Long, slow, less out of passion, more out of a need to grasp and cling to the life on each side of our lips. When we parted, I stole a moment and sank into her gold-flecked green eyes. How they could be so brilliant yet colored with such sadness, I had no idea. Such beauty and such darkness.

"Are you gonna be okay?" I asked.

"I don't want to be okay," she replied. "I don't want to be fine. I don't want to be locked up in this bed. I don't want to be brokenhearted. *I don't want to feel what I'm feeling right now.*"

"Dee, I—"

"No. You listen to me. *I don't, not for one second, want you to think that I'm going to give you some speech about law and justice. Do you understand me?*" Her lip quivered. She fought emotions as potent as acid. "*Holly did not deserve this. Of all the people on the earth—not Holly.*"

I could only nod. If I spoke, something would have broken. Andy put her hand at the back of my head and pulled me against her shoulder.

"*This was not your fault,*" she whispered.

"*This was not your fault,*" I whispered back. "I'll stay with you, if that's what you want."

"No. You heard what Earl said."

Get your ass out here. I had used Andy's phone to call him. His voice carried, even if the audio wasn't on speaker.

"Go," she said. "Hurry back."

95

I took just enough time to change clothes and share one more lingering kiss with Andy despite Margie hovering over her trying not to cry as she sorted damaged monitor cords and sensor leads and doted over her patient. I broke out of the house and hurried across the lawn. The EMTs loaded two bodies in the rescue squad. A smaller ambulance had arrived. The bodies loaded into the boxy rescue squad were handled like cargo, like evidence. The body loaded into the ambulance might have still been delicate crystal. Most of the EMTs knew or knew of Holly.

I locked my teeth and pushed hard against the tight twist of emotions threatening to choke me.

Wheeling around on the lawn, I took off again, ignoring the speed limit despite the cluster of police and sheriff's cars sitting in front of my house.

PIDGE STOPPED me at the FBO office door.

"How's Andy?"

"Not hurt."

"I know that. But *how is she?*"

I had no idea what to say.

Pidge reached up and placed her hands on my cheeks. For a horrifying moment I thought she meant to kiss me. Instead, she squinted into my eyes. "Can you see straight?"

"Straight enough."

"Good. He's got 'em in the shop."

She led me past the darkened office, down a hallway, through the part of the shop cluttered with power tools—the drill press, the band saw, and others specific to aircraft repair. We hooked right and went through a door that opened on a hangar-sized aircraft workshop. Two airplanes in varying stages of disassembly occupied opposite corners of the shop, undergoing either annual or 100-hour inspections.

The scene staged on the glossy concrete floor didn't surprise me.

Two men in white shirts and black ties occupied a pair of office chairs in the center of the shop floor. Pilot's epaulets decorated their shirt shoulders, one with four stripes, one with three. Both men wore creased black dress pants and nicely shined shoes. One looked younger than me, maybe in his late twenties, with sandy brown hair and a high school jock's face. The other, the captain, had some years in the lines of his face and some hours in his logbook. Gray at the temples, but still looking fit, he presented a movie idol look from the days when every leading man was in his fifties and his love interest barely cracked thirty. His eyes were sharp. They took rapid measure of me when I entered. I caught a flash of recognition—or thought I did. If so, he suppressed it quickly.

Earl paced the floor, a bowlegged specter that would have inspired me to run. I wondered why these two sat patiently, until I saw that their hands had been zip tied to the chairs on which they sat.

Oh, Jesus, I thought. The news about Holly must have blown the lid off of Earl's standard simmering rage.

The captain wasted no time confirming my fears.

"I don't know who you are, but if you're not here to get us outta these restraints and away from this lunatic, then you just signed on to join the defense in one motherfucking massive lawsuit not to mention criminal charges for—."

"Shuddup," Earl growled.

I asked Pidge, "What did they fly here in?"

"Phenom. It's out on the ramp."

Any worry I had about wrongful detention melted quickly.

I stopped in front of the two men. To the captain, I asked, "Did you drop off three passengers?"

"None of your goddamned business."

"It was two," the first officer said.

"Shut your mouth," the captain warned.

"Go fuck yourself," the kid replied. "It was two guys and whatever they got up to, I got no part in it. I'm just filling a seat, man. I got a slot with Endeavor and my class starts in three weeks. I really don't need this shit."

"Two men?" I asked.

"Affirmative."

I looked at Pidge. "Did they rent a car?"

"Nope," she said. "Got picked up by someone. This was just before I left for the day, and before you called me."

"Was some guy," Earl muttered. "Couldn't see him real good, but it was a guy."

"Your passengers. Did you get any names?" I asked the kid.

"Only what's on the manifest. Ertley or Evans or something like that. What's this about? Because, like I said, I just signed on to fill right seats these last few months. This asshole wouldn't even let me take a leg."

"Fuck you," the captain muttered. "I got connections at Delta. You can kiss your career goodbye."

Earl leaned down until the breath that carried his words hit the captain in the face. "I got connections at Delta, too, shithead. People you only dream of knowing. Those fellas you delivered here tonight committed murder. It sounds to me like this kid knew nothing about it, but you're startin' to give off some stink."

The man grew defiant. "Back off! I don't know anything about any murder. I don't know who our passengers were other than what was on the manifest."

"Brothers, I think," the copilot added. "Same last name."

"Look," the captain switched to a solicitous tone. "Let's just dial it down here. How about you cut us loose and we call it a day. No harm. No foul."

"Not so fast." I stopped to think.

"And stop treating the meat in the right seat like shit," Earl growled. "I had my fill of martinets like you in my career." Earl sent a supportive nod in the direction of the first officer, but I think it only scared him.

"Your airplane is registered to a law firm," I said to the captain.

"So?"

"Is that all you do? Fly lawyers around?"

The captain didn't answer.

"Law firm," the kid chuckled. "What bullshit. Last week I picked up a hop in one of the G700s. That Phenom may be registered to some law firm in Rochester, but the crews circulate in and out of a huge flight department. They promised me G time when they signed me on. Said I'd get time in most of the aircraft."

"Bigger flight department?" I turned to the captain. "Time to decide how much of a fall you want to take for accessory to murder. Who?"

"I got nothing to do with murder." The captain looked past Earl at me. He put on a friendly face. "You look like a pilot. Am I right?"

"All day long."

"Then you know the game. You hire on. You fly where they tell you. You live by a phone with a packed bag at the door. If you're lucky you only have one divorce under your belt, right?"

"Who?"

"I just want to establish that I'm answering your questions from a position of—"

"It's Guardian Worldwide," the kid blurted. "I don't care what the registration says, they're the ones who operate the Phenom out of Rochester. They have a fleet hangar in Westchester, New York. The Phenom flies in and out of Westchester all the time. The crews are all under Guardian. That's what my last paycheck said. I don't even know anything about a law firm, for chrissakes! Those guys we brought in tonight sure as hell weren't lawyers. We picked them up at Midway in Chicago."

"They carry any equipment? Any gear?" I asked.

"Just overnight bags."

"What about fishing or hunting equipment?"

He shook his head.

The captain glanced warily at Earl, then at me. "Okay? This is me cooperating, okay? Nobody wants to escalate this to false imprisonment and potential civil action. You get what I'm saying? Maybe you should cut these loose and we all take a breath here."

"Who's Guardian Worldwide? Who is it really?"

"Man, you don't know?" The kid blinked, mildly astonished. "Christ, that's Bin Foss. If he's not the richest guy on the planet, he's a close second to Musk."

I stepped back and looked at Earl.

"I gotta make a call."

"You calling Tom?" Earl asked. "Because I can probably get more outta this four-stripe asshat. Hand him over to the cops and he'll likely clam up."

"Not calling Tom. Not yet."

"Good. Use my office. These guys ain't going anywhere."

96

I used a shop rag to hold Earl's greasy phone to my ear.

"Can you reach out to Lieutenant Greg LeMore and ask him to call Will Stewart at Essex County Air Service. It's urgent. Emergency. Here's the number."

The Milwaukee Police Department dispatcher said yes and read the number back to me.

"As soon as possible. I'm waiting by the phone."

I remained standing in Earl's office. Nothing on the planet would induce me to sit in his office chair. He probably had it rigged to tip backward and throw intruders the hell out.

Pidge appeared at the door. "You gonna bring me up to speed on this? Like…are we maybe blasting off somewhere tonight?"

"Maybe," I allowed. "I think I'm starting to see the picture here, but I want some information. And if we blast off tonight, we're doing it in style."

She lifted her eyebrows. "Jet style?"

I gave a Maybe-Yes shrug, prompting the shadow of a smile.

Earl's phone rang.

"This is Will."

"What's up, man?" I recognized Greg LeMore's voice.

"Were you able to do a deeper dive on that girl found in the lake?"

"No pun intended."

"Did you happen to look at that camp we talked about? Up on that island in the Straits of Mackinac?"

"That part? No. Not yet. Why?"

"Remember something Andy said? How…we need to connect the dots, from the other direction. How this started with a mother looking for her missing daughter and the thread now goes through the intentional homicide in Three Lakes and in New York. She said the line starts at the other end. Not with the daughter."

"I remember."

"Two things, and then I need to ask you to look for something."

"Me? What about your FBI pal?"

"I got a bad feeling she's on a cargo plane to Anchorage right now."

"Ouch. What's the ask?"

"First…" I told him how Andy discovered that an actor posed as Baxter Gaffney at Penn State.

"That's fucked up," LeMore said. He asked for the name. I told him to call Andy.

"Now here's part two." I brought him up to speed on the tortured path this night had taken. The part about Holly came out hard. On the other end of the line, LeMore said only three words.

"Mother of God."

"Greg, I'm at the airport. The pilots that brought in the hitters are here. I don't think they're in the know. For one thing, it wouldn't make tactical sense. But we just found out who owns the jet they flew in on."

"Who?"

"I'm going to give you the company name and I want you to see if you can find any connection to Saint Martin Academy in Upper Michigan. It's that camp we mentioned. Ready?"

"Hit me."

"Guardian Worldwide."

"Fucking Foss? Seriously?" Then, as the next thought hit him, Greg said, "Oh, my God. Chaney Foss was on the magazine."

"Find out if Foss owns or has anything to do with Saint Martin Academy —which is where the mother thought her daughter Baxter was when she disappeared."

"Where are you going with this?"

"We talked to a boat captain up there." I didn't mention the visit to the island or Hollis. "He said there were rumors of parties at the camp. Boys from the town who got busy with girls from the camp. But he also said there were visitors."

"You're thinking trafficking?"

"I don't know what I'm thinking. Can you look into it and call me? I

don't have a phone with me, so call this number when you have something."
I recited Pidge's cell number. She blinked at me.

"*I can't believe you actually know my number*," she muttered.

"Got it," Greg said. "You do know your wife hates coincidences, right?"

"She thinks unicorns are more probable. Gotta go," I said. I dropped the handset on the old touch-tone phone on Earl's desk, tossed the rag, and wiped my hands on my pants just because.

Pidge blocked the exit.

"What?"

"A. You're not fucking taking another step without me. And B. What the fuck is going on?"

"I have no idea."

97

"Last chance," I said, clicking my heels across the concrete of the hangar floor. "Option A, I leave you in his hands." I gestured at Earl. "This is a small town. Everybody knows everybody. My wife was the intended victim and he adores her so this is not his happy face." As if they had any doubt. "She's also a cop, so if you expect protection from the cops, you're delusional. This guy knows the chief of police, so he knows all the places the chief won't look for bodies."

The captain stared. The kid blurted, "You have my full cooperation."

"What's Option B?" the captain asked.

"Depends," I said. "Bindle Foss. Ever fly him around?"

"Nah," the kid answered quickly. "He gets the senior guys. His regulars."

"Where is he tonight?"

"Europe," the captain answered.

"No, he isn't," his copilot said.

"Jesus, you stupid…" the captain shook his head helplessly.

"Where is he tonight?" I repeated to the kid.

"He *was* in Europe on one of the 700s. He got back yesterday. Unless he went somewhere, he'd be at home, I guess."

"What home?"

"I dunno. Some mega-mansion up on the Hudson."

The captain, clearly unhappy with the loose lips of his former copilot, repeated his question, "What's Option B??

I glanced at Earl, then at Pidge. I saw no objections.

"We gas up that Phenom and take it back to New York."

"Rochester?"

"Westchester."

The captain looked uneasy. "Look, I gotta take that jet back to Rochester. It has to be—"

"You'll be lucky if it isn't impounded by the local police," I said.

"Easy there," he said. "I might have gotten off on the wrong foot with you. I mean, you weren't exactly—"

"Friendly?" Earl growled through gritted teeth.

"Come on. You know how it is. You serve the client. The customer. The boss. Whoever. My instinct was to protect my passengers and their privacy, but I didn't know anything about them or what they were up to. You have my word."

"Noted." I turned to Pidge. "Cut this kid loose and go with him and gas up the jet. Kid, you get to fly the leg. She's your copilot."

"Wait! What about me?" the captain protested.

"You get to ride in coach. I'll be back in an hour. Be ready to go."

98

Before I left, I asked Earl not to use any power tools on the jet captain. Earl said he could not commit.

For the second time tonight, I broke every speed limit when I raced from the airport to my home. The rescue squad and ambulance were gone, along with the cars from the Sheriff's Department. Several Essex PD units remained parked beside the road and in the driveway. Tom's personal SUV sat near the back steps. A van I didn't recognize trailed hoses from its interior across the lawn and into my porch. I found out why when I arrived inside and saw two people in hazmat suits wiping the wood floors, the walls, the furniture. The spray of blood and brain on the pockmarked dining room wall was gone; so were the curtains.

Chief Ceeves supervised. The massive cleanup effort made sense. Andy couldn't be moved, and she couldn't be left in a scene of unimaginable horror. I didn't know where he found the cleanup crew, but somebody jumped when he called. The makeshift curtain remained in place, shielding Andy from a process she herself had supervised at least once in her career. I appreciated that Tom treated her as the victim, and not as one of his cops, even if she didn't see it that way.

I slipped into the curtained space just as Andy's phone rang. She checked the screen, then said, "Hi, Greg."

She listened. Closed her eyes. Took a deep breath.

"I'm okay but thank you."

"She was."

"She did. Incredibly brave."

"Thank you. Will just walked in. Let me put you on speaker. My boss is here, too. You remember—yeah. Him. Hold on."

She laid down the phone and touched the necessary buttons.

"Are you there?" Andy asked.

"Yup. Will, I got that information you asked for. I called the number you gave me. She told me to call Andy."

"What did you find?" I asked.

"A screwed up path of ownership, but in the end, that whole island and all the construction on it belongs to an LLC that eventually adds to the net worth of Guardian Worldwide, held by one Bindle Foss whose glowing and pregnant wife is on the cover of *Vogue*."

Andy tipped her head back against the pillow and gazed up at the ceiling.

Tom stepped closer as one of the curtain units was carried away by a member of the cleanup team. The second member coiled hoses and gathered supplies. They had finished. The floors looked wet, but it wasn't blood. Under the scent of cleanser, however, I either smelled or convinced myself that I smelled blood.

"Lieutenant, it's Tom Ceeves. Anything new on the Jane Doe?"

"No. But we asked Sault St. Marie to renew the notice they originally sent out. This time they put it out nationally."

"Why?" Andy asked. I could tell she knew the answer.

"Your missing girl case. Baxter Gaffney. She was from New York but now it looks like she went missing from that academy or camp or whatever they were running up there. We assumed the first one came from the Great Lakes. Now we need to consider that she may have attended the same camp and could have been from anywhere."

"So maybe it is trafficking. Like you said."

"I don't know," LeMore confessed. "What's weird here is the scale of response. Missing person cases end up in the files all the time. Nobody pays attention. Why go to all this trouble? We generally don't get involved unless a body turns up? Yet somebody has now committed murder—twice—for reasons we don't have a handle on. Toss in the triple lookalike thing including a billionaire's wife, and my head spins. For sure."

I explained about the jet crew, the jet, and the Chicago origin of the two men who traveled to Essex. I added, "They were carrying the same ID as King Kong."

"Gallica," Andy said. "There's a through-line that includes Gallica."

"Is there?" Tom asked, lifting an eyebrow in my direction.

"Gallica's huge. International. I can't confirm that they work for Foss, though. They're more secretive than the Secret Service. How did you find out about those guys in the first place?" Greg asked.

Andy made a face at me.

"My friend in the FBI. She may have dealt with them before." It was a weak lie and Andy let me know with an eye roll.

"Well, you're not going to get anywhere taking a run straight at those guys. I never dealt with them, but I have had run-ins with private security before. Especially the ones that cover big money. They know all the angles. You can't get past their phone menu without them rolling out some judge who issues a cease and desist. They might have dispatched the two hitters tonight, but you can bet there's no trail back to the Gallica offices. They're pros."

"Do you think Gallica provides security for Foss?"

"No idea," Greg replied. "Lemme work on that. Oh. One more thing. Chief Schultz called me a little while ago. He got a call from his brother. You remember David? Chicago PD?"

"Yeah," I cringed. "I remember him."

"Yeah, I guess there was an incident at the Hyatt Regency tonight. I'm not sure why I got the call, but Chief Schultz—our Chief Schultz—said his brother got wind of it and saw the security footage."

Nobody spoke. I felt my cheeks burn.

"My Chief Schultz said his brother wanted me to pass along that he's taken personal charge of the incident, feels it won't amount to anything, but that if it does, he has already taken possession of the hotel security footage."

I could hear the smile in LeMore's voice.

"Good to know," I said.

"Yeah. He said it was revealing. He sounded impressed."

"Change of subject," I said quickly. "The crew that flew the hitters into Essex are flying back to New York tonight."

"The hell they are," Tom declared. I held up a hand, hoping to press the pause button on his protest.

"Earl and I had a chat with them. I don't think they have anything to contribute about what happened here tonight, but based on what you just told me, I see some value in hitching a ride back to New York with them, which they kindly offered." I gave Tom a pointed glance.

"Why?" LeMore asked.

"They work for Guardian Worldwide. They work for Foss."

99

After the call with LeMore ended, a debate broke out about Andy.

"I appreciate all this," I said to Tom, "but she can't stay here."

"She can't be moved, either," Margie protested. "There's been too much movement already, and we've lost our ability to monitor her. I put in a call to the doctor. He's supposed to call me back."

"I'm staying here," Andy announced. "I'm not risking this child any more tonight."

"Dee, just staying where you are is a risk. The third shooter—the one that got away—he works at long range."

"Then assign a couple units to stay," she said to Tom. "Tell them to bring night vision gear with infrared and put them on foot patrol around the house. We'll tack up some blankets over the windows."

"That won't help if he has thermal imaging. He can put a round through the wall."

"Not if we warm it up in here," Tom said. "We can pump up the temperature inside. We can set up space heaters outside, too. Mess with the imaging."

"I want to put the question to Dr. Maserati," I said. Andy released a twitch of smile. "I want him to weigh in."

Andy took my hand. "I'm staying."

"Dee, I don't want to risk moving you. I really don't. But if that sonofabitch comes back here to finish the job, I'm not sure there's a way to stop a bullet from several hundred yards away."

"He can't shoot what he can't see. I'm staying."

I looked at the Chief.

"I'll set it up, Will. And I'll be right here. Where can I find blankets, a hammer, and some nails?"

I gave Tom instructions. He headed upstairs for the blankets.

"Margie, can you give us a minute?" Andy asked.

The nurse smiled at her. "Sure. If the doctor calls back, I'll put you on the line." She walked to the kitchen.

I sat down beside Andy. The chair was too low. Standing was too high. I hated every bit of everything happening and fought tension inside that had the potential to snap at anyone, including Andy.

As if she knew that, she turned her head and soothed me with a look laden with affection. "Thanks for calling earlier."

"Aw shucks, ma'am. Tweren't nuthin' much."

"I'm sorry."

"For what? This wasn't your fault."

"I should have left it alone. All of it. I should never have listened to Lydia. I can't—Holly—I can't—"

"Stop. I won't tell you not to feel horrified by what happened. I feel it, too. She was such a goddamned simple soul. I mean that in a good way."

"And those children..." Andy whispered. *"I didn't know she was hurt like that, Will. I didn't know."*

"You couldn't. And maybe she didn't know either."

Andy steadied herself. It wasn't her first struggle with composure. It wouldn't be the last.

"She said something before...you know. She said something about Chaney Foss. About the rich lady. I think she was kind of in awe of her, being on the cover of a magazine like that. But what she said, it was true and deeply sad."

"What?"

Andy told me.

We both needed a moment.

Andy said, "It got me thinking. Will, hand me that magazine."

Along with some of the medical debris in the room, the stack of reading material had been shuttled from place to place. Andy pointed at an end table that had been shoved aside. I fetched the glossy periodical.

"Coincidence," she said. "Everything has been coincidence. You know how I feel. But this business with the photos of Baxter Gaffney, and the therapist connecting to Foss, and the girl in the lake, and then that look-alike at

Penn State, and now what Greg said—it's so damned coincidental. Perfectly so. Which must mean it isn't."

"I'm pretty sure it isn't. I just can't figure out how."

She opened the magazine and flipped pages until she came to the photo spread of Chaney Foss. I had looked at the photos but had not read the article. Andy had. She turned past the first couple pages of perfectly staged and lighted candid photos of the woman in a variety of settings that oozed wealth, each of which draped new fashions over her early-stage baby bump. Andy pointed at a picture of Chaney Foss with her young son; Foss posed as if introducing the boy to his future sibling. In the picture, Foss held the child's hand on her belly.

"See this?" Andy held up the page.

"Yeah. They already have one kid. What is he? Three? Four?"

Andy stroked an elegant finger down the length of the text. She found what she was looking for and handed me the magazine.

"Here. Read this."

100

After collecting two fresh power units from the mudroom, I left Andy in what felt like a fortress. Tom nailed blankets over any window that had a line of sight to Andy. He effortlessly reached the top of each window frame. When he finished with the blackout curtains, he contacted Alicia at dispatch and gave her the names of additional officers to call up for duty, along with a list of equipment to bring to the farmhouse. The list included night vision equipment, a recently acquired drone with infrared imaging capability, and a pair of kerosene heaters that looked like small jet engines. The department used the propane-powered heaters when a remote incident or crime scene lacked power but required warmth. His plan, he explained, was to set them up in the yard and aim the heat blast at the exterior of the house. It would, he assured me, turn the wall of the house into one giant glowing blob in any thermal imaging equipment. I wondered if it would peel the paint, but didn't ask.

Tom also issued instructions to gather and review camera images and plate reader data from the main roads in and out of the county. We all agreed that the shooter with the long rifle was five counties away by now, but no one disputed the steps to be taken.

I didn't know what car he drove. I didn't know what roads he took or where he was headed, but I knew who the shooter was. Murphy. The name imprinted on the black thing lurking in my heart.

I kept the name to myself.

Andy pulled me into a kiss when I told her that it was time to go. We held on and held each other and transmitted love and sadness and relief and a thousand promises across our touch. The embrace ended reluctantly.

"Be careful." She lifted her eyes to mine.

I checked my watch.

"It's after midnight. You're in luck."

101

Tuesday

"We're fueled and filed. There's a shitload of texts from company dispatch." Pidge and her flight bag leaned on the Essex County Air Service counter. She held up a phone that was not hers. "These guys carry company phones."

"We should do that."

"What?"

"Carry company phones. I keep losing mine."

"*I know!* I've been telling that old fucker that for months. His idea of new technology is the telegraph. Anyway, this is the captain's company phone." She held up the device. Text messages ran the length of the screen. "Somebody's got their hair on fire."

We set off down the hallway to the shop. I noted that the Phenom jet waited at the Jet-A fuel pumps.

"What do they want?"

"Update ETA Chicago. Update status passengers. Update fucking everything."

"That's coming from Gallica. It means they're tight with the Guardian Worldwide flight department. We also have to assume they know their mission tonight went bust."

"Why?"

"Because the third man got away and reported it. So now they're trying to figure out if the flight crew is in custody and what damage has been done. Do you get the feeling *el capitan* is not being forthright with us?"

"I don't trust the fucker. Can we throw him out?"

"If you can get the door op—"

I stopped short of entering the maintenance shop.

"What?" Pidge asked.

The door open.

"You look like you just learned what to do with your man parts, which, if I may say…" Pidge leered at me. "Kudos to Andy."

"I just…I just had a thought…"

"Don't hurt yourself."

I followed her into the hangar. Kid Copilot had been released but the captain remained bound to the chair. Earl hovered nearby. He wore an ancient leather flight jacket that had almost as many cracks and creases as his face.

"Where are you going?" I asked Earl.

"With you. Told you. I don't trust the sonofabitch."

I stepped past Earl and stood in front of the captain.

"How many airplanes does Foss own?" I asked.

He shrugged. "I don't know. He's got a hangar full. Two G700s, a Citation, the Phenom. He's got a Boeing Business Jet, but that's parked at LaGuardia."

"Does he have toys? A P-51? An L-39?" I asked. "I'm asking if Foss is a pilot."

The captain looked reluctant to answer and my trust in him plummeted. Earl's offer had merit.

Kid Copilot answered. "Yeah. He used to fly. I don't know if he had a Mustang, but I know he used to fly all the time, until his dad passed away and junior took over the company. I heard the board of directors put a hard stop to him getting in a cockpit. Jeez, if I had that kind of money—"

"He doesn't fly anymore?" I asked.

The captain shook his head.

"Last chance. Where's Foss tonight?"

"Like I said. He's in—" the copilot said.

"I asked him." I stared at the captain long enough to make him uncomfortable.

"What he said," the captain answered reluctantly. "He was in Europe. He flew back to Westchester yesterday. They're taking 700 Blue to Washington, D.C. tomorrow."

"I tried to get assigned but there was no opening," the kid chirped.

"Do you ever shut up?" the captain asked sourly.

I looked at Earl. His standard glare grew fierce.

"Told you I was going with you. Now it's time for you to tell me what in blue blazes is going on."

"Fuck, yeah," Pidge seconded.

"I wish I knew," I said. "Let's get them loaded. Then I'll tell you as much as I do know, and you can decide if you're still in."

102

The Phenom 300E rendered a beautiful night flight to Westchester County Airport. Before boarding, I thoroughly confused Pidge and Earl with what I knew. Both declared it made no sense but if I planned to go after the people who hurt Andy and killed Holly, they would not be left behind. Earl called the captain a snake and said someone needed to keep an eye on him. Pidge insisted that someone needed to sit up front. Kid Copilot flew from the right seat because he said he felt more comfortable in the first officer's position. I gave him credit for not exceeding his training. Pidge took the left seat and adapted quickly to handling radios and navigation and checklist tasks. The captain, with his hands bound, grumbled about us only making things worse for ourselves. He sat strapped into a rear-facing seat across from Earl, who never took his eyes off the man. I took a seat across the aisle from the two of them, thinking I might catch a nap to dampen the fatigue creeping into my bones. Sleep didn't come. I tried to put some weight on my eyelids by reading the *Vogue* article that I had torn from Lydia's magazine, but rereading the section Andy showed me only upped my blood pressure.

I didn't know what was worse. Chaney Foss believing she embodied humanity's shining example of womanhood, or the writer who put her on that pedestal. The article lauded Foss's struggles to begin a family, her failures marked by miscarriages, her battle with depression induced by physical trauma as well as the emotional devastation. Then triumph. The successful birth of her son three-and-a-half years ago. And now again. Pregnant. A miracle. A daughter on the way, blessing the Foss Dynasty with perfection and a future. In the glossy photos, she posed with at least one hand on the baby bump, sometimes gazing down at it, sometimes looking into the camera.

I could not let go of what Holly said, her exact words, so gentle in the dark.

I could not look at the Chaney Foss while those words haunted me.

The woman looking at the camera let no one mistake how she felt about lesser people. In haughty lined eyes and the supremacy that money endows, I saw someone capable of hating a Holly Bennett simply for being. I convinced myself that if this icon of fashion, power, and wealth learned that Holly's life ended, she would dismiss the death as an improvement on the human condition.

But that was just me.

"The landing was a little rough," I told Kid Copilot, "but not horrible."

"I know," he admitted as the engines spooled down after he taxied to a private hangar set on a private ramp on an airport awash with gleaming executive jets.

"It's trailing link gear, goddammit," Earl muttered. "How do you bounce trailing link gear?"

Pidge smirked from the captain's seat. "We gotta get one of these, old man."

"Over my dead body."

"Incentive," Pidge replied. "Okay, what now?"

I remained in my seat. I pulled out the Guardian company phone.

"Now we wait," I said. "I texted them while we were taxiing in. *Big problem. Landing KHPN 0315.* I got a bunch of replies. Kinda rude."

What problem?

Report.

Report or you're fired!

The phone had also vibrated in my pocket. A stack of missed calls came from a number listed as Private.

I didn't underestimate the task at hand. Getting the world's second richest man to leave his silk sheets and drive to the airport before dawn looked like a long shot to me. I began thinking about visiting whatever gilded castle he occupied on the shores of the Hudson River.

I examined the huge hangar. New and polished and perfect. Built on a corner of the airport well away from other hangars, it was the best money could buy. Subtle embedded security lights all around gave it a mystical glow. Glass lined the walls just below the curved roof and invited daylight into the hangar, but not uninvited eyes. The glass also said that spending tens of thousands of dollars to heat the four-story building meant nothing to the owner. No matter the season, the family Foss boarded their personal jets in shirtsleeve comfort.

I held up the phone and glanced back at the captain. "You're in a world of shit, captain. They are super unhappy with you for flying here instead of back to Chicago. Especially after everything went south. Bad judgment."

The blood draining from the captain's face made the half-lie worth it.

Earl leaned over and looked through the window on my side of the aircraft.

"Whaddya say we break into this whorehouse."

"Kill the interior lights," I ordered Kid Copilot. The cabin went dim except for annoying LEDs and the glow from the cockpit instrumentation. "Do you keep anything aerosol onboard? Spray can?"

"We have two Halotron fire extinguishers."

I shook my head. "Won't work. Doesn't leave residue."

"Wait! What about this?" He twisted in his seat, dug in a side pocket, and pulled up a tiny can of WD-40. "There's a squeak in the liquor cabinet door."

"That'll do." I said. "I don't suppose you've got a..."

He held up a remote that looked like an ordinary garage door opener. He pressed his thumb to the remote. Lights flashed a brief warning, then the giant hangar door began to rise. Interior lights blossomed.

"Perfect," I said. "Everybody, wait here."

It was a bit of a trick. After opening the cabin door but before stepping out, I made sure both the captain and copilot could not see me.

Fwooomp! I vanished and heaved myself out the side of the aircraft. Ten minutes later I returned after a slow flight around the hangar interior during which I found and sprayed the lenses of half a dozen security cameras. I then located four more outside the hangar and applied the same treatment.

Fwooomp!

I reappeared outside the aircraft near the wing.

"Let's go," I called into the cabin from the foot of the airstair. "We're going to have company soon."

The captain came first.

"What about me?" the copilot asked.

"If I were you," I said, "I'd wait five minutes, then get the hell out of here and don't look back. Good luck at FO school."

The young man looked genuinely relieved.

"Hey," Earl snapped at him. He flinched. "You run into any shit at Delta, you call me."

I wasn't sure if the kid was smiling or trying not to pee himself.

"Dammit," Pidge muttered. She climbed out of the pilot's seat. "I was getting used to this."

With the survival knife from my jacket's shoulder pocket, I sliced through the zip ties binding the captain's wrists.

"Move."

103

We didn't have long. The text messages to the captain's phone had grown increasingly hostile before they stopped. The sabotaged security cameras also gave us away.

After crossing the newly paved ramp, we stood under bright lights in the most beautiful, cleanest, brightest aircraft hangar I'd ever seen. The glossy white floor did not show a single spot or scratch. Mirror perfect, it reflected the sublime lines of Gulfstream's premier jets, two G700s, parked like poised thoroughbreds. Between them, a crouching Cessna Citation Longitude seemed sadly junior, despite being Textron's top-of-the-line model. The back of the building featured a glass wall like the Foundation hangar at home, but this one rose two stories and contained a mix of offices and luxurious lounge spaces. Except for a powerful aircraft tug, I saw no sign of aircraft maintenance supplies, or cleaning supplies, or any of the detritus that normally infests aircraft hangars. Nor did I see exotic toys. No P-51 World War II fighter or L-39 jet trainer. No antique biplane. No row of parked motorcycles. A second tall door granted aircraft access at the side of the hangar. A flight office jutted into the hangar space in one corner. Beside the office, a line of tidy white metal cabinets hid the working tools of a flight department from sight.

One item, however, stuck out like a red-headed stepchild. Tucked in the corner of the hangar, a turboprop Beechcraft King Air 90 akin to the King Air that Earl had purchased a little over a year ago, looked woefully out of place among the continent-hopping armada.

I had seen model 90s like this before. They often filled a very specific role.

"What about that one?" I asked the captain. I pointed at the King Air. "Does Foss fly that airplane?"

"I don't know."

"Don't know or won't say?" Earl snapped.

The man huffed in frustration. "Maybe. I guess he used to, but not for three or four years."

Three or four years. I studied the King Air and one more piece of the puzzle slipped into place.

We stopped in the center of the huge space. Earl stepped close to me and lowered his voice to a raspy whisper.

"How do you want to play this?"

"Either we get Foss to come here, or we go to him. Any minute now, somebody's going to show up here and make that decision for us."

Earl looked around. To Pidge he asked, "Think you can make yourself skinny behind that office door over there?"

"She shops in the children's department, boss."

"Fuck you." Pidge stalked off. Over her shoulder, she said, "How long are we gonna stand around?"

"Long as it takes," Earl muttered. "I'll be behind that row of cabinets."

A space between the last cabinet and the wall offered just enough of a nook for Earl to position himself out of sight.

"Seriously, you're just going to stand here and hope the richest man in the world gives you the time of day?" the captain muttered. "You're in deep enough, pal. Let me make a call and end this." He held out his hand for his phone.

"We wait."

"Yeah, well you can go to hell, because I'm not—"

I pulled Andy's Beretta M.92 from a deep pocket inside my other flight jacket. The weapon had been reloaded in both magazine and chamber. I pointed it at the captain.

"What? You gonna shoot me?" He oozed bravado.

I lowered my voice and the weapon. "Yes. In the femoral artery. Just like your passengers did to an innocent young woman tonight. Then I'll watch you bleed out on this sparkling floor. You'll have about a minute. Maybe two."

He froze.

"We wait," I repeated.

104

Less than ten minutes later, a black Cadillac SUV rolled around the corner of the hangar and made a turn tight enough to cause the tires to squeal. It pulled into the hangar with attitude, leaving tire scuff marks on the spotless floor. I had time to think that some nameless, faceless minimum wage earner like Holly would be tasked with scrubbing those marks away before Foss saw them.

The vehicle stopped with the headlights aimed at the captain and me. The driver's door opened and disgorged a man in dark clothing. He slammed his door, produced a weapon and stomped toward the captain, aiming at the man's face.

"You fucking came here?" A familiar voice demanded. "Where are Killian and Rudder? You were supposed to—"

His attention shot from the captain to me. Recognition blossomed. The hostile muzzle end of the gun swung to me.

Angry Bald Man.

"Are you Rivers?" I asked. "What did you do with my clothes?"

Smug satisfaction washed over Angry Bald Man's face.

"You."

"Me."

He took a breath. Switched his aim again. And shot the captain in the face.

105

F *wooomp!*
I slammed the levers in my head all the way to the stops and kicked the floor. Rivers' weapon swept back to where I'd been standing. Despite my launch for the ceiling, I knew my body could not clear his line of fire in time. Only one thing saved me.

The shot did not come. Startled by my disappearance, he did not pull the trigger because filling his gunsight where I stood a moment ago was the gleaming fuselage of his boss's eighty-million-dollar jet.

"Wha—"

"DROP IT!" Earl stepped out from the cabinet nook holding out his vintage .45 with a bead on the bald head.

From above, just before I hit the white steel trusses of the hangar roof, I saw Rivers crouched and pirouette, whipping his gun arm around for a shot at Earl.

BANG!

The flash came from Earl's side of the hangar.

Rivers' body slapped onto the white floor beside the spray of blood from the back of his head.

I clutched the steel truss thirty feet up, fighting to get my heart out of my throat.

From the office at the corner of the hangar I heard Pidge shout, "IF YOU ASSHOLES ARE DONE SCARING THE SHIT OUTTA ME, I'M COMING OUT!"

106

"Well, this isn't getting us anywhere," Earl muttered, frowning at the two bodies on the hangar floor. "And you're welcome." He dropped his big Colt 1911 in a deep jacket pocket.

"I don't know about that." I knelt beside Rivers' body and tried not to look at the hole where his right eye had been. Earl's shot had been impressive, taken from at least 30 feet. Maybe more.

I probed Rivers' pockets until I found a phone. Remembering my experience with the passcode in Chicago, I held out little hope.

Instead of a passcode, the phone asked for facial recognition.

"Think this will recognize him with that hole in his head?" I shifted around for a better angle on his face. I held out the phone and heard a compliant beep. The screen opened. "Damn. Good to know that if you ever get shot in the face, your phone still works."

Basic icons populated the home screen. No extra apps. No games. I suspected the phone served one purpose. Touching the message icon, I saw one entry. One contact. *The Man.* Cute.

I scooted back on my haunches, aimed the phone, and snapped a picture of the dead man. Opening the photo, I touched the upload button and selected Message. I picked the single contact and attached the photo, then typed.

Baxter Gaffney.
I know everything.
The hangar. Come alone.

Bring 2 Billion.

"Two billion!" Pidge leaned over my shoulder. "How's he supposed to bring two billion dollars? In a duffle bag? Or…a hundred duffle bags? Fuck."

"Fine." I backtracked and retyped the last line.

Be ready to transfer 2 billion.

"He's not gonna bring money," Earl griped. "He's gonna bring a goddamned army."

"Don't be too sure. I think he will take me for someone who can be bought and disposed of later. And if I'm right about what's really going on here, I think keeping everything quiet is his top priority."

I hit Send, then held my hand out to Pidge. "Gimme your phone. I need to call Andy to ask her to look up the tail number for that King Air."

107

Like so many who loom large in the media, Bindle Foss was a small man in person. Athletic, the way people with personal trainers can be. Tanned, the way people with private islands culture their skin. With perfect hair and perfect teeth and clothing from Paris or Milan or some such. He wore a black ball cap with no logo. He tucked expensive sunglasses in the neck of his designer t-shirt. He wore deck shoes without socks, killing his last hope for mercy from me.

He rolled the predictable Porsche Panamera into his extravagant private hangar and skidded to a stop, leaving more tire marks on the spotless floor.

Climbing out from behind the wheel, he slammed the car door.

I waited alone in the center of the polished floor.

"Who the hell are you?" He glanced at the two bodies.

"Rivers didn't send my photo? I figure they got a decent shot of me at the Gallica offices in Chicago."

"I don't know any Gallica, and I don't know any Rivers."

"Rivers is the one-eyed ugly over there." Foss paid no attention.

"Are you the one who texted?"

"Affirmative." I held up Rivers' phone.

"You said you know everything. What is it you think you know?"

"Truthfully, I didn't know shit until tonight. It's been one massively messed up set of facts seen from our side."

"Our side?"

"Me. My wife the cop—the one you tried to kill. Twice. And my friend in the FBI—the one you had your puppets in the government fire. And the Milwaukee PD. The Chicago PD. The national guard. The United Nations. NATO."

"I don't have time for this shit. If you know anything about me or Gallica or Rivers, then you know you've made a horrible mistake."

"Wouldn't be my first," I said. "And you just said Gallica. I thought you never heard of Gallica."

"*I fucking OWN Gallica,*" he snapped. "I own over a thousand business entities, but Gallica—that's something special. Gallica is the reason your body will never be found. Gallica is the reason your wife isn't going to get to the thirtieth week of her pregnancy. Gallica is the reason your friend in the FBI won't be able to get a job as a letter carrier, you stupid sonofabitch."

"Is Gallica the reason Baxter Gaffney is carrying your child?"

Foss said nothing.

"Did you have Gallica inseminate her? Or did you give it the personal touch? Either way, you had to contribute your genes. Did you do it in person? At Saint Martin Academy? Party time up at camp?"

He remained silent. Thinking.

I gave him time.

Predictably, he said, "I don't know what you're talking about."

"Sure, you do. Baxter Gaffney." I let the name sink in. The flicker of anger in the eyes gave him away. "Yeah. You know who I'm talking about."

I waved one arm in the air.

Pidge emerged from behind the hangar office door and strolled to where I stood. She handed me Andy's M.92 which I trained on Foss. She walked to Foss and patted his jacket, his pants, his ankles.

"Want his phone?" she asked.

"Nah."

Declaring him unarmed, she stepped back.

Earl emerged from behind his cabinet nook and walked across the ramp to join us. He stopped to examine the rear seat of Foss's Porsche, then pocketed his .45 again.

"It's good you didn't pull a gun. That girl can shoot the nuts off a squirrel at fifty feet. Your balls never would have had a chance."

He chuckled.

"That's it? You're going to point a gun at me and make accusations? That's hardly worth my time."

"I don't know," I said. "I think this story has legs. Maybe an exclusive in *The Atlantic.* I'd take it to *Vogue,* but they would have some back pedaling to do. Not their fault, of course. But editors hate that shit."

He shook his head. "You're a joke. You have nothing. And even if you did, it's all fake news and *I will bury you.* Whatever you think you know will never see the light of day. Whatever you post will be stripped in seconds. Whatever you blab to the press will be bought off the wire."

"I know this: Three and a half years ago you were blessed with a bouncing baby boy. He has his mother's looks. The writer at *Vogue* said so. You liked that. You were quoted in the article as saying 'Chaney is so much better looking than me.' That's some saccharine false modesty, I gotta say."

"Fuck you."

"The birth was a blessing after a very private pregnancy. And the kid's arrival was a huge surprise to the public. You told the writer you went to extraordinary lengths to keep the pregnancy quiet because you were never sure Chaney would make it all the way to term."

"You can read. Bravo."

"That's the public story. The thing is…your wife was never pregnant. I don't think your wife can get pregnant."

He maintained a stone face. "Says you. You know nothing."

"Says the autopsy on the girl that was found in Lake Superior who had recently given birth. A girl who looked remarkably like Chaney Foss."

He twitched. A fissure appeared in the billion-dollar cool.

"I'll admit," I said, "this part had holes. We don't know who she was or where you found her, but we'll see to it that her image is splashed all over *Good Morning, America* and cable news. Someone will recognize the composite photo. Someone will come forward. Someone who never stopped wanting to know what happened to their sister, or daughter, or granddaughter. Maybe someone who knew the girl went to a camp on an island in the Straits of Mackinac and never came back. A camp that only ran for one season. Then closed. Long enough for troubled girls and townie boys to party. And for a well-heeled stranger to pop in by seaplane for a little fun."

"Absolute nonsense."

"The door comes off."

"Huh?"

I gestured at the King Air.

"The door comes off on the 90. Not every airplane offers you a stable platform, a good autopilot, and a door that comes off. That's why they love the 90 for skydiving. That's where you bought this one. Used to fly skydivers at a jump school in Arizona. Certified to fly with the door off. The only way a single pilot can dump a body over one of the Great Lakes."

He shook his head. I continued.

"Your son looks like his mother because his mother looks like your wife," I said. "I'm gonna guess that round one was serendipity. Chance. Opportunity, perhaps. You saw a young, fertile woman who could pass for Mrs. Foss. Got yourself an heir. Maybe that was enough, until you and your wife ran into the Gaffney family at some social affair. Or gala. Or gallery opening. Whatever it was, you took one look at Baxter Gaffney and saw a way to add to the family. You couldn't get too close, but there's nothing your guys at Gallica can't dig up. The girl has behavior problems. The girl sees a therapist—one who trades her integrity for social standing and a shitload of cash. Macallen urges the family to enroll Baxter in an exclusive camp, which you reopened and restocked. God, that must have cost tens of millions of—oh that's right. Chump change for you.."

Foss eye-rolled silent contempt.

"A woman has twelve cycles in a year. Thirteen if the calendar lines up right—an extra period just like a Blue Moon. The camp was perfect. Gave you time to stick the landing, so to speak. A couple trips up to the island when her cycle hits its peak—information I presume Dr. Macallen provided. And then all you had to do was hide her away and wait for the baby to arrive. Is she a prisoner somewhere? Or is she waiting patiently thinking you will divorce your wife so that you and she can run away to your private island?"

Foss said nothing.

"But here's a twist. This time, your wife put it all out there in public—with a fashion angle. What better way to explain how, in a few months, you're the proud father of a sweet baby girl who looks just like her mother? And Baxter Gaffney ends up in a frozen lake. Or maybe a woodchipper, since the last body didn't quite disappear like you hoped."

"All bullshit."

"No. It's all true. You just certified it for me."

"How?"

"Because you're here. Because I sent you a picture of the only other person you trusted with all the moving parts. He's dead. Now you need to shut me up."

"I'm not paying you two billion dollars. That's absurd."

"That's okay. I never planned to collect or to shut up. Not for two billion. Not for everything you own."

Foss held a cold boardroom stare on me. His dark eyes labored to drill me with barbs honed by ruthless success.

"Let me tell you how this is going to go," he said. "I'm going to keep my money. You're going to make a bunch of unfounded accusations. Maybe get some press. Meanwhile, you'll be defending yourself against a murder charge. And the child porn discovered on your laptop. And a tax evasion prosecution by the IRS. And any of twenty other major offenses I can arrange with as many government agencies simply by snapping my fingers. And your insane claims about my children? DNA testing will conclusively prove they are mine. *Guaranteed.* Oh, yes. I can buy results guaranteed to be in my favor. And while you're mourning the death of your wife and little Miss-Shoot-The-Balls-Off, your legal bills will pile up. Assuming you can find a lawyer that I can't buy first. And let's just say you get some traction with a prosecutor or an investigation. Do you know how many years I can tie up the courts with counterclaims and motions, and trips to the appeals court, or the Supreme Court? Do you know how many of the judges who rule along the way I play golf with? Judges who I take on private jet fishing trips to the Yukon? Pay for their grandchildren's exclusive schooling? *Nothing you've described can be traced to me. NOTHING.*"

Foss's outcry echoed in the huge hangar.

A long silence hung in the air. Beside me, Earl shuffled his feet.

"He ain't wrong." Earl said.

"Fuck," Pidge muttered.

Foss sensed victory and turned. He started for his car.

Earl stomped his bowlegged stride to intercept Foss, whose eyes grew wider with each step Earl took. Foss staggered backward.

Earl kept coming. He cut across Foss, cocked back his right arm, and smashed the side of Foss's head with his forearm. Foss fell.

"Don't mean this is over," he said to Foss. He turned to me and Pidge and tapped his arm. "Always use this fleshy part by the elbow. Won't leave a mark."

Foss crabbed away from Earl and tried to push himself up. Earl flinched a menacing step in his direction. Foss sank back to the floor and stayed there.

"Now what?" Pidge asked.

Foss rubbed the side of his face. "Go ahead. Beat on me. I'll document every bruise. How's that going to look for you in court, asshole?"

"You can't testify if you can't talk," Earl muttered.

"You're all finished!" he cried. *"Murder! Assault! Kidnapping! No one will believe a word you have to say! No one!"*

Pidge drew up beside me and spoke in a low voice.

"He has a fucking point. What are we supposed to do? Call the cops?"

"YES!" Foss shouted. "Call the cops! Call the goddamned police right now!"

Earl shook his head. "I don't think that would go so good."

A sick feeling invaded my gut, but I wasn't ready to give up. Parts and pieces going all the way back to Lydia's deck spun around in my head, condemning the man who cowered in front of us.

He believed he remained out of reach, protected by wealth kings could only dream of, authorities bought, and media channels hypnotizing millions.

Pidge looked at me.

Looked at Foss.

Looked at the King Air and the open hangar door.

"Fuck this." She muttered. "I got an idea."

She walked across the hangar floor and picked up Rivers' Glock. In a deft stroke, she pulled back the slide to confirm a round in the chamber, then spun and lifted the weapon until her aim and any bullet governed by her aim converged on Foss's face.

"Move, asshole," she snapped. "Over by him." She waved the gun at Rivers' corpse. "MOVE!"

"No," Foss refused defiantly. "You're not going kill me. Just go. I'll let you go. I'll give you all a ten-minute head start."

Earl growled at Foss. "She told you to move. Want me to make you?"

Foss looked at Rivers' body and shook his head. "You're not gonna shoot me. You're not."

Pidge took two steps, pistol held on Foss. She swung her arm and fired. Twice.

Foss screamed. He threw his hands over his face. It took him a moment to realize he had not been hit. He looked up. Pidge's aim remained locked on Rivers' chest where two new holes sprouted.

"Cover your ears, motherfuckers."

I did as she commanded.

She shifted her aim and fired again, this time into the grille of the Porsche Panamera. The grille. The windshield. The tires. She rapid-fired, puncturing metal, shattering glass, blasting plastic into the air. She fired until the last cartridge flew from the weapon and pinged across the hangar floor. The slide locked open. Bitter gun smoke drifted in the hangar air.

"Whew!" She exalted.

"Great," Earl muttered. "You made a bunch of noise and killed a car. That's your goddamned idea?"

She looked over her shoulder at us, then at the King Air. Mischief sparkled in her eyes.

She grinned.

108

With Rivers' Glock in one hand, and Andy's M.92 in the other, I followed Earl and Foss across the hangar floor and onto the ramp. Earl dragged, kicked, and pushed Foss. The King Air waited for us where Earl had pulled it using the tug parked in the hangar.

The left engine began to whine as Pidge, seated in the pilot's seat, ran through turbine engine startup procedures.

"Get up there," Earl shouted at Foss over the rising engine noise. "Get in."

Foss tripped and staggered but climbed the steps into the plane. I hurried up after him. Earl remained on the ramp, now blown by prop wash. He reached down and heaved the door up behind us.

"Don't forget to lock up," I shouted to Earl. He flipped the door up. I snapped the latch in place.

Foss hunched over in the aisle. I pushed him forward and then down into the rear-facing seat directly behind Pidge. Foss gaped at the seatmate facing him.

Rivers.

A black hole substituted for his left eye. A line of blood from the hole seeped down his face. Two additional holes marred Rivers' chest, the result of Pidge's surprise gunfire.

"Who's guilty of murder now, asshole?" Foss shouted at me over the sound of the second engine starting.

I took the forward-facing seat on the other side of the aisle.

"Not that you'd believe me, but that was self-defense. Your man here overestimated himself. Mistake."

"A fucking grave." He shook his head. "You're digging a deeper and deeper fucking grave for yourself."

"You have a point," I agreed. "Which is why we're going to take you out over the lake and give you the same chance you gave Jane Doe. What was her name, by the way?"

"No idea what you're talking about." He laughed. "Really? You're going to dump me over the lake?"

Pidge had both engines running. Off the left wing, the big hangar door descended. They would find Foss's car in a locked hangar, shot to pieces. They would find the captain's body in the front passenger seat. Earl would see to it before he slipped away.

We began to roll. The nose bobbed as Pidge pulled a tight turn and worked differential braking.

"What's wrong with dropping you in the lake?" I asked.

He laughed again and sat back. Smug in knowledge he held but we didn't.

"Fuck you."

"Buckle in. Tight." I reached up and snatched the ball cap from his head.

I leaned into the cockpit and laid the Glock on the copilot's seat after pulling out my shirt and wiping down the parts of the weapon that Pidge and I touched. I didn't have to look over my shoulder to know that Foss followed my every move.

I tapped Pidge on the arm. She lifted the headset cup off her right ear.

"You got this?"

"Fuck, yeah. Can't wait to hear what they say."

"Just don't talk to anybody. And don't overdo it."

"Roger that." She grinned.

"And don't kill me."

The grin widened.

"I mean it. Andy will come after you. Also, remember, they're touchy about terrorists. If you get wind they're sending someone after us, get it on the ground. Fast. I don't want to get shot outta the sky."

"Roger that."

"Here," I handed her the ball cap. "Put this on. I don't want anyone seeing blonde hair."

She flipped me the finger then grabbed the cap.

I swung back into my seat, slipped on a headset, and pointed my gun at Foss.

109

"Aircraft taxiing on Kilo, identify yourself."

Pidge had tuned Westchester Ground Control. A woman's voice carried a note of understandable irritation. Aircraft movement without authorization does not meet with joy in the tower. Pidge ignored the call. Continuing down the taxiway, we passed general aviation parking, and then the Atlantic Aviation and Signature Aviation FBOs. Between us and the structures, a Who's Who of general aviation business jets populated the ramps.

Pidge reached up and tapped the radio stack, waking up the recorded ATIS broadcast. She caught the tail end of it, then waited for the recording to repeat and disclose the ceiling, visibility and wind information, the crucial piece being wind.

"…winds two eight zero at five, altimeter…"

Over the back of the copilot's seat, I watched out the front of the King Air. The high instrument panel obscured the taxiway ahead, but most of runway 11/29 to our left remained visible.

Ground control repeated their call, spicing urgency with a touch of anger.

"Aircraft taxiing on Kilo, identify yourself."

Over the intercom, Pidge said to me, "They're getting twitchy. Wait until they see this."

We approached a left turn at an intersection where Taxiway Kilo running parallel to 11/29 tangled with Taxiway Lima for 16/34. Pidge swung the nose onto Taxiway Lima. I lifted myself in the seat. Pidge plowed undaunted toward the hold-short lines protecting Runway 11/29.

"Unidentified aircraft on Taxiway Lima, hold short of Runway 29, repeat hold short of Runway 29."

"They're gonna love this," Pidge muttered. She glanced left and right to check for traffic. Simultaneously, her hand closed on the throttles and eased them forward. The aircraft surged. We shot across the forbidding yellow hold-short lines, building speed.

Pidge reached for the radio. With a deft touch she switched Ground Control to Tower.

"Unidentified aircraft crossing Runway 29, do you read Westchester Tower?" It was the same woman, working both stations in the tower.

Pidge pushed the throttles up their channels. The engines pulled us into rapid acceleration. Pidge swerved left. We exited the runway and lined up on the empty taxiway.

"Here we go."

The King Air, almost completely unladen against the abundant power she carried, heaved forward, pressing me against the seat.

Tower called again, this time using the aircraft tail number.

Somebody got out the binoculars… which made me realize that dawn had cracked the eastern sky. A line of luminous red and orange streaked the horizon and would soon be spreading to a high layer of clouds.

There was no mistaking our intentions now. The King Air's tires reported each crease and tar line in the taxiway as it raced toward takeoff speed. The end of the taxiway came up fast, but the airplane leaped into the air and climbed sharply.

"Well, that just busted a few dozen regs," Pidge commented.

Foss, at first wide-eyed, grew smug again. He shook his head, then chuckled to himself.

"What's funny?" I asked loudly over the cabin noise since he did not wear a headset and was not privy to the intercom.

"You. You're an idiot. Your threat is to drop me over Long Island Sound?"

"The Great Lakes. Probably Ontario."

He laughed. "Like I said. You're an idiot. You can fly this with the door off, but you won't get that door open in flight. So, let's get real. This isn't about tossing me in the lake, or revenge for some girl. This is about money. I'll give you two million." He pulled his phone from his pocket. He waved it in the air between us. "I can transfer two million to any account in the world.

Let's do this deal and then you can drop me off anywhere. Keep the airplane. I don't give a shit."

"The offer was two billion. With a B."

He laughed again. "You're outta your mind."

Pidge banked sharply to the right and leveled the airplane at a low altitude; I guessed around five or seven hundred feet. She held a turn that swung the nose through north, then east, then south, finally rolling out on a southwesterly heading. Foss glanced at the landscape below.

"You know that you're heading into some of the busiest airspace in the world."

"No shit. Two billion."

"Five million. Five million transferred right now." He waved the phone. "Come on. Be real. You win. Let's do this deal."

"And you get to keep the baby?"

Foss pointed a finger at his ear and shook his head. "I'm sorry. I don't know what you're talking about." He grinned.

"Oh, you think I'm after a recorded confession." I shook my head and twirled a finger in the air. "Too much cabin noise."

Congested suburban landscape streaked beneath our wings. I guessed that the cluster of lights off the right wing belonged to White Plaines. Beyond that, I could not have named any of the bedroom communities that loaded daily trains for New York.

"Three minutes out," Pidge announced.

"You're not going to own up to any of it, are you," I said to Foss.

"You mean this kidnapping? Your murder of my associate? I'm happy to testify. We do this deal and you walk. I won't say a word."

Pidge slowly lost altitude. Foss noticed. He furrowed his brow.

"Ten million. Final offer. And since you're not from around here, here's a bit of advice. You're headed straight into New York Class B airspace. At this time of day, LaGuardia is sending up loaded airliners every thirty seconds. I suggest you turn this thing around."

"Noted. Two Billion."

"Come on! That's impossible. You wouldn't even know what to do with ten million dollars!" Anger lines embossed Foss's forehead. He glanced out the window. We dropped lower.

I leaned into the aisle and beckoned him to come closer. He complied. "Do you know how many candy canes you can buy with ten million dollars?"

He wrinkled his brow, confused and impatient. *What the hell?*

I leaned back. So did he, but not before I saw him take note of the gun on the copilot's seat.

"Two minutes," Pidge said.

"What's your skin in this game, anyway? Besides being married to some cop. What's your deal?"

"Did you know your guy Murphy shot her?"

"Who the hell is Murphy?" Foss looked genuinely unaware.

"Yeah…I guess you wouldn't know. You paid Rivers to insulate you. Even if the whole thing came apart at street level, you set things up so nobody can touch you, right? I bet if things got bad enough, you had a deal with Rivers to take a fall, do a few years in prison, and collect a big payout when they push him outta the gates on an early release. Maybe get one of those judges you play golf with to set it up."

"Fifteen million. What the hell is she doing?" Foss looked at the earth rising to meet us less than three hundred feet below.

Shoreline raced beneath the wing on Foss's side of the plane.

"One minute. Buckle up," Pidge said smoothly. She wiggled a bit in the seat she had pulled all the way forward. I noticed she had found a cushion and sat on it.

Pidge abruptly banked left and dove in a way that lifted me against the seatbelt. I gave Foss a smile and shoved the Baretta into the inside pocket of my jacket, then grabbed both armrests.

"Here' we go," Pidge said. "I'm switching to LaGuardia tower now."

Instant busy chatter crowded my headset. Caffeine-fueled morning controllers worked their urgent magic with dozens of aircraft. Transmissions were sharp, clipped and minimal, well-rehearsed by pilots and controllers who made a living in this intense airspace. I would have been cowed.

"What the—!" Foss braced in his seat as flat placid water raced up beneath the wings. He braced for impact that did not come. G-forces pressed him down in his seat when Pidge leveled off. "Is she—OH GOD!"

The suspension span of the Whitestone Bridge flashed overhead.

"SHE FUCKING FLEW UNDER THE BRIDGE!" he shrieked. "You gotta stop her!"

"Sit still!"

Pidge lowered the left wing. I wondered if the tip might touch the water. That would be bad. She banked through a steady left turn. Ahead, I saw an airliner rise against the dawn sky, climbing over us.

"Don't hit anything," I said softly into the intercom.

"Pucker up."

At over 200 knots we roared toward the departure end of LaGuardia

Runway 31, flying opposite the departing traffic. I lifted myself against the seatbelt and looked in amazement at the busy New York airport. Jets of every size and livery lined up for takeoff. A 737 raced toward us on the runway. Pidge skidded slightly to the right side of the runway.

The Boeing, committed, lifted off, its lithe wings bending under the weight it carried. The nose swung up and any question of a collision vanished. It shot skyward over us. Caught on tape, the proximity of our passage would have looked suicidal.

"Tower, what was that?" A pilot exercising astonishing calm inquired.

Pidge dipped the speeding King Air. Any lower, and we would have clipped taxiway lights. The airport and its maze of pavement flowed past like a high-speed conveyor belt carrying model airplanes.

Pidge abruptly climbed thirty or forty feet to clear the high tails of the aircraft lined up for takeoff. They shot beneath us.

LaGuardia tower frantically broke the orderly transmissions.

"All aircraft! All aircraft! Cease operation. Hold position. Arriving aircraft, all landing clearances are rescinded. Climb and contact departure. Repeat, arriving aircraft, all landing clearances are rescinded. Climb and contact departure."

The tower that issued these frantic instructions passed above us on the left.

"ARE YOU INSANE!" Foss shrieked. "Get me the fuck down! I'll give you—"

Abrupt G-forces cut him off. We reached the airport's southern perimeter. Pidge yanked the airplane into a steep climb and then a vertical bank. She pulled the nose through the New York skyline in a tight right turn. Densely populated city streets rotated below us. Our bodies sank in our seats. The gun in my jacket pocket tugged the garment down.

Seconds later, Pidge reversed the bank and heaved the airplane around in a tight left turn. Sunrise that had been adding color to Foss's white face now appeared on my side of the plane. She rolled out sharply, pointed back at the airport, and dove.

"STOP IT! STOP IT!" Foss shouted. "You're gonna kill us!"

The control tower appeared dead ahead. First, as landmark. Then as an obstacle. In shaved seconds, the concrete and glass spire filled the forward view. At the last instant, Pidge cleared the structure by banking hard to the right. She dropped the wing that would have clipped the tower. The King Air cleared the structure by mere feet.

People inside the tower dove for the floor. I saw a coffee mug fly.

"AIRCRAFT INTRUDING LAGUARDIA AIRSPACE! YOU ARE IN VIOLATION! DEPART THE AREA IMMEDIATELY!"

Pidge laughed as she heaved the wings level again and skimmed the surface of Flushing Bay. She performed a graceful chandelle, lifting the nose through the horizon, banking 45-degrees left, and swinging the nose back down again to line up for another opposite-direction pass over Runway 31. On the congested airfield, all movement ceased.

The tower repeated frantic commands for us to go away, then repeated instructions for all aircraft movements to cease.

Pidge's voice sang in the intercom.

"God, I love this!"

Pidge guided the diving King Air down on the runway, this time lining up on the centerline. A jet in position for takeoff sat helplessly at the departure end. She pushed the throttles to full power and gained incredible speed. The jet applied power and surged to its right, trying hard to clear the runway.

"Anything! I'll fucking give you anything!" Foss cried. "They're gonna shoot us down. Do you realize that?! They're gonna shoot us out of the sky!"

"Yeah," I said, forcing a calm that was the inverse of his panic. "Probably. I figure we got a few more minutes before they blow us outta the sky."

"WHAT DO YOU WANT FROM ME?"

"Nothing."

We raced down the runway. The waiting jet tried hard to get out of the way. I felt bad for the flight crew staring at some lunatic playing chicken. It had no chance. Pidge issued a glorious shriek that hurt my ears.

Foss gaped at me, dumbfounded.

"I don't want anything from you," I said. "I don't want your money. I don't want to take your life. I don't even want to try to make you understand how disconnected you are from the rest of humanity. You're a piece of shit that floated to the top where you think you're out of reach."

"That's it? That's all you got? Some fucking speech, as if I haven't heard it all before. Fuck you!"

Pidge reached the end of the runway and pulled hard, shooting skyward over the jet still trying to taxi clear. She banked left. She raked the airplane's nose across the ball of sun peeking over the horizon. Swinging around, she took up a path in the opposite direction of the pass we just made. She leveled off at around 1,000 feet and pulled back the power. The cabin grew eerily silent.

Is she gonna kill us? Is that what this is about?" Foss clawed at his seatbelt. I pulled out the Beretta and pointed it. He froze.

"No," I said. "She's not gonna kill us. This will all be over in a minute."

"How?"

"Pleasantly, I hope."

In contrast to the high-powered, high-speed runs she had made, Pidge now executed a smooth circuit, drawing back the power and letting the airplane catch a breather. She eased through a smooth, curved approach to the runway and lined up. Our speed was high, and the wind was wrong, but she guided the plane to the pavement without flaps and without extending the landing gear. She gingerly bled off speed. A warning horn blared in the cockpit.

We sailed over the approach lights for Runway 13, above the overrun chevrons, over the numbers. Pidge abruptly killed both engines. She leveled off less than twenty feet above the asphalt. Centerline stripes swept beneath us. We floated. Fifteen feet. Ten. The props spun until they began to tick-tick-tick against the pavement.

Things grew loud and rough after that. Despite Pidge all but kissing the runway with her gentle touchdown, the sudden grinding of pavement on the belly of the plane rattled our bones. Metal shrieked. The props stopped, bent back at the tips. The nose dipped.

We skidded straight for hundreds of yards, then began a slow swing to the left. Soon, we slid sideways. Foss cringed. He gripped his seat. He clamped his eyes shut. The terminal passed across the windscreen, then the tower. We rotated until we faced the thin trail of smoke we left behind. The plane made a full one-eighty and came to a grinding halt. Put it on wheels, and we could have rolled for takeoff.

Silence fell abruptly.

Pidge broke it by snapping open her seat belt. She threw off her headset and kicked the seat all the way back.

"Hey," I said, careful not to use her name. She glanced back at me. I showed her how I used my shirt to rub the leather armrests on my seat. She did the same with the yoke and throttles and bits of the radio stack. Then she swung out of the pilot's seat into the aisle. She hurried past me to the cabin door.

I followed. Pidge used her shirt to crack the lock. She pushed the door open with her shoulder. It fell partway, hit pavement, bounced, then settled, half open. Pidge and I lined up to leave.

"STOP!" Foss shouted from behind us.

We both turned.

He stood in the aisle grasping Rivers' gun. His chest drew and released panicked breaths.

He opened his mouth to speak. No words came. Instead, he pulled the trigger. Again. Again. And again.

Nothing happened.

He gaped at the gun in his hand, then at us.

Sirens broke the silence. From the terminal, a fleet of emergency vehicles followed a vanguard of law enforcement units onto the taxiways.

"They look pissed," Pidge deadpanned.

We had seconds before being surrounded.

I hooked Pidge's arm. I raised my own arm and pointed at the King Air windscreen behind Foss.

I leaned close to Pidge and said, "Hey, look. A baby osprey!"

Foss, shaken, hesitated. Then seeing Pidge break into a smile, could not help himself. He turned to look.

Fwooomp!

EPILOGUE I

She cut a sublime figure, an icon of womanhood, a dreamy image that elegantly symbolized procreation. Her gown had been planned weeks in advance by one of the hottest designers in New York. It shimmered, draped, and accented the growing baby bump and her prominent and healthy breasts. Photos taken at a session staged before departing for the gallery opening guaranteed the gown would appear in *Vogue.*

Police pushed the paparazzi halfway back down the block, but intrusive lenses zoomed in to read her celebrity face for signs of stress. Reporters shouted questions from both barriers. Cameras and lights locked on her.

How do you feel?

Have you spoken to your husband?

Does being here tonight signal support for your husband?

What can you tell us about his breakdown?

Who are you wearing?

Chaney Foss concentrated on the drape of her gown, the challenge of the slightly dangerous heels she wore, and the potential for catching a pavement crack between the curb and the red carpet leading into the gallery. A host of men and women in black tie and signature gowns watched the world's (potentially) richest woman descend from her armored SUV.

Police guarded the entrance. The opening had been planned for over a year, but duty assignments had doubled since the events at LaGuardia and the arrest of Bindle Foss. Putting on a brave face, Chaney Foss issued a video statement declaring that despite her husband's sudden and tragic health issues, she would not be swayed from her duties to the arts and the community that supported them. The news came as great relief to the gallery owners, who counted on millions coming from the Foss coffers and from all the collectors eager to keep up.

The expression "brave face" dominated network and social media coverage. And while layouts for the next issue of *Vogue* had already been typeset, the task of putting a new spin on the tragic downfall of a titan of finance and enshrining the noble and courageous rise of his pregnant wife in his place injected fresh adrenaline into the editors.

Chaney Foss displayed her strength and resolve with a confident wave to both barriers. Her handlers and bodyguards guided her forward. She looked past a woman with short black hair who waited at the door and focused instead on the reception she anticipated inside. The genuinely important reporters and influencers had been granted admission to the gallery to witness and proclaim the undying support exhibited by Foss's wealthy peers.

The woman Chaney Foss overlooked, flanked by uniformed officers, wore a black blazer, a black t-shirt, and black jeans. The only thing preventing her arrest for a glaring fashion *faux pas* was that her garment colors matched the tuxedos waiting inside the glass gallery doors.

The entourage approached the entrance. The woman raised an FBI badge to eye height.

"Good evening, Ms. Foss," she said, offering a polite if slightly crooked smile. "Special Agent Leslie Carson-Pelham, FBI. I just need a moment."

"Now? Don't be absurd. You can speak to my lawyer," Foss replied.

"I'm sure I will, but perhaps you could answer one quick question for me."

Without warning, Leslie lifted her free hand and flicked open a stiletto blade. She flipped the blade and plunged it into the sleek fabric of the gown. The vertical stroke penetrated the curve of the pregnancy bump.

The crowd gasped. Cameras flashed. Foss flinched, then froze.

Everyone stared at the hilt of the blade left sticking straight up.

No one moved or spoke. Including Foss.

"You're under arrest, Ms. Foss, for accessory to the murder of Marie Sandoval, Caroline Gaffney, and Holiday Bennett."

"Who?" one of Foss's handlers, a young man wearing too much mascara, asked with disdain. "Who did she say?"

Someone reached for the knife. Leslie slapped the hand away without looking down at it. She stared at Foss whose face adopted a cold, hard glare.

"Hands behind your back, please," Leslie said.

Cameras clicked and flashed.

EPILOGUE II

Floating lightly above the wooden cabin floor, I studied the man through a bank of windows without fear of being seen. Compact and fit, he walked toward me on a path that drew a direct line between the cabin and a small lake. The features of his face gathered tightly beneath a high forehead and above a square jaw. He kept his hair short, the way the military liked it.

I gripped the edge of a workbench. Tools and supplies for homemade ammunition formed tidy rows and stacks on the bench. The equipment suggested expertise. I knew nothing about the process except to guess that he could modify the potency of a bullet by adjusting the amount of gunpowder or grain or whatever comprised the cartridge charge.

Andy explained the dynamics to me during a remarkably academic conversation about the bullet that pierced her body.

"Subsonic rounds travel under 1,125 feet per second. They're used with suppressed weapons to avoid the loud crack you get with a supersonic round."

"The crack being a…what? Sonic boom?"

"Yes."

"Seems like something to avoid."

"Sometimes. But there are considerations. Supersonic ammunition travels faster and is more accurate at long range because it has a flatter trajectory. Subsonic rounds can jam in semiautomatic weapons because the charge is insufficient to push the slide far enough to rack the next round. That's not an issue for a bolt action weapon. For a sniper shot, where the shooter accounts for the heavier round and greater drop, a subsonic round can help hide the shooter's location."

She smiled at me from her bed. I smiled back.

"Do you have any idea how hot you are when you talk about ammunition?"

Torturing me, she used a breathy, sensual tone to describe the type of rifle her shooter probably used, licking her lips provocatively and derailing my train of thought entirely.

Lust aside, she accurately described the rifle I found in a black case on a shelf under the workbench in the cabin. Protected by soft foam packing and silky cloths, the also-black rifle fit Andy's description of the weapon that would have been used to kill Caroline Gaffney. A long suppressor tube in the case verified the find as far as I was concerned.

It was Leslie who found Murphy. Off the books, just as I asked.

A clue had been the car picked up by plate readers before and after the shooting at the farmhouse—a bland Buick sedan with a cleverly weathered Wisconsin license plate that proved unreadable. From that thread, Leslie performed some FBI magic. She found a handful of potential suspects, including a former Marine sniper named Murphy who owned a remote property near Ashland, Wisconsin.

Convenient to Three Lakes, I noted.

She provided the information to me several weeks after Dr. Maserati deemed Andy capable of extremely light mobility. Margie continued to work for us as a day nurse, but Andy rejoiced in being able to trek all the way to the first-floor bathroom by herself or join me on the porch when Leslie dropped in for a visit.

"I thought you were fired," I said to Leslie.

"I thought you were bedridden," Leslie said to Andy.

"They let me walk this far—although unplugging all the monitors is a giant pain. At least the stent is out. I felt like I was being watched."

"I wanted to sell tickets," I said.

Andy rolled her eyes. "I'm something of a medical miracle. I think Dr. Maserati—oh, crap!" She slapped my arm. "Now you've got me saying it! I think Dr. Maharashtra wants to do a paper on me."

"Exciting," Leslie said.

"I'm declining. It's…it's not a good idea." To Leslie's quizzical look Andy simply added, "Too intrusive."

I changed the subject. "How did you avoid getting the ax from Big Bob?"

"Big Rog." Leslie spread her crooked smile. "You know…guys like him who constantly have the volume cranked to 11 always miss subtlety. They're so busy exploiting other people's vulnerabilities they fail to account for their own. It took a few conversations with the man and his minions to make them realize that derailing my career might have unintended consequences."

"Did they actually fire you?" Andy asked.

"For about five minutes. I made a few phone calls to people outside the FBI who persuaded the new Acting Assistant Director that he would be better off selling furniture than he would be messing with me. I know too much."

"Nice position to have," I mused. I couldn't help but wonder who Leslie had in her corner in the world of power politics. She didn't share.

We gravitated to Baxter Gaffney. The very pregnant girl had been found keeping house at a property owned by a chain of entities that eventually connected to Guardian Worldwide. The glowing and growing mother-to-be occupied her time buying baby clothes and setting up a happy home for the moment when, as she was promised, billionaire Bindle Foss would divorce his wife and commit to true happiness with his newfound soul mate. When Gallica Protection Services abruptly withdrew from secreting the girl away, they left her without a credit card. Determined to continue filling the house of her dreams with the baby-raising equipment of her dreams, she used her own. Soon after, the FBI arrived.

"Honest to God, she bought something like seven cribs. They were all over the house," Leslie told us. "The girl really does have serious mental issues. She refuses to accept Foss's arrest at LaGuardia as real. She insists Foss loves her and is meant to be with her."

"That's not necessarily mental issues," Andy said. "Foss probably made her believe he was trapped in a loveless marriage, and deeply and desperately in love with her."

"The good news for her," Leslie added, "is that she's carrying a baby with a legit claim to half of the fortune of the former richest or second-richest man in the world. Gaffney's lawyer dad is back in the picture and already clamoring for conservatorship. The same for Marie Sandoval's family regarding the boy. The DNA results—genuine results—are already back and undeniable. Cha-ching!"

"Damn," I said. "I should have taken the fifteen million."

We didn't discuss Foss. Weeks of salacious stories about his arrest for terrorism, murder, and a host of other charges, fed bottomless cable news appetites. Celebrity psychologists discussed to death his insane claims that he'd been kidnapped. Pundits and comedians glommed onto the wildest details, one of which was his insistence that a petite blonde woman was the skilled maniac pilot who brought east coast air traffic to a standstill. Late night TV talk show hosts began calling this figment of Foss's imagination Tinkerbell.

Leslie spent the bulk of her quiet afternoon visit talking with Andy about her health, her thoughts about the coming birth, and about Holly. I slipped out when Holly came up. There were tears. I kept mine to myself.

When Leslie parted from Andy's company, I walked her to the car.

"Here." She handed me an envelope. "A little light reading. I wouldn't share it with your wife."

"I share everything with my wife," I said.

"Your call. But you never got it from me."

Murphy.

He lived in the only cabin on a small lake southwest of Ashland where he fished and hunted and—I assumed—waited for the next call from Gallica Protective Services who, thus far, avoided being mentioned in context, legal or media, with the biggest news story in the country. Murphy's house at the end of a half-mile dirt lane hid from satellite imagery under a thick crown of pine trees.

I parked a mile away and arrived at the cabin by air on a bright, sunny November day. The approach over water reminded me of my approach to the Gaffney house in Three Lakes weeks ago. Smoke rising from the cabin's chimney smelled good and promised warmth inside.

I spotted Murphy when I arrived just after sunrise. He walked toward the lake carrying his fishing gear. I drifted overhead in silence, giving him time to establish himself. Then, while he enjoyed coffee from a Thermos and dragged his breakfast from the lake, I broke the latch on his front door and slipped into his rustic refuge.

He wasn't away long, but it was long enough. When he returned, I waited. His heavy bootsteps halted midway across the cabin porch.

The severed latch lay on the wooden boards. The door hung open.

Murphy carefully laid down his fishing gear and the morning's catch. He checked the windows and searched the yard. Using stealthy moves prescribed by his training, he bobbed his head in the doorway several times before swinging his body through the frame.

He did not relax when he saw that the cabin was empty. He examined every dimension of the one-room structure.

He paid particular attention to the curious arrangement placed in the center of the open floor.

The sophisticated black rifle leaned against the seat of a wooden chair.

Casually. Carelessly. No one with firearms training would lean a weapon like that against a piece of furniture.

Murphy studied the setup from several meters away. He checked the room for other disruptions, then surveyed the yard once more before advancing.

He moved carefully toward the rifle, constantly scanning, treating it like a trap, a distraction, but one he could not ignore. The precarious and irresponsible placement of the weapon probably offended him.

As he approached, the rifle slid sideways along the chair seat. Easy to explain. The vibration caused by his footsteps broke the rifle's tenuous contact with the wood.

He quickly bent to catch the barrel, perhaps hoping to prevent damage to the optics.

Mistake.

The rifle went off.

Without the suppressor, the confined space blast slammed my eardrums. I cursed myself for not wearing earplugs. The man had a plastic jar full of them on his workbench.

Dumb luck. The barrel had been pointed at Murphy's midsection when it fired.

Murphy doubled over and staggered one step backward before dropping to the floor. His legs splayed and his back banged against the wall beside the door. He gripped his guts. Blood seeped between his fingers and joined the red flannel of his woodsy shirt. He gasped for air.

The weapon clattered to the floor.

Fwooomp!

I appeared taking a knee beside the rifle. His astonished face grew more so at the sight of me. I peeled off a pair of latex gloves and stuffed them in my back pocket.

"Who the hell are you?" he asked. His voice remained strong. I didn't think that would last long.

"Rather careless of you to leave a weapon like that."

I remained kneeling, face to face with Murphy. He groaned.

"Help me," he begged.

"You've got a phone. Call 911. Do you get a signal out here? Or did Gallica give you a satellite phone? You know; for those rush jobs."

A hint of awareness penetrated his agony.

"I bet an ambulance can be here in half an hour or so. Just one quick question before you pass out. Outside the Three Lakes Police Department… that shot you took…where were you?"

He didn't answer, but tightening of the skin around his eyes gave him away.

"You gotta help me," he pleaded, fighting a gurgle in his throat.

"Actually, I don't. When they pull that bullet out of your gut—either at the hospital or during the autopsy—it will prove to be a ballistic match to the one they recovered from the pregnant cop in Three Lakes."

Near the sac containing my unborn child, you piece of shit.

There it was again. A flash of recognition.

I drew a slow breath and released it into the silence.

I smiled.

"And those rounds you're cooking up over there on the workbench. They probably tell a story, too."

Blood wicked through his pants, rapidly staining his lap. Sweat rolled down his blanched face.

I stood up.

"Yeah. Terrible accident, this. Gun safety, pal. You can't be too careful."

Fwooomp!

DIVISIBLE MAN - THIRTEEN MOONS

Sunday, January 5, 2025 to Wednesday, April 2, 2025

ABOUT THE AUTHOR

HOWARD SEABORNE is the author of the DIVISIBLE MAN™ series as well as a collection of short stories featuring the same cast of characters. He began writing novels in spiral notebooks at age ten. He began flying airplanes at age sixteen. He is a former flight instructor and commercial charter pilot licensed in single- and multi-engine airplanes as well as helicopters. Today he flies a twin-engine Beechcraft Baron, a single-engine Beechcraft Bonanza, and a Rotorway A-600 Talon experimental helicopter he built from a kit in his garage. He lives with his wife and writes and flies during all four seasons in Wisconsin, never far from Essex County Airport.

Visit www.HowardSeaborne.com to join the Email List and get a FREE DOWNLOAD.

THE DIVISIBLE MAN FRANCHISE

**BINGE-READ INDIVIDUAL NOVELS THAT INJECT
AN ASTONISHING TWIST INTO THE CLASSIC THRILLER.**

The media calls it a "miracle" when air charter pilot Will Stewart survives an aircraft in-flight breakup, but Will's miracle pales beside the stunning aftereffect of the crash. *Will's new ability might make the difference between life and death…if it doesn't kill him first.*

A *BookLife from Publishers Weekly* Editor's Pick - **"A book of outstanding quality."**

"Will Stewart is one of the most believable unbelievable characters currently running in fiction." — *Kirkus Reviews*

"FIVE STARS." — *Reader's Favorite*

"Seaborne keeps the concept fresh and readers guessing…proves he's a natural born storyteller…" — *Kirkus Reviews*

"Even more than flight, Will's relationship with Andy—and that crack prose—powers this thriller to a satisfying climax that sets up more to come." —*BookLife*

"Seaborne knows how to mix genre thrills with heart and humor in a way few authors can." — *Reader's Favorite*

Available in print, digital, and audio.

Search: "DIVISIBLE MAN Howard Seaborne"

Join our Reader Email list at **HowardSeaborne.com**

9 781967 895076